At Shutter Speed

a novel

REBECCA BURRELL

Cranesbill Press

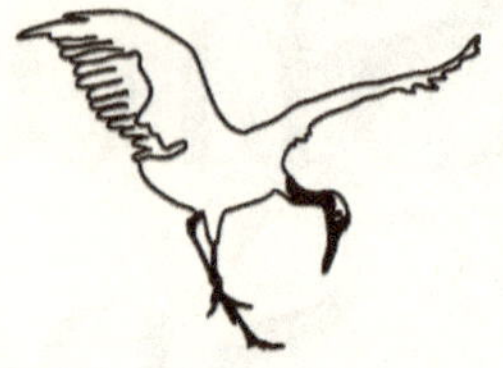

Published by Cranesbill Press, 2018

This book is a work of fiction. Any references to historical events, real people, or real places are used fictitiously. Other names, characters, places, and events are products of the author's imagination and any resemblance to actual events or places or personal, living or dead, is entirely coincidental.

Edited By: Sue Laybourn
Book cover design by BespokeBookCovers.com
Cover Photography from Shutterstock.com
Publisher's Cataloging-in-Publication data:
Names: Burrell, Rebecca, author. 1974-
Title: At shutter speed: a novel / by Rebecca Burrell.
Description: First trade paperback original edition. | Massachusetts: Cranesbill Press, 2018.
Summary: A newly minted human rights attorney gets a trial by fire when her conflict photographer husband goes missing during a crackdown in Cairo.
Identifiers: LCCN 2018904458 | ISBN 978-1-7320828-0-9 (trade paperback) 978-1-7320828-1-6 (epub)
Subjects: 1. Marriage–Fiction. 2. Love–Fiction. 3. Journalism–Fiction. 4. PTSD–Fiction. 5. Family--Fiction. | BISAC : Fiction / Contemporary Women. | Fiction / General

At Shutter Speed

REBECCA BURRELL

Cranesbill Press

Coming Soon

Resurrecting Micah
How High the Moon

What readers are saying about
At Shutter Speed:

"Rebecca Burrell stunningly and sensitively reconstructs a marriage that transcends distance in the face of difficulty. *AT SHUTTER SPEED* is a beautifully wrought tale that is at once political and personal, heartbreaking and affectionate, global and very near to home." *— Jessica Brockmole, internationally bestselling author of LETTERS FROM SKYE*

"Burrell has crafted a smart tale that could be ripped from today's headlines... As the story unwinds, it asks us to grapple with the high toll war takes, not only for those on the front lines but also on those who are compelled to document it. Readers will find this a complex, gripping story." *— Liz Michalski, author of EVENFALL*

"Rebecca Burrell plunges us into a tangled web of politics, revenge and desperate courage that stretches from Washington, D.C. to Cairo, Chad, Syria, and Kurdistan, in which senators ally with war lords and a photo journalist's search for truth and family lands him in a deep state's "black site." Yet at heart *AT SHUTTER SPEED* is a love story, an odyssey of return, a triumph of loyalty and devotion over lies." *— Pamela Schoenewaldt, USA Today bestselling author of WHEN WE WERE STRANGERS*

For anyone who's ever felt difficult to love

and for Kevin, Leigh, Josh, and Dylan
(who aren't)

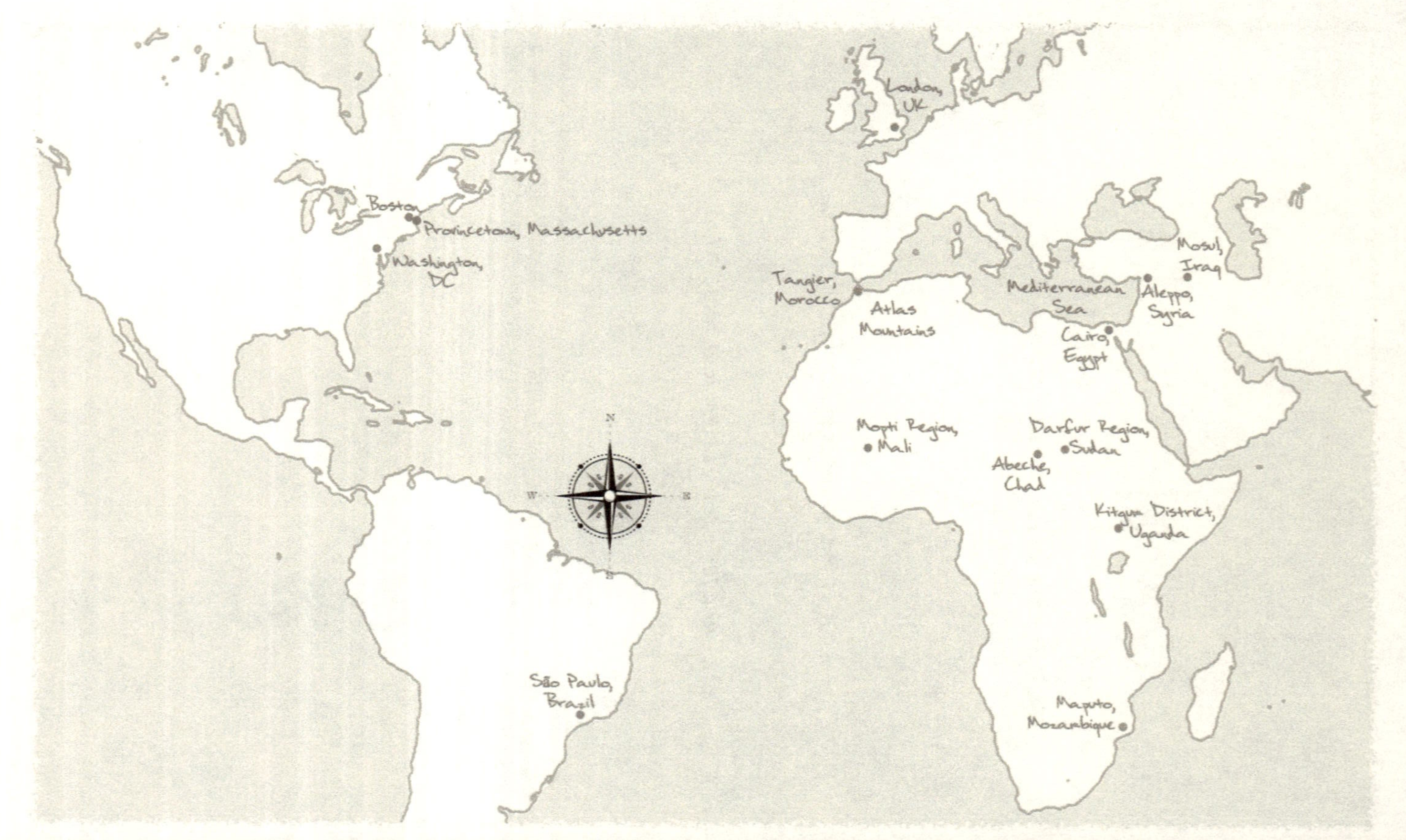

London, UK
Boston
Provincetown, Massachusetts
Washington, DC
Tangier, Morocco
Atlas Mountains
Mediterranean Sea
Mosul, Iraq
Aleppo, Syria
Cairo, Egypt
Mopti Region, Mali
Darfur Region, Sudan
Abeche, Chad
Kitgum District, Uganda
São Paulo, Brazil
Maputo, Mozambique
N
S
E
W

Chapter 1:
Crackups and Crackdowns

CAIRO, EGYPT

In a split second, Matty can tell you a story.

With a click of the shutter, he captures a life—beginning, middle, or end. His photos tell tales, expose truths, open worlds. If journalism is a dying profession, I've been watching it kill my husband for years. But at the same time, it's keeping us alive.

A sea of humanity undulates through Tahrir Square, respiring with simmering fervor. Sirens have been blaring since evening prayers, punctuated by dull explosions from police-fired smoke bombs. Casualties litter the streets, while rescuers staunch head wounds with T-shirts and flush each other's eyes with Maalox cocktails. Hissing canisters snake through the gardens near the Egyptian Museum. Masked protestors hurl them back. *Death to the dictator, death to the regime!*

The museum's been closed for ages. No one in the immediate vicinity gives a damn about antiquities, so I've got a front row seat in the Grand Saloon between a statue of Amenhotep and an arched window facing the square. The air tastes flinty, like gunpowder. Pinpricks of fire are creeping down my throat from the gas. In theory, I'm studying, but you can't exactly study in the middle of a crackdown.

"Dear me, Leah." A bespectacled face pops up beside Amenhotep—the curator, Yusef Hafez. In his cream linen suit, with a perma-smell of aged vanilla and musk, he's something of an antiquity himself. "He hasn't returned?"

"Soon, I'm sure," I say. Though I'm not. Matty is somewhere in the chaos outside. Which means he has his eye to the lens, so he'll be the last to notice when the police don their masks for another round. It means he'll come home coughing, clothes reeking of smoke, on a rush that'll keep him from sleeping for weeks. Weeks he'll spend restless, wandering from room to room because he keeps imagining the smell of tear gas. Where he'll lose ten pounds because he'll forget to eat. Where he'll catch one whiff of a Lucky Strike or diesel fumes and it'll be as if someone opened a window to some long ago and far away hell. It means being locked in a constant state of vigilance, watching for signs, so I can run to the icebox for the frozen orange I keep in there, because sometimes, something cold and fragrant can bring him back before it gets worse.

It means he'll be unfocused and get lost doing simple things, then pick fights with me over stupid crap because it's easier than letting me help. But then he'll finish the story and—poof—he'll be himself again, the guy who holds me close and promises me that someday, the world will be what we both desperately want it to be. It's our thing. We're broke and spend our lives dodging bullets or sleeping under the stars, and time was, I wouldn't have traded it for the world. He's the adrenaline junkie. These days, I just hang on at the fringe.

It wasn't always this way—I spent my twenties as a humanitarian aid worker in Sudan and Uganda. The short version is that I got spooked, left the field, and went running for law school. Now I stay behind while he takes crazy risks. I should be out there too, but when one's husband has been killing himself to put one through law school, one has no excuse for failing the bar exam. At least not twice.

"It was kind of you to let us stay here," I say to Yusef, blinking as the dots swim on my practice test. Hours ago, as the clashes over the rigged election intensified, the government declared all foreign journalists 'purveyors of fake news', the new favorite epithet of authoritarian regimes everywhere. After they yanked our hotel permit, Yusef, an old friend of Matty's, offered us a spare room in the basement.

Jowls turned down, he strokes the bristles of his beard. "You may need to make other arrangements. The museum is at risk. The Night Hotel has been set ablaze."

Outside, a flickering orange glow lights the square. I tuck my study guide behind me, then stand on pins-and-needles legs for a better look. Even the palm trees are in flames. There goes the best fourteen-dollar-a-night hotel in Cairo. "When did that happen?"

"Some time ago."

Students dance in front of the burning building, bare seconds before being swept away by police water cannons. "They could put it out if they wanted," I say. "Guess it's more fun to squirt protestors."

"This is Egypt." Frustration courses through Yusef's voice. "We say 'God will take care of it'. Then we do nothing."

Our last trip to Cairo had been during the 2011 revolution, and so much has changed. Shop windows once filled with honeyed cakes and risqué clothes are burned and boarded. Once, students danced on the rooftops, because where else would you go when the world tipped on its head? Now, if you dare go outside, you watch the rooftops for the glint of a sniper rifle sight. Revolution isn't binary, it isn't an endpoint, it's a fluid state of mind, and Egypt's has been dark for years.

"Maybe that's what the people outside are trying to change."

It's not that I think arson is a good way to solve problems, but I grew up with a giant of the civil rights era telling my bedtime stories. What's happening outside goes beyond buildings and things. Matty's photos of sheet-wrapped corpses prove it.

Yusef clings to the crimson ropes around the colossus, contemplating his world, the hieroglyphs of Isis, the soaring majesty of Horus, the gold in Tut's death mask. "Egypt's greatest treasure is her history.

In their anger, youth forget such things. They forget the past contains the answers."

To me, it's simple. These clashes are rooted in three things: power, money, and sex, which are pretty much all that people ever fight about anyhow. The men in power have all the money, and this being Egypt, they're damned determined to control the sex, too. No one under thirty has a job, which means they can't get married, which means they can't get laid. So instead, shit gets lit on fire.

Someone—a teenage girl—slams the window, crazing the glass. A dozen cops in riot gear give chase, shields and batons raised. *We will be free,* she screams at them in Arabic, scampering into the crowd. The police start beating everyone near her.

I toss the world of contracts and torts aside. The way I should've done four years and a shit-ton of money ago. "That's it."

Yusef eyes his mummies. "Where are you going?"

"Out." I wrap a scarf around my face, then make sure the long skirt I'm wearing covers my ankles. 'Out' is where people need help. 'Out' is where the old Leah would be. "I'm not doing any good sitting here."

"Your husband will not like if you leave."

Too damn bad. I snap a pair of swimming goggles on my forehead. Yusef's been hovering all night. I figure Matty asked him to babysit, which is ironic for any number of reasons. "Probably not."

Maybe I look like a bug-eyed Calamity Jane, but my dad, the Honorable Dale Atkins, Esq., would be ashamed if his daughter sat on her ass while thugs in riot gear form ranks across Tahrir Square.

While I'm doing the one-foot hop with my sneaker, my phone dings. Twice.

Stay put Leah

And get away from the goddamn window

I peer outside. A line of armored vehicles stretches to the cornice at the Nile end of the square. Matty is perched on the wall of the lotus pond, wearing faded jeans and a flak vest, a checkered scarf over his mouth and nose. With his wheat-colored hair and dishwater-grey eyes, he's the kind of guy who stands out in any crowd, but it's really damn obvious here.

It's different for me—my Mom's French and my Dad's roots are Igbo, which makes guessing my race some weird game show for strangers, who seem to think I'm either Mediterranean, Hispanic, or 'wow, for a white girl, you can really tan'. The good news is that at this time of year, I can pass for a local in Cairo. The bad news is that the secret police are out in force, so nobody's safe out there tonight.

I dial Matty's mobile, to remind him to cover his head, but then shots start popping and he hits the deck. The crowd scatters. He scrambles away, and I hang up, fast.

Banging my temple with the phone, I watch him scurry into an alley behind the museum. My mobile rings a few seconds later.

"Hey, babe." His breathing is labored. "How's the studying?"

"Are you okay?"

"Far as you know."

A wiggle of relief hits my belly. "Butthead. I'm coming out."

The crowd sounds go quiet. "Leah, it's bad. There's nothing you can do." He sounds defeated, which is never a good sign.

"Is anyone with you?"

"Reuters has a couple stringers out here. Or maybe they're AP. Not sure they know either."

"Not what I meant." Matty's parents were missionaries who dragged him from one godforsaken hotspot to the next, and it messed him up pretty good. What I care about is whether he's working with someone who knows him. Knows what his mind can do to him when things are 'bad'. Which they have been. For months, ever since he got injured on his last job in Syria. On the outside, he's still healing, but something worse is eating him from the inside, something he won't talk about. Which isn't exactly unusual, but it's never been this bad for so long. We're doing our best to smile through the pain and pretend everything is getting better. It's killing me that it's not.

In the background, I hear a wolf whistle. "Cahill, is that your wife? Man, I had no idea she had tits like that."

Matty swears. "Christ, Sal."

Saleh is Yusef's son, a producer for CNN's Africa desk, and I can guess what he's looking at. A normal guy would carry a wedding photo. Maybe a vacation snap. Something that involves, say, clothes, but this is a photo of me that Matty took the first night we made love. Like…*right* after, and he's been schlepping it around ever since.

He comes back on the line. "Sorry."

"Since when are you showing that to people?"

"I wasn't, Leah, I just…needed to see it, okay?" His voice sounds distant. Sad.

"Matty, come home. You can have the real thing."

He exhales. "God, you have no idea. As soon as things calm down, I'm yours."

"Hope that's a promise."

"It is." He coughs, away from the receiver. "How's your stomach? Did that tea I brought help?"

It's a loaded question. The water in Egypt never agrees with me, and as far as he knows, that's all it is. The two pregnancy tests I took before we came agreed, and then there's the get-it-while-you-still-can-because-fuck-the-patriarchy IUD I had put in after the election. None of which does a damn thing to explain why I can't even remember the last time I had a period. Or make me feel any less jumbled up inside.

"Yeah, better," I finally say.

"Liar." He pauses. "How about I scrounge up some of that honey candy you like?"

All I need is him. Screw that. I need him to *be* him—the guy who lets me help when he's messed up, not the one who shuts me out and keeps secrets, who feels like he's one bad day from giving up. Because from the minute we landed, my body has been doing its damnedest to convince me those stupid pregnancy tests were wrong. "I'm okay."

Water jets sweep the crowd. The line of black uniforms holds. Fresh volleys of smoke burst forth. "Hey listen," he says, "rumor has it the government is shutting down the internet. Can you get to my website?"

Matty, who's a freelance journalist these days, likes to joke that he got kicked out of the Fourth Estate and into a trailer park. We met at an Iraq War protest, and even then, the news orgs were refusing to print some of the photos he took—too controversial, or they didn't fit the narrative somebody wanted to spin. His blog is his voice, in all its raw, unfiltered glory.

"It's been loading like a ninety-year-old turtle with a piano on its back," I say, waking the tablet beside me. Truth told, I've been paying more attention to that than my review books.

Mizaru's Window, reads the site's header. The letters twine around a graphic of the Three Wise Monkeys—See No Evil, Hear No Evil, Speak No Evil, a copy of one tattooed on his arm. All I know is it was some kind of farewell screw-you to his dad.

"Check your flights while you're at it," he says.

Originally, they were 'our' flights, but one of us is in the middle of documenting a war and the other has the bar exam in four days. "They're looking for observers down in Suez. The military says eleven dead, but Amnesty thinks it's higher. Maybe we should—"

"No."

"I could fly out tomor—"

"I'm not going to be the reason you miss that damn test again."

Okay, so I didn't exactly fail the bar the first time. Long story. This time, I have a job waiting for me in DC, which I *have* to take if we have any hope of paying back my loans. It's immigration law instead of human rights, which means diving into a system I know nothing about, which I'm only doing because the way things are going at home, it feels as if I have to. Except taking it means an office instead of the front lines, which comes with the guilty reminder of the moment I walked away. When we started out, Matty and I were a team, and deep down, I'm scared to admit those days are gone forever. But something has to change.

Yesterday, before we left to come here, I found him naked on the beach by my parents' house—in February, no less—throwing sheaves of story notes and photos onto a campfire he'd started. High as a kite to boot. Once he'd sobered up, I told him that unless he got his act together, he wasn't coming with me to DC. In hindsight, getting on a plane with him to Cairo wasn't the best way to convince him I'm serious about leaving, but I was terrified of what might happen if I didn't. If there's a baby involved, I can't bear to think what it means.

Maybe my stomach…thing…is just stress. People who accidentally get pregnant don't have to take the bar, or soul-sucking law jobs. They get to dress up their baby girls in frilly outfits and drink Starbucks all day, don't they?

Right Leah. Keep telling yourself that.

"I got a one-ninety-one on my practice Bar today," I say. "Finished in under two hours. With a twenty-minute Angry Birds break."

"Funny that your staunch opposition to the death penalty stops with cartoon pigs."

"The evil green porkers deserve it." And like he's any different. "You realize two hundred is perfect?"

"I heard you," he replies. "I'm sure the Egyptian military will be impressed if they decide to detain you for a few weeks."

Or Borders and Customs. Sighing, I click refresh. "You realize I'm going to make a shitty lawyer if I can't even negotiate with you."

"You only suck at negotiating when you're wrong."

The cursor keeps spinning. "They must've pulled the plug."

He curses. "The US producer must be having a fit. He wanted a live feed ready as soon as Jake Tapper finishes feeding some White House Nazi his own nutsack."

"Which one?"

"I can't keep them straight. The dude who looks like his mother fucked a lightbulb."

That's my Matty. "I bet Jake Tapper would tell me to stay."

"Don't get me in the middle of your unholy crush on JT." His voice grows muffled. "Hey listen, let me go take care of some things, then I'll come find you."

"Will you be long?"

"I'm staring at a nekkid picture of my gorgeous wife. Part of me is."

"I happen to like that part. Try not to get it shot off."

Even the happiest couples have secrets. When we met, I saw him as this exotic world traveler—born in Brazil, he spoke five languages. He grew up in places like Mozambique and Iraq; I'm an attorney's daughter from P-town, Massachusetts, who'd dreamed of seeing the things he'd seen, and yet to realize they'd nearly killed him. He says he fell in love with me because I proved to him the world could change. I fell in love with him because he showed me what had to.

Billows of sweet, noxious smoke cloud the air as I slip out of the rear service door, needing to see for myself that he's okay. The goggles and my scarf protect me, though I can't stay out long. His silhouette is visible through the haze. Head tilted a little to the left, elbow raised, camera ready. I'd know it anywhere.

I've always loved watching him work, getting to look through his photos at the end of a day. Matty has this desperate search for humanity, but he sees it in things that are fleeting and hard to find. He lives in the infinitesimal space between the best and worst of human nature, and some days, the camera is all that keeps it from crashing down on him. Even in the worst situations, he manages to find some shred of hope. Dignity. But it's rare to see him this at peace while he's doing it, and I can't help but wonder what's changed.

Near the American University, students hold vigil beside a stone church which is set up as a makeshift field hospital. Mourners gather around a lifeless body, surrounded by others who form a solidarity wall, protecting them from the riot troops. Matty moves to an alcove by the front gate, transfixed by something on his camera LCD.

All he wants is one photo that changes the world. Nobody but journalists and history buffs remember who took the Kim Phuc photo, the naked girl running from her napalmed village, but it altered the course of the war. Nobody remembers who got the shot of the guy staring down the tanks in Tiananmen Square, but the world still wonders what happened to him. It took a while before I understood why Matty lets life take so much from him. He rejected the life his parents led, but parts stuck with him nonetheless. The need to see justice done, to give a voice to the voiceless. He keeps searching for that one seismic photo because it's the only way he'll ever figure out how to live with himself.

A woman with a dark, shiny braid comes over to Matty. Thirty-ish, she's dressed in a loose olive pants and a black tunic, with a rose print scarf over her hair, an Assyrian-style cross around her neck, and a downcast expression on her face. A few words pass between them. He opens the memory slot on his camera and gives her the card, which she reluctantly accepts. After that, he draws her into an embrace, planting a tender kiss on her forehead.

Just like that, I can't breathe.

At the same moment, she glances across the square to where I'm standing, and a flicker of recognition lights her eyes. Matty notices me then too, and freezes. I catch a musky smell, a man's smell, and I realize someone is standing behind me.

Before I can even turn, the man slides into the crowd. Western clothes. Dark, flowing hair, and a pair of silver sunglasses perched on his head, though I can't see his face. He circles the mourners like a great cat guarding a kill. Or stalking the next.

His expression flits between bemusement and rage, the latter directed at the woman with Matty, who's now kneeling in prayer inside the circle. "Come out, whore," he taunts. "Do you think I can't see you?"

Her gaze lifts. The fear is gone, replaced with anger and grief. She shifts off her knees and exits the circle, towards a young father and son standing at the gate. The boy, ragged and rail-thin, holds out a shaggy brown mongoose, which hops onto her shoulder.

The father steps protectively in front of his son. "Leave us in peace. We have beaten you. You lost." His accent is Syrian, not Egyptian, which likely explains the haunted look on his kid's face. "You have no power over us now. Or this woman."

With a bemused smirk, the jerk flicks ash from his cigarette. "This is the thanks I get? Perhaps I should not be surprised." He flashes a knife. "Offer her a place to sleep and she'll fuck you too."

The mourners break up in a chorus of peace-be-with-yous and *as-Salamu Alaykums*. The jerk shoves the father aside, then lunges for the woman. A *pop-pop-pop* comes from the rooftops. The crowd screams and scatters. And then my idiot husband goes and tackles the jerk.

Matty barely dodges the knife on the first swing. On the second, the mongoose leaps, sinking its teeth into the man's neck. The knife clatters to the pavement, and the mongoose prances away, chittering triumphantly.

The woman grabs the boy by the hand and escapes down an alley. The jerk gut-punches Matty, shoving him away. Inaudible words pass between them. Matty gapes at me, white-faced and startled. Grinning, the jerk flips his knife, then skips off after the woman.

Matty is slow to get up, clutching his ribs, which he'd broken six months ago during an airstrike in Syria. I run over and help him out of the line of fire. "You're hurt."

He's got this lost, anguished expression on his face. Sweat mixes with ash, and greasy black smudges run from his temple to his chin. "She's just someone I know, Leah—that guy…"

Mixed with the pain, there's guilt, and I'm not sure I want to know where it came from, so I replace the lens cap. "It's fine, you can tell me later."

The crowd swells as we make for the safety of the museum. Smoke and flames leap through the roof of the building across the alley. "I told you to stay put," he grouses, as a tank rumbles past.

"You know me better than that." I stab Yusef's spare key into the service entrance door. "What were you thinking, going after that guy?"

"I was having another goddamn flashback, okay?" He squeezes his eyes shut. "Can we not talk about it?"

Something hits me hard, deep in the stomach. We've spent half our marriage dealing with his flashbacks. It's not why he did it.

"Fine," I say, struggling to figure out what he's not telling me. Which seems to be how I spend most of my time these days. "Then let's talk about her."

He peels the goggles off my head, hands coming to rest on my face. His skin feels raw, about a million degrees. "Stop looking at me like that." He walks me into the darkness of the unlit entryway. "You know I'm no cheat. She's a source. A friend."

What I want him to say is why the 'friend' with the jealous eyes and curvy figure was acting as if she knows me. Why he was comforting her. I'd settle for some hint of why she's in trouble in the first place, but if she's a source, with Matty, that's the end of it. I know he's no cheat, sure, but he's never been as secretive and self-destructive and just plain messed up as he's been the last few months either.

I want to blurt out *I think I'm pregnant,* but the words won't come. I've seen too much of the world to want to bring a child into it, and any time it's come up, he jokes that his brain should be donated to science, not inflicted on another generation. Kids were never in our plan. But here we are, and I need him to tell me he'll find a way to crawl out from whatever he's under, that he'll do it for me and the baby because he loves us. Yet I love him enough to know it's not that simple.

The basement smells of must. A strange, sweet salt tickles my nose. Down here, it's a maze of painted metal boxes and shelves, filled with dusty artifacts collected god knows when. He's wandering between them, lost and unfocused, so I take his camera and set it on a nearby crate. "Matty, where are we?"

He blinks, scanning around. "Cairo, right?"

Anxious, I step between his knees, resting my forehead on his, but when I move my hand to his arm, he flinches. My hand comes away warm and sticky. I grab his wrist and pull up his sleeve, revealing a two-inch dig right below the monkey tattoo on his biceps. I know it's from a bullet, which is bad enough, but he's written his name and my cell phone number in thick, permanent marker on his arm. Suddenly I'm fighting tears.

"Hey, ssh, ssh," he says. "It's nothing, don't worry about it. I'm here, right?"

Over our years together, I've watched him bury a dozen friends, sometimes nothing more than memories in empty coffins. I've been stuck half a world away when the internet discovers the latest video of some fuckwit beheading a journalist. Worry isn't a choice, it's something that tattooed itself onto my heart long ago.

"C'mon, tough guy. You and I have a date with the first aid kit."

He buries his face in my neck and slips his hands under my skirt, cupping my rear. "Leah, I don't need a damn Band-Aid. I need you."

His kiss swallows the night, deep, wet, and lingering. He wants me to let this go, but we both know I can't. "What's wrong?" I say, caressing his temple. "Are you in trouble?"

"Nothing a good lawyer couldn't handle." He nudges my knees apart with his hip, shucking his T-shirt. "Though I've got something else for her to handle instead."

I count the scars on his torso, making sure there are no new ones. Darfur above his left hip, Kirkuk across his left pec, Aleppo all down his right side. "You're burning up."

"Can't help it." He lifts my top over my head. "Is this okay?"

He asks, because once, someone didn't. It's not something I think about much these days. "It is if you tell me what's going on."

A kiss, a nibble, a caress of my hip. "I'm making love to my wife." He peels down the cup of my bra, flicking his tongue over my nipple. "Who should know I'm completely mad about her."

"Completely mad about something." I say, surrendering in a swirl of emotion, dust, and our own tangled history. Fine, I need him too.

But then comes a commotion upstairs. Smashing glass, running footsteps. Bitter, angry shouts. Looters. Yusef's muffled shouts rise above the fray.

Matty's weight drops onto me. With a groan of frustration, he rolls off, contemplating the ceiling. "He's about to get himself killed over some clay pot, isn't he?"

As he buttons his jeans, I sit up. "Where's my skirt?"

Leaning over for a quick kiss, he snags his shirt. "Stay. I'll only be a few minutes."

I snag it back, draping it over my breasts. "Seriously—what's got you so spooked?"

He stops, wiping sweat from his forehead. "I don't even know where to start."

Does that mean he knows? I bite my lip. "For starters, you could tell me how you feel about it."

His brow furrows. "Are we talking about the same thing?"

I can't make myself say it, so I put my hand over my midsection. His jaw goes slack, and a rush of breath escapes from his lungs. "God, Leah, I—"

There's another crash, a scream. Eyes closed, he kisses my forehead. "I love you, but right now I am scared to death. I'll be right back. Then we'll talk. I swear."

Scared to death is better than I expected. "Okay. Go."

As the sound of his footsteps fade, I slip on his shirt, and while I'm buttoning it up, I notice he didn't take his camera. Given that it's his sixth appendage, it's odd. Not to mention the frustrated way he tossed it onto his bag. As if he's tired of it ruling his life.

When I turn it on, an error comes up on the display, and that's when I remember him passing the card to that woman.

Who is she? What did she want with it?

The looting upstairs reaches a fever-pitch. Ear-splitting scrapes, floor-shaking thuds, triumphant shouts. It's either looters or a herd of zebras dancing *Swan Lake*.

My phone buzzes. Matty's number comes up on the display. I hit answer. "Hey, where are you?"

"Out," he says, breathing heavily. "Needed a smoke."

Everything inside me goes cold. We have a code phrase. In case something ever goes bad. That was it.

Adrenaline puts a tremor in my hands. My legs. My pulse pounds in my ears, loud enough I can hear it. Forcing down the panic, I try to remember the questions we worked out, the ones we agreed to use if someone could be listening. "Could you get some ibuprofen while you're out?" *Can you get away?*

Muffled sirens, people shouting. "Stores are closed, babe."

My legs go weak. "Matty—"

"Check my bag," he says. "Side pocket. Should be some in there."

I dive on his old green duffel, hands trembling. The pocket is empty, but the lining is ripped. Inside, I find a Brazilian passport in my name. He has dual citizenship—there are places he goes where being American is a bad idea—but if I have it too, it's news to me.

"What's going on? Where did this come from?"

"I got your back, baby."

"Is this about—?"

"Stop." A rush of breath comes out of the receiver. "You don't know anything. I haven't told you a thing, right?"

"Matty please…"

Echoing sounds, like footsteps in an alley. More than one pair. "Say it, Leah."

"Would I be asking if you had?"

He drops his voice low. "Listen to me. Put on my sweats. Tie the biggest goddamn knot in the waist you can because there are gangs out here who will make you regret it if you don't. Then get your ass to the embass—"

A low *pi-too* sounds, like gas escaping in a rush. He gasps and drops the phone. My heart stops. "Matty, say something, please."

When he picks it up again, his voice is slurred. "I love you—you know that, right?"

I lose it. "You're supposed to come home, Matty. You promised you'd always come home."

"No choice," he murmurs again. "You're the only home I ever knew.

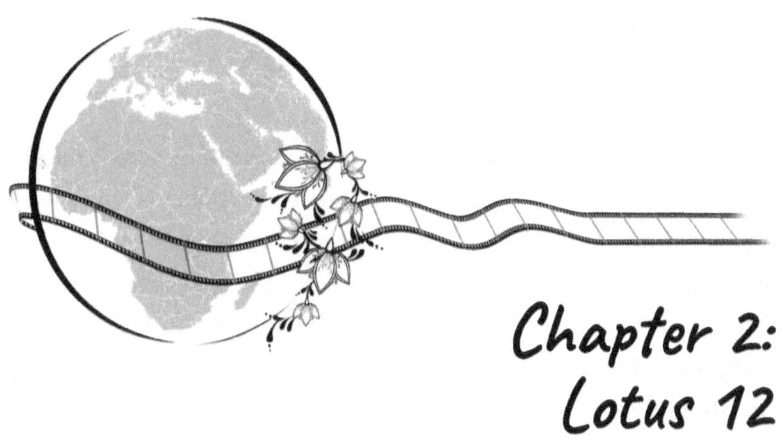

Chapter 2:
Lotus 12

WASHINGTON, D.C.

SIX MONTHS LATER...
(PRESENT DAY)

The law offices of Godderall & Coventry occupy a city block not far from the Capitol, where I've developed a reputation as the associate most likely to suffer an aneurysm before her next birthday.

Outside, the leaves are quaking in a late summer drizzle of rain. It's been six months since Matty disappeared. The bar exam is a distant speck in the rearview mirror, along with my sanity.

Finishing my last swig of coffee, I hit send on the email I wrote to him, part of my morning ritual whenever he was traveling. Silly, mundane things about my classes, what's on the news, what color underwear I'm wearing. Pathetically, I keep sending them because it makes him feel a little less gone.

Dear Matty. Today I sat next to a naked man and a pigeon on the metro...
Dear Matty. Today, nobody tried to deport a single one of my clients.
Of course, that's because the government was shut down...
Dear Matty. Today was supposed to be the day our baby was born...

Numb, I close the lid. For ten weeks, I had a little piece of him with me, a reason to hope, something to keep me going, then one day, the heartbeat was gone. Just one of those things, the doctor said. Except it felt as if my heart had stopped too.

As far as the world is concerned, Matty is one of hundreds missing in the crackdown. Amnesty classifies him as a prisoner of conscience, but between shooting, imprisoning, and brutalizing every journalist and dissident they can get their hands on, Egypt denies they have him. Reporters Without Borders says 'Missing, whereabouts and welfare unknown'. The network that sent him to Cairo washed their hands of the whole thing as soon as the first ransom demand came in. *'Due to Mr. Cahill's status as a freelance journalist, we regret that we are unable to provide further assistance. Mr. Cahill was advised of the need to provide his own kidnap insurance.'* Most of our friends think he's dead, which isn't a possibility I'm willing to consider. At least not out loud. But in the lonely, small hours of the night, sometimes I wake up talking to his ghost.

To hear people talk, I've gone off the deep end. *'He's obviously dead, she's in denial. She's better off without him anyway.' 'His own fault, going those places.'* Social media? Forget it. Turns out, posting an appeal for a captured journalist is a surprisingly effective way to generate rape threats.

The fact is, the 'kidnap insurance' Matty was supposed to buy cost more than the assignment paid. He covered the Syrian Civil War in Russian surplus body armor he bought on Craigslist. We both knew the risks. But not getting Matty back means accepting a world where journalism is expendable. Even the truth itself. If fighting that makes me crazy, then so be it.

I found this tiny apartment after he disappeared, a one-bedroom off Columbus Circle. A bay window overlooks the street, floor to ceiling bookcases in the hall, filled with framed photos and books, plus dozens of sandpipers Matty had carved out of driftwood while we were shacked up with my parents. He'd spend hours watching them dart along the shore, lost in his thoughts.

Oops, like me. Late for work.

I'm wearing his favorite T-shirt, which doesn't smell like him anymore, but I pretend it does. I slip it off, then throw on a navy skirt suit—the universal female junior associate attire. It's my suit of armor, defense against the whispers that I only have a job because of my dad, but it can't stop me from feeling like a fraud on the inside. *Silly old Leah can't even get the Egyptian Government to answer her inquiries anymore.*

After grabbing a pair of heels, I run out the door. Though I know Matty would yell at me for doing it, I leave it unlocked. I always do. Just in case.

The days after he vanished are a blurred nightmare, stumbling through fields of bodies in the makeshift morgues, until my visa got revoked and the State Department threw me on a plane home. The first thing I did was call the firm to let them know I couldn't take the job. Not with Matty's trail growing colder by the second. One of the founders, Julie Coventry, who'd clerked for my dad back in the day, picked my ass off the floor and drove me to the bar herself. *'Pull it together. You'll need your license. You'll need our resources. You'll need advice. This is not the time to go it alone.'*

Junior associates at God & Coventry—nicknamed for either the other founder's legal reputation or the fact he's approximately six thousand years old—carry between fifteen and twenty cases. Including Matty, I have thirty-two. It's partly because immigration attorneys who speak passable Arabic are few and far between, partly because the administration hasn't met an immigrant it doesn't want to deport, and partly because I begged for the extra work. If I stop moving, I'll drown.

What it means on this particular day is that I have to be at the courthouse by eight a.m. to ambush a judge who makes a game of hiding from lawyers who need his signature, because if I'm not, one of my thirty-two clients will be deported to his home country and killed. I have to be at the firm by nine a.m. to meet with Julie for my thrice-delayed performance review, which is about to get delayed a fourth time because I have to go and prostrate myself in front of Senator Nance to get Immigration to stop sitting on a different asylum petition that's about to expire. Which would undoubtedly go better if I hadn't lost my shit with him last week over a 'sanctuary city' defunding provision he caved on, because apparently, refugees are only worth saving if they're victims or saints instead of ordinary, flawed people like the rest of us. Basically? It's going to be a fun morning.

Brushing raindrops from my hair, I sprint up the courthouse steps, after spotting Judge Lawrence Q. Underwood skulking behind the Civil War monument by the south entrance. It's judiciary-only, which means I have to use the western entrance, take my chances with the pervy security guard because his line is invariably shorter, and then catch Underwood before he reaches his office, because the lawyer-hating architect who designed the courthouse thought it would be *great* to have separate corridors for judges, juries, defendants and attorneys, so none of us ever have to talk to each other. Except when we do. Which Underwood finds hilarious.

Panting, I catch the old coot as he ducks into the sixth-floor men's room. With peaked grey eyebrows, bowed legs and an overstuffed belly, he's a chimera of a horned owl and a basset hound. He waves his copy of the *Post*. "Nature calls, Counselor. You'll have to wait."

I debate following him, but rumor has it the last attorney who did found his client on a plane to Uganda an hour later. "Your honor, it won't take a minute," I say, pushing the door a crack. "I just need a signature."

All I get is a fart and a whistle. To the tune of the United Airlines theme song.

"I'll be outside, your honor."

"Ms. Atkins—"

"Atkins-Cahill, your honor."

"Is this that homosexual client of yours? The Armenian?"

"Mr. Nimazi is Azerbaijani, your honor."

Another fart. "That's what I thought."

Given that lately, the best advice I can give my clients is to go off the grid and disappear, he knows he can screw with me as much as he wants. Frustrated, I retreat to the wooden bench across the hall and close my eyes.

Being married to a photographer has a way of making images stick in your head. Sometimes, I'll see him standing in the bedroom door with the cup of chamomile tea I'm just realizing I want. Or sitting in the branches of a mango tree near Lake Victoria, listening to me ramble about the latest bureaucratic aid crisis. Other times, it's him bleary eyed and shirtless in the kitchen at four a.m., absentmindedly rubbing his ribs. Or shackled to a wall in some dank Cairo cell, wondering whether I've given up on him.

Maybe I won't close my eyes after all.

The courthouse is waking up. Clacking heels and over-applied aftershave fill the halls. Since it's been twelve hours since anyone in the Egyptian government ignored me, I pull out my phone, intending to be a good lawyer and harass someone, but it's ignoring me too in favor of software updates.

Apparently, an Angry Birds update. A little mindless pig-killing. Just what I need. If I'm lucky, they've added a judge piggy.

Clearly, I've got Egypt on the brain—the level looks like the Egyptian Museum, pillars and palm trees in front of a pink building. But then, a brilliant blue lotus flower unfolds on the screen. A dozen petals spread in bloom before fading to blackness.

It launches a video. Dark and grainy, a small room somewhere. An aluminum chair tilts to the left, then right, like the room is moving. There's a running timestamp in the corner.

From yesterday.

Scraping sounds, a moan. "Get him up."

Sweat-stained arms haul a limp body into the chair. My breath catches in my throat.

Oh dear God, "Matty—"

His face is gaunt, almost skeletal, eyes bloodshot and dim. He's naked, at least from the waist up, filthy, arms bound behind his back.

He's alive. Or was yesterday at least.

"His memory's fucked," the other voice says. "Show it to him again."

In English.

American English.

My brain rebels at first. It means the Egyptians weren't lying. They don't have him.

We do.

His own country did this to him.

My hands are shaking too badly to hold the phone. At the start, I had my suspicions—how could I not? NSA surveillance…the justice department going after journalists… the administration's raging hate-on toward the whole profession… the praise they lavished on dictators in Egypt and Russia and Turkey for journalists murdered or imprisoned. There was nothing. Not a shred of evidence pointed anywhere besides the Egyptian military.

Which means someone went to a lot of trouble to make it appear that way.

Disembodied hands smack a folded newspaper on a table, making me jump. "Focus, Cahill. Where do we find him?"

Matty's head lolls to the side. "Find who?"

The interrogator throws up his hands. "Christ, you know who. Are you that stupid?"

"Guess so." Matty pushes his tongue through his lips, as if he can't figure out how his mouth works. "Y'know my wife's a lawyer?"

The camera bobbles. The shadows shift, revealing a broad chest wearing an army green T-shirt. Someone grabs the sides of Matty's head, forcing him to look at the paper.

"She's not here, reporter. I am."

Bloodshot eyes flutter open. Matty gets agitated, straining at whatever keeps him tied to the chair. "I've got nothing to lose, man. Can't give you what I don't have."

He starts convulsing. The video goes dead.

"No no *no!*" Mashing the screen, I try everything to get him back, but he's gone. It's as if someone poured drain cleaner down my throat. Who sent this to me? Why? What do they think Matty did?

An email flashes on the screen.

> From: Senator Anthony J. Nance
> To: oaclark@af.mil.gov
> Subject: Senate Armed Services Committee, Emerging Threats Division.
>
> You are hereby called to testify on the date and time below. Hart Building 212. Due to ongoing leaks from staff and committee, per Executive Order #1925, only members cleared by the Justice Department will be in attendance. Agenda: briefing on status of Section 1021 detainees, per requirements of Section (f).

Section 1021 is the so-called 'Indefinite Detention' provision. *Indefinite.* Forever. Nauseated, I throw a hand over my mouth and run for the bathroom, heaving into the trashcan by the door.

It's a bullshit law dating from the Bush era, a purposefully vague travesty that can get a journalist arrested just for meeting with the wrong source.

Is that what happened?

Who are they looking for?

Wiping my mouth, I stumble towards the sinks. No, he knew better. His former editor, Jack Solomon, is part of a massive lawsuit against the Department of Justice that's still making its way through the courts. The ACLU and Amnesty keep fighting it, but every administration keeps defending it. And winning. Combined with NSA surveillance, it's carte blanche for the suppression of journalists.

Sick and shaking, I splash some water onto my face. Whatever they want, why did they need to make him disappear to find out? How the hell am I going fix this?

I'd forgotten about Judge Underwood until a grunt comes through the vent.

The hearing is today. Twenty minutes from now. Missing Underwood's signature might mean my client's life. Missing the hearing almost certainly meant Matty's.

Think, Leah.

Outside, in the hall, a familiar voice echoes off the marble. Scott Burgess, a divorce attorney at my firm, talking way too loud into a cell phone. Could be God himself for all I care. I run out and dive on him, thrusting the asylum petition in his face. "Please, Scott, you have to help me—"

He hangs up, brushing latte foam from his tie. "What's the matter?"

Everything. "I don't have time—I'll do anything you want in return, but you have to stay *right here* until Underwood comes out and get him to sign these."

It seems to dawn on him that there's only one reason I'd be so freaked. "Where does it need to go?"

"Immigration. Before noon."

"I've got court all day, Leah."

God, please. "I'll call Julie and borrow her paralegal."

Nodding, he takes the folder. "I'll call her. Go."

I yank off my heels, then sprint for the stairwell and fly out of the building, pushing my way through a crowd of tourists on Constitution Avenue. A cold sense of paranoia floods in. This is Washington. People are watching.

Getting into the Senate offices will be easy—I'm there all the time, have a visitor's pass in my purse and everything. But how the hell am I going to crash an intelligence briefing? What am I going to do if I get inside? Hold the entire Senate Armed Services Committee hostage? If we're lucky, they'll throw us in the same cell.

He's alive. That's all I need.

At 8:34, I get to the metal detectors at the Senate offices. The security guy checks my pass. "The schedule says you're not supposed to be here until ten."

I stepped on some broken glass running over here, it's stuck in the bottom of my foot and it hurts like a sonofabitch. The good news? It's taken the edge off my panic.

"Must've misread my calendar," I say, biting the inside of my cheek. "I'll find a corner and get some work done."

Limping, I head up to Room 212, a conference room off the main hall. The American and Senate flags flank each side of the heavy oak door. Maybe I'll tear them both down and set them on fire. Maybe I'll go rip down the copy of the Constitution that Nance keeps behind his desk and bash his face into it until he remembers what it says.

Beside the flags, Senator Nance's senior staffer, Cole Warren, is guarding the doors. Cole is a quintessential Southern gent. I'm a die-hard New England girl, so Dixie guys come in two flavors as far as I'm concerned—cowboy and porch-sitting mint julep sipper—but we've been friends since my first ill-fated attempt at the bar.

It was last July, the night before the exam. I'd been home studying when Matty left me a rambling, incoherent Skype message about a teenage girl caught in an air strike in northern Syria. She'd been right next to him when the missiles hit and wasn't going to make it without long-term first-world medical care. Matty, who had a half-sister in Iraq who died in the war, took it personally.

I ended up bailing on the Bar and camping out on the Capitol steps in what I knew was a futile quest to find someone to sponsor an emergency visa. Cole, who'd found me sobbing in the gallery, had come to the rescue with Nance.

'It's personal for him too, Leah. Everybody knows he's a Gulf War vet, but not too many know he was a refugee himself—his family fled from Lebanon during their civil war and came here. He's been our chief voice on Iraq and Syria for eons. We've got a genocide going on over there and the administration won't lift a finger. You say this girl is an Iraqi Chris-tian? We can use that, maybe. Let's see if we can get creative.'

Nance is a four-term independent with a reputation as a power-broker and dealmaker, someone willing to reach across the aisle. Since it tends to happen when military action is on the table, I'm not a fan. Not to mention I had no intention of letting him use a teenage refugee as a political prop but, whatever. I was desperate.

I slip off my shoe and limp past, leaving a generous smear of blood on the floor. My inner feminist howls, but it does the trick. Cole fumbles his phone. "Goodness, Leah, are you all right?"

"Cut myself." I hop to the wall, where I can inspect my wound. There's a shard of glass stuck in the ball of my foot. Fresh blood trickles onto the floor as I yank it out. "Ow."

He pulls out a handkerchief. "You're white as a magnolia. What were you doing running around barefoot?"

"I'm such a klutz," I say, glaring at my stilettos. "From now on I'm sticking to sneakers." I make a dizzy feint, then let him catch my arm. "Guess I shouldn't have skipped breakfast this morning."

"Well dang, girl, you've got too much going on for that." He glances at the door. "I've got bandages in the office. Might be able to find a muffin too. It's just…"

I press my thumb over the wound. "I can watch the door for you. Promise, I won't let anyone in."

"It's not that," he says. "He's pretty sore at you. Doubting him, after what he did for that girl? She's one of millions, Leah and you know it. Don't you want to help the others?"

Half the time, Nance can't even remember Maira's name. I push my hair out of my face. "Cole, right now, I have a Haitian client sitting in a detention facility because yesterday, when INS raided the plant where she works, they found out that last year, some racist cop pulled her over for Driving While Black. I only *know* she's being detained because her kids' school called me and said nobody came to pick them up and oh-by-the-way, her eleven-year-old was having a panic attack that her mother had been crushed under a building like her father. So before you talk to me about who I do and don't want to help, tell your boss to stop making it harder."

Cole grimaces. "I expect he's trying harder than you think." My foot is gushing, so he hands me the handkerchief. "Keep the pressure on."

As soon as he rounds the corner, I dive on the door. I need to walk out of here with proof. Evidence. Grounds for a habeas petition to challenge Matty's detention.

In the end, I smooth my hair and tug down my skirt, and try to pretend I haven't just found out the U.S. Government is torturing my husband. *Deep breath. Let's do this.*

Staying calm buys me a few seconds. The room is darkened, which helps. It's the usual committee set-up, a bunch of overstuffed white guys sitting around a dais. Nance, fiftyish and Lebanese, looks as out of place as I do.

A man in uniform stands in front of a projector, the Army emblem lighting up his face like grey-green war paint. The rest are arguing so no one notices me at first. A junior senator, some first-term Silicon Valley bajillionaire, is about fifty shades of incredulous. "So Colonel Clarke—you're telling me the administration sent an *American* journalist to a black site? That's a thing we're doing now?"

Clarke has a Midwestern accent, a greying flat-top haircut, and a silver eagle on his shoulders. "With due respect, Senator, the statute authorizes the detention of anyone who supplies material support to terrorists." His response is directed more at Nance, pronounced bone structure making his disdain apparent. He switches the slide on the screen. "The optics suck, but DOJ sees this as a slam-dunk case."

PRISONER CODE NAME: LOTUS 12
- Detainee on CIA/Homeland Security radar since 2003.
- History of prior knowledge of bombings and attacks.
- Unexplained access to highly classified U.S. Intel.
- Multiple points of contacts within ISIS and AQIP.

AUTHORIZATION FOR DETENTION
- Present at major attack last year against Christians in Aleppo.
- Evidence at scene implicates detainee in long-range plan for attacks on American interests.
- Interrogation provided key intel in thwarting attacks.

NOTES: Prisoner on prolonged hunger strike. Receiving forced nutrition.

The room starts to spin. *Hunger strike? Forced Nutrition?* There's no name, but given the video, it all fits. Not to mention that apart from the places and dates, winding up on the brink of death from some stupid, noble, and ultimately futile gesture would be exactly Matty's style.

Before I lose it, I snap a picture with my phone. Then it occurs to me that it's my only link to whoever knows where he is. My only proof. Shaking, I slip it into the ripped lining of my purse. *Slam dunk my ass.*

"Some of us would get primaried over this," chides the junior senator. "What kind of attacks are we talking about?"

"Who cares?" The senator next to him helps himself to some coffee. "The intel thwarted the attack. We leak it to the press and we're heroes."

"Not in my state," someone else shoots back. "The civil liberties people are all fired up. If it gets out that I allowed the detention of an American journalist, I'm cooked. At least tell me he's Muslim."

Nance loses his temper. "You're in luck. The crazy bastard is Brazilian."

Months of pent-up emotion spill over. "That's a lie!" I cry. "He's American! His parents are American! Why are you doing this? What are you doing to him?"

A dozen heads spin. Coffee guy spits out a mouthful, spraying Nance. Someone picks up the phone, senators jump out of their chairs. "How'd she get in here? Who's that?"

"The detainee's wife." With a baleful glance towards Clarke, Nance gets up and snaps off the projector. "Ms. Cahill, how did you learn about this hearing?"

I'd ask how he knew, but shouts echo down the hall. Half a dozen Capitol policemen storm in.

Good. Now I have witnesses.

"I'm sorry, was this a hearing?" I try like hell to channel the patented Dale Atkins stare down. "I could've sworn that in a hearing, the defendant has a right to hear the evidence against him. You know, confront his accusers, that kind of thing."

"Enough." Nance, wiping coffee from his suitcoat, gets right in my face, his voice low, with barely controlled anger. "Leah, I feel we've gotten to know each other rather well over the past few months."

Months he knew. Months he spent lying to my face. Months faking sympathy, months pretending he wanted to help. Hot shame washes over me, thinking of things I told him. Stories he encouraged me to tell. He was using me to gather information. How could I not see it? "How could you?"

He doesn't miss a beat. "You're a lot of things, chief among them a self-righteous pain in the ass, but one thing you are not is stupid. Do you realize what a felony trespass conviction will do to your career?"

"Do you realize what violating the Constitution should do to yours?"

Someone pins my arms, so I let my body go limp. I've been going to protests with my dad since I was five, so I know the drill, but this time, I don't have Dale Atkins as my shield. I'm staring down the full force of the U.S. government by my lonesome. If I blow it, there's nowhere to go but down.

Desperate, I scan the room for a friendly face. "Ever watched a democracy die, Senators? I have. Step one? Go after the journalists. Tell people they're inciting all the problems in the first place. That they're sympathizers. That they're associating with the people they're afraid of. Call them troublemakers. Then collaborators. From there, it's an easy step to traitor."

"Shut her up." Clarke says. He looks drawn and nauseated, with a perceptible tremor in his right hand. "You're giving her exactly what she wants."

Chills crawl up my neck. "What I *want* is my husband back."

"Quiet," Nance snaps. He and Clarke confer, heads together, arguing over who's going to wrangle the committee and who's going to wrangle me. Nance motions for the guards to release me.

My nerves feel as if they've been hooked up to a car battery. Mentally, I'm ordering the motions I need to file. Running through a list of dad's old friends. Judges who might give me the emergency petitions I need. How I'll spin it when I go to the papers. Matty will hate it, but whatever. I'll have to pull up all the detainee case law, from Boumediene back to Eisentrager.

He marches me out of the conference room, where Cole is standing with a dismayed expression. I go to say something, but Nance does some kind of Vulcan pinch on my elbow. "I said quiet."

I stifle a yelp. "Not until you tell me everything you know about Matty."

"You're in no position to negotiate." His private office is around the corner, wingback chairs and a paneled oak desk. The walls are solid with photos, him with a group of Marines in Iraq, him as a young boy in Lebanon. There's a flat screen above a grey marble fireplace, tuned to a news channel. He shoves me inside, closing the door. "Your mobile, Mrs. Cahill."

I flex my injured foot, showing the gash. "It got run over by a bus when I tripped."

"It is in the lining of your purse and you are fortunate I'm the only one who saw you put it there." He leans forward. "You may not believe this, Leah, but I know little more than you about what's happening. Today's hearing was a chance to rectify that situation. A chance you have now all but destroyed."

"You're right. I don't believe you."

"If it were me, I might care to learn whether the person who led you here was trying to help or hinder your efforts."

"The good cop routine might work better if you hadn't spent six months lying to me. I don't have to give you anything. You said yourself I'm not under arrest."

"That depends greatly on your cooperation. Beginning with your assurance that none of today's foolishness leaves this room, and after that, the name of your source."

"Sorry. Don't have a clue." I sit back. "Look, let's cut the crap. If whatever torture techniques you've been using haven't worked by now, they're not going to. Either Matty doesn't have what you want or he's not giving it to you. I'm your best chance. Get him on U.S. soil within 24 hours or I go to the press. Trust me. I've got the contacts."

A red chyron breaks across the television screen, a news alert. The screen shows a GoPro-style video, turbulent and chaotic. Whatever is going on is obscured by roiling billows of gas.

SARIN GAS ATTACK IN PROGRESS AT SOCCER MATCH IN MONTREAL. LIVE-STREAM FROM SOCIAL MEDIA ACCOUNT BELONGING TO SYRIAN REFUGEE.

Everything in me goes numb. With a hard, frustrated curse, Nance hurls his keys at the desk. After a heavy silence, he regains his composure. "Go ahead. Try it. You know the playbook. The response will be a series of leaks portraying his involvement with certain persons of interest. They will tie him to this incident. Other perhaps to come."

Tears well up, both from the horror on screen or the suggestion that Matty had anything to do with it. It's not that I believe him, but given all we've lost, what we spend our lives trying to do, it's about the worst thing anyone could say to me. "Matty has as much sympathy for those nihilistic fucksticks as you do. He was trying to do something about it."

"Then perhaps you should ask yourself what he's protecting."

Matty would never reveal a source. "Obviously you don't know my husband."

This is for Aleppo, the attacker shouts in Arabic. Then he collapses to his knees, sobbing. *For Mosul. For Idlib. For a world which watched our children die and did nothing.*

A sickening realization takes root. If there was anything Matty and I both understood about the world, it was the way one terrible thing drove another, then another. I'd spent my career struggling to head those things off, and Matty had spent his struggling to get people to stop looking away. Was it possible? Had he tried with this man and failed?

Nance leans forward, elbows resting on his knees. "You need to accept that he's not coming home."

Fighting not to lose it, I stand. "Then you obviously you don't know me either."

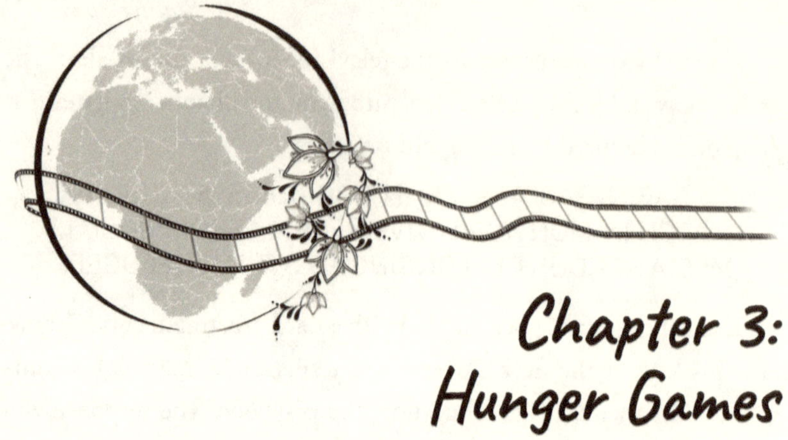

Chapter 3:
Hunger Games

SOMEWHERE ON THE MEDITERRANEAN

Matty

Dizziness comes in waves, colliding with the pitching of the ship. Groans roll through the hull. The sea is restless, like the mood onboard. Something's going on. It's in the air.

Leah's voice floats by the infirmary door. She's arguing with the warrant officer. *Where are his medical records, I want copies of all interrogation tapes.*

There's zero chance it's anything but a hallucination, but the door squeaks open and there she is, fumbling with my straps. "Baby, what have they done to you?"

Her face is a blur of soft angles. Whispers of dark hair fall on my face, too real for a hallucination. My mind floods with the smell of an ocean wind. It's the way she smells when we're at her parents', the way she smelled the day we got married. It's the smell of freedom, of better days, of things they've made clear I'll never have again.

Leah is hope when I lose it, she's a light that never goes out. She makes sense in my life when nothing else does. The ache for her is a hundred times worse than anything else. Gritting my teeth, I turn away. "You're not here."

A gentle hand caresses my cheek. "Yes I am, baby. You've been asking for me, right?"

The blackness of the room is disorienting, more than whatever they shot me up with. Sugar, water, and vitamins, they said. No. It's poison, twisting hope into a weapon. "Not real."

She loosens the restraints on my wrists. "Ssh, I'm here, I finally found you, I'm here. Why is this happening, what do they want?"

Warmth flows up the vein in my arm. Caught by delusion, I'm about to spill, but my tongue feels all twisted and wrong. Somewhere through the fog, it bubbles up what she said first. How she said it. 'I'm here', not 'hea-uh', the way Leah does.

"Get away from me, whoever you are." I sit up, ripping out the IV. Blood spatters the table and floor. "Couldn't you idiots find someone with the right accent?"

Someone clocks me. My shoulder hits the wall. I fight, but after a month with no food, they slam me onto the table like a rag doll.

"Push another five mils." Someone lashes webbing straps around my wrist. A sharp pain hits my elbow. A burning sensation trickles up my arm, then a flooding sense of calm.

Voices drift through a distorted fog. "So his wife knows now? What are we doing about that?"

"The boss sent Hendricks," comes the reply.

Can't think. Hendricks… I know that name.

"Try again when he wakes up. He won't remember."

"Hell I won't," I slur. Good or bad, memories are all I have.

Chapter 4:
Chaos Theory

NOVEMBER 2002
BOSTON, MASSACHUSETTS
(15 YEARS EARLIER)

Until the day I met Leah, I was convinced certain things had no power to affect the world. Butterflies, cyclones, all that. Or hey, one of my photos. Bottom line, if you'd told me one girl, standing against the winds of the world could make me believe in something again, I'd have said you were crazy. In the end, a parking spot changed my mind.

It was one of those rare fall days in Boston where the sun was shining and everyone was getting one last dose before winter blew in. I was slumped over a couch in the student union at BU, where my editor, Jack Solomon, moonlit as a lecturer. I was fresh off an eight-week shoot in Mozambique, which was supposed to have been a ten-week shoot, except my buddy Rani Camilos had decided to go tearing off after a farmer's kid who'd run into a minefield. The idiot had died in my arms, and once I'd dumped the footage on Jack, I was seriously contemplating the idea of taking a header in front of the Green Line. If it hadn't been for the girl with messy pinned-up hair and knobby knees running around the lounge, I'm almost certain that's what would've happened.

She was handing out flyers for a peace rally, shoring up a disheartened smile for everyone she approached. It was the day of the big BU-BC hockey game, so she wasn't having a ton of luck. I spied Jack jumping the line at the coffee shop, but she got there first, heading me off.

"Morning, Professor Solomon," she said brightly.

Jack hadn't been 'Professor Solomon' to me since freshman year. He was a relic of the old guard, a napalm-for-cologne journo who'd made his bones in Vietnam. He still wore a flak jacket, but only on lecture days. It was part of the mystique.

"We're holding a protest march at noon," she said, handing us a red, white, and blue sheet with 'No Blood for Oil' scrawled across the top. She had a blue peace symbol painted on one cheek, an American flag on the other. The words *Not in Our Name* stretched across her T-shirt, above a picture of tanks racing across the desert. "Will you come?"

I had my best friend's blood on my shoes and thirty rolls of film that'd put it there. What I saw was a cliché, a bleeding heart in designer jeans bouncing from one cause to the next. "You're wasting your time, sweetheart."

She turned on a sweet, dimple-cheeked smile, and blew a wisp of dark hair out of her eye. "Every voice counts. If enough people join in, we'll be heard."

At that point, the war was just an itch in Bush's pants, but it didn't change the fact it was coming. "The people in charge are deaf. Blind and dumb too."

"All the more reason to fight." She pressed the flyer into my hand, revealing a dove-shaped tattoo on her wrist. "I'm Leah, if you change your mind."

I crumpled it up, then chucked it in the bin, hoping she'd take the hint.

"Don't mind him, dear," Jack said, with a faux-paternal expression. "He's pretending to be allergic to idealism."

"Bite me, Jack."

As she wandered off to her next victim, Jack's 'daddy' mode abruptly switched off. He slurped his coffee, leering at her ass. "God's balls, Matt, you look like hell. When'd you get back?"

All I did was hand him the bag of film rolls. "It's there, the whole shoot. Do whatever you want with it."

He fished a pack of Djarums out of his vest. "Dumping the story won't bring Rani back."

I followed him outside, blinking in the sunshine. "You weren't there."

The trip to Maputo had been my idea. Rani and I had been friends ever since I ran away from my folks in São Paulo, and we'd been working together about that long. I'd had a thing for years about landmines, all the neocolonialist, Marxist, racist, holy-war bullshit that had been strewing them around the world for a hundred-odd years. Rani and me, we were going to do something about it.

Jack stuck the cig into his mouth, then struck a match. "No. But I heard what you did. Thought you were past this suicidal crap."

I'd been out of my freaking mind, not suicidal. That came later. "You weren't there," I repeated.

A wreath of clove-scented smoke curled around his head, trailing away in the breeze. "So two more of journalism's boy heroes fell to earth. Suck it up and write the story."

Rani was the writer. I was just the guy who took the pictures. "I can't, Jack."

"Why not?"

Because I couldn't close my eyes without reliving it. Because I'd been hearing Rani's voice in my head non-stop and the pictures would make it a thousand times worse. Except you didn't admit that crap to your editor, not if you wanted to keep working. "Rani would rip me a new one for making it about him."

"So don't."

We headed toward the Charles, walking a brownstone-lined street which ran through the heart of campus. After eight weeks in a country where people farmed mined land because it was the only place things would grow, culture shock was killing me.

"People don't get it." Jack took a thoughtful drag from his cigarette. "Why risk your life for a three-hundred-dollar photo? How you can stand back and shoot while someone's dying instead of lending a hand?"

Not what I did, but, whatever. On a good day, I would've said you went for the shot because people had a right to know why the guy died. Or because you secretly harbored a dream that someone might decide to do something about it next time. Today wasn't a good day.

"You really think that's what I need? A lecture about journalism ethics?"

He stopped in front of his beater Toyota. "You think I don't know what it's like to watch someone die? Forget all the wars. I've been watching you die for years, because *something* in that messed-up head of yours knows how to take a photo that grabs the world by the nuts. I'm trying, Matt, I'm giving you every shot I can. But it'll be a miracle if you make thirty."

I slid into the passenger side. "You said that about me turning twenty-five, too."

A commotion started down the street, old-style peace songs competing with slogans and chants. Leah's protest group was at the far end, by the ROTC detachments.

Jack banged his fist on the glove compartment, retrieving a pill bottle. "Look—forget the *Globe*. We'll say you were on a sabbatical. I'm headed out west tonight. I'm having drinks with the chief editor at *Mother Jones*. They're looking for alternate lines to hit the administration and they're not afraid of journalists who take a position. This is a chance to write your landmine story the way you want to write it." He shook a few white pills into his hand, offering me one. "Your first national. In or out?"

I swallowed the pills. Didn't give a shit what they were. There was no way I was going to be able to look at those pictures. "I'll think about it."

"A month," he reminded me, tapping my camera bag. "Go get drunk, get laid, whatever you need to do. Just finish the story."

Finish the story. Right. "I'll get him something."

The landmine story wasn't gonna happen, but I wasn't about to let a feature at MoJo slip either, so I grabbed my Leica and got out of the car. What I needed was another story. Fast.

Though I hadn't spent much time in the States since 9/11, the country was splitting apart at the seams. Two protestors threw red paint on the steps of the ROTC buildings, which brought out every soldier, airman, sailor, and Marine inside. What started as a pissing match grew into chest-bumping and shoving. Leah was pleading with a guy in a field uniform.

If it hadn't been for where Jack had parked his car, I never would've given that girl in the union a second thought. But it took about five seconds to realize this wasn't just anyone to her, this was someone she loved, someone who was pissed as hell at her. What I saw was a peacenik who loved a warrior. It was the pain in her expression as she reached for his cheek, it was the cold fury in how he pushed her away.

I took the shot the moment her eyes got wet, the moment his hardened. A photo is life's truths captured in silver, the ones that happen too fast to see. A great photo doesn't capture a moment, it captures emotion—jubilation, grief, fear. But the second she touched his face, he flipped out and shoved her into a hedge.

Rule one: you're not the story, you're a witness. Report, don't influence. I was sick and damn tired of the rules. So I did the paparazzi strut and started snapping like mad.

The guy spun around, a second lieutenant, a single gold bar on his uniform, along with a pair of copter wings. His chest was heaving, as if he couldn't quite get it together. "Mind your goddamn business."

I tucked the camera safely under my arm. "Hey, man—an officer in uniform assaulting a peaceful protestor? Goes *way* beyond my business."

He straightened up, scowling. "What are you, a reporter?"

"Like Jimmy Freaking Olsen."

He made a grab for the camera, but a campus police cruiser turned the corner. A flame-haired Army cadet, who'd been watching them argue from the sidewalk, popped a handful of Altoids into his mouth. "Ain't worth it, Dino."

Glancing sidelong at the cruiser, the lieutenant backed off, pointing at me. "Print those and you'll regret it."

Since I had him by the balls and he knew it, I turned to his buddy, squinting at his name patch. *Hendricks.* "Care to give a statement, Cadet Hendricks?"

Hendricks cracked his neck, giving me a death glare that reminded me of a pissed-off scorpion. "You're trespassing on government property. Be a shame if anything happened to you." He flicked an Altoid at my head, then clapped the lieutenant on the back and led him towards the stairs. "Come on, man, forget her."

Clutching her wrist, Leah followed them to the railing. "Jason, you have to believe me. I didn't know they were planning to come here. I didn't know about the paint."

Something in his expression changed. He knew he'd hurt her, but instead of apologizing, he swore under his breath and yanked open the detachment door. "You make me crazy, Leah. We're done."

The door slammed behind him. "Your boyfriend is a dickhead," I said, picking a broken holly branch out of her hair.

She'd had it up before, but now it fell around her face in shiny waves, reaching halfway to her waist. It was the color of the Chesapeake sand at sunset, and her eyes were deep brown, flecked with the green of the water.

"He's not... I mean we're not..." She looked down, struggling to keep her tears at bay. "He's not himself at the moment. Please, you can't print that picture. He'll get in trouble."

"Maybe he should."

She shook her head. "He just got back from SERE. Capture training. All Army pilots have to take it. It… it didn't agree with him."

Whatever. "It might help your cause. Get you some attention."

She stiffened. "No. We don't need tricks. War is wrong. People will see that sooner or later."

I rolled my eyes. "Sure they will."

She rubbed her wrist, staring at the paint on the stairs. "They will. One heart at a time, if we have to."

She came off more devoted than naïve, but I couldn't put my finger on why. Women in my world tended to be jaded and distant, not that I wasn't. You had to be. Leah was different. She wasn't as worldly, at least not then, but I got the sense that not much scared her.

"I'll look at the photos and see if there's anything else I can use," I lied, slinging the bag onto my shoulder. "Mind giving me your number?"

She leaned on the hedge. "Personally or professionally?"

Maybe she got to me because she was willing to take the fight where it hurt. Maybe I needed another reason to keep from jumping in front of the T. Maybe Jack's happy pills made me loopy, because all I remember is Rani's voice saying *'you gonna be fine, boyo—you gonna marry this girl someday.'*

"Would it change your answer?"

"I have a boyfriend," she said softly.

"Two minutes ago you said you didn't."

"It's complicated." Her nose wrinkled. "Either way, aren't you a little old for me?"

I shrugged. "How old do you think I am?"

"Thirty…five?"

"Close. You're only a decade off." I handed her my card, making a mental note to get some sleep. "Look, what I said in the union—it's been a bad week. I do care what happens in Iraq. I care quite a bit."

"What does that mean?"

I flicked the card. "You'll have to call me to find out."

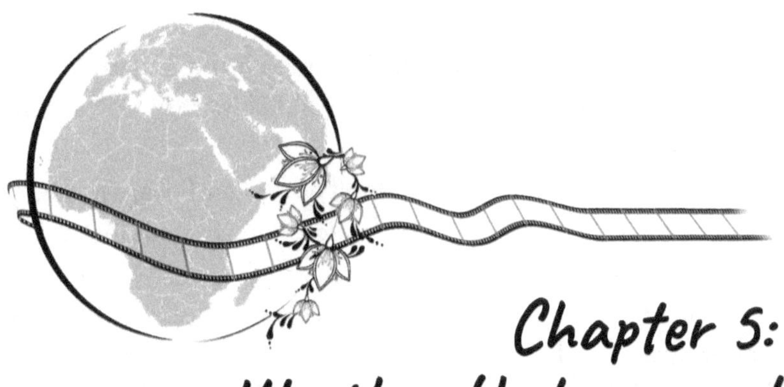

Chapter 5:
Weather Underground

DECEMBER 2002
BOSTON, MASSACHUSETTS

The next time Leah and I saw each other was at a city-wide peace rally on the Common. Between drinking binges and other futile attempts to make Rani's death go away, I'd been pitching an Iraq story. Screw landmines. Nobody gave a shit about Africa. Bring on the UN inspectors and WMDs.

The war was all anyone was talking about anyway. The sky was grey, and the air tasted of the first winter snow, but five thousand signs bobbed and wove across the green, amidst songs and chants, the odd whiff of weed. Rumors ran wild—the government was about to reinstate the draft. The Pentagon had ordered fifty thousand body bags. Bush was going to declare martial law and we were all going to have to start saying 'nucular'. Whether or not the stuff turned out to be true, people were nervous.

Leah was by the Frog Pond, where a crowd had gathered around an aged black guy in a frayed Army field coat who was delivering a fiery rant. I knew him by sight—Dale Atkins—famed civil rights attorney, though long shunned by the movement for marrying a white woman. More recently, he'd become a patriarch to the tattered anti-war community.

"Raise your hand if you've heard their lies before," he said, pointing at a couple of Vietnam-era vets. "God knows they fed the same lines to my boy…"

After grabbing a shot with my 4x5, I headed for Leah, who was off to the side, rapt. She had on another protest shirt. This one read '*Silence is consent*'. I figured she had a collection.

Content, I slung the strap of my Leica over my arm and bumped her shoulder. "I still picture this guy with an Afro from his Weather Underground days—he looks almost respectable now. What's a civil rights radical doing at a war protest?"

"He lost his son in Vietnam." She put her finger to her lips. "Besides, what more important civil right is there than the right to speak out against an unjust war?"

A true believer. That was Leah. "I take it you're a fan?"

The speech ended, to raucous cheers and applause. She started to laugh. "You could say that."

She ran to Dale, who'd broken through the circle, and kissed his cheek. "You were brilliant, Daddy."

Whoops.

I'm not sure what I was thinking, other than the same things clueless white guys always have a habit of thinking. Leah was so light-skinned she was barely darker than me, but up close, I saw the resemblance. "Should've known. Like father, like daughter?"

That made her happy. Smiling, she fiddled with her hair. Dale turned. "I presume you mean she shares my ability to drive her mother crazy."

I stuck out my hand. "Honored to meet you, sir. Matt Cahill, Boston Globe."

He shook it. "How do you two know each other?"

"She tried to draft me into a peace rally over at BU." I glanced at her arm. "How's the wrist?"

Dale raised an eyebrow. "What's this?"

Leah rubbed her arm. "It's nothing, Dad. You know how protests go sometimes."

"I'm working on a photo essay about the Iraq situation," I added, wondering why Dale Atkins's kid was making excuses for her boyfriend's anger management problem. "Leah inspired a new angle. I was hoping to talk to her about it more."

Dale scanned the crowd. "There are scads of Gulf War vets here. People who truly understand the country. I'd be happy to make some introductions."

"I've got the Iraq part covered," I said, noting that he'd ignored the idea she might have something to contribute. "Lived there a while when I was a kid."

Leah's brow went up, and she thumbed a stack of index cards she was holding. "Seriously?"

Thanks to my bastard of an old man, I had a seven-year-old half-sister there too. With or without the war, it wasn't my favorite subject. "Told you I cared."

A large group had gathered by the Soldiers and Sailors monument. *1-2-3-4, WE DON'T WANT YOUR BULLSHIT WAR!*

As the police migrated in the direction of the chants, Leah frowned. "Is this where you try to convince me to let you use the picture you took?"

5-6-7-8, STOP THE KILLING, STOP THE HATE!

"You were in a public place. I don't need permission." I scratched my head. Way to sound like a dick about it. "Don't you want a chance to let people know where it came from?"

She whispered into her father's ear, probably hoping he'd tell her I was wrong, but he gave me old man's slow nod. "You won't win an argument with a reporter over the First Amendment, Leah. Learn to manage the press instead."

"That's what I was doing!" she insisted. "He was with Professor Solomon, and I remembered seeing his picture in the alumni newsletter and—"

"Wait—you knew who I was?"

Her face reddened. "A sympathetic reporter is an activist's best friend."

Dale winked at me. "Never trust the friendly ones."

"I need to get back to campus," she said, looking at him. "I have the LSATs tomorrow."

Dale kissed her forehead. "No review books tonight. Get some sleep."

Her face fell. "I thought we were going to have dinner."

A banner near the carousel read 'Vietnam Veterans for Peace', attended by some greybeards in field coats. He handed her a twenty. "I promised your brother's friends a drink."

Reluctantly, she took the money. "Can't I come?"

He gave her nose a tweak. "No girls allowed."

She forced a smile. "Okay. But you owe me dinner next time I'm home."

The overcast skies were about to let loose. Dale maundered off across the pond, I knelt, zipping my Leica inside the case. The thing was a pain to lug around, basically the photographer's equivalent of a shiny red sports car—but you couldn't beat the shots it took. "If it bothers you, you should've told him."

"I'll be happy if he doesn't get himself arrested this time." Wistful, she pulled a knitted blue hat from her pocket. "Besides, I should've realized today wasn't about father-daughter bonding for him."

"Then what was it?"

She stuck the hat on her head. "Making sure some other father doesn't spend thirty years missing his son."

Over the years, I came to realize that Dale loved Leah fiercely, but as his little girl, not the protégé she was killing herself to be. She came late in life, from his second wife, a girl child when he only wanted the boy who'd been taken. She pretended she understood, but her childhood was one long struggle to live up to the memory of a brother she'd never met.

"About that not-realizing-he-was-your-dad thing…"

"What, like you're the first person?" Though she smiled, it wasn't as sunny as before. She picked a strand of her hair, rubbing the end. "My mom says I'm lucky I can pass. She used to chase me around every summer with a squirt bottle of lemon juice and a tube of SPF50." She watched her father walk off with the veterans. "I mean—I get it, trust me, but some days I just want to be able to stand next to him and have people think I belong."

It hadn't occurred to me that she might've been standing aside for a reason. "Who says you can't?"

"You'd be surprised." She pulled a face, then glanced at the sky. "Hope you got your pictures. I think we're about to get soaked."

With the first patter of freezing rain, half the Common started piling onto the T. "How about I give you a ride to campus. We talk about the story, and then you can go back to making excuses for the people you care about without my interference."

A wry smile played at the corners of her mouth. "Gee, how can I pass up an offer like that?"

We started down towards Beacon Street, dodging a game of snow Frisbee. "So how does your boyfriend feel about you being here?"

"He's back at flight training." She zipped her coat. "Look, I get that you've convinced yourself I'm some sort of battered woman, but he knows if he ever does anything like that again, we're done. He spent the last month getting hunted, interrogated, starved, and waterboarded on the off chance the Iraqis not only shoot down his helicopter, but he survives it and they capture him. If you're looking for a victim, look at him, not me."

I had a spiel set to go, war has a human cost, it's my job to show it, people can decide for themselves, blah blah, but then it sunk in what she'd said. "Wait, they waterboarded your boyfriend?"

Her cheeks went pink, a combination of cold and fluster. "I shouldn't have said that—they're not supposed to... I mean..." Biting her lip, she glanced up the hill. "My dad was right, you should've talked to those veterans, not me."

The protestors melded into a crush at the gate. Families, moms and dads in uniform. It pushed us closer, hands almost touching, and suddenly I felt all warm. "The other day, you asked whether me asking for your number was personal or professional. First off, you're gorgeous and a guy would have to be dead to not want you. But that picture proves you have as big a stake in this war as anyone here. I wouldn't be asking about Iraq if I didn't think you had something to say."

With an uncertain smile, she bounced in her shoes. "You really lived there?"

I bumped into a guy in Birkenstocks waving a banner which read '*My God can beat up your God*'. "My folks were missionaries."

"I'm sorry, I didn't…" With a shocked expression, she kicked the toe of her Sketchers on the ground. "Was it Saddam?"

I realized she thought they'd been killed. My mother had recently discovered email, which meant my spam filter heard about once a week that it was never too late for Jesus. "Far as I know, they're still at it."

"You don't know?"

Ahead of us, there was a little kid asleep on an airman's shoulders. My fingers started itching for the shutter. "I haven't seen them since I was seventeen."

"Oh." A counter-protest had gathered outside the gate, all 'Freedom isn't Free' signs, pictures of the Twin Towers and effigies of Bin Laden and Saddam Hussein. Leah pressed her lips together. "Look, forget me. You know the country. You should be writing about it. Explain why sanctions need time to work, and—"

"Why would I do that?"

She stared at me as if I had two heads. "Uh, so we can avert the stupid war? Find a peaceful way to stop Saddam?"

The crowd started closing in. The warm feeling faded. "The sanctions are killing more people than he is."

Someone jostled her. She slipped on the ice and grabbed my elbow. "Are you sure you're on the right side of this gate?"

I shoved my way out of the crush and made for the wrought-iron fence. "I don't do sides."

She followed. "I want to hear what you have to say. If this is really what you think, convince me."

A layer of wet snow covered the bricks. Frustrated, I knelt, drawing a rough outline of Iraq. "Know what that is?"

She crossed her arms. "My last name is Atkins, not Bush."

"Good to know." I pulled her down beside me. "Since you're so smart, draw the borders of Iraq a century ago."

She hesitated. "Trick question. It didn't exist. It was part of the Ottoman Empire."

"Half right." I drew three circles. "Even the Ottomans were smart enough to divide it up. Remember T.E. Lawrence?"

A guy in a ski parka stuck his head over, chomping down a pretzel. "The Lawrence of Arabia guy?"

"Yeah." I rubbed out a line, joining the lower two partitions. "This was his way—the Kurds and Assyrians had their own area up north, the Sunnis and Shiites had the south, which wasn't real smart either, but whatever. The guy knew the region. Better than anyone in the west. His way would keep the peace. Trouble was, that wasn't what the British wanted."

I merged the areas, then added borders for the rest of the Middle East, the Suez Canal, and the Persian Gulf. "They needed an excuse to stay, so they reversed what Lawrence said and created the most instable country they could. Same thing with Syria, Jordan—the whole damn region."

"Bastards," someone muttered.

When I glanced up, a crowd had gathered. A cold pit cratered into my stomach. "Look, if Hussein falls, someone will replace him. He exists because if he didn't, the country would tear itself apart."

"Maybe that's what needs to happen," said a woman standing beside Leah.

Leah studied me. "Are you saying we should be asking ourselves why it hasn't?"

"Easy," someone said. "We like their oil."

"It's not that simple," I said.

The chants of *No Blood for Oil* blew up again. Yet they were competing with a charismatic street preacher and a round of '*Stand up for Jesus*' coming from outside the gates. At first, all I saw was a shock of black hair. The rest of him was hidden behind a sign with a big black arrow pointing to the Common, *Free Ticket to Hell Inside*.

"Peace, they want?" the preacher shouted. "From Saddam Hussein? The guy is a madman. *Matthew 10:34*. Jesus said, I came not to bring peace, but a sword…" A chorus of *Amen, Rev'rend Elijah* rang out.

The sign bobbed out of the way. The instant I saw his face, all the oxygen sucked out of my lungs. The crowd started pitching, and suddenly I couldn't see past a forest of legs. I stood, shoving my way past the crowd.

Leah grabbed my vest. "What's wrong?" She sped up, walking backwards in front of me. "Why did you freak out? People were starting to listen to you."

Once I got past the fence, into Beacon Street, I could breathe. I pressed my thumbs into my eye sockets, wishing for the millionth time that Rani was here. "Put it this way. Either I'm seeing things or the leader of the pro-war fan club there is my old man."

She spun around. "The guy with the megaphone? The one with the grey hair?"

Grey?

I didn't look. Going crazy was better than being on the same continent as him.

"Matty, you look like you're going to be sick. What's wrong?"

What was wrong was by the time I was twelve, I could spout chapter and verse of every book in the Bible, only to realize the guy who was making me do it didn't believe a goddamn word. I spent seventeen years watching him control crowds as if the Lord Himself was speaking through him. It all flooded back, the brainwashing, the beatings, the hiding and fear, hunger, death and disease. My entire adult life had been one long struggle to unlearn all the toxic male bullshit he'd pounded into my head. She was right. It made me ill.

"Religious hangover. Nothing jumping in front of a bus wouldn't cure."

She stiffened. "That's not funny."

My head felt all confused and disoriented. We'd gotten to my beat-up GTI, one round headlight, one square, the windshield covered in sleet. I jabbed the key into the lock, forgetting it was busted. "Didn't say it was."

"Matty, look at me." She reached out, touching my arm, something she always did, right from the beginning, and somehow, it never failed. "You wanted to talk, right? Let's go talk. Somewhere else. We can talk about anything you want. Your story, your family—anything."

Leaning on the car, I kicked at the slush, and all I could think was God she's beautiful. "I thought you had to study."

"I'm Dale Atkins's kid, remember?" She forced a smile. "Pretty much the only thing I'm not worried about with law school is getting in."

We ended up hanging out for the better part of the evening, shooting the breeze, arguing, blowing Dale's twenty bucks on a pizza. I'd given up trying to convince her that the war was already bought and paid for, she was clinging to the idea it wasn't going to happen, so we'd moved to safer subjects, like excommunicated nuns in Africa.

Mostly, I sat there with a dopey expression while she tried to pull out my life story. What does the Serengeti smell like (wildebeest farts and German tourists), had I ever seen a lion (not if they saw me first), would I teach her to curse in Swahili (maybe if she got me drunk enough).

A houseful of frat boys piled in around the counter. "Hey, do you mind if we change seats?"

She gave me a funny look, but got up. "Sure, why?"

Because they were blocking my view of the door and I was ready to jump out of my skin. "No reason." I popped the top on my third Corona, then slid around. "Seriously, if you're so hot for this stuff, why law school? Hit the Peace Corps or something."

She picked a burnt onion off her slice. "My dad and I have plans."

Any idiot could see her dreams weren't where she said they were. "Plans change."

"Speaking of that." She licked sauce from her thumb. "How did you go from kid missionary to conflict photographer?"

Childhood had been one long blur of overcrowded diesel stations, always either shivering or sweating, usually thirsty or starving. It was Chick tracts and Leviticus, fiery sermons and the shame of my wicked soul. "I was a piece of human luggage, not a missionary."

The reason I'd picked up a camera and started documenting the stuff I saw was because otherwise, no one was ever going to know what people were doing to each other and to me that sucked. But if I'd told her that, I would've had to admit there'd been a time I'd been all starry-eyed about it, that I'd thought it'd make a difference, and I wasn't real proud that it hadn't.

Instead, I fiddled with the beer cap. "You know the old joke about bringing a knife to a gunfight? I'm the idiot who takes a camera."

She twiddled a crust. "I didn't mean to pry."

I took a pull from my beer. "What, I'm serious."

"No you're not, you dodged my question.

I took another swig. "Yep."

Undeterred, she tore a piece off the crust, popping it into her mouth. "You knew who my dad is, which means you know the deal with my family."

"Doesn't everyone?"

She frowned. "Right. Which means the world sees me as the result of Dale Atkins betraying everything he stood for."

I raised an eyebrow. "I read his biography once. Boston society girl renounces family fortune, joins forces with radical black firebrand, pisses off entire country in the process. Ask me, you're everything they fought for."

She turned, knuckle to her eye. "The only thing my mom fights now is me. Your turn."

It got real quiet, only clanking pizza trays in the kitchen. I picked at the beer label. "Mine was a wild child in the '70s—Studio 54, all that. Some sicko cabbie drove her and a friend out to the middle of nowhere and shot them both in the head. Took her three days to crawl back to civilization. She swears Jesus carried her out of a ditch on Route 202."

Leah's face clouded. "Wow."

"Yeah."

"Please tell me this leads into some impossibly romantic happi-ly-ever-after love story with your dad…"

"Uh…no." My mother had a textbook case of Stockholm Syn-drome. "Picture Jerry Falwell and Satan getting it on. He's the unholy offspring that resulted."

She took a noisy sip of her lemonade. "Thanks, I needed that men-tal image."

I stole the last piece of pizza. First time in weeks I felt like eating. "You're welcome."

With a pensive frown, she dropped her chin into her hand. "After you told me how old you are, I reread that alumni profile on you. It said you'd been covering wars since the Balkan crisis. You couldn't have been more than fifteen."

"So?"

"So when I was fifteen, my summer job was lifeguarding at the Chatham Country Club. My biggest worry was finding crap in the kiddie pool. You've had this amazing life. Why does it feel like you're ashamed of it?"

I shifted in the booth. "My old man was more con man than preacher. First time he stuck a camera in my hand, he told me to shoot him laying hands on this Dinka woman in the Nuba Mountains. It was supposed to look like he was healing her, so we could send the pictures to our church at home and people would keep sending us money."

"Did she die?"

"Put it this way—the only miracle he could do was make other people's money disappear."

Tucking an errant strand behind her ear, she stared into her straw. "Didn't it bother you, shoving a lens in someone's face at a time like that?"

I raised my eyebrow. "Or when someone's boyfriend is knocking her into a hedge?"

"We're not talking about me."

"You get used to it." I drained the Corona, then grabbed her coat off her chair. "Come on, I'll walk you home."

She frowned, sticking her arm into the sleeve. "You're blowing me off, aren't you?"

"If I told you the rest, you wouldn't go out with me again."

"Boyfriend."

"Don't care."

"I do."

"I'll tell you the rest if you break up with him."

"I'm not *that* curious."

I swiped the cup of ice left over from her lemonade. "Yeah you are."

We took a walk down Comm Ave. She ran her fingers along a snow-covered brick fence. "Since he went on active duty, I swear, he sounds like Bush. The other day, he actually said he thinks the war is God's plan for America."

I shrugged. "Can't fight a war if you don't believe it's worth fighting, right?"

"Shouldn't that tell him something? I've been killing myself to graduate early… we had this whole plan to get married, but now…" She leaned on the wall. "I just need to know there's a chance he'll get back to normal someday. Like you."

"If you think I'm normal, we've got problems." I crunched an ice cube. "Especially if you're seriously considering getting hitched to that dickhead boyfriend of yours."

She stuck her tongue out at me, then pressed the walk signal. "I'm asking if you ever bought into what your father was doing. Or why it changed."

At first, it sort of pissed me off. The only person I'd ever talked about it with was Rani, the kind of stuff that comes out when you're drunk or stoned and lying flat on your back in the desert, just two guys and a billion stars. God, girls, the state of the world—we could talk about anything. I wasn't ready for someone to take his place. What did Leah know about my life? Nothing.

But the thing was, she wanted to. And for a guy struggling to convince himself to keep doing his job, that was huge. I finally had a face to put on the person I'd envision when I was getting shot at in an alley or freezing my nuts off waiting for a source or getting cooked in the middle of some godforsaken desert village. She was the person who'd see the photo I was there to take, the one who wouldn't look away. The one who'd do something about it.

I shook the last bit of ice into my mouth. "My seventeenth birthday. We had a close call at a fueling station in Johannesburg."

"Close call?"

I crunched down, needing the melt to cure the dry mouth feeling. "The trucks would come along and dump petrol right into open trenches, and people would scoop it out in jerry cans or whatever they had. I was taking pictures, my mother was handing out 'literature', while my old man was spouting off a sermon." I chucked the lemonade into a trash barrel. "All of a sudden, he decided God wanted us to fly back to Brazil."

She pulled a face. "God makes travel arrangements? To Brazil?"

"My mother was born there. And he was wanted in the States for tax evasion."

"Oh."

Her 'oh' had that pretending-not-to-be-shocked sound, so I squinted at the sky and made like I hadn't noticed. "So later that day, the station went up. The fireball was so huge, we saw it from the plane."

To my mother, it was just one more miracle, but he'd been off talking to some scuzzy Komanddokorps Afrikaners two minutes before his 'revelation'. Once we'd gotten home, I holed up in my darkroom, my one refuge. There was something about slipping a sheet of photo paper into the developer bath, watching the shot appear. For some guys, the lens was a filter, a way to distance themselves from the stuff they saw. For me it burned them indelibly into my head. Under the red safe light, the photos confirmed what I knew I'd seen. For him to hustle us out of there like that, the bastard had known they were up to something. For some ungodly reason, he'd let fifty-seven people burn to death anyhow.

I'd confronted him, he didn't deny it. While I was figuring out what the hell to do about it, I'd shacked up with an artist friend in the *favelas*, an opium princess, all blonde dreadlocks and pierced nipples. Between getting me stoned and fucking my brains out, she inked my arm. After she went nuts and came after me with a lit cigarette, I slunk home. My old man belted me when he saw the tat. *See no evil, hear no evil, speak no evil.* It wasn't as if he actually believed that telling people to lay their suffering at God's feet would magically feed and clothe them, raise their children from the dead or heal their wounds, but he did it every goddamn day anyhow and I was sick of getting dragged into it. It was the last time I'd seen them.

"This is me," Leah said, pointing at a three-story brownstone with a bright blue door.

The past few hours, I'd felt alive and human. I didn't want the night to end. "When can I see you again?"

She toyed with her hair, looking all uncertain and conflicted. "There's a pre-law party tomorrow, after the LSATs. I doubt you want to hang out with a bunch of college kids though."

"Why not?"

She hesitated. "Let's just say I struggle with the idea of you playing beer pong with kids whose biggest worry is getting carded at Julian's. You really made it through four years here? Without killing anyone?"

College had been sort of a blur. Freshman year was dealing with the God-shaped hole in my life, searching for whatever the hell was supposed to fit in its place, and when the answer had come back as 'nothing', I spent sophomore year suicidal. Rani literally talked me off a ledge more than once. '*Come on*, gatão, *get in here. We'll blow off class, go chase a story somewhere.*' In the end, work was the thing that saved me. It gave me the space to get out of my own head, to stop forcing myself to breathe out everything I wanted to breathe in. Things were better the last two years, until they weren't. Let's just say it wasn't a time I'd go back to. But I would've hung out in a lion cage if it'd meant spending more time with Leah. "I'm easy. It's a date."

"Just friends, okay?" She touched my shirtsleeve. "But I had fun tonight."

"Me too." A rush of endorphins kicked in. "Good luck tomorrow."

All that bliss didn't last five seconds after she disappeared inside. When I turned, the Reverend Eli Cahill was on the corner, beneath a streetlamp, which cast a sinister shadow on his face. This time, I was pretty sure he was real.

Out went the endorphins, in came the bad chemicals in my head. "Are you lost, *cachorro*? Told you I'd see you in hell."

"We heard about Rani." He shifted off the pole, like a serpent curling out of a tree. "Your mother is worried."

I kept walking. "So why isn't she here? Since when do you care about your kids?"

His hand twitched, as if he was itching to belt me, but I was a grown man now. "The Lord needs her elsewhere. She sends her prayers. You would do well to put aside your resentment. Let us help you find your way back into the light."

I spun around. "You know who needs your goddamn help? Ari. Do you even care there's a war about to start?"

His face mottled. "You blame me for the child's existence, yet nothing for her mother, the temptress?"

It took everything I had not to punch him in the throat. "Drop dead."

As I walked off, he followed. "We thought Rani's death might be the epiphany you needed. It breaks your mother's heart to think of you standing unrepentant before the Lord. Come back to the fold."

"You're fucking delusional." I rounded the corner. "Hope you managed to con those morons at the protest out of enough to cover your ticket."

His head lowered. He stepped off, heading for a homeless guy wrapped in blankets, who'd holed up in a doorway for the night, and tucked a few small bills into the man's pocket. "The view must be pretty good from that high horse you're on, Matthias. We're not so different. We both went to sleep one night believing in something and woke up one morning to find it gone. We searched and searched, but somehow wound up doing nothing more than profiting from others' misery."

It was like a poison seed planted in my head. "The day I start believing I'm anything like you, I really will kill myself."

My phone rang, and this time, when I stalked off, he didn't follow.

The caller ID said Jack, which usually meant there was a plane to get on, a war waiting, whatever senseless patch of ground people were fighting over today. This time, it was to tell me the magazine wasn't interested in the protest story.

"Sorry, Matt," he said. "He wants the landmines or nothing."

It was the last thing I could deal with right then. I ground the heel of my hand into my eye. "Come on, Jack—you know I can't."

"What I know," he said, "Is this is why you two went to Mozambique in the first place. All that happened is life made it personal. It has a shitty way of doing that, in my experience. Man up. Stop screwing around."

Maybe he was right. But I was a mess of grief and warped memories and dying ideals, so I went off to make one of the biggest mistakes of my life—developing the photos from the day Rani died.

The photos gave roost to a lifetime of demons. I spent the night ripping stuff out of my archives, throwing negatives on the lightbox, stoned out of my tree and pulling straight from a bottle of scotch. I dug out pictures of a buddy from Reuters who'd been hit by a sniper in Belgrade. An old girlfriend from Moscow who'd vanished without a trace of her or the story she'd been writing. I'd lived, they'd died, and for what? None of the stories ever saw daylight, nothing ever changed.

By midnight, the voices were telling me I was just a collection of problems, no help to anyone, a curse living inside my own head. Death was the taste in my throat, it was the grasping branches of trees, stripped bare and beseeching the forsaken sky.

It was snowing like a bastard, so I gathered my photos, the lives I'd watched slip away, and threw them into a shoebox on the car seat. After the plows came, I backed the GTI onto a side street by the Esplanade, a spot where I could see the river. Once I felt the crunch, my hand lingered on the shifter. The stench of exhaust drifted up. I closed my eyes. That was it. I was done.

Next thing I knew, someone was dragging me out of the seat. My cheek was stinging, and if my head hadn't already exploded, I wanted it to hurry up. At first, I couldn't hear a thing, then I heard her calling my name. "—Matty, open your eyes."

It didn't seem like a particularly good idea, but I did it anyway. I was lying in the road by my car, slush soaking my jeans. Leah was kneeling over me. I rubbed my eyes and tried to sit up, nauseated and weak. "What happened?"

Heaving a sigh of relief, she balled up her coat under my head. "Your tailpipe was in the snow bank. What were you doing sleeping in your car?"

It all came back, and I couldn't help it, I started bawling. She must've figured it out, because a little noise escaped from her throat, a hitch in her breath. By that point, I wasn't sure I wanted to be dead anymore, but I wasn't sure how I felt about being alive either. Mostly ashamed.

To this day, I have no idea what had sent her out there. She didn't push. She didn't judge, she didn't ask questions. She was exactly what I needed—a guardian angel. A friend. Maybe, despite everything, there's a god after all.

"Come on, you're shivering," she said. "You're staying with me tonight."

Chapter 6:
Minefields

DECEMBER 2002
BOSTON, MASSACHUSETTS

Leah stood by the stove in her tiny kitchen, clad in flannel pajamas. The world outside was head-splitting white. There was a ridiculous amount of food on the counter, pancakes and toast, a pile of crisp bacon, half a melon, and she was tracing swirls through scrambled eggs in a frying pan. Purple wires snaked out of her ears, eyes closed, hips swaying to the beat. Despite the jackhammer in my head, the way my muscles felt all seized up and weak, maybe being alive wasn't so bad after all.

She pivoted, opened her eyes, and jumped a mile when she saw me.

"Hi," I said.

With a relieved expression, she tugged the buds out of her ears. "You're up."

"I'm up." I yawned, scratching my belly. "Thanks to you."

She pulled a blue china plate from the cabinet. "Hope you're hungry."

Food was a definite no-go the way my stomach felt. "Nice place," I said instead. Her apartment was cozy, but a hundred times better than anywhere I'd ever lived.

"My roommate, Sara—she's in Belize for the semester." It must've been as much small talk as she could manage, because the plate clattered to the counter. "Matty, what happened last night? Why did you…?"

Here we go. "Don't ask."

"You seemed fine and then I saw you with—"

"Leah, I'm begging you, drop it."

"No." Lips pressed together, she wound her earphones around a pink iPod. "You can either talk to me or I'm calling Professor Solomon and telling him what you did. Your choice."

The walls started closing in. "Trust me, he'll be shocked." I grasped the doorframe as a bout of lightheadedness came on.

She reached out to steady me but I was feeling stubborn and pulled away.

Wearing a cool frown, she stirred her eggs. "You know what? Last night, I made this really great new friend. He's smart. He's cute. He's got a wicked sense of humor. He's lived more in twenty-five years than most people live in a lifetime and unlike me, he's not afraid to say exactly what he thinks."

I ground the heel of my hand into my eye. "He's also bugfuck nuts."

She banged the handle on the pan. "God, Matty, I couldn't *sleep* last night because I couldn't stop thinking about you and your stories. We had this amazing night, and all of a sudden, the stuff I want to do with my life seemed seriously lame. I went for a walk to clear my head, and then I spied your car and I saw you inside and I got all excited because I had a million questions for you and I didn't think you'd mind. Instead I found you almost dead next to a bunch of old pictures. If you don't want my help, fine. One night doesn't make us best friends. But forgive me for being a little freaked out that you almost killed yourself last night."

She stood there in her PJs, indignantly choking the daylights out of a spatula, and suddenly it was the funniest thing I'd ever seen. Life sucked and the world was a mess and my best friend was still dead, but Leah was there, jumping into the void.

Was I in love with her then? Probably. Love to me is something captured at shutter speed, it's either there or it's not, you can't dodge it out or burn it in. I fell for her because she showed me her soul that night, because she saw mine and didn't run.

There were tears in her eyes, so I just held her. When I'd been looking through my photos, it'd felt as if my pilot light had gone out, but now it was back on. It was the way her head came right up to my chin, the way it felt when she rested it against my chest, the way her arms wrapped without hesitation around my waist. Boyfriend or not, she'd been lonely too.

I buried my face in her hair, which smelled like warm beach sage and swore to myself that I'd remember this feeling the next time I decided to do myself in. "Did you have to give me mouth to mouth?"

Her expression was dead serious. "First time in six years of lifeguarding."

I fought a smirk. "I don't remember—can we try it again?"

She wriggled away, pretending to be mad, then threw the dishtowel at me. "Are you always this impossible?"

I sat at the table and bit into a slice of toast. "Usually worse."

"I believe it." She pushed aside a pile of papers and set a plate of eggs in front of me. "Here. Eat."

"You didn't need to do all this. But thanks."

She tried, but couldn't hide her smile as she neatened the paper stack. "You're welcome."

That was when I noticed what she was holding—her LSAT forms. "Aren't you supposed to be at the exam?"

She put the pan into the sink. "I wasn't going to leave you alone. Besides, I've taken them once already and did fine."

I choked down a bite of eggs. "Then why were you taking them again?"

As she turned on the tap, a hiss of steam rose from the pan. "I signed up when I was hoping to go to Columbia like my dad—my first score was borderline." She sloshed the water around. "I mean, they'll probably let me in anyhow, but I wanted to earn it, you know?"

Feeling like a complete jackass, I scratched my chin stubble. "I didn't mean to screw things up for you."

She shook her head. "You didn't. My score is fine for the schools near where Jason will be."

My appetite dried up. I pushed the plate away. "Big mistake, Leah."

The pan clanked against the sink. "Someone who's five hours past a suicide attempt doesn't get to give relationship advice."

Wife, submit to your husband, go where he goes, wear what he tells you to wear, screw when he wants to screw. I'd grown up with that crap and it pissed me off. I forked a glob of egg. "If you want to go to Columbia, go to Columbia. Don't let him decide for you. Just saying."

She reached for the dishtowel, then dried her hands. "The couch is yours as long as you want it. Your stuff is by the bookshelf. Including your box of pictures. If you want to talk about anything that doesn't involve my boyfriend, I'll be in the other room studying."

I pushed the eggs around my plate, until my phone went off in the other room. When I got there, Leah was at her laptop with my mobile. She pushed it towards me. Jack's number was on the display.

"Rough night?" he said when I answered.

"You could say that."

"The state of my basement seemed a pretty good indication."

Jack let me keep my darkroom stuff at his place. I lived out of a duffel bag, so spending money I didn't have on rent was stupid. Technically, you could say I was homeless. "My bad."

"Dare I hope the environmental disaster down there means you've started on the story?"

I didn't answer. Leah slid the lid off the shoebox of photos. *I'll help,* she mouthed.

I closed my eyes and surrendered. "Yeah, I have."

Looking back, I should've known she'd be the love of my life. We were more or less living together by that night.

With snow falling outside, we'd gone over to Jack's to pick up my crap. While I packed chemicals and equipment, the two of them talked in hushed tones. From the sadness in her eyes, I knew he'd told her about Rani.

Forget two weeks—Jack said the editor at MoJo wanted five thousand words plus photos before Christmas. *Go edgy*, he said. *You're angry—make him angry too.*

Angry. Maybe I was, but until Rani got killed, I would've said 'concerned'. I was 'concerned' about the minefield markers I saw wherever the hell we went. I was 'concerned' by the English or Chinese or Hebrew or Cyrillic markings on the damn things in places Americans and Chinese and Israelis and Russians had no business being. I was 'concerned' by one-legged kids hopping through fields or wearing eye patches, or worse, their mothers prostrate and sobbing in some makeshift field clinic. Iraq, Sudan, Uganda, Mozambique—the damn things were everywhere.

While I switched negatives around on the lightbox, nursing a Heineken, Leah was lying on the rug, ankles crossed, going through my archives while she hummed along with some old Ella Fitzgerald recording she'd stolen from her dad. It was a little bittersweet, a little sad, and completely perfect. Having her there kept the evil thoughts at bay, but they came back any time I tried to come up with words to go around the photos. Words were Rani's job. Me taking it over meant he was really gone.

"I can't believe you still use film," Leah said, flipping between contact sheets. "Wouldn't this be easier on a computer?"

"I'm old school, baby." Digital sucked. Faces came out flat and uninspired, colors weren't natural, lines were too sharp. The grains in real film gave better images. It was the feel, the rhythm, the yield of the shutter under my finger, the sound when I flipped the advance lever, the game of timing the shots that counted. Or maybe I was just stubborn.

"Think of it like sex."

She rolled sideways, head resting on her hand. "Oh boy. This should be good."

Couldn't help it, the way she was lying there, I could see right down her shirt. "Digital is like porn—it's quick, easy, gets the job done.

Film is like the girl you've had your eye on for months slipping you her room key."

Mischief danced in her eyes. "If your daddy could hear you talk…"

"My dirty mind was the least of his problems." Grease pencil in hand, I grabbed a random contact sheet and sat next to her on the floor. The sheet was a few years old, from the Intifada, a rock-throwing exchange between a teenage Palestinian girl and an IDF soldier who wasn't much older. "It's a whole different process when you've only got thirty-six exposures on a roll. You can't construct a scene, you have to figure out how to structure the shot from what's there—what you fit in, what you leave out, all of it."

She scanned the sheet, which was covered in grease paint scribbles, rectangles and crosses. "What do all these marks mean?"

"Blue is me, red is Jack. If we both boxed a certain frame, good chance it's the money shot. The rest are crop marks, areas that need dodging or burning, things like that."

Leah's troubled gaze hovered between two marked-up frames in the third row. I'd probably blitzed through the whole roll in under a minute, and it hadn't ended well for the girl. "Why did you both pick this one, where she's curling the rock in her hand? Didn't you want to show what happened to her?"

The sheet was radioactive one way or the other, especially for an American paper. "Look again. Tell me what she's thinking in the first one."

"Maybe she's deciding where to aim. Or whether it's worth the risk of throwing it."

"Could be anything. That's what a photo is. The person outside a photo can ponder it forever if they want, but the person inside is frozen at that one moment in time." I stuck the sheet into the box. "Besides, showing her as a victim robs her of agency. She was a person who made a choice, and something drove her to be there. Same with the soldier who shot her. Whether it was a good or bad one isn't my place to say."

She stretched back on her hands. "Be honest. You have an opinion on the subject."

"Yep."

"But you're not going to tell me what it is."

"Nope."

She dug out the sheet, studying it. "It's here," she says softly. "The way you follow both of their movements—you saw it coming and couldn't stop it. You're right. I didn't look hard enough at first."

I got up and went back to work. Mostly because I didn't trust myself to say anything else.

She flipped through the proofs again, and at some point, she started giggling. When she turned it around, it was a shot of me and an old girlfriend goofing around on a beach in Spain. Both of us butt naked, of course. "Hello! What's this? Another big story?"

On a different day, I probably would've been embarrassed, but last night, it'd been the photo that sent me over the edge. "It's what happens when your buddy gets hold of your camera on Spring Break. Her name was Misha."

"Russian?" She studied the photo. "Is she a model? She's pretty enough."

"Now and then." My head started to hurt. "She wanted to be a journalist."

Sensing it was a sore subject, she tucked the photo in the box. "Past tense...I take it she's an ex-girlfriend?"

The corner was up, so I lifted it out again. "This was senior year. A few weeks later, I was back at school, she was back in Moscow. She sent me this weird email, that if I saw photos of her on the wire service with some Gazprom oligarch not to read anything into it—she was doing a story on him. Nobody ever heard from her again."

A swirl of emotions crossed Leah's face—confusion, shock, pity, outrage. As if the world had just opened up and showed her its ugly side. She stuck the cover on the box. "I'm sorry, this isn't helping."

In a weird way, it was. The photos didn't have the same power in daylight. I took the cover off and dug towards the back. "You were asking about Africa—there are a bunch here somewhere about a school building project in Kenya. Sorry, it's not usually this disorganized."

Things fell silent, only the hum of the lightbox and melting snow dripping from the eaves. She sat up with a photo from the stack. "Is this Rani?"

The beer almost came back up. I was expecting Kenya, but he was on his knees beside a lean-to shack, taken after we'd found a kid's mutilated body in the *favelas*, the Saõ Paulo slums. We'd had no idea who he was or what happened to him, but Rani's face was pure agony, the same expression every guy gets in this job the first time he sees the devil walking among us.

"Yeah. Day we met."

She fingered the corner. "Will you tell me about him?"

I switched off the lightbox, then reached for it. "His father was the features editor at *O Globo*—biggest paper in Brazil. Rani was in the office when I showed up looking to sell some photos."

"You can walk in off the street like that?"

"You can if you have pictures of a local preacher with a Neo-Apartheid terrorist cell."

At seventeen, I'd been as full of self-righteous piss as anyone, but I'd run off from my folks and I needed money. Fuck that, I'd needed someone to know what my old man did. Mr. Camilos skimmed the contact sheet I'd brought and said unless I could get my father on the record, all I had were pictures of a gas station.

It'd cheesed me off—until then, nobody had ever questioned the photos I wanted to sell. You've got talent, *menino*, he'd said, but editors are paid to twist what you give them into what sells papers. Report the truth and only the truth. Never, *ever* burn a source, because there's a word for reporters that do: unemployed. Place a higher value on your ethics than you do on the law. Don't let anyone dictate your story. Keep the personal crap out of it. Treat people, even the bad ones, as people—people have flaws and strengths and you'll need both. No one is perfectly evil or perfectly good. Keep searching for trouble and someday, you'll meet the exception. You'll tell yourself you'll know it when it happens. So did all the other dead reporters I know.

After that, he'd called Rani in and told the two of us to head out to the slums and not come back until we had a story he could print. "The dead kid was our big break." I picked at the beer label. "Which sorta sucked."

"Did they ever find out who killed him? Who he was? How did you find him?"

Though I shrugged, it was something Rani had wondered aloud more than once. "Wasn't exactly a rare occurrence in the *favelas*. O *Globo* used it to shame the local police into keeping closer tabs on abandoned kids. Guess we felt like we'd done something useful and started looking for what else we could fix."

She straightened the contact sheet. "What were you looking to fix in Mozambique?"

"Land mines." Between fifteen years of Marxist civil war, apartheid-driven sabotage from Rhodesia and South Africa and the Portuguese raping the place, the Maputo borderlands were lousy with mines. Ten years later, they still blew apart a few thousand civilians a year. Rani and a little farmer's boy included. So basically? Yeah, I had my issues with the damn things.

"We wanted something that would pressure the Bush Administration into signing the Ottawa Treaty."

She frowned. "So you were delusional before all this?"

"Jack used to call us Don Quixote and Sancho." My voice came out thick. The truth was, there were reasons Jack was pushing the story somewhere else. A year after 9/11, the country wasn't in the mood. "We figured it was worth a shot."

She pushed the film bag towards me. "If it was, it still is."

Wishing I could've believed her, I took a mental inventory of what was inside. The negatives I'd processed last night. A tape recorder. A palm-sized pad filled with Rani's scribbled notes. Interviews, quotes from locals. Stats and facts to find or check. Angles we'd thrown around. Stuff he would've used to write the story. My eyes started to sting. "It's not that."

"Then what is it?" she said softly.

I didn't know how to put it in words. Both she and Jack were right. We'd gone to Mozambique hoping to show the world a terrible thing, and naively hoped it would change. But all we'd proven was that we weren't the avenging angels of truth we thought we were. We weren't untouchable. We weren't gods. We were flesh and bone, ashes to ashes and all that. It was a hell of a price to pay for that lesson, given that on some level, we'd both always known. We were supposed to have each other's back, and that was supposed to be enough to keep fate at bay. But I couldn't say any of that, so I just shrugged.

She must've realized I wasn't going to open the damn folio. With cautious deliberation, she reached for it. "Will it damage anything if I look?"

Besides me? I shook my head. "Not sure it matters anyway."

She dug in and came up with the negatives and the notebook, the latter of which she handed to me. Squinting, she held a strip up to the lamp. "Maybe you could start with these," she said. "It's just some kids playing soccer."

When she flipped on the lightbox, it was as if someone plugged ten-thousand volts into my spine. Suddenly I was seeing the world through a sun-flared lens. The shutter clicked. Disembodied voices speaking Portuguese came out of nowhere. The stench of manure. A child's laughter. Rani screaming at him to stop. My body flooded with the urge to run, but I couldn't, my legs felt frozen.

Distantly, I heard a chair scrape the floor, and then next thing I knew, Leah was helping me onto the couch, though she didn't seem to realize the problem at first. "Dammit, I knew I should've made you go to the hospital last night. Are you all right?"

"It should be me who's dead." *There, I finally said it.* "It shouldn't be him."

She wet her lips. "Matty…"

It all started to tumble out. "We'd hooked up with some friends in the aid convoy. The truck broke down, so Rani was playing soccer with some kids near a flooded cane field. We knew the mines were there, we saw the signs."

She sat beside me. "It wasn't your fault."

"I was the one who kicked the ball." I got up, then fitfully arranged the rest of the negatives on the lightbox. I'd snapped a shot of the ball rolling into a culvert, another of the boy chasing after it, Rani running after him. The last exposure on the roll was a blur, a shower of mud in the air. I couldn't look at it without hearing that split-second *zip* of a charge jumping out of the ground. Strength ebbing, I sank into the chair. "The damn thing pretty much decapitated the kid. The shrapnel caught Rani in the gut."

She didn't say anything at first, just stood behind me, rubbing my shoulder. "There was nothing you could've done."

I flexed Rani's notebook, struggling not to lose it completely. "You know the stupid thing? I actually thought we could save him. I thought he had a chance, but the second we tried to move him, something let go. He bled out right there on the roadside."

What I didn't tell her was that I was so out of my head that I ran straight through the field, screaming at God, *hey fucker, blow me up too, go on, I dare you!* I heard later that one of the Red Cross guys tackled me after my third time through.

I turned over the notebook, so I didn't keep seeing the stick figure porn Rani had drawn on the cover. "Swear to god, I have no memory of packing this stuff. I stayed sober long enough to get the body sent back and that was it. I woke up at the gate in Lisbon with the bag on my lap. Only thing I can figure, my buddy from the Red Cross put it there."

She folded her hands around mine. "I have a feeling you packed them yourself. Somewhere buried under all this guilt and grief is a guy who knows he's the one who has to tell the story. I can see him, even if you can't right now."

Resigned, I rubbed her thumb. "You're not giving up on this, are you?"

"I'm not giving up on *you.*" A little smile broke on her face. "Try to get started. You'll feel better."

Rani's 'notes' were pages of Portuguese chicken scratch. "I'd feel better if I'd started three weeks ago like I was supposed to."

Brow furrowed, Leah flipped his check sheet. "What does this stuff mean?"

ORS: Pentagon won't give up 'force multiplier' of landmines, but Gulf War UXO complicating war plans—<u>need alt source!!</u>

"ORS is off-record source. UXO is unexploded ordinance. It means the Pentagon should've thought about invading Iraq again before they vomited a few million mines around the no-fly zone."

"He expected to find a military source willing to discuss their own screwed-up operational planning?"

"Don't ask me, I'm just the guy who took the pictures." I flipped the page. "Don't suppose you know a Korean government official willing to go on the record about landmines in the DMZ."

"How'd we get from Mozambique to South Korea?"

"It's the main excuse the US uses for not signing—they claim we own the mines in the DMZ, we'd have to take them out, and the North Koreans would plow right through to Seoul."

She tucked her hair behind her ear, this one crazy strand that never stayed put. "The ambassador and his wife have been to our house to go sailing. Do you want me to call my dad?"

I stared at her. "You're pulling my chain?"

With a mysterious smile, she went into her bedroom. Ten minutes later, she came back with a slip of paper, a DC phone number and some neatly organized notes. "His name is Sung Chul Yang. He's expecting your call."

I could've kissed her. "You're an angel."

The ambassador liked to talk, and clearly had some stuff to get off his chest, so we'd been on line for an hour. "It is untrue that the United States owns the DMZ ordinance," he said. "Only a foolish nation would rely on another for survival."

I decided to push. "So if the United States wanted to sign the Ottawa Treaty, that'd be okay with South Korea?"

There was a long pause, which preceded the worst words a reporter can hear. "I no longer wish to have this conversation on the record, Mr. Cahill."

"Don't hang up," I said quickly, drawing a dark 'x' in my notes. "I'm marking the spot where our conversation ended. Anything else we talk about can be on background. It doesn't see daylight. No 'senior Korean official', nothing. You have my word."

Another long pause. "Your question was posed by the Clinton administration. With certain guarantees, our foreign minister was receptive."

"So the deal fell apart when Bush came in?"

"No. Much sooner. It was rescinded the following day by your Pentagon."

Click.

Leah wandered into the room, a spare blanket in her arms. "Get what you needed?"

I sat there holding the phone. Then started scribbling. This story had better legs than I'd thought. "Yeah, thanks."

She padded over with the blanket. "I thought you might've been cold last night."

My watch said it was after midnight. "You don't mind me staying here again?"

"I like the company," she said softly.

Her eyes were all puffy, which meant she'd been talking to the douchebag again. "You okay?"

A troubled expression flitted over her face. I raised an eyebrow. Even then, she must've looked everywhere in the room except at me. "His buddy, Ryan Hendricks—he saw us together when we went over to Jack's."

"The red-haired guy? The one with the Altoids?" It took a minute to sink through my skull. "Are you telling me that dickhead has someone following you?"

"N-no. It was a coincidence. At least I think." Clutching the blanket, she leaned against the wall. "I love Jason's ROTC friends, but

Hendricks…" She shuddered. "He's a jerk. His girlfriend cheated on him last year, and he's become this he-man, woman-hating creep."

"Pretty sure the Army isn't real big on stalkers."

"He doesn't need the Army. Rumor has it he's got a job with the CIA after graduation." She forced a thin smile. "Guess I was practice."

"Leah—"

"Don't," she said, her voice wavering. "It's over."

God knows I wanted to believe her. I pinched the bridge of my nose. "You're not practice to me. That's all I was going to say."

With a hundred other unsaid things hanging in the air, she set the blanket beside me. "What about you? Are you okay?"

Fighting the urge to pull her down with me, I flopped onto the couch with Rani's tapes. She wasn't really done with her boyfriend and I wasn't really done with my story. "Yeah, I'm fine. Night."

When I hit play, he was in the middle of interviewing some corrupt government weenie. I'd jogged up all excited and out of breath. *'Hey man, I got a line on some flooding last night in Metuchira. Might've unearthed a bunch of APL's. Tova's headed that way with a food drop. He said he'd take us.'*

For a second, Rani was there beside me, all *fuck-yeah boyo, let's go,* and then the ground exploded again, but when I opened my eyes, all shaky and weak, it was Leah.

"The hell with fine," she whispered. "You're not. Neither am I. It's okay."

Then she curled up next to me, put her head on my shoulder, and with my dead best friend's voice in the background, we stayed like that until we fell asleep.

Chapter 7:
And So It Begins

The guards drag me through the sally port. Rain plinks like gunfire on the deck overhead. A steel door squeaks. They remove the shackles. A dull ache sets into my wrists.

I stare ahead. In two minutes, they'll leave and I can curl up in the corner, forget the aches and hunger pains and pray for sleep. Since they put me on suicide watch, I never get more than fifteen minutes at a time. Life has become one mindless, exhausting routine.

There are others: a pair of Egyptian students, three Turkish journalists, an assortment of Iraqis and Syrians, most of whom have been here for years. The guards come and taunt us through the "bean" holes, tell us our wives have moved on. Not Leah. I've seen her work miracles before. It's not in her nature to give up.

The guard shoves me forward. This one, a cowboy by way of Ukraine, wears a beat-up straw Stetson, has a snake tattooed on his arm, and carries a can of pepper spray he shakes like a rattler's tail. "Nighty night, Cahill."

I focus on the electrical tape covering his name tag. Standard detainee protocol says I'm not supposed to know their names, but I do anyway. "You got a wife, Orlyk?"

He looks down and checks the tape. Grunts. Then he sucker punches me in the gut. The bottom falls out of my lungs, I hit the deck. Stars fly. I can't get a breath.

"It's started," he rasps. "Last night. You better smarten up and help us stop it or else."

Picture this. You're a reporter. Last you remember, you'd finally worked up the courage to tell your possibly pregnant wife about the bombshell you're about to drop on the world. The one involving a bastard arms dealer named Adnar Kıraç who you've been investigating since before you got married. The one you last saw ten minutes before in a Cairo alley, when he told you exactly what he planned to do to her once you were out of the picture. That you'd learned he was involved in a plan hatched by some assholes who thought the world was being a little too generous towards migrants and refugees, and who figured a few well-placed attacks would scare the world into seeing it their way. That you found out after they dropped a missile on your little sister's apartment in Aleppo, because the evil green smoke rising from the rubble meant the genie was out of the bottle, that they'd realized too late how foolish they were, because all the bastard wants is to watch the world burn.

Now picture that the people behind it will kill everyone you love if you expose what they've done. That even when you woke up in shackles, you cooperated with the government, you told them what you could. That two days ago, the guards all changed, and this time, your captors were the assholes themselves. That their dim view of your continued existence rests with your ability to locate the bastard arms dealer before anyone finds out. That ever since, you've been struggling to figure out where you went wrong. And realizing that, with a storm descending, you have no one left to trust.

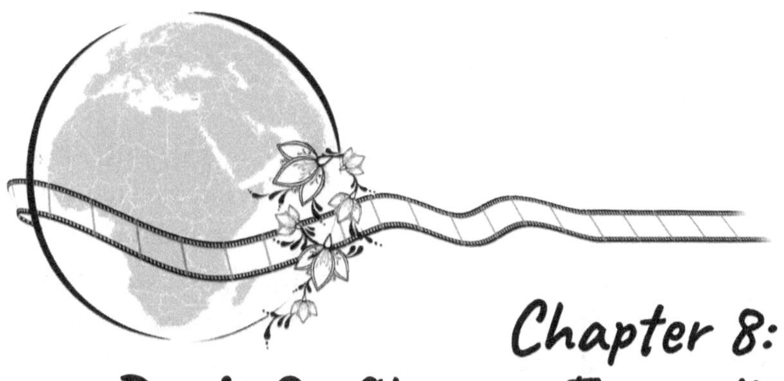

Chapter 8:
Don't Go Chasing Firewalls
WASHINGTON, D.C.
PRESENT

Leah

Even in broad daylight, Washington Highlands isn't the kind of neighborhood a woman with a foot full of lidocaine should go traipsing by her lonesome. Brick row houses molder beneath overgrown brush and graffiti. Tots and drug dealers wander the same trash-strewn streets. If you don't live here, you don't belong here. But I have a client who does, one I desperately need to see.

Matty's interrogation video keeps playing on a loop in my head. I'd have bled on every monument and government office in the city until I got some answers, but Nance ordered the Capitol police to drive me to the hospital. He also told them he'd searched me and didn't find my cell phone, which means he hopes I'm stupid enough to lead him to my source. Which is also probably why a man with reddish hair has been following me since I got off the Metro. From the way he walks, squaring off his corners, he's military.

Before ducking into the complex, I check the rear window of a parked Bronco, and see a familiar face in the reflection, albeit one I haven't seen in years: Jason's douchebag friend from ROTC, Ryan Hendricks. Coincidence? Doubtful.

I ring the buzzer at the gate, ignoring the stinkeye I get from a Filipino woman who's scrubbing the walk with a straw broom. On the second floor, a faded curtain brushes back. The gate clanks open.

Poet and 'hacktivist' Izar Nimazi was an outspoken critic of Azerbaijan's ruling government, until they got fed up and disseminated photos of him in bed with his partner, an Iranian journalist. His partner was executed within hours and Izar barely escaped the same fate in his village, an Islamic enclave on the border. He fled to the US and applied for asylum. I've been working his case since my last year at Columbia.

Smelling of sandalwood and patchouli, his apartment is dim, the paint dingy and grey. He's made it home with canvas paintings, secondhand books, a wicker chair and a woven rug he sleeps on in the corner, near a sketch of his lost love.

"Come in, come in," he says, kissing my cheeks. "Peace be with you."

I return his greeting. In the end, everything worked out with Judge Underwood. Scott got his signature, and Julie's paralegal brought me the paperwork while I was at the hospital, where the computer system helpfully decided I was supposed to be in labor and not getting my foot stitched up.

I set Izar's finalized asylee form on the table. "Next stop, Green Card, Mr. Nimazi."

He moves his computer off the chair. "Please, for the thousandth time, call me—"

His features contort in pain, and he pitches forward. I catch his arm. "Are you all right?"

At forty, with grey-stricken black hair, Izar is Matty's age, but some days he looks as old as my father. He spent a year in an Azerbaijani jail, and his back hasn't been right since. Among about a hundred other things. Breathing labored, he straightens. "I think tomorrow, it will rain."

The paperwork blurs. "Do you think it will ever go away?"

He shuffles away, putting a kettle on the stove. "I do not see myself as a weakened man. I see myself as one who has been made strong. I am as steel. So will it be for your husband."

"I hope so," I say softly.

"Have you had any news?"

My poker face apparently sucks, because his face lights with intrigue. "You can't get involved," I whisper. "If you tell me what to do, I can do it."

A lopsided grin breaks on his face. "And where would I be had you let me argue my own case?"

"Izar—"

"Psht." After stretching his fingers, he pokes the wakeup button on the computer. "I have been too long without a challenge. Life in your country makes a man soft."

I go to the window. The sweeper stands by the courtyard gate, broom clutched to her breast like a weapon. Hendricks offers her a tin of Altoids, along with a folded bill.

Crap. "I'm sorry, I shouldn't have come. I have to leave."

Izar shuffles over, glancing over my shoulder. "I have gained nothing if I accept that fear and repression control my destiny. Would you have me believe they follow where I go?"

Yes! I want to shout. Instead, I close my eyes, drifting from the window. "Matty's alive. I've seen proof. I need a way to reach the person who sent it."

He goes silent until the kettle whistles. "How did they contact you? Phone? Email? How is your security?"

"Phone." Given that my job involves people in foreign countries who might be killed for talking to an American lawyer, I take precautions. "I use Tor. Matty used it for communicating with sources too."

"Without a VPN on top? Tsk." Izar clicks a sound file on his desktop. A haunting melody of Sufi instrumentals and chants comes from the speakers. "Tor can be compromised. Your NSA would have been able to de-anonymize you if you repeatedly use the same networks. Voice calls are child's play. Open Whisper, plus Tor, plus a VPN—that will stop them. These games you play—the one with the birds and pigs? Did you say yes or no when it asked for access to your data?"

Clearly, I am the world's biggest idiot. "So what do I do?"

"You trust Izar."

There's another app open on his desktop, streaming the aftermath of the attack in Montreal. A smoky haze lingers around the stadium, amidst a chaotic sea of police activity and rescue workers in haz-mat gear. "How bad is it?" I ask numbly. "All people were talking about at the hospital was that he was Christian instead of Muslim."

He switches to an American news feed. "See for yourself."

The chyron at the bottom does its maddening crawl. 'ATTACKER WAS SURVIVOR OF SARIN GAS ATTACK IN IDLIB EARLIER THIS YEAR. WIFE, INFANT DAUGHTER KILLED. PRESIDENT ISSUES TWEETSTORM BLAMING CANADA'S LAX REFUGEE POLICY.'

Above it, the anchor is getting schooled by a buzz-cut CEO-type in a polo shirt, who, according to the graphic, is Bradley Gleason, head of some global security firm.

"You keep calling this an 'unprecedented' chemical attack," Gleason says. "The hell it is. It's what these people know, and it's exactly why they don't belong here. Christians, Muslims, Yazidis, I don't care. You heard what the bastard said: more of these attacks are coming and they're coming here. *Your* mall, *your* school." With a vindictive smirk, he sits back. "Ask me, all those people who said Saddam had no WMDs should feel pretty stupid."

Hopeless and lost, I put my head down. "I hate the world so much right now."

Izar closes the stream and rises from the table. "There is much to be angry about, yes. And much to fear. I choose to be grateful for those who see the difference. If you and your Matthias are any indication, most Americans do."

I bang my forehead on the table. "Apparently, not so much."

While I fill him in as much as I dare, he shakes loose tea into a pair of mugs, then pours steaming water over them. "Did the person who contacted you indicate willingness to be contacted in return? Perhaps a distinctive signature?"

"There was this flower that came up—a blue lotus with a dozen petals." *Lotus 12.*

He gets a pensive furrow in his brow when I show it to him. He opens a secure browser window, then fires up Twitter. "Create a new handle. Incorporate the bona-fide into your avatar. A single tweet should suffice. If your new friend wishes to be contacted, she will reply by a different channel."

"She?"

He raises an eyebrow. "You think a man such as me knows little of women?"

"No, but —"

"Am I not saying what your own intuition is telling you?"

I'd been sort of blindly hoping it was him. The flower did look a little girly, but with everything else, I can't handle the idea of another woman being secretly involved with my husband.

My mind wanders to the crackdown, the night he was taken. The woman Matty was with. *'You know I'm no cheat. She's just a source. A friend.'* Maybe my instincts weren't totally wrong. Maybe they had a secret. A secret too big for him to share with me? If the past day, the past eight months have taught me anything, it's that I don't know Matty as well as I thought.

Through a storm of hurt and confusion, I try to focus. "What if someone else sees it too?"

Hiding a sly grin, he stirs his tea. "It is unlikely. You picked a good day. An exploit was posted that allowed us to access your IRS system. Your FBI and NSA are otherwise occupied."

"I'm going to pretend that didn't sound like my client just admitted to hacking the U.S. Government, Izar."

With a cheeky wink, he takes a noisy sip from his mug.

I really am going to get disbarred today. I upload a copy of the flower. "If this hacker chick spent half as much time figuring out a way to tell me how to contact her, maybe I could get somewhere."

Izar fiddles with my phone. "You must understand the mindset. It is not enough to fool the system. It is the elegance of the solution that shows greatness. A sign of respect."

Oh good, my husband's secret girlfriend respects me. "Or maybe she has way more free time than I do."

He shows me a screen of cryptic text. "The worm on your phone appears to have originated in Russia, but it was spoofed. There are hops to an anonymity service popular in the Middle East."

"English, please."

"Your friend is very well hidden." He scrolls down the screen. "There. I've decrypted the headers."

Nance didn't just send the email about the Senate hearing to Clarke—there are a dozen hidden recipients. All addresses on private domains. Not government servers. Given how he felt about me crashing his secret hearing, there must be some reason he wants them to know.

Which means there are people both inside and outside the government with an interest in Matty's detention. In keeping it a secret. And that, Nance, our 'Chief voice on Syria and Iraq' is happy to oblige them. Corruption 101, with a side of autocracy and dictatorship. Welcome to the New America.

"Can we find out who these people are?" I say. "Without them knowing?"

Izar's cocky expression fades. He ambles towards the window, peering through the curtain again. "This is a game of cat-and-mouse. Sometimes, the mouse loses. A safe approach will take time."

Time is something Matty just doesn't have. When I scheduled my day, it didn't include a singlehanded attempt to take on the Patriot Act, but I've got a brand new theory about why someone has it in for me at Immigration. Not to mention Maira, the Iraqi refugee he rescued.

INS blindsided me with a denial on her case yesterday. She'd only gotten her feeding tube out a few weeks ago, and with the refugee ban on hold, it should've been a slam dunk for her to stay. It's the whole reason I had a meeting scheduled with Nance this morning, so he could tell whoever had it out for her to back off. So much for that.

I stop at home to grab Matty's photos from that trip, desperate for clues. Through the window, I see Hendricks in the alley, poking through the trash barrels. Apparently, no one told him pickup was yesterday.

After pulling the curtains shut, I go to the hall bookcases. Buried amongst the Africana and tchotchkes is a grey shoebox, sitting beneath a shopworn copy of *Scheherazade's Tales* we found in Mosul. The box contains a stack of jewel-cased CDs, labeled with a date and place, and whatever media outlet paid for the assignment. I flip through, not having a clue where to begin. Iraq, Mali, Sudan… our lives, our marriage—they're in this box. And I went through every damn one six months ago. Frustrated, I dump the whole lot into my bag.

But when I go to stick Scheherazade on top, a notecard falls out. Tucked inside, I find the last photo I've ever seen of his sister Ari.

It was taken in a village somewhere in Iraq, before the war. She can't be more than seven, the same age as she was when she died. She's sitting on his knee, dark hair in plaits, wearing a purple T-shirt and a toothless smile. The photo always kills me to look at—there's a fatherly protectiveness in the way he's holding her, and on some level, I'd always understood that what happened to her is the main reason he didn't want kids. Beneath it, there's a note in his left-slanted scrawl.

Dear Leah,

Things are such a mess I don't even know where to start. You losing your job, missing the bar... I can't fix any of it. Maybe it's too late for that. Maybe it's too late for truth

You're right, I broke my word, and it's killing me that I can't tell you why. I wasn't mad at you for wanting answers—I'm mad at myself, I'm mad at my father, I'm mad at the world. This is the third time I've had to face losing you, and I barely survived the first two.

'Broke his word' was the understatement of the century—my third year of law school, Matty had been embedded with a group of White Helmets, the Syrian Civil Defense force, near Idlib—one of the few foreign journalists left in Syria. After a series of near misses, my last shred of sanity had beenwas hanging by a thread. One complete emotional breakdown later, we made a pact that he'd stay out. As far as I knew, the plan was working great—he'd found a niche covering the refugee crisis in Turkey, I'd managed to stop bursting into tears every time my phone rang. Then all of a sudden I got a call that he'd been caught in an airstrike in Aleppo. For all that, not a *word* of explanation, and I'd finally had enough. Things between us were awful for months.

But the note ends there, leaving me no closer to his secrets than before, and suddenly I'm furious with him. Like, want-to-hit-something pissed. Did I not know him at all? Did he not know me? Whatever his big secret was, how bad could it be?

Seething, I find a pair of flats that don't irritate my stitches and leave. This time, I lock the damn door.

On the first-floor landing, I run into my landlord. Clearly, the universe is nursing a grudge.

"Hi Leah," he says. "Late lunch? You should've stopped by."

When I moved in, his wife had just had a baby. She moved out a week later… and in with the baby's real father. As the two most pathetic people in all of DC, we'd share takeout occasionally, until he had too much wine one night and tried to kiss me.

"Sorry, gotta run," I say.

He pads after me in his stocking feet. "How about dinner on Friday? Completely sober this time. No wine."

"My firm has a dinner thing."

"Need a date?"

I hold up my hand, showing the silver moonstone I wear on my ring finger.

"It's been a year, Leah," he replies quietly. "Yours isn't coming back any more than mine is."

"Six months." Exhausted, I head downstairs. I'm sick and damn tired of having to justify myself. "Nice talking to you."

As in-house pro bono counsel, our semi-annual 'client appreciation' events are how I earn my salary. I'm expected to show up looking poised and resilient, while people talk behind my back about how well I'm holding up, as if they can't see I'm holding my soul together with Band-Aids and rusty staples. They're pure Washington-style schmooze, and given the last one netted a society page mention in which *Form-Fitting Gown Fuels Pregnancy Rumors for Missing Journalist's Wife*, I hate them with my last ounce of strength.

The lidocaine has worn off, leaving my foot with a pins-and-needles ache. New York Avenue is busy with afternoon pedestrians darting between shops. Since Nance is out, my best option for my refugee problem involves convincing my father to make some calls. Which involves talking to my mother, which will involve breaking a blessed silence that's been going on a month. Mom and I don't exactly see eye-to-eye where Matty is concerned. Or much of anything, really.

I'm wound up in my own head and had forgotten about Hendricks until I get the sense of someone walking way too close. I catch a flash of red hair, dodge sideways, but he grabs my arm. A cold ring presses against my back.

Click.

"Keep walking, Law School," he says. "Make a sound and you'll be in need of a kidney. And yes, I will shoot if you make a scene."

Spend a decade in post-colonial Africa, you *almost* get used to people waving guns at you. You take a deep breath and tell yourself if they don't shoot right away, they're just waving their pathetic little dicks around to get your attention.

"Last I knew, the CIA wasn't allowed to operate inside American borders, Ryan. You freaks didn't think to send someone I wouldn't recognize?"

Adjusting his grip on the gun, he nudges me into an alley. "For the chick who did my buddy dirty?" He grabs a fistful of my camisole, twisting it around my neck like a garrote. "I volunteered."

Until thirty seconds ago, I was clinging to the idea that it's all one giant misunderstanding. That Matty is a victim of a national security apparatus run amok. Clearly, it's time for a new theory.

"Matty must *really* have something bad on you," I say, as he yanks the strap so tight it burns. My vision goes fuzzy and I grit my teeth, fighting for consciousness. "Can't wait to find out what it is."

The grating squeal of car brakes comes from the open side of the alley. Hendricks curses. The pressure on my trachea releases. "Last warning, Law School. Back off. Next time, you get a piece of his corpse."

By the time my vision returns, he's gone. I draw a shaky breath, in time to see a black town car drive off. I can just make out Nance's face behind the sun visor.

So that's how it is, huh?

Fear gradually morphs into anger, and with it, a realization dawns.

They just screwed up.

Coming after me in broad daylight is impossibly brazen. What I told Nance is true—I could call half a dozen editors and have it splashed on every news site in ten minutes. '*Missing Journalist's Wife Wears Boring Suit, Reports Domestic CIA Harassment over Efforts to Free Him*'. They want me to know they'll make good on their threats.

Sending Ryan was supposed to scare me, to prove they're in control of my world, and let's get real—mission accomplished. But they forgot one thing: the scariest monsters are the ones you can't see. This one just showed its face. And in the process, it gave me a way to figure out who I'm really dealing with.

A hasty plan takes shape in my mind. Even *years* after I broke up with Jason, the government would call me any time one of his ROTC buddies was looking for a security clearance. The questions were always the same—were they trustworthy, did they drink or do drugs, did I have reason to think they'd ever betray the US. Who else had they worked for?

My hands won't stop shaking as I dial the phone. Even armed with Izar's encryption protocols, I'm taking a risk. With Matty's life. With my own. With things I'd much rather forget.

Jason's mother and mine are still best friends, though Connie hasn't forgiven me for breaking up with her darling son half a lifetime ago. She picks up on the second ring. "Hello?"

A sick feeling craters my stomach. I doubt she'll recognize my voice, but I throw in a little accent, just to be safe. "Ma'am, I'm calling from the US Office of Personnel Management. We need to speak with your son Jason about a security clearance for a friend of his, Ryan Hendricks, but we've had trouble locating him. Could you give me a current phone number?"

The line goes quiet. "You lawyers are all the same. You tell that ex-wife of his she's not getting a dime. Stop calling me."

Uh... I'd heard Jason married some nitwit he'd met on base, who'd done nothing but cheat on him and cash checks for hazard pay. "Ma'am, I couldn't care less about your son's personal life." *See, now that was true.* "Our interest is in Mr. Hendricks."

She answers slowly. "Then I'm sure you won't mind if Jason confirms with Ryan. Give me a number where he can reach you."

A shadow rolls past the alley and my mind goes blank. I hang up in a panicked flood of adrenaline. Fighting tears, I sink to the wall. "Smooth, Leah. Real smooth."

Needing better advice, and possibly an economy-sized bottle of Xanax, I head for the office, a granite-faced monolith two blocks from the Treasury. The receptionist sits at a glass desk in front of a two-story water wall. She hands me a thick white and green mailing packet.

"The courier brought this for you, Ms. Cahill. Ms. Coventry wants to see you right away."

The return label says it's from Immigration. *Christ, what now?*

I limp up the stairs. At the third-floor landing, Scott Burgess comes out of his office, tie hanging loose. "This is what I get for doing you a favor, Leah? Thanks. Thanks a lot."

I'm in the middle of opening the envelope, so it doesn't register at first. "Huh?"

His buddy Joe Maynard isn't far behind. "Other people are paying for your screw-ups, as usual."

Joe, who's a corporate tax guy, isn't fond of paying for anything. Politically speaking, we're like napalm and banana trees. "What are you accusing me of?"

"Crash any Senate hearings lately?"

Uh… You don't get hired here unless you have connections, but if Joe knows about the hearing, somebody's talking. A staffer. A campaign donor. Something. "Where'd you hear that?"

He pops his knuckles. "Babe, this is Washington. Gossip spreads faster than crabs at a Black Lives Matter protest."

"You're a pig."

"Chill out, Angelina," he says. "If you lose your license, bet you can take the bar as many times as you want in Kraplakistan."

Why the hell do I let him get into my head?

Usually he's a bit more subtle with this underminy crap. Which starts to make me wonder if there's more going on here. The guy is a douche, but conversation at your average law firm isn't supposed to sound like a YouTube comments section.

"So tell me, Gaslight Joe," I finally say." Did somebody put you up to this?"

"Cole Warren told me," Scott says quietly. "After I was wondering why I had a judge grant custody of three kids to the guy who was beating their mother. He lost his job for letting you sneak into that hearing. Told me I should think twice about helping you. I hope whatever you found out was worth it."

It's like someone punched me in the heart. Retaliating against me is one thing. My otherwise reliably liberal father kept a loaded 9MM in his briefcase and there were days when a very friendly, very muscular Marine named Lucky waited outside my elementary school classroom. Strange as it sounds, intimidation is supposed to have rules. "I'll fix it, Scott, I swear."

Joe snaps his wrist, fiddling with his cufflink. "That's the trouble with you bleeding hearts—always sticking your nose in, thinking you can fix everything. Cahill deserved what he got. You're too blind to see it because you're married to him."

Maybe I'll go ahead and deck him. Julie will probably give me a raise. "Blind? Talk to me about blind when you've seen *half* the stuff I've seen. Why does being my husband make Matty different than any other political prisoner? He deserves to have someone defending him. I am doing my job."

Joe rubs his nose, eyes shifting towards my mail packet. "Not what I hear."

A cold fist seizes my spine. With shaky fingers, I slide the contents out of the envelope. Maira's immigration petition. Denied—along with a charge I falsified her paperwork.

Case Status: Temporary Protected Status conditions not met. Per Executive Order #2310, undocumented Syrian nationals are threats to National Security and considered high priority for deportation.

Case Notes: Major irregularities identified in legal filing. The circumstances of this case would have required full knowledge of case attorney. Evidence supporting charge of perjury has been forwarded to DOJ.

"The hell?" I didn't falsify anything.

This 'National Security' bullshit could bite my shiny metal ass. Maira had been through hours of 'reasonable fear' interviews with Immigration, facing questions that no matter how many times I'd done it, always made me want throw things at the person asking them. *'You told us your brother was killed before the missile hit. Which eye was he shot through? Was there an exit wound? How big was the hole? You said an American soldier raped your sister when you were twelve, but she made you swear not to tell anyone. How many stripes were on his uniform?'* She hadn't exactly flown through, but who would?

I had medical records. Letters from her doctor in Syria. Citizenship papers. An MSF report on the attack. Interviews with survivors. A flyer with her name on a death squad hit list. Between me begging senators and scrounging up a medical team and skipping the bar, Matty had sent everything I said I needed to file an asylum petition. He'd sat next to her for a fifteen-hour flight on a cargo plane with six broken ribs and a collapsed lung while a physician friend of mine struggled to keep her alive. Even half a world away, I'd understood: he'd needed to do what he hadn't been able to for his sister. At least that's what I'd thought.

What else could it be? Matty wouldn't lie to me. Would he?

All at once, it hits me. *What if he did?*

It's not about the legal consequences of signing my name to a lie. It's that the lie seems to involve people who—for reasons I've yet to uncover—orchestrated the disappearance of a journalist. And their shot over the bow involves the piece of paper in my hand. Which is a death sentence. For a teenage girl.

My brain simply doesn't want to believe it. "It's a mistake, some-one made a mistake."

"You," Joe shoots back. "Everyone's always covering for you. We all know they only hired you because of your dad. Affirmative action much?" He leans closer, poking at an angry welt on my neck, the one courtesy of Hendricks. ""Wait a sec—is that a hickey?" He bursts into laughter. "Well, boys, looks like the mourning period is over—who had August?"

"Enough." snaps a voice from the corner. Julie steps out of her office, rocking natural white hair and vintage Chanel. "I'm running a law firm, not a schoolyard. Leah, my office. Now."

I follow her inside the glass walls, wishing they were made of lead. I'm tired of being on display, tired of everything. I sink to the leather sofa by the window, tossing the envelope beside me. The contents promptly spill onto the floor. I drop my head to my hands. "I give up."

Julie goes quiet, probably waiting for me to take it back. "In that case, we have bigger problems than I thought."

My throat feels as if I've swallowed a rock. "Julie, I'm trying, I swear to god, but I'm failing at everything. I'm failing at helping my clients because I'm failing at helping my husband and deep down I'm scared to death that it's an impossible task to begin with, and now..." Tears start streaming. "Was Joe right? Am I fooling myself? Am I really?"

"Get your appeals filed and go home, Leah." She hands me a tissue. "*Home* home, not that memory trap you call an apartment. Go see your father. At Friday's benefit, I expect to see the woman I hired again."

Struggling to pull myself together, I kneel to pick up the spilled papers. "I have other clients."

"We'll make arrangements." She squeezes my shoulder, but she catches the welt with her ring and I flinch. Her head cocks. Reaching out, she lifts my hair to the side. Though her expression barely registers a change, she cups my chin. "You're much more like Dale, than you realize, my dear."

I gather the last of the papers. "I wish I believed that."

She walks behind her desk, sticking on a pair of tortoiseshell reading glasses. "Dale never told you how your brother died, did he?"

DJ had been killed in Vietnam, long before I was born. "Half-brother. Someone put a gun in his hand and told him to shoot people. They shot back. It happens."

She keys a few strokes into her computer "Consider having a closer look at your father's case history, Leah."

"What's that supposed to mean?"

After taking off her readers, she stares out the window. "Only that I meant it when I said you're too much alike. May you never know the pain of losing a child. It changes you, dear."

The papers are all jumbled up and I'm way too frustrated for this conversation. "Julie, if you're trying to tell me to drop it, you can forget it."

"Your father would never forgive me if I didn't try."

Maira's immigration photo slips out of the pile. Matty had taken it the day of the attack, gashes, burns and all, barely recognizable as the girl she is now. But when I go to slide it into the envelope, I notice what she was wearing around her neck. It's a hand-carved wooden cross, the letters IHS inscribed in gold paint.

Shaking, I undo the clasp on my bag, dig out Matty's note, and flip over the picture of him and his sister. Around her neck is a small wooden cross. And a faint glint of gold paint.

This is it. His big secret. Matty's sister didn't die in Iraq. Ari-eil is Maira. Maira is Ari-eil. She's alive. She's the one he's trying to protect.

Julie sighs. "I suppose at least there's no one left for them to go after."

I can't make my voice go above a whisper. "I'm not so sure that's true."

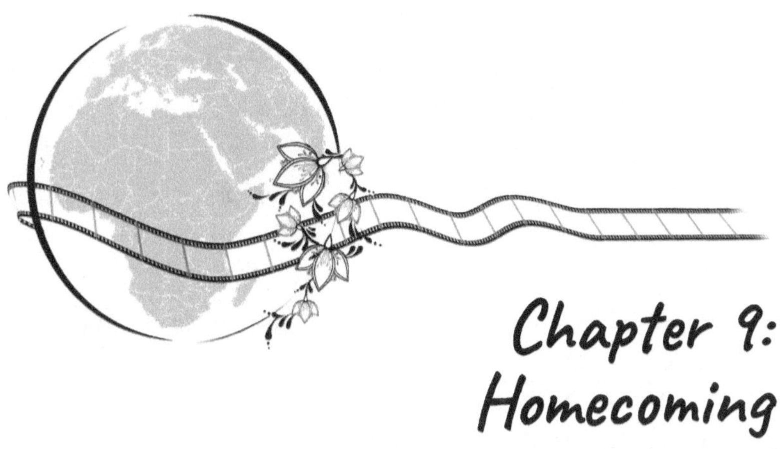

Chapter 9:
Homecoming

PROVINCETOWN, MASSACHUSETTS
PRESENT

Clam shells crunch under my feet as I enter the driveway, surrounded by familiar scents of salt and wisteria. My parents' Cape rises above the dunes. P-Town is the very tip of Cape Cod, a mixture of shingle style boxes and sherbet-colored Victorians, long a gay haven, grown from turn-of-the-century artist communities. For a mixed-race couple in the late 1960s, it was the kind of place that wouldn't give them any more trouble than they'd already been through. Now? It's the height of tourist season, with mobs of sunburnt New Yorkers tootling around in SUVs.

Armed with a trowel and pruning shears, Mom is on her knees by her hydrangeas, a floppy hat on her head. Fighting the urge get back on the ferry, I slink toward the carriage house. Maybe Dad is working on his sailboat.

She gets up, brushing dirt from her hands. "Leah, you should have called."

I stick my thumbs under my backpack straps, pulling them in front like a suit of armor. "Nice to see you too, Mom."

"I mean a month ago." She comes over, pulling off a polka-dotted glove. "You look like hell, baby."

"Thanks."

Squeezing my waist, she gives me a peck on the cheek. "I'm glad you're home. I have lemon bars. Dad's on the front porch. I'll bring some out."

My mother firmly believes that life's problems can all be solved with citrus and a bit of tea. Gin, if you're desperate.

"How's he been?"

Her face clouds. "Go easy on him, Leah. Julie rang. I know why you're here."

And she wonders why I haven't called her in months. "Matty's alive," I blurt out. "It's all some bullshit conspiracy—he must've uncovered something—I don't know what, I just know he's alive, I know who's holding him."

The ocean breeze blows ash blonde hair across her eyes. "You're sure?"

I wipe my nose. "If you had any idea what the past twenty-four hours have been like…"

"Sweetheart, you've been sure who captured him three times now," she says quietly. "I don't want you to get your hopes up again. You need my advice, not Daddy's. It's time to start cutting your losses. Think about moving on."

I turn, heading for the porch steps. Matty and I had been married a year before she stopped calling him 'Leah's little project'. "Go back to your flowers, Mom."

She catches my sweater. When I look back, there are tears in her eyes. "Dad and I have had forty years together. Fifteen wouldn't have been enough."

My parents met in '68, while Dad was prosecuting a housing discrimination case. After hearing him speak, she came to him with the evidence he needed… about her own father, who promptly disowned her. Which means somewhere buried under that housewife exterior is a woman passionate enough to risk her future for the things she believed in. I've never met that woman. As far as I can tell, she stopped existing somewhere around 1982. *That* woman would understand. God knows this one doesn't.

"It'll be sixteen in November."

"Together," she repeats, more forcefully than she needed to. "You're not twenty anymore, Leah, time is running out. I want more for you than you seem to want for yourself. If you hate me for that, I'm sorry."

Trust her to turn unlawful detention into an opportunity for grandchildren. Ever since I lost the baby, she's been impossible. "You've never had a clue what I want."

The veranda wraps around the house, past a forlorn porch swing, a reminder of first kisses and first loves, swaying in the breeze. I knew it was a mistake, coming home.

Closing my eyes, I take a deep breath of ocean air, and remind myself why I'm here: to find whatever Pandora's Box Matty opened and shove its demons back inside. I have two days and twenty thousand photos to try.

My breath catches when I saw the old man asleep on the wicker love seat. He's gaunt, his eyes sunken, skin translucent, hair like the thinnest lamb's wool on his head. Did he look this old the last time?

When I was younger, I thought it was cool that my father remembered Prohibition. The New Deal, FDR. At twenty, he stood inside newly liberated Dachau with the 45th Infantry, though you'd never know from the history books there had been a Negro unit there. I only heard him talk about it once, to Matty, when neither of them thought anyone else was around. Nine years later, he'd been in the room when the Brown vs. Board decision came down. Through the turmoil of the 60s, as a new war dragged on, he took on corruption in local draft boards, fought to open segregated neighborhoods, which he saw as a tool to keep blacks unemployed and funnel them into the military. People started calling him a radical. Then two weeks before King's assassination, my half-brother was killed in the Se San Valley.

All DJ has ever been to me was a picture on the wall. There are more in a drawer, Dad with a handsome black boy and woman who wasn't my mother, and when I asked about them, Mom tucked them away and said I should never mention them because they'd make Daddy sad. I learned more about my brother from books and speeches than my father ever told me himself. From the time I was a little girl, the plan had been for me to get my law degree, join the practice, and Dad would gradually retire, the way he'd always planned to do with DJ. For reasons I never fully understood, or maybe didn't want to, 'the plan' went awry when I married Matty.

There's a chill coming off the salty breeze, so I grab Dad's patchwork afghan from the chair, tucking it around him. A gull screeches by the porch, startling him awake. He blinks twice. "Well hello, stranger."

He pats the seat beside him. I kiss his cheek. "Hi Daddy."

The screen door swings open with a squeak. Mom comes out with a tray of iced tea and her special lemon bars. "I called the salon," she says, handing me a glass. "If you leave now, they can squeeze you in for a cut and highlights."

Seriously? "How about a bikini wax while I'm there? What part of my husband being held hostage by the U.S. government says 'spa day' to you?"

Dad raises his eyebrow. Mom sets the lemon bars onto the table beside him, nearly knocking over a sandpiper carving of Matty's. "Don't be insufferable, Leah. You're not living in some godforsaken refugee camp, you're a professional now. An hour for yourself won't kill either one of you. And besides, Connie is coming over. I didn't think you'd want to be here."

Crap. "She lives two miles away. Can't she come over tomorrow?"

Dad takes a sip from his glass. His face brightens.

"We have a church supper to plan," Mom says breezily, switching my glass with his. "Maybe if you'd called…"

When I go to protest, she sticks a lemon bar into my mouth. The screen door bangs behind her. I bite off a hunk and chuck the rest into her hydrangeas. I'm about to do the same with her iced tea, but Dad pipes up. "It'd be a shame to waste the gin, sweetheart."

I take a sniff, then a sip. "Ginned tea?"

He winks, downs half his glass, then holds it out. "Have pity on your poor old pop. She'll never know." After I oblige, he squeezes my hand. "Now what's this about Matthias?"

Plovers dart on the sand as I fill him in. Mostly, he listens, although he gets misty about me crashing the Senate hearing. "That's my girl."

Numb, I gulp some tea. "'Your girl' needs to hurry up and figure out why her husband lied about his last trip to Syria. The girl he rescued? Maira? She's his sister, Ari."

Dad squints at the sun. "You're sure of this?"

"As much as I can be." She's not returning my calls and no one answered the door when I swung by their apartment on my way from the airport. "They're threatening to refer charges against me too. It's not like they don't have a case—for starters, she's like twenty-two, not eighteen."

"Clients lie. Courts know that. They're trying to scare you, girl." He takes a sip of his tea. "Why would Matthias keep something like this from you?"

Because I made it easy for him. Because I was furious with him for going into Syria in the first place. Because we were both drowning for a change, instead of one of us pulling the other out. What it means is that he made a choice, a choice that kept him from introducing the sister he's been grieving for over a decade to the wife he loves, and as hurt, pissed off, and anxious as it makes me, it's a choice it must have killed him to make. He would've had to have felt it was the only way to protect her. And maybe, in his own twisted-up way, me. Which means he knew the threat was powerful enough to follow them here from Syria.

I press my thumbs into my eyes. "Because he's Matty."

Mom has the TV on in the kitchen, where the news—along with most of the country—is riveted to the attacks in Montreal. Last night, another would-be attacker got caught at the border, detonated a sarin-laced bomb, and when the footage hit the airwaves, America lost its damn mind. Overnight, several mosques and Assyrian churches got burned. Videos were circulating on social media of gun-toting militias blocking access to others, though what passed for 'journalism' seemed to be acting like stenographers for the incoherent rage-tweets coming from the White House, who chief occupant is clearly giddy that someone went and lit off the Reichstag Fire for him.

"I don't recognize this country anymore," she says, her voice weary. "Honey, don't bite my head off, but is this related to Matty's detention?"

It kills me to admit it, but we're past the denial point here. "They claim there's evidence he knew something was coming," I admit. "But I think they knew too." I dig into my bag for the list of email addresses the hacker sent me. "If they're so intent on keeping it quiet, why is Senator Nance keeping a bunch of his donors in the loop?"

Dad's brow furrows. "You have names?"

Last night, it took me until 2 a.m. to finish my appeals, about the same time a major hack of IRS records dropped through Anonymous. About two minutes after I got an unsigned WhatsApp message saying it would. Between that and Julie 'accidentally' leaving a post-it with her password to the firm's tax archives, I know way more than I did twelve hours ago.

"I don't get it. It's all through various SuperPACs and bogus charities rather than directly to Nance, but most of these people are hard right military types who wouldn't be caught dead voting for him." I thumb through the copies I made. "This guy? Bradley Gleason. He runs a company specializing in high-risk security and foreign strategy: Sierra Tango Global Strategies. They made a fortune in Iraq after the war, until Gleason got barred for 'callous disregard for the lives of Iraqi civilians'."

"Certainly could be a link there with Matthias or his sister," he muses.

"Yeah. And then there's a scientist who founded a big chemical conglomerate based in Baltimore...I thought it was a dead end, because all I could find was a bunch of thirty-year-old environmental lawsuits, but turns out they used a German subsidiary to sell stuff they weren't supposed to be selling to Iraq back in the eighties. Including the precursors for sarin."

He tugs his ear. "Don't suppose it was Elcola Chemical."

Who needs LexisNexis when you have Dale Atkins? "Did Julie mention that when she called? She's actually the one who pointed me towards them."

He ponders the plovers. "No. But I could hear it in her voice."

"What does that mean?"

At first, he doesn't answer. "She came to me as a young mother with a son dying of cancer. We tried everything, but I couldn't make a case against the people responsible for it. A mother never forgives or forgets that kind of thing, but she's not necessarily objective."

"I mean, yeah, but..." *Why is he fighting me on this?* "These guys... they're bad news. I didn't remember it until she reminded me, but I ran into Elcola my first year with ReliefNet. This plant of theirs gave cancer to a bunch of women in Mali, and when we tried to do something about it, they hired a local militia to run the entire village off the land. Same thing though, we couldn't prove it."

He scrunches his feet in his slippers. "Hunches won't make a case. Julie should've known better than to set you off chasing ghosts. What else do you have?"

Disheartened, I move down the list. "Okay, so, Colonel Clarke? The guy who testified at the hearing yesterday? He was Sierra Tango's military liaison during the war. And I found out that Nance was CIA during the Gulf War—they've all worked together for years."

After a contemplative swig of his bootleg gin, Dad shuffles his feet. "Can you pinpoint times where they crossed paths with Matthias?"

That'll have to come from Matty's photo archive. Or at least I'm praying it will. "Not yet, but the pieces fit. Gleason is big in anti-refugee circles. He was all hair-on-fire on the news yesterday, banging on about the attack in Montreal." I fish out a copy of a deposited check. "So why is he donating $200k to a dodgy charity pushing for resettlement assistance for refugees?"

"You're thinking Nance is blackmailing the others?" Squinting in the sun, Dad reaches for the plate of lemon bars. "I've never known Matthias to take an interest in political corruption."

Mom's voice floats through the window screen. "Could he ever focus on anything for more than a few months? First it was landmines. Iraq, Darfur, now Syrian refugees…"

Like Dad was any different? "It's Matty's job to shine light where it's needed, Mom."

With a loud crunch, she turns on the icemaker. "Leah, you do realize you're the only person on earth who still idolizes journalists…reporters, lawyers, and politicians are the world's three least favorite professions."

"Speaking for the porch and the unlawfully detained, we resent that."

Dad brushes powdered sugar from his pajama shirt. "Your mother has a point, Leah—with this administration, the cost of disappearing a journalist is far greater than the risk of a bribery conviction."

"Think how easy it would've been to discredit him," Mom adds. "Some falsified detail or doctored photo. A MeToo accuser."

Where the hell is the gin? "Seriously? You're going there?"

"It wouldn't have to be true," she says quietly. "Think what would happen if it got out about that Russian girlfriend of his that went missing. No one would ever listen to a word he said again."

All the exhaustion, fear, and worry catches up with me and suddenly I'm in tears again. "Dammit."

She comes out and tries to rub my back, then sighs when I flinch away. "You know I'm right, baby. I'm not sure I can watch you do this to yourself."

Her footsteps pad off the porch steps, back to her hydrangeas.

Dad's been rocking, waiting for me to pull it together. "If he's alive, they need him for something."

I push my hair out of my face. "In the video, they kept asking him how to find someone. A source, probably. I'm beginning to wonder if the job in Cairo was just a setup for them to get him out of the country. The head of the network is on Nance's donor list."

Dad strokes the white bristles on his chin. "Can you find proof?"

"It's a theory at this point," I admit. "My priority is getting Matty freed, not his investigation."

"Then you leave yourself exposed."

"I know, Dad, okay?" There are times when I appreciate his relentless perfectionism, the way everything I do can be improved. This isn't one of them.

"I'm working on a habeas petition—there's no immediate custodian, which means they'll ding me on respondent and jurisdiction, so I pulled up *Braden* and *Boumediene*, along with *Rasul v. Bush*."

He unfolds a set of reading glasses, then skims the brief. "Overwritten and formulaic," he harrumphs. "Three years of law school and they undid everything I ever taught you."

Dad's not a fan of modern anything, least of all current methods of legal training. "Is it my writing or my case?"

"Your arguments are sound." He hands it back. "Why haven't you filed it?"

Because I took Julie's advice and went through your case history?

I spent half the night on Nexis and found a bunch of sealed case records from the time DJ was killed. Dad had gone after the well-connected head of a local draft board, charging him with taking bribes for deferments from the wealthy and privileged. The case never went to trial.

"Is it true?" I whisper. "Was DJ killed because you pushed too hard on a case?"

Something in him seems to turn inward. His breathing slows, and becomes labored, a tremor in his jaw. He stares out over the waves. "Not that I could ever prove."

The expression on his face just guts me. I lay my head on his shoulder. "I'm sorry I brought it up—I shouldn't have. I just...need to know what you'd do."

He folds his glasses, blinking. "Your generation's battles are different than mine. Your mother's right. I can't help you, Leah."

My stomach craters. "I'm not asking you to plead his case, I—"

He pats my hand. "My girl, you're dealing with people with no respect for the rule of law. You will not beat them with it."

My vision blurs. Is the greatest attorney I've ever known really admitting that even his faith in the law has limits? "So how *do* I beat them?"

"Broaden the fight." He reaches for Mom's tea. "Get someone else on your side."

"Who?"

"Are you or are you not married to the press?"

It's not like I haven't tried before. But Hendricks made it clear what will happen if I do it now. "Dad, they said they'd kill him."

He takes a long, slow swig of his tea. "I warned you your decisions would always have that potential."

"I know, but—"

"But nothing. Find your courage. You fail because you are timid."

From my mother, I expect this. From him it hurts. "The Armed Services Committee didn't seem to think so."

"You were flailing. You had no plan, beyond hoping they would provide you with one. Instead, you showed your hand."

I drop my head to my hands. "I know, okay? I'm completely over my head."

"Horsefeathers."

I press my thumbs into my eyes until I see stars. "Nowadays we say bullshit, Dad."

He grows distant, fixed on the surf. "Your mother took you out there once, when you were a newborn. It was a day like this, after a storm, and the undertow was terrible. A giant wave came along and knocked her off her feet. She tumbled and tumbled, and all she could do was clutch you tighter, certain you'd both drown. It seems she was swimming towards the bottom. All she needed was to figure out how to put her feet down

Actually Dad, I was three. I remember. I draw a shaky breath. "I'm going for a walk."

"Leah—" He picks up Matty's carving, running a gnarled finger over the beak. "The storm washed up the driftwood. You might collect some. He'll need something to still his mind when he returns."

I kiss the top of his head. "Thanks, Daddy."

Clamshells crunch under a set of tires, which means Connie is here, so I beat a hasty retreat, limping across Route 6 for the dunes. Get my feet back under me. Right.

To the roar of the Atlantic, I trudge up the hill, running my fingers through the tall grass. Memories prickle at the sharpness. When Matty and I lived in the carriage house, this was always where I'd come to find him. He'd be at the water's edge with his knife, a piece of driftwood, and his Nikon around his neck, watching the birds and the waves.

The surf is up. I scrunch my toes in the warm sand, wincing as salt water floods the slice on my foot. The tourists rarely venture out this far, so it's secluded and peaceful. Of course, that's the other reason Matty likes making me come fetch him out here. A roll in the sand usually cures whatever ails him. I could use a bit of his cure myself.

Sometimes it feels like I'm losing sight of my own identity. Sometimes I wonder if I ever had one in the first place. I've been daughter, a friend, a lover, then a wife. Am I even that anymore? Even a widow can grieve. All I can do is wait. It has to stop. Now.

When I open my eyes, someone is watching from the dune nearest the highway. Not Hendricks. This one has dark hair, a fisherman's jacket and ball cap pulled low over his eyes.

Like a zebra who spotted a lion in the grass, I get up, heading towards town. Whoever it is follows me past the breakwater and up Commercial Street, all the way to the pier.

Marine Specialties, P-town's Army-Navy surplus store, is more glorified pirate cave than a shop. It's older than dirt and smells twice as funky, but it might have things that'll make life difficult for my new friend. Things like police batons and pocket knives, maybe a bit of fishing line, if I can find them between the doll arms and legs, old license plates and dried puffer fish.

At the entrance, the antique dive suit that's been hanging overhead for generations holds a sign reading *'Beware of Attack Lesbian'*. It's over a bathtub full of cat's eye marbles. They're 89¢ for a handful, so I dig in, dumping them into a beach bag with light-up flamingos on the outside.

Between the marbles, the bag, and a pen knife concealed in a lobster-shaped keychain, my booty costs me a grand total of $28.36. The lobster even has a little penlight where its antennae should be. Whether cornered by government goons or a man-sized crustacean, I'm as ready as I'm going to get.

But halfway out, my pursuer stumbles into the store and takes off his cap. I freeze. His skin is doughy, blackish hair unkempt and blending into a scraggly beard. His eyes are glassy and unfocused, and they've lost that skyward gleam. Beneath the coat, his flannel shirt is stained, and his sneakers are mud-caked. For someone who used to get up at 4:30a.m. to make sure his combat boots were polished, a kid who grew his pilot's swagger the first time he rode the helicopter ride at the fair, it just…isn't *right*. "Jason?"

He gives me a sheepish smile. "Been working up the courage to say hi for twenty minutes. Your mom mentioned you were in town."

I can't make my fingers unclench from the lobster. "Did she now?"

My mind starts racing. If he knows about the call yesterday, he's not letting on, but the chances of this being a coincidence are nil. Best case, his mother figured out it was me on the phone and this is some plan she and mine cooked up. Worst case… I can't even go there. Because it probably means Matty's dead.

He taps the bill of his cap on his thumb. "How have you been?"

The whiskey fumes on his breath make my eyes water. "Are you kidding me?"

He leans on a bin full of seahorses. "Lee, give me a break. My life sucks as bad as yours does at the moment, and don't even try to pretend you don't know what I'm talking about, because I know your mother better than that."

Beyond the divorce, his time in Iraq ended when the Army stripped his wings and slapped him with an other-than-honorable discharge after an 'incident'. Last I heard, he spends his time on Tindr and bumming around various couches to avoid the alimony payments. "Didn't realize it was a contest."

"It's been fifteen years. Can we try being friends again?"

"No." Hell no.

Growing up, Jason and I had been inseparable. Seaweed fights on the beach, riding our bikes to Race Point, but we were just friends until my sophomore year, when we convinced ourselves we wouldn't ruin it if we kissed, just once. Fast forward five years, past prom night promises, first everythings on the beach, past us both starting college, him joining ROTC, me diving headlong into my grand plan to be the next Dale Atkins…and stop when the planes hit the towers.

Overnight, we fell apart. *They* were out to get us, we had to get *them* first. I was sad and scared and angry like everybody else, but I saw the country I loved drawing into a burrow like a wounded animal. I saw us giving up our freedoms for empty promises. I heard my father shouted down at what had started as a vigil. And the boy I'd grown up with, who knew exactly what my father had given this country, to whom I'd give myself heart, body, and soul… I watched him turn around and call us both traitors.

We hung on for another year, breaking up and getting back together, cutting our hearts to pieces in the process, but it wasn't until Matty came into the picture that we broke up for good.

"No?" Jason finally says. His hands clench. "That's all you have to say?"

I back away. "I see your temper hasn't improved."

"My te—" Face red, he dances on his feet. "Lee, you're the one who dumped me. I'm trying to be a good guy. If I'd been captured or killed on duty, I'd hope my wife had people looking out for her."

"Matty knows I can take care of myself."

He mutters something, looking towards the street. "Have you gotten any news on him lately? Who's got him, or what they want?"

He's asking for a reason, and I know *damn* sure it isn't out of concern for Matty. I call home, needing a quick way to cut through the lies. Eyes closed, Jason hangs his head.

My mother picks up. "Hi honey," she says brightly. "Hair looking better now?"

"Forget my hair." I eye him sideways, struggling to gauge how much he knows. "Did you tell Jason I was on the beach?"

"Jason's in town? What a lovely coincidence. Connie, why didn't you mention it?" From the muffled background reply, his mother didn't know either. "Tell him to call his mum, sweetheart. You two should catch up!"

"Uh—sure. Talk to you later." I hang up, mind racing. So his mother didn't figure it out. Which means he did. Which confirms he's talked to Hendricks. Do I scream? Run?

He scratches his knuckles on his neck. "So my mom calls, saying some chick called about my old buddy Ryan. Figured I'd give him a call, see what's up. Funny thing though. He starts asking me a bunch of questions about you. Except he won't say why. Made me curious. Figured if you were willing to lie to my mom to get in touch with me, maybe we should talk."

Unless I'm imagining it, he sounds a little suspicious of Ryan. Which, if I was Ryan, was exactly how I would've told him to approach me. "So what's with the stalker routine?"

He throws up his hands. "We were best friends for fifteen years. Like I didn't know you'd be on the damn beach."

My heart slams against my ribs. "So what did they tell you to do? You play dumb, see what you can get from me and then they disappear me the way they disappeared Matty?"

"Do you realize how nuts you sound?"

"Yeah, imagine that." I turn on my heel out of the shop, heading for home by way of a passage between the art gallery and the burlesque theatre.

Jason follows. "So what's the deal? Why'd you call me?"

"I didn't." Having him this close is seriously making me queasy. "Since you're here, don't suppose you're willing to tell me who Ryan's working for these days."

"Don't see why I should."

"If one of my friends committed treason, I'd want to know."

"Doesn't seem to apply to your husband."

Fuck you. Rubbing my arms, I change direction and speed up, heading for the public beach. "You can tell Ryan I figured it out on my own. Sierra Tango Global Strategies, right?"

Confusion blossoms on his face. "Hold up." He gets in front of me, turning to walk backwards, nearly tripping over his own two feet in the process. "How sure are you about that?"

When I force myself to look at him, he's not just confused, he's... hurt. "Check for yourself. His tax records were part of the data dump Anonymous put out last night."

"But it's a recent thing, right? Like the last couple months?"

"Try ten years. Why?"

His sigh envelops me in a cloud of alcohol fumes. "While back, they were looking for a pilot. My CO from Iraq got me on the short list. Said they wanted someone who could handle both fixed wing and chopper, including military. Somebody willing to fly anywhere. The head honcho was willing to 'overlook' my discharge, but had reservations." His gaze drops, and he kicks at the sand. "I asked Ryan if he knew anybody who could put in a word. Told me he didn't."

"When was this?"

"Maybe a year ago?" He squints at the sun. "Colonel Clarke was always saying something else would—"

My breath gets short. "Clarke? As in Oswald Clarke?"

"Yeah, why?"

A year ago would've been right around the time of Matty's last trip to Syria. And now, the same guy feeding Congress information about Matty's detention just happens to be Jason's former CO. What it means? Is that whatever Matty was investigating not only went back years, but it somehow just crossed over from his life to mine.

Needing to get home, to start putting the pieces together, I duck behind the boardwalk. "Trust me, you dodged a bullet. They're bad guys, Jason. Including Clarke."

He keeps following me. "Bullshit. He's a patriot. You know his wife and daughter died on 9/11, right?"

I didn't. But it put an interesting spin on his willingness to accept Matty's detention. "What's your point?"

"That tremor in his hands? It's from exposure to sarin, or mustard gas or something. He got exposed in Iraq, then got ordered to pretend it never happened. This attack yesterday—"

"Let me see if I have this." I'm dimly aware that I'm about to restart a fifteen-year-old argument but can't stop myself. "We *had* to attack Iraq because they had WMD. Except they didn't. What they *did* have was a thirty-year-old chemical weapons program we gave them, which someone has now decided to return to us. And all it cost us was two trillion dollars, a quarter million dead Iraqis, five thousand dead American soldiers, not to mention the thirty-five thousand others who came back like you or worse…"

"For pete's sake, give it a rest, Lee. The guy killed himself last night."

The shock takes a minute to set in. He certainly didn't seem suicidal at yesterday's hearing. "Are they sure that's what happened?"

"OD." His face turns sad. "Totally sucks. He was a good guy. I've never met a soldier more dedicated to his country. Or his men. He even spoke for me at my court-martial, for all the good it did."

Matty, who'd been embedded with a Marine counterinsurgency squad when it'd happened, was the first person who'd told me about Jason's 'mistake': he'd fired a Hellfire missile into a mosque in Diyala province—three miles from the insurgent nest where it was supposed to land. Twenty-four people died, mostly women and children. The military claimed he had drugs in his system, the JAG lawyer blamed faulty targeting software, and basically? Right now, I'm wondering how much more Matty knew than he let on.

"Let me guess," I say. "Before Clarke offed himself," *or before somebody killed him,* "he got you to come talk to me with a promise to reopen your case."

His chest rises, and he turns his face to the sky. "You have no idea what it would've meant, getting my bird back."

As if I didn't know he wanted to be a pilot since he was five. As if I hadn't spent most of college struggling to balance my dreams on his. As if he didn't throw it all in my face in the end.

"Actually I do," I say. "But if I were you, I'd be asking what the Army would gain by re-instituting a rusty pilot with a drinking problem."

Nostrils flared, he scrambles up, but he's so drunk he lurches sideways and falls on me. The booze must've short-circuited in his brain, because all of a sudden his hands are on my shoulders, in my hair. "It wasn't supposed to be this way, you and me."

I grab a pinch of skin and twist until he yelps, but I can't stop myself, I hit him and keep hitting him. The last time he came at me like that, it nearly destroyed me. "Don't touch me, don't you *dare* touch me!"

He seizes my wrist, then shoves me away so hard I hit the ground. "The guy's a loser. He's been lying to you all along. What the hell did you ever see in him?"

I pick myself up, hating him as much as I ever did. "I see the only person who ever stood up for me."

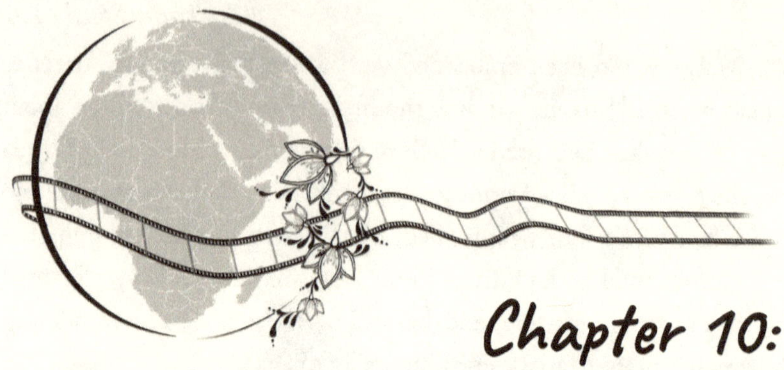

Chapter 10:
That's What Friends Are For

MEDITERRANEAN SEA
PRESENT

Matty

After the last dose of Haldol wore off, I got a cell mate.

Rani is by the door, mopping sweat from his nose with his São Paulo FC jersey. The same one he died in. "Hey boyo," he says, "Long time no see."

The ship is sweltering, so it might be the heat, but I can't make myself move. "Am I dying?"

"Na, man, you just losin' it."

I want to ask him if he forgives me. If he thinks Leah would. "Can you stay a while?"

The cockeyed grin he always wore evaporates. He comes and sits next to me. "You better eat something, boyo."

There's a dragon gnawing at my insides, but the untouched tray sits, as it has for the past thirty-four days, near the floor slot. "Pass."

He cocks his head. Then gets up and slinks towards the door, flattening himself along the wall. Craning his neck, he peers out the beanhole. "You gotta get out of here, man. Can't do nobody no good if you're dead."

Next thing I know, Orlyk's ugly mug pops up in the hole. Rattling sounds echo outside the door. "Yo, reporter." Three sharp raps clank off the steel. "Who's he talking to?"

"Hell if I know," his buddy replies. "Toss in those pictures of his wife. That'll snap him out of it."

With a suspicious sniff, Rani picks up my untouched tray of grub. "You think she wants you back like this?" He makes a point of sticking a few congealed beans into his mouth. "I bet your dick don't even work no more."

A shower of glossy paper flutters through the hole. The dragon stops cold. Rani lights up a cigarette and turns away.

The shots are grainy drone surveillance photos, taken from overhead. Leah's in a city, glancing over her shoulder. Seeing the real her after this long knocks the breath out of me. Strong, determined, beautiful—for a second, I'm the luckiest guy in the world again. Until I see the next shot. It's from the side, and Ryan Hendricks has her by the arm, his jacket pressed to her back.

Fuck. Fuck fucking *fuck.*

Her family name, her father's connections—I'd been counting on them as a layer of protection, no matter how thin.

"You've been wrong about that before." Rani peers over my shoulder. "Wait, I thought you knocked her up? I don't see no big belly. Guess you was wrong about that too."

Hearing that... realizing he's right... something snuffs out inside me. I guess if she decided she couldn't go through with it, it's not like I can blame her, but truth is, I'd gotten used to the idea.

Aching, sad, and confused, I pick up the rest of the photos. I need to see her any way I can get her. In the last shot, the angle of the sun is lower. She's alone on a bench on the Provincetown ferry, staring into the waves, as if she's utterly destroyed. But whoever took the photo got the guy watching her from behind the bulkhead. The *last* guy I want anywhere near her. "What the hell is Jason Barnes doing there?"

Orlyk's smirk broadens. "We are all old friends. He said to say hi."

The dragon takes a bite at my insides. "You sent that asshole after my wife?"

He snorts. "You think we are stupid? That guy is dumber than bag of dicks. She called him."

Everything in me clenches up, a sickening feeling that goes right down to my nuts. "Bullshit. She wouldn't. No way."

When an evil grin spreads on his face, I realize how badly I just screwed up. How much ammunition I just gave him. Gleeful, he flips a final proof through the grate. "Chew on those. We'll be back in an hour."

The camera is the most powerful tool man ever invented. In the right hands, it can topple governments, bring down giants, turn the voiceless immortal. It's the only weapon I've ever needed, and in the simple act of taking it out of my hands, they rendered me powerless. Now Leah's paying the price.

I crumple the photo. She's the smartest, most resourceful person I ever met, but when she feels hopeless or trapped, her judgment goes to shit.

"You're one to talk, *gatão*." Rani flicks a bean at my ear. "Least you know she ain't given up on you, right?"

"Shut up, will you?"

This is my fault, all of it. She shouldn't be dealing with armed goon-squad freaks, though god knows she's done it before. Shouldn't have Jason Barnes anywhere inside a five-mile radius after what he did to her. Feeling a dozen broken promises crash down on my head, I look at Rani. "How the hell do I get out of here?"

A wreath of smoke trails around his head. "Wanting to sounds like a start."

Chapter 11:
Love And Other Disasters
DECEMBER 2002
BOSTON, MASSACHUSETTS

Leah knocked on the bathroom door. "Matty?"

Red safelight illuminated the mess I'd made of the place. Trays balanced precariously on the tub. Haphazard strands of clothesline and drying photos stretched between the walls. There were brown bottles of fixer and developer on the floor, wash baths in the tub, the fruits of a marathon editing session now entering its second day. I glanced at the enlarger, which was sitting on top of the toilet. "Do you need to go?"

"No, it's fine, I peed in the kitchen sink."

"What?"

"Kidding."

It was a week before Christmas, and I was putting the finishing touches on the landmine story. My deadline was that day, the post office closed in an hour, and I'd been trying to salvage one badly lit shot all afternoon, two brothers swinging from a banyan tree, the younger of whom was missing a leg. "Wouldn't put it past you."

She'd taken me in like the homeless puppy I was, and life was on a serious upswing. Between her thesis and finals and law school applications, she found time to help me look through my photos, to listen to my stories. To hear about Rani. To make me see he'd made his own choices, that it wasn't my fault. I even started to believe her. Of course, by that point, I was completely, madly in love with her, so that helped.

She knocked again. "It's almost four—can I make you a sandwich?"

Stomach rumbling, I hit the switch on the enlarger. Once the article was in the mail, I wouldn't have to think about it anymore. "I'll grab something later."

"We could start with breakfast."

Breakfast made me think of bed. Bed made me think of sex. But sex made me remember she had a boyfriend. "Don't you have class?"

"Class schmass." Her footsteps retreated. "I'm staying until you finish."

She started banging in the kitchen. Twenty minutes later, I'd reframed the shot and had it back in the fixer when the smell of molasses and spice weaved through the developer chemicals. When I opened the door, she was crouched at the threshold, holding a cookie the size of Texas. A triumphant smile broke over her face. "I knew this would get you out."

Stomach rumbling, I helped her up, going for the cookie. "You found my weakness."

With a cheeky grin, she pulled it back. "This one's mine. If you want yours, come and get it. It's next to your sandwich."

I went to snatch it and she darted into the living room. So I chased her. Over the sofa, twice around the table, down the hall, onto the balcony—three stories of rickety black iron. "Gimme the cookie, Leah."

"No! It's mine!"

There were probably two dozen more. "Not for long."

She shoved half the cookie into her mouth. "Oh yeah?"

"Now you're in trouble."

My last bit of restraint dove off the balcony. What started as us wrestling for the other half of the cookie ended with us against the railing, hip to hip, her back to the post. We just fit. I couldn't move, couldn't breathe, couldn't stop myself from getting hard.

Flushed and breathless, she glanced down between us. "I dropped the other half."

It felt like now or never. Everything I wanted was right there in my arms. I brushed her temple with my thumb. "You've got sugar on you."

I couldn't stop, not now that'd I'd touched her. I tangled my fingers into her hair and got lost in her eyes, savoring what it'd be like to taste her lips for the first time. Her breathing slowed, and we sort of melted together, and all I could think was *kiss her.*

Over the next few months, I'd want that moment back more times than I could count. I should've done it, I should've gone the last inch, pressed my lips to hers. I should've wrapped those killer legs of hers around my waist and carried her inside the apartment. I should've laid her down on the bed and asked her to be mine then and there, but I needed to hear her say it, say she was done with him and she wanted me instead.

But inside, the phone started ringing. "That's Jason," she said, without moving. "He's supposed to hear whether he's going Chinook or Apache today."

It was a call she'd been dreading for days. Chinook meant she could tell herself all he'd be doing was driving troops around. Apache meant he'd be the one firing missiles. Deep down, that wasn't something she could live with, and the trouble was, he was playing her guilt over it like a mandolin string. One day she'd be killing herself to graduate early so she could move to Alabama. The next, cursing him and downloading a Columbia Law application for the nineteenth time, which she somehow never managed to finish. I kept hoping she'd figure it out.

Kicking myself, I shifted away. "I need to get to the post office."

"Don't forget your sandwich," she said softly. With that she went inside and closed her bedroom door. Through the window, I heard a muffled *you too, sweetie.*

We went on like that for another couple of weeks, until everything hit the fan her last day of classes. I'd heard from the editor at *Mother Jones* the night before. *I hear you're worried what your friend would think–don't. It's a hell of an article, a hell of a tribute, and I'll bet it was hell to write. He'd be proud.*

Leah's stuff was in boxes all around the apartment. I got up early and drove down to the Cape, walking the dunes with my Leica, just me and the gulls and terns. The best shot was a pre-dawn silhouette near the pier, of jutting pilings and an ancient fisherman in a pale blue boat. So I made up a frame from slats of an old gate that'd washed up and gave it to her when she came back from the library.

"You made this?" She ran her fingertips over the smooth wood, the tenons I'd cut in to get the joints right.

"Carving was a good way to pass the time when I was a kid. Give me a knob of acacia root and I can make a pretty mean leopard." Plus, driftwood was free, which was what I could afford at that point. "I can get you a better one once my check comes through."

"It's beautiful," she said softly. "Is this why you disappeared this morning?"

It wasn't about the frame. It was about hoping she'd realize she didn't want to leave. "Thanks for putting up with me."

Her nose wrinkled. "Wait—you said check. They accepted the article?" When I nodded, a broad smile broke on her face and she gave me a hug. "It was brilliant. I knew they would."

"Can I take you out to dinner to celebrate?"

Her expression turned uneasy. "I have to turn in my thesis by midnight."

Things had been weird since the cookie incident, so I wasn't surprised she turned me down. Instead, Jack and I ended up at some trendy joint in Lower Allston. He ordered us a round of fancy scotch, which he was under the mistaken impression I was paying for.

"To becoming immortal," he said, clinking my glass. "And the ones who aren't."

The contents burned down my throat like liquid smoke mixed with guilt. I motioned to the bartender for a refill.

Jack did likewise, surveying the scene at the bar. "We in editorial have a sacred tradition when one of our cubs hit it big. Your next assignment is to use that pretty boy face of yours to chat up that stunning pair of ladies at the far end of the bar. I suppose I'll have to take the brunette, but such is my sacrifice."

At that point, I couldn't have possibly been less interested. "Aren't they a little young?"

He leaned his elbows on the bar. "Oh dear. You do have it bad for this one, don't you?"

I stared into my scotch. "I should just tell her I don't want her to go, right?"

He slid off his stool, then clapped me on the back. "Never too soon to get started on the first ex-wife."

The bars closed at two, so I suppose I got back around then, but the door was locked, so I had to go up the fire escape. It was the first sign something was wrong.

Leah's sublet was this drafty old brownstone off Comm Ave. She only had one set of keys, and usually, it was her getting back late, so we'd been leaving the door unlocked. The lights were off. I was so drunk I flopped right onto the couch, fighting the urge to crawl into bed with her. First thing tomorrow, I'd tell her.

That was when I heard her. Just the smallest sound, as if she was trying not to breathe. She was curled up in a blanket, hiding beside the radiator. From the second I saw her face, saw the way she was sitting, there wasn't a doubt in my mind what had happened.

"Oh Jesus, Leah," I said, stumbling to her side.

She flinched and pulled away. "Please don't touch me."

It was as if someone put my guts in a blender. "You're safe. I won't let anyone hurt you."

"Jason's father had a stroke." She started rocking, knees to her chest. "He didn't make it in time, he came here on his way home from Hanscom."

In the field, the lens gives a veneer of emotional distance, a way to shrink-wrap all the suffering into a slow cancer eating at your soul. It sucks, but you live in fear of the day something strips away the shell. Watching her, feeling her recoil from even the smallest touch, it was all my nightmares laid bare. "God, Leah… I'm so sorry I wasn't here."

"I was taking a shower," she said, head resting on her knees. "He came in throwing your stuff and yelling." She squeezed her elbows around her head. "I told him we were just friends, I swore nothing happened."

She'd been completely faithful to that bastard. "Even if it did, the guy had no right to—"

"Look, I let him, okay?" She pushed a tangle of hair out of her face. "It's like it wasn't even him, like he'd snapped. I promised I wouldn't leave him, I thought that was all he needed to hear, but he started pushing me into my bedroom, and…"

I felt sick. I wanted to tear his goddamn head off. "That's still rape, Leah."

"Get out," she said, softly at first. "That's not what it was, get out."

"I've spent half my life in war zones, for Pete's sake. This isn't the first time I've seen a woman who's been—"

"Get out, leave, just go." She put her head down and started sobbing. "Get out, Matty, I don't want you here."

By then I was shaking as badly as she was. If I'd come home one drink earlier, taken a goddamn cab, anything. It was like watching Rani chase that kid into the gulley all over again, being too far away, too utterly freaking useless to do anything about it. "Please don't make me go. I will if you want, but please don't make me. Tell me what to do, tell me how to help."

Huddled inside her blanket, she rested her head on the wall. "I just need sleep." She drew a shaky breath. "I won't be able to face him at the funeral otherwise."

There was no way I heard her right. "Uh—what?"

"My mother and his are best friends," she said. "We all go to the same church. If I'm not there, people are going to ask why."

"Then let him explain," I said bitterly.

She shook her head. "I'm not going to blow up two families just because he had a bad night."

Ask me, it was a hell of a lot worse than a 'bad night', but she'd been there for me. The least I could do was shut up and be there for her. "I'll make you some tea," I sighed.

She turned away, rubbing her arm. "My birth control is in the medicine cabinet. Could you get it?"

Numbness took over. "You should see a doctor, Leah. I'll go with you if you want, but you need to get tested. He might have—"

"We've been together since I was fourteen," she said quietly. "There's nobody else." After pressing her knuckles to her eye sockets, she moved away from the wall. "Do you mind if I take the couch to-night? I don't feel like being in my room. "

The bathroom was in such a state, it was as if a bomb had gone off. Overturned bottles, broken glass. I almost left it, hoping it'd convince her to call the police in the morning, but I felt sick looking at it. While the tea was steeping, I changed the sheets, then brought her the medication. "Here."

Her face was pale and drawn, barely registering a change of expression as she swallowed about four of the pills. "The sad thing is, he was right about a lot of what he said."

I handed her the steaming mug. "I find that very hard to believe."

She stared at her feet. "Including how I feel about you."

I stayed up all night while she slept, guarding the door. In the morning, I drove her out to the Cape, waiting out of sight, telling myself she knew where I was if she needed me. I watched her flinch when he hugged her goodbye, I felt the twist in my nuts, and when she walked back to the car, I watched her crumple, then held her while she cried. And I promised her that so long as there was breath in my body, she'd never have to deal with him again.

The next few weeks sucked. She tried like hell to pretend nothing happened, I tried like hell to help, but she kept withdrawing. Stopped eating. Her mother hadn't spoken to her since the funeral, and while Leah wouldn't say, I knew she hadn't let on what Jason had done to her.

As awful as it all was, it brought us closer. I quit thinking in non-platonic terms and started thinking of her as a friend. We told ourselves all the things that you do when you're in love with a friend, that what we had was amazing and deep, that we didn't want to ruin it, which worked great until I realized she was lying too and trying to force herself to get over it for me. So when an opportunity came up to do a story in Iraq, I took it.

She stared at me for a long time after I'd told her. "How long will you be gone?"

We were sitting at the kitchen table, me fiddling with my new digital SLR, which I'd bought to replace the Leica Jason had trashed. Though I was less fiddling and more trying to gauge her reaction. I needed some glimmer of hope that she'd miss me, that things would be better when I got back.

"They want me to report on conditions in the no-fly zone," I said. "Maybe a couple weeks, unless the war starts."

She slid her index finger up and down a gin and tonic, which had come to replace her evening chamomile. "Will it?"

I squinted at the viewfinder, getting the feel of the shutter. "No sane commander plans to launch an invasion in the middle of winter. Or wants to be there during summer. My guess, first day of spring."

Her lips pursed. "How can you even get there? There are all these travel warnings, and I mean… can you even get a visa?"

"The rules are different for journalists." I pointed the lens at a radiator shadow on the floor, testing the light meter. "The magazine gives me press credentials—they send a few faxes and give me a letter I use to talk my way across the border."

Truth told, it was a killer assignment—no propaganda-spouting Baathist minder, just me going wherever the spirit moved. Plus, it was a chance to see Ari, along with what was sure to be another futile attempt to get her someplace safe. "That area is under Kurdish control, so it's not hard if you know the right people."

"You do?"

I shrugged. "That's why they're sending me."

"Oh." She drained her drink, then poked the leftover ice. "Guess I was hoping I could go too."

Squinting, I clicked the shutter. "Why the hell would you want to do that?"

"Because we're about to go to war and you've made me realize I don't understand why we should or why we shouldn't. The only way I'm going to do that is to see it firsthand."

I frowned at the shot on the display. *Flat flat flat.* "Leah, if my photos can't do that, then I'm not very good at my job."

"Please don't do that," she said softly. "Don't treat me like my father does."

"Huh?"

She coiled her hair into a loose knot. "You saw him at the protest. I'm his sheltered little girl who doesn't have the first clue what he and DJ and his friends went through. Maybe I haven't known you for that long, but I see how the things you've experienced affect you. You're part of the club."

"So what? You want your own nightmares?"

"No." She moved behind me. Hands coming to rest on my arms, she traced my tattoo with her thumb. "I don't want to be a 'See no evil' person anymore."

I closed my eyes. She'd broken the distance between us and I wasn't sure what that meant. "Come on, Leah…"

She wrapped her arms in a comforting embrace around my neck. "Wouldn't it help to have someone who can carry your stuff? Hand you a new lens when you need it?"

On some level, I knew it wasn't my stuff she was offering to help carry; it was a different sort of burden, of things I'd seen. "I'll manage."

Her chin came to rest on the top of my head. "You know what? I think talking about it makes it bearable for you. We both have plans for our lives, Matty, and mine doesn't work if I stay the little girl who watches from the sidelines. It's time for me to grow up and start being part of the world."

With a sigh, I set the camera on the table. "I'll make some calls."

Chapter 12:
Hail Hail The Gang's All Here

JANUARY 2003
NORTHERN IRAQ

Leah and I crossed the Turkish border just after New Year's. The invasion was still two months off. She took a disconcerted gander at the chaotic sea of supply trucks, HumVees, and artillery sprawling around the complex and exhaled a deep lungful of oil-choked air. I could see, it was the moment when it finally hit home that the war was inevitable.

Truth be told, I was glad to be back in the field. The magazine was picking up my expenses and all I had to do was exchange my memory card every other day with a runner at the border. They'd take what they wanted, my agency would update my contact sheet with the rest. Digital was officially the best invention since sex.

The desert looked like whitecaps in a sea of tan, with a light snow fallen overnight. Rays of sunlight broke through the clouds, illuminating the eastern mountains which led toward Iran. Leah had this schoolgirl hiker thing going on, with her hair in braids under a navy bandana. Basically, too damn cute for her own good.

"It's prettier than I thought it would be," she said.

"Parts of it are."

She shored up the straps on her pack. "How do we get to Mosul?"

We were meeting Tish Harding, a friend working the UN Oil for Food program. It was a jumping-off point for the shoot, and a chance for Leah to get her feet wet in aid work. Plus, Tish was someone I trusted to be with her while I worked some dodgier angles. Leah was happy. I was happy. It seemed like a brilliant idea.

"I've got a driver lined up." I ducked around a rumbling troop carrier, then headed for the road. "Someone I've known since I was a kid. We can trust him."

Daniel Pearl's murder had been less than a year ago. You had to think about stuff like that now.

Ishai was smoking a cigarette by a rough-idling Renault on Highway Four, which rambled along the banks of the Tigris. Olive-skinned, with a ski ramp cowlick over his right eyebrow, he greeted me with a double kiss. "It is good to see you, Matthias."

Ishai Maloof was Ari's other brother, one of three siblings. The whole family drama thing was mortifying, which was why I was still working up the courage to tell Leah. Her dad was a legend, mine was a philandering hypocrite. At some point, I was going to have to suck it up. My plan was to bring Ari into town to meet her tomorrow.

"It's good to see you too," I replied, doing my best with the neo-Aramaic he preferred to Arabic. "How is your mother?"

"She is nervous," he admitted. "As are we all."

Assyrian Christians didn't have it much worse than any other minority in Saddam Hussein's Iraq, but with the war about to start, it wasn't a great idea for Ishai to go running around with a couple of Americans. Bottom line, they needed the money.

"*Al salaam alikuum*," Leah said, introducing herself, using about half the Arabic I'd taught her on the plane, part of a crash course in correspondent life. Mostly stupid stuff, like not taking naps under convoy trucks and how to deal with the runs and the attitude she was going to get from Iraqi men. She was supposed to be finishing her law school applications, but she'd barely opened them once. Not that she seemed to care.

Without warning, a pair of Strike Eagles screamed over our heads, zooming off to the south. A deafening roar trailed behind. Leah managed to not act rattled until one launched an AGM, a burst of fire and smoke streaking across the sky. "Is that it? Is it starting?"

Ishai scowled. "There would be far more than two."

"They're taking out a missile battery or something," I said. "You'll get used to it."

She gave me a stern expression. "No babying me. You promised."

"Whatever you say, boss."

Ishai pitched his butt down the riverbank. "Come. We must go."

He didn't stop grousing all the way to Mosul, about his studies at university, what a pain in the ass his middle sister, Hana had become, which didn't surprise me. Apparently, she'd been tagging along to his engineering classes, and doing better, which didn't surprise me either. Their father had been a professor there, until the regime had him executed. Two years earlier, Ishai had applied to MIT, part of my grand plan to get Ari out of Iraq. He got in, but neither government would grant him a visa. I was there the day the Twin Towers fell, and had to watch him give up and burn the acceptance letter.

As he careened down the twisty mountain roads, Leah watched the jets patrol the sky, taking in every village, every watering hole. It'd been killing me, watching her struggle the past month. She seemed at peace now. I almost started thinking bringing her along was the right thing.

The market was in full swing as Ishai dropped us off at the Al-Hadba minaret in central Mosul, a cacophony of haggling, squawks, and honking. A lazy breeze curled around the tent stalls like a witch's finger, bringing with it a tart smell of sumac, the sweetness of smoked fenugreek, mixed with the sour foulness of decaying produce and meat.

Leah's eyelids fluttered. She threw her sleeve in front of her face. "What *is* that?"

"'That' is UN-sanctioned Iraq." I pulled my T-shirt over my nose. "Sucks twice, because real Iraqi food rules. After the sanctions, it took me two months of living here before I could get through breakfast without puking."

That god-awful rot was laced with bad memories. My old man would haggle for food, proselytize when he could get away with it, while my mother and I sat on a blanket passing out disguised New Testaments paid for by our church back home in Virginia.

It wasn't all bad. The book strand was off the market, a dozen stalls with stacks of paperbacks, surrounded by shisha cafes where Iraq's literati would sit and argue for hours, smoking and drinking their coffees.

A slinky brown mongoose was bopping down the aisle of stalls, begging for scraps. Halfway down, we found Dagen Serhati, head of the bookseller's co-op. A Kurd with jet black hair and striking blue eyes, he was picking his teeth with a hooked dagger when he noticed us. He thrust the dagger into a green cummerbund, where it joined two friends. "Matthias! What brings you to Kurdistan?"

"The usual." I introduced him to Leah. "She's joining the aid corps for a few weeks."

"Then she will need something to fill the time." With entrepreneurial flourish, Dagen straightened a stack of books. "Anything you want, I have—or I will get, *insha'Allah.*"

Dagen had been my savior when I was a kid. I never got my hands on a book other than the Bible until I was ten, a travesty he'd been eager to rectify. I winked at Leah. "Tell him you want a copy of *The Satanic Verses.*"

He gave me a stern finger wag. "Yours nearly cost me my head."

"Impossible Matty strikes again." She blew the dust off an illustrated volume that'd seen better days. "Ooh, is this *Scheherazade's Tales?*"

I chucked. "He's been trying to unload that since I was like six."

Smiling, she added a small Kurdish independence flag from a display on the wall, a show of solidarity which conveniently put Dagen in a talkative mood. Armed with the local scoop, we headed for a yellow mud brick café with a faded white sign, the Foreigner's Club, which adjoined the only western hotel in Mosul at the time. The joint was dark, a series of vaults dug into a cellar, which was about as air-conditioned as it got there. The low light made it a good place to go if you didn't want to be seen.

Near the back, a couple of spooks and Special Forces types were sitting around a table with a map. A heavyset American with a hawk nose and lots of jet black hair was at the desk, signing the register, which I made a mental note to check later. Though the rest were dressed as locals, the youngest guy had his feet up. Rookie mistake.

When I reached for my Nikon, one of the spooks nudged a forty-ish guy with a greying flat top. "Yo, Clarke."

Clarke folded over the map, all steely-eyed and square. There was something familiar about him, but I couldn't put my finger on it. "Don't even think about it, son," he said in Arabic.

You pick your battles where the military is concerned. The fact we already had boots on the ground wasn't exactly a scoop, and the guy you play ball with one day might decide to give you the shot the next. So I loosened the camera strap and kept walking.

At the back of the cantina, a pushed-together collection of rickety tables was piled high with camera bags. Tish sat with the AP pool, who were all scrunched in tight on the far side. Nobody in this job sat with their backs to the door.

"Matty, you made it!" Blonde wisps spilled out of Tish's checkered hijab. She Euro-kissed me, then Leah. "He's told me all about you—so good to meet you."

Tish was as balls-out as they come, a Londoner from one of those society families where people had been doing what they wanted for centuries without question. She spent her time bossing around Baathist goons and UN bureaucrats, so it came in handy.

Her friend Rosalyn, a pain in the ass from Le Figaro, inhaled from a Gauloise. A crochet cap covered her dark hair, and the silk scarf slung around her neck made little effort to conceal her tits, which was a convenient way to get the photos of enraged Muslim men her paper wanted.

"Why should we bother getting to know dis one? Let us call her Tuesday, *mais non?*"

A hot flush crept over my neck. The others snickered. Someone passed me a Heineken, and I took a much-needed pull. "Eat me, Rosie."

She gave me a wicked leer. "Aich, you know the rules—you first."

Aleksei Kusnitch, a paunchy Russian with a thing for hookers, waved his cigarette. "Don't mind her, nichevo. When these two make love, the rest of us come too, eh?"

Christ on a cracker. Aleksei was Misha, my college girlfriend's, big brother. Since we both assumed the other knew more about her disappearance than he let on, the shit-talking was how we dealt with it. "Your next girlfriend is on me," I said, flipping him a silver dinar. "Keep the change."

It occurred to me that there were aspects of life on the road I'd failed to mention to Leah. "Ignore them. This is journalist for 'nice to meet you'."

Undoing her scarf, Leah smiled sweetly at Rosie, introducing herself in passable French. "Rosalyn Giroux? I remember seeing your name on a fashion article near one of Matty's about the airstrikes in Yemen."

"How nice for you." Rosie chain-lit a fresh cig. "I have many talents. Unlike your *petit copain.*"

Leah's devious side rarely came out to play, but it was a thing of beauty when it did. She returned a mysterious smile to my raised eyebrow. "I've been clerking for my father since I was nine," she whispered. "Never know when a detail can come in handy."

Snappy retorts aside, she was less okay with it than she wanted me to think. "You know Tits McGee over there isn't my girlfriend, right?"

She shuffled her feet. "Was she?"

"God no."

"But you've slept with her?"

I pinched my nose. All Rosie and I had in common were our hypocrite fathers. Hers was a Catholic bishop from Toulouse. "Now and then. Ignore her, okay?"

Dave Nasser, a BBC old-timer who'd covered every MidEast conflict since Lebanon, ambled over. In a profession where most people either got burned out, blown up, or shot within a couple of years, Dave was a dinosaur, although at this point, he only worked to cover his alimony payments.

"Dreadful shame about Rani." He ran his hand through wispy white hair. "So sorry."

The teasing stopped, the jokes stopped. Everyone got very interested in their drinks or shoes. Leah squeezed my hand. I stared at the small window to the outside. "Yeah, me too."

Rosie tapped cigarette ash into an empty beer bottle. "I am curious, Ma-tee—what were you doing when Rani went careening into a minefield?"

Screwing Rosie was like charming a cobra—you never knew when she'd turn tail and fang you. "Talking to the kid's mother."

She settled back, eyes narrowed. "But of course, you were with the woman."

"Lay off," someone said.

For a split second, Rani was there, sitting in his seat. Then the ground turned to jelly, I felt the shockwave, and then it was pieces of flesh and earth raining from the sky, the god-awful smell. "I never said it wasn't my fault."

"It wasn't," Leah said sharply.

"And you know dis how?" Rosie flicked the cherry from her cig. "He goes hunting for shots which are suicide, and if the rest of us want to eat, we must follow."

"No one is forcing you." Blood stung my eyes as if it was actually there. I ground it out with the heel of my hand. Leah was right, I had no business being back in the field.

Rosie laughed bitterly. "Oh yes. You say here, we all run along behind. No one questions when Matty thinks there's a story." She glared at Tish. "Even you—he convinced you to go along with this? A girl with a lifetime of privilege, hoping to ease her guilt? Is that not why she is here?"

"No," Leah snapped. "I am here because he needs someone who believes in him." She turned me away, cupping my cheek. "Matty, you have more power to affect change in one finger than most people have in their entire bodies. Please tell me you can see that."

The flesh smells began to dissipate. Rani's ghost faded to a shadow in the corner. I didn't say anything, just rested my forehead on hers.

Rosie sniffed. "I wish you luck with him. You will need it."

Clouds rolled the desert skies as we left Mosul. Ishai drove us past the Kurdish checkpoints to Bashiqa, a restless town on the edge of the no-fly zone, in the shadow of the Sinjar Mountains. A mural of a faded peacock graced the city's high stone walls, though graffiti was scrawled over the seven jars beneath him.

"*Shaitan amusalin'*," Leah said, sounding out the lettering. "What does it mean?"

Tish pulled a goofy face, fingers making horns on her head. "Devil worshippers."

"Yazidis believe Melek Taus was a fallen jinn who created the universe from a cosmic egg," I said. "The seven jars are full of his tears, which put out the fires of hell. Muslims think he's a form of Satan."

"Assyrians think they're both crazy," Ishai added in English, glancing into the rearview mirror.

"People here don't like each other very much," Tish warned. "We have to be careful not to look like we're playing favorites."

We were meeting an aid convoy which was supposed to be carrying food and water, but when we rolled up, a riot was in progress. Two UN Oil-For-Food trucks were parked by the Assyrian temple, empty, save for some rotting produce. People shouted, waving jugs and baskets at the drivers. Water barrels had leaked their contents onto the grain, which had begun to ferment. The last few gallons streamed through the floorboards of the truck into the sand. People were trampling each other to fill their jugs with whatever they could catch.

I scrambled on top of the second truck, shooting like mad. Tish pushed Leah towards the back. "Get them under control!"

Leah's jaw dropped. "How?"

"Figure it out." Tish shoved her way into the crowd. Clutching at her head scarf, she ran at the driver, an overstuffed Iraqi in a marshal uniform. "Where is your UN escort?"

The driver stroked his wooly mustache. "Perhaps they are lost."

The edge of the no-fly parallel was across the highway, a mined stretch of desert marked by ten-foot-high warning signs with skulls and cartoon feet stepping on Claymores. A tank platoon of Iraqi soldiers had gathered at the far edge. As they jeered and egged him on, the driver climbed atop the cab, gesturing at a wall-sized mural of Saddam Hussein plastered on the village school.

"Mighty America would have you starve!" he shouted, waving his arms at the villagers. "Do not fear, for the Great Saddam Hussein shall bless you with Allah's bounty!"

Leah twisted through the crowd, and eventually made it to the truck I was standing on. "I get that you're working, but what does Tish expect me to do?"

I framed Tish and the driver with the chaotic crowd on the left edge. To unload that trailer, someone had to get rid of the UN escort. Executed, bribed, whatever. This was huge. "We talked about this, Leah."

Tish leapt into the cab and stole the keys. I clicked the shutter as the driver lunged. If he drove off before she managed to learn what had happened, it was over.

Leah scanned wildly, at Tish, at the people fighting to get supplies, at me. "I know, I get it, you can't compromise your objectivity, but —"

"Then why are we talking?"

"Because you're the only one of us who speaks Arabic?"

"Then I guess you're screwed," I said, still snapping.

With a *thunk*, Leah banged her head on the truck's dented side panel. "I'm not worried about me."

Tish broke free, tossing the keys into the melee. The driver dove after them. I kept my eye to the camera. "What would your father do?"

"Indict somebody? How the hell should I know?"

"Calm down and think."

It was part me not wanting to lose the shot, part giving her a chance to remember why she wanted to come here in the first place. If she was really in trouble, I would've gotten down.

She ran to Ishai, who reluctantly got out of the car. The two of them wormed their way through the crowd. "Can you tell them more is coming?"

Ishai threw an elbow at a guy who tried to push him out. "It won't. Tomorrow they will say it has been stolen again."

Leah froze. "Tell them anyway. There must be some way to fix it. We have to salvage what we have."

At first, her plan worked. People calmed down and got back in line. She and Ishai recruited helpers to help divvy thing up. I knelt, broadening my focus and spied a small Kurdish girl in a red striped jumper, cupping her hands to scoop spilled water from the sand.

Snap.

When I glanced into the truck bed to check on Leah, she was handing a squashed head of lettuce to a twentyish Iraqi in a broad white turban. With a howl of prideful rage, he shoved her into the lift gate.

Shit. I jumped down, but Tish and Ishai got there first. Ishai, who he seemed to know the guy, pulled him away.

Tish got in my face. "You told me she knows the customs!"

My neck went hot. "How much did you expect her to learn in a few days?"

Face ashen, Leah scrambled up, holding her elbow. "I didn't use my left hand, I didn't touch him, I said a blessing—what did I do wrong?"

Tish scowled. "They're Yazidi, not Muslim. They don't eat lettuce."

"I should have realized," Leah said. "None of the others were taking it."

"Don't let her bully you," I said, picking greens out of her hair. "Is your arm okay?"

"Dad would be proud," she said dryly, checking a scrape on her forearm.

"He would," I said, knowing she needed to hear it.

The tension in her face relaxed. "Lettuce? Seriously?"

I shrugged. "Something about the devil taking a nap in a lettuce patch. Or maybe what they grow it in here. Depends who you ask. You're really okay?"

"I'm fine." She hopped onto the gate. "We'll get the rest of this garbage distributed. Go back to work."

Ishai, who'd been off having words with his buddy, returned with a sheepish look. "I ask your forgiveness for Tal. We were classmates at school. Last week, he was forced to leave by Baathist decree. I reminded him you are not the one he should be angry with."

The truck driver inspected his handiwork, smirking. Tish whipped off her hijab, eyes burning holes into his gut. "I'm going to strangle that fatherless goat with his own testicles. He's bribed the escort." When I raised an eyebrow, she shook her finger. "That's off the record, Cahill."

"Which—the goat strangling or that someone in the UN is for sale?" Nobody outside knew how bad the corruption was in the program at that point.

"Try it and I'll be having testicle stew for supper." She balled up the fabric. "We've got a medical shipment scheduled for tomorrow. If I can't find out who's behind this…"

I scratched my chin. "If only you knew someone who was good at that kind of thing."

"Matthias Cahill, if you're waiting for me to beg, you will be roundly disappointed."

While they finished unloading, I took a walk inside the local hospital. The place was in shambles—empty shelves, no lighting, a woman in labor on the floor, a doctor screaming for someone, anyone, to find him some catgut. A local strongman had been making trouble for weeks. Nobody was brave or stupid enough to say why.

In a dingy, unlit exam room, a man sat up on a gurney, rubbing sleep from his eyes. He wore pigeon grey scrubs, had a bald head and scruffy black beard. "I never forget a face I have stitched, Matthias Cahill."

Given the number of stitches I've had in my life, I couldn't reciprocate. I had a vague recollection of being about seven and going off to play with Ishai, until my father came running up and belted me, ranting about the Republican Guard. Never did figure out what set him off.

Making a deep reach for the memory, I got voices, snatches of conversation, blurry faces, but there was no way I was going to come up with a name. "I'm sorry, I don't remember."

"I am Dr. Sherzad Alatassi. I also delivered your sister." The woman in labor screamed. Something spattered the canvas drapes from the far side. Alatassi staggered past. "My hospital has enough trouble without your questions, as you can see. Give my blessings to Ari and her mother."

"Maybe I can help."

It took some serious pressure, but once I told him what was going on with the truck outside, he opened a crack. "There is sickness in this village. Without the supplies the UN has promised, many will die." Face haggard, he lit a cigarette. "Last month, a Kurd was brought to me. A spy for the Americans, I was told. His captors demanded my assistance, in order he survive their interrogation as long as possible. They found my efforts lacking." He waved away the smoke. "You see the result."

Leah had said she wanted to see the real Iraq for herself—this was it, where a healer could find himself complicit in torture with no recourse. But for someone in the local UN group to be accepting bribes, this went way beyond local retribution. The real question was who was skimming and what they were getting in return.

"If you want those supplies, you need to tell me what you overheard."

Chapter 13: Old Friends

MEDITERRANEAN SEA
PRESENT

Wade's black surveillance drone hovers overhead. He peers down from the observation deck, holding the controller, its antennas whipped by the wind. "Get up, Cahill. Playtime's over."

It's my one hour a week of sunshine. Fresh air. Me and a hundred square feet of AstroTurf, rolling with the Mediterranean. I can close my eyes and be on a beach somewhere. Pretend I'm lying down by choice, not because I'm too weak to do much else.

The drone lowers, blocking my rays. "Move your ass, reporter."

"Fuck off." At this point, there isn't much else they can do to me. Although I'm sure they'll try.

He flicks a cigarette butt at me. "Guess you don't want the little treat I have for you."

"Not even if you beg, Agent Wade." I stretch my hands behind my head.

Doug Wade is a Virginia boy, a big guy with a big chin and a lion's head. He talks slow, but only because he's usually busy plotting something. Faux-Leah was probably his brilliant idea. "We'll see who's laughing later, a'ight?"

The bulkhead squeaks open behind me. I crane my neck. The third guy, Mike Quinn, nearly fills the opening. Quinn is Army Intel, a deep-woods Mainer with a lumberjack build and a beard to match. He and I go way back, and unlike Wade, he's made an effort to get me to trust him. I don't, and given that they spent most of yesterday showing me pictures of my wife at gunpoint and being stalked by her rapist, I'm not exactly in a trusting mood.

"You still had ten minutes," he says. "We've got some photos for you to look at. Cooperate and I'll bring you out after."

Resigned, I drag myself up. Chances are, whatever's on those photos, I'll need the fresh air.

Following the red stripe on the floor, Quinn marches me below, into the windowless coffin they call an interrogation room. Wade is waiting with his BFF, Orlyk. The two of them used to share an office at the Pentagon, until some Saudi assholes flew a plane into it. Hard to say who holds the bigger grudge, but for the past six months, I've been the target of it.

Orlyk has a smirk on his face, which always means trouble. "Sit."

With a wary glance at the restraint table in the corner, I take the chair. On any given day, they're convinced I'm holding out on any of a dozen different things. Some days, it's truer than others.

The photo Orlyk lays down, of a corpse with a bullet wound in its left temple, means it's going to be one of them. My eyes sting with recognition, but I play dumb. "Who's this?"

"Sherzhad Alatassi." Wade pushes the photo closer. "But you knew that, right?"

God knows I did. Alatassi, who'd fled to Syria years ago, was the only reason Ari survived the airstrike last year. He saved her life. It's not like I expect the world to be fair, but right now, it can go fuck itself. "Sorry. He's not my type."

"Quit stalling." Wade leans right in my ear. "See, I've got friends in Syria too. Mine keep me posted on what's going on there. *Your* friend Alatassi tried to be a hero and got himself shot by security forces in Idlib last week," he says, poking my chest. "That's when *my* friend called and said your phone number was on this guy's mobile. So you wanna tell me why, or should Quinn here start digging?"

The person they really want, the one that can lead them to Kıraç, is Hana, the woman Leah saw me with in Cairo. I told Leah the truth—Hana's like my kid sister. There was nothing going on. Plus, these guys already know about her. They just think she's dead. For all I know, they might be right. If she's alive, she wouldn't come out of hiding to save my ass. But she would for Ari.

I flip the photo across the table. "The guy gave me info now and then, sure. He was into kink, so I'd copy stuff off PornHub for him in exchange for casualty info—where they were coming from, who was fighting, all that. Standard reporter stuff, nothing earthshattering. Ask around. Christ, you guys must be desperate."

The first part is true. So is the second. But if they know about Alatassi, they'll find out about Ari soon enough.

And that makes me desperate too.

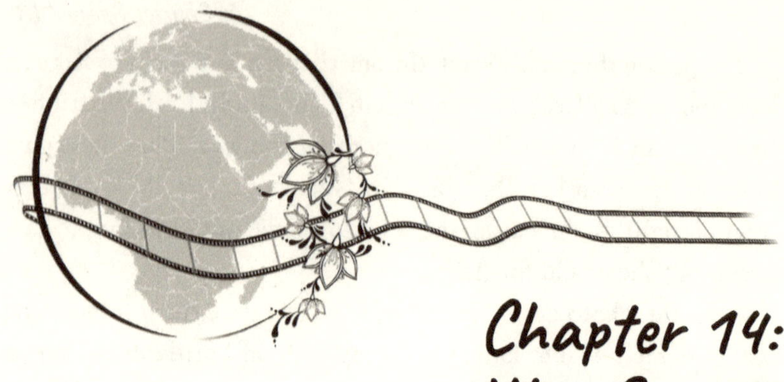

Chapter 14:
War Stories

JANUARY 2003
NORTHERN IRAQ

With his hospital in chaos, Alatassi had better things to do than talk to me. The supply truck idled by the roadside. Ishai was in the car, impatiently tapping his thumbs on the wheel. People were collecting their meager provisions and their children. No sign of Tish or Leah.

The little girl in the red jumper, who was about five, was still struggling to drink from the puddle. A slender guy in a T-shirt knelt and gave her water from his canteen. I turned the camera on them, squinting through the viewfinder. The blur came into focus as the guy glanced up. Dirty blond hair, Brazilian nose and jungle green eyes. Plain as day, it was Rani.

A metallic taste flooded my mouth. Legs rubbery, I forced myself to blink. Twice. His face swam. When the blur cleared, it wasn't him, it was Ishai's friend Tal from university, doing something Rani had done a thousand times, watching out for a kid. Though my hands shook, I clicked the shutter, if for no other reason than to prove to myself later that it wasn't him. My stomach felt ropey, and I knew whatever else I shot that day would turn out like crap, because all I wanted to do was go find Leah before he showed up again.

I took two steps towards the truck, then started to laugh. An awful unhinged laugh, thinking what the crew at the Foreign Club would say. Crazy Matty, the nutter who gets the pictures they don't and they think it's because he doesn't care if he lives or dies, though it's really because he hasn't the first freaking clue how to live with himself otherwise. Here he is, running for a twenty-one-year-old girl, hoping she'll protect him from his best friend's ghost. They would've said I was losing it. They would've been right.

Near the truck's rear wheel, Tish's voice came from the back. "Rosie and Matty? Oh darling, it's nothing—they're all like that, you know, all these daft journalists, war photographers, whatever they're calling themselves this week. People blowing up and screaming and dying all around, twenty-four by seven, so they fuck like mad rabbits until they feel human again. It's the same in the aid corps. You'll see."

Leah sounded worn out. "He hasn't even tried to kiss me."

This was news to me. That day on the porch, the only thing that stopped me from kissing the daylights out of her was her dickhead ex-boyfriend. Now he was gone, but he'd taken a piece of her with him. She flinched every time someone tried to hug her. Her smile had become as elusive as desert rain. Being able to kiss her was just an ache, a dream I was struggling to keep from getting buried in the graveyard with the rest.

When I hopped onto the liftgate, Leah went pale. She wetted her lips. "Get your shots?"

She was sweaty and smudged, but her hair was falling in wisps around her face and I'd never seen anything more beautiful in my life. I went over and kissed her like I should've kissed her on the porch, kissed her until she was breathless, kissed her until I felt alive inside again. She tasted like sunlight and hope and she felt like coming home. When I finally came up for air, she was smiling.

A warm sense of ecstasy washed over me. I smoothed her hair, forehead resting on hers. "Yeah, I did."

"Well now." Tish winked at Leah. "That's sorted."

Leah blushed, slipping her hands into my pockets. "It's a start."

All the way to Mosul, she rode on my lap, trading kisses and secret smiles. Tish's supply line crack-up couldn't have been further from my mind. I had new territory to explore, the hint of skin where Leah's top rode up, the satin-trimmed lace I found a bit higher, and thank god the Interior Ministry finished screwing with our visas, which meant we could get into the room.

"This is us?" Leah peered into a tobacco-stained second floor cell at the end of the hall, two iron cots and a busted lock.

A six-inch scorpion scuttled around the doorframe and fell to the floor. She screamed and jumped. "Jesus Mary and motherfucking Josephine!"

Chuckling, I scooped the thing up and flung it out the missing window screen. "No freeloaders."

She peeled herself off the ceiling. "Feeling suicidal again?"

"Nah, they're not deadly. Although that reminds me—sleep with your shoes on."

She edged closer, eyeing the screen. "Why couldn't we have done that with Rosie?"

"Next time," I murmured, beckoning her closer. "C'mere. You look like you need kissing again."

After two months of living with her, keeping my distance, I wasn't looking for just a kiss, not this time. What happened in the truck was even better than I knew it would be, and so help me, I was savoring whatever came next. But she broke the kiss, tugging at my camera strap. "Can I see the pictures you took?"

What I really wanted was to throw her down on the cot and make love, but I realized a kiss was as far as she was ready to go. I ducked out of the loop. "Knock yourself out."

She sat on the cot, turning on the display. The desert wind had put the pink in her cheeks. "Hey." I waited for her to tear her eyes off the camera. "It's good to see your smile again."

"Yours too," she said softly.

Diesel fumes wafted through the window, along with voices in English. Animals gather around a watering hole at the end of the day—Americans gather for beer. Apparently, the spooks were done for the day too. Which reminded me of Tish's missing supplies.

"I gotta run downstairs," I said. "We'll grab some chow after that. Brace yourself."

Clarke was out back, along with the hawk-faced wall of muscle who was signing the hotel register when we came in. Thanks to the desk clerk falling asleep on the job, I'd learned his name was Bradley Gleason, a retired Army Ranger from Fort Bragg, in Iraq setting himself up for a piece of the post-war action. Most of the brass expected it to be over in a month. The smart ones got in early.

Gleason was swearing his fool head off at a ruggedized field laptop, while Clarke leaned against the hood of the HumVee, reading a dog-eared letter, which he folded when he saw me. "Something I can help you with?"

Army guys want everything laid out nice and neat. "C'mon, man, you look old enough to know how this works. I've got info, you've got access. I need pictures, you need to help your boss convince the world to go along with his cowboy bullshit."

He lit a Marlboro. "Speak English, Cahill."

If he'd gone to the trouble of finding out my name, I figured I was in. "How about Arabic. Rashid Tann Qazim."

Gleason's eyes flickered away from the laptop screen. Clarke took a drag on the cigarette. "What about him?"

"Saddam's cousin. Head of Tribal Affairs. My source says he stole a UN Oil-For-Food shipment today, and he's looking to do it again tomorrow. I'd like to make sure it gets through."

It was that magic hour of twilight when shadows were starting to merge. Great for photography. Impossible for reading a face. "I suppose you'd like to be there if we decide to intercept?"

"This war won't be the cakewalk people think," I said. "Better to make friends now."

A photo fell out of his letter, fluttering to my feet. It was of a pregnant woman with reddish hair, sitting under a tree at sunset. I handed it back. "Your wife? Bet you can't wait to get home."

Eyes closed, he tucked the letter inside his coat. "Thanks for the tip."

There's an old joke in the Army that if at first you don't succeed, call in an airstrike.

Clarke made it clear that whatever he was doing didn't involve reporters, so I left Leah with Tish, snuck off to chase down some old sources, and found where the payoff was going down. By morning, I'd have my story. A big one.

At ten that evening, the usual gang gathered at the Foreign Club. The Mosul water had caught up with Leah, but after a double dose of Flagyl, she was dealing. I knew I was in trouble when Dave set a bottle of Chivas in front of me, along with a filthy tin tumbler. "To Rani."

It was the strangest funeral you've ever seen. What started as a remembrance devolved into a pissing contest, the way it always did, everyone smoking, bragging about the crazy shit we did. Shootouts in Kosovo, Stingers in Kabul. Most of it was bullshit. Leah being fresh blood, everybody thought they'd get away with it, but she figured out we were screwing with her and got sneaky. She'd play Aleksei off Dave, or Dave off Rosie. It turned into a game, to see who could fool her. Me… I knew better than to try.

In a roomful of Magnum-sized egos, she might as well have been poking holes in the Hindenburg, but everyone except Rosie found it hilarious. "What about 'im," Rosie demanded, waving her cigarette at me in exasperation. "He is as full of shit as the rest of us!"

I poured another Chivas, wishing it was just Leah and me alone in her apartment. "She wouldn't dare. She's too afraid the scorpion I evicted has friends."

"Wait until she meets her first camel spider." Aleksei rolled up his sleeve, revealing a quarter-sized scar on his forearm. "Big as dinner plate, this one."

Dave snorted. "Five minutes ago that was a sniper round in Chechnya."

Leah, who was on my lap, put her arms around my neck. "Matty only lies by omission. It's harder to find the truth in what someone doesn't say than the lie in what they do."

It caught me so off-guard that all I could do was drain my tumbler. "Ladies and gentlemen, the next Dale Atkins."

By the time the party broke up, I was too drunk to do more than pass out on my cot, but the damn war stories kicked my subconscious into overdrive. The dreams were bad that night. There were pieces of Rani all over me, gore dripping from the ceiling, and I couldn't move, then a landmine with legs started vulture-hopping towards the kid, then—boom—he was gone too.

Next thing I knew, Leah was there next to me, *'ssh, ssh, it's okay, you're safe'*.

I was freezing cold, drenched, pain in my heart, pain in my chest. I was dying, had to be. But her face was there, all side-lit in moonlight, and it brought me back. She brushed sweat-soaked hair off my face and kissed my forehead, like a mother with a scared child. She started to say something, but she didn't get through it because it was either start bawling or kiss her back.

The warmth from her lips was a tenuous thread to a safer world, where no one was bleeding or starving, where my friends didn't keep dying. With a little hitch in her breath, she shifted, hair falling against my shoulders like warm summer rain. Her lips parted and she deepened the kiss, a hesitant sweep of her tongue on my lip, a taste like midnight and wintergreen. She was shaking too. "You kept saying his name."

Need spiraled out of control. If we stopped, the dream would come back, she'd disappear and all that would be left was the blood, so I kept going, stripping her shirt over her head.

Her forehead rested against mine. "You're burning up."

With a creak of the cot, I rolled her onto her back, kissing her lips, the hollow of her throat, exhaling into her neck, tasting the tips of her breasts. But when I got between her legs, she instantly went tense.

I froze, pushing myself off. "Jesus Leah, I'm —" Sorry. *An idiot. A complete asshole.* "I wasn't thinking about—"

She looked away, reaching for her shirt. "Yeah, neither was I, for once."

I got up, pacing. "You know I'm not like him. I mean, I'd never—"

"I know." She drew up her knees. "We both just want to feel human again, right?"

That didn't help. "If Rosie and Tish made you think I expect this or something—"

"For god's sake, Matty, stop." She pushed her hair away from her face. "Nobody made me think anything. Except that it sounds really freaking nice to be able to have sex with whoever and whenever you want instead of feeling like a giant mess about it."

I wanted out of that club, not to drag her into it. I flopped on the cot, head in my hands. "Yeah, well… I've been trying that since I was fifteen. Seem like it's working?"

She laid beside me, fiddling with my hair. "Just lie with me, okay?"

We stayed like that until the sun came up, but that kind of peace can't last in Iraq. So much had changed, yet it hadn't, at least not enough. We'd broken the first seal. Every preacher's kid knew what that meant.

Some kind of apocalypse was inevitable.

Chapter 15:
All In The Family

JANUARY 2003
NORTHERN IRAQ

When I woke with Leah in my arms, a pre-dawn glow lit her face, and for the minute, everything was all right. "Morning, beautiful," I murmured as she stirred.

Drowsily, she brought our clasped hands to her lips and kissed my thumb. "Morning."

Warmth begat hope, hope begat serenity. Part of me was more up than the rest and she didn't seem to mind, so I brushed her hair aside and kissed my way up her neck, hoping to redeem myself.

But Tish came busting in and punched the light switch. A spark flew overhead, and the lights zapped on with a burning smell. "Oh dear. Room 29's dodgy lock strikes again. Thought you'd be dead to the world, luvs."

Squinting in the harsh light, I reached for my shirt. "Mmfph."

Tish knew I wasn't a heavy sleeper—she was making sure I didn't skip out on her missing supplies in favor of staying in bed with Leah.

I dragged myself up. "Can you two find something to do for the morning?"

Leah rolled to her side with a suspicious frown. "Why? What are you doing?"

A dull ache set into my head, the kind that comes from too much whiskey and evil dreams. I grabbed my flak vest, hoping she'd take the hint. "I'll show you the pictures later."

Leah's frown deepened. Tish took a matchbook and some smokes from her pocket. "Does this involve my missing supplies?"

My stomach went queasy. "No," I lied.

Which of course, Leah realized, and got out of bed. "Who's going with you?"

The warm feeling went up in smoke. I knew where this was headed. "No one. It's my story."

Brow furrowed, Tish struck the match. "Maybe you should take Dave or Aleksei."

It was the sulfur. The acrid flare. When Rani died, my buddy in the aid convoy had just lit up, and the smell kicked off that pure dread that always walloped me right before a flashback. Your body feels an explosion a split second before your mind realizes it. That split second was where I was living.

Leah reached for my arm. "Matty—"

I shook her off. She didn't get it. Something bad was going to happen and I didn't want her anywhere near me when it did.

"Haven't you heard? People who go out with me get killed."

When I stumbled into the hall. Leah tried to follow, but Tish stopped her. "Let him go. You can't fix him when he's like this."

Maybe she listened, maybe I ran off too fast, but by the time my head cleared, I was in the marketplace, near Dagen's book stall. In a blind rage, I ripped down one of the shelves, but before I actually started baying at the moon, somebody took me by the back of the neck.

"Yo, man, get a grip. You know where you are?"

Through sheer force of adrenaline, I twisted free. It was one of the Special Forces guys, the hulk-sized rookie. Nauseated, I sank to the ground, head below my knees. "More or less."

With dark, close-cropped hair, the guy was about my age, an intelligence officer by his insignia and a Mainer, by his accent. For whatever reason, he was up before dawn, thumbing a copy of the Quran from

Dagen's stall. He rapped a packet of Marlboros on his hand, shook two out, and offered me one. "Someone bite it on you?"

I took the butt. Never mind that I'd quit a year ago. A little hair of the dog. That'd fix me. "What makes you say that?"

He gestured at Dagen's scattered books, which were lying on their sides, pages fluttering in the breeze, then flicked a Zippo. "My fiancée died a few years back. Got pretty good at tearing things up myself."

He offered me a light, but with the question hanging in the air. Closing my eyes, I inhaled, hot air filling my lungs. "Yeah, my buddy. Not here though. Been a couple months."

"Rough, man, rough." A jet patrol near the mountains turned his eyes skyward. "I was afraid you were going to tell me something happened to that pretty little thing sitting on your lap yesterday. What kind of idiot brings a girl to a place like this?"

Ten minutes, or maybe a lifetime ago, I was in bed with her and everything was aces. "Leah has a funny habit of making up her own mind where she goes."

"None of my business, I guess." With a contemplative stare, he rolled the cig between his fingers. "Maybe I got a sore spot about unprotected women."

"Careful there," I said, gesturing at the Quran. The cherry was so close to text that the edge curled. A wisp of smolder trailed skyward. "Your CO isn't as covert as he thinks, but that's a surefire way to make sure they have you all hanging all from a bridge by dawn."

That put a rod in his spine. "Cahill, right?" He closed the book. "Mike Quinn. He says you're a'right. For a reporter at least."

The tobacco finally took the edge off, leaving a dull ache around my heart. "What happened to your fiancée?"

Distant, he exhaled a cloud of yellowish smoke. "Egypt Air 990. Co-pilot ditched the flight off Nantucket."

It occurred to me then that maybe he meant to burn the book. "Sorry, man." I pressed my thumbs into my eyes, struggling to focus. "So if your CO thinks I'm a good guy, does that mean he's decided to do something about that stolen relief shipment I warned him about yesterday?"

A light-skinned foreigner with long, flowing hair appeared at the edge of the marketplace. He wore a blue crocodile leather jacket, a pair of silver sunglasses on his head, but I didn't get a good look, since he retreated to the shadows when he saw me.

Quinn shifted away from the stall. "No idea what you're talking about, Cahill." He stuck the Quran on Dagen's shelf, turning to where the foreigner last stood. "If I did, I'd tell you to keep your nose out of it."

Like that was going to happen. "Thanks for the smoke."

Ten minutes later, Ishai skidded up at the edge of the market-place, nearly taking out a stall full of sumac and preserved lemons. As I jogged over to the car, he was scowling. "We must make a detour," he said. "You will be able to talk sense into her."

'Her' was Hana, seventeen at the time, which was about ten years after the last time anyone succeeded in talking sense to her. I stubbed the butt, which had mostly succeeding in making me remember why I'd quit. "What's she done now?"

"You will see."

We drove east along the Tigris, past the ruins at Nineveh, my old man's favorite haunt in Iraq. The Book of Jonah calls it 'an exceedingly great city of three days' journey in breadth'. More like five—he decided we had to walk across it once. That was his thing, to tread in the footsteps of the prophets, to see what their eyes had seen. I didn't get it, either then or now, but it gave me a river to splash in and other kids to play with. Ishai and Hana were two of them.

The Renault sputtered into Wadi Dusyan, the Assyrian settle-ment where the Maloof family lived, an eroding basin of mud brick houses, livestock pens and a lime-washed church, populated by peo-ple who'd fled or otherwise been kicked out of the city. The second I stepped out of the car, a Tasmanian blur attacked. "Matty Matty Matty Matty!"

The grumpy fog lifted. "Somebody owes me a hug."

Ari threw her arms around my neck, legs dangling off the ground. "Ishai promised you'd come!"

Clad in a yellow Mickey Mouse T-shirt and cotton pants, she'd shot up two inches since I'd seen her last, with a new set of front teeth to boot. A wooden cross dangled from a black leather cord around her neck. That and her wide hazel eyes were the only things my father had ever given her.

Seventeen years traipsing around the Third World. Uganda, Nigeria, Brazil, the Middle East. Hiding from the Republican Guard, three different infections that nearly killed me, and all my mother ever said was 'this is God's plan for us, Matty'. She believed it, my old man didn't, although I think he wanted to. Ari came along after he got sick of pretending to be a saint and spent one night living like the bastard he is. He came back sobbing and confessed everything.

Any self-respecting wife would've screamed, cried, kicked his ass out—something, but my mother decided the devil had made him do it and never said another word. We spent months in and out of Wadi Dusyan, while rumors swelled with the size of Widow Maloof's belly. The day Ari was born, I overheard him threatening her to keep her mouth shut. We left Mosul the next day, and far as I know, he's never been back.

I grabbed a wrapped package I'd brought from home out of the car—a bright purple shirt and pants, purple hair barrettes, and a Little Mermaid doll. "Merry Christmas, pretty girl."

Smiling, she climbed onto a nearby boulder. "You being here is the best present."

A little money when I could, a gift here and there. It wasn't much. I felt like shit every time I left, but the fact the asshole never acknowledged her didn't leave much in the way of options. Truth was, her real family was here.

Her face was guarded while she carefully tore the wrapping. "How long are you staying?"

I glanced at my watch. "Only a few minutes right now." When her face fell, I sat next to her on the rock. "I'll come back later. Promise. I've got a friend I want you to meet."

"A girl?"

Hana emerged from the house, bouncing on her toes as if she had some great secret. The mongoose was behind her, standing on two legs, mimicking her excitement. I tousled Ari's hair. "Yes, a girl. I need to talk to Hana."

With an impish glint, Ari clipped a barrette to her braid. "She washed her hair for you."

Hana turned bright red. "Ari!"

Ari stuck out her tongue. "Eema will yell if she sees you in that shirt."

Hana wore an embroidered white blouse, which did look a little tight. "Tell your mother I'll get her a new one before I go."

For some reason, Ari found that amusing. Ishai grabbed my hand and yanked me towards Hana. "Go ahead. Ask her where it came from."

Hana pulled something from behind her back. From the reverence on her face, you would've thought it was the Grail itself. "Please, Matty, tell him how wonderful this is—I can keep it, can't I?"

'It' was a battered field laptop with a solar array on the case, and I was fairly certain I wasn't going to like how she'd gotten it either. "Hana?"

She rocked on her bare feet. "I fixed it for them."

"Who?"

"The Americans."

The air suddenly felt dangerous. Heavy. "Blond guy? Flat-top hair cut?" I said, running my palm over the top of my head.

She drew the computer to her chest. "He said he wanted to be my friend."

Hana was impulsive, but her IQ must've been north of two hundred, give or take a million. She knew perfectly well that American spies did not give laptops to teenage Iraqi girls without expecting something in return, and whatever it was, she wasn't about to let Ishai—or me—talk her out of it.

Since I figured it was the same thing soldiers away from home usually wanted from local underage cuties, I was more pissed off than worried. It meant a pointed chat with Clarke later. At worst, the threat of a front page picture and a headline that wouldn't play well with the family values crowd. But then she started talking.

She'd been waiting for Ishai near the book strand, playing with the mongoose, where Clarke and Gleason were having trouble with the computer. She jumped in and got it running again. Clarke was so "impressed" that he showed up the next day, computer in hand, the hard drive newly wiped. '*Fix it and it's yours*', he said.

Ishai fumed. "What were you doing talking to the Americans?"

Her lips pursed. "Perhaps now you wish you had let me come to class."

My head was too far up my ass to deal with this. The intercept of the UN truck was supposed to be happening any minute. "Look, stay out of town for a few weeks. No more making 'friends'. If they come back, walk the other way."

Ishai threw up his hands at the sky. "God help us."

Their mother, Magdala, who mine referred to as the Whore of Babylon, came up from the river. She set her water jug beside me. "You have aged ten years in two, dear boy. I thought you were Eli."

I didn't look a damn thing like my father and she knew it. "Like he'd be here?"

She tweaked my chin. "God gave you and me the same burden—we try to help those who are beyond help. He repaid me with Ari. One day, for you it will be the same."

Ari wandered over, clutching a photo of us from my last visit. She tugged at my camera strap. "Matty, I want a new picture of us. Will you take one and send it to me when you get home like before?"

"I can do one better." I handed the Nikon to Hana. "I can put it on her new toy—you can have it today."

Ari hopped on my knee and threw her arms around my neck. "I love you, brother."

It hit me then, hard. A week, a month—it didn't matter when the war started. She'd be here when it did. Nothing I did would change that. Bringing Leah here to meet Ari meant asking her to understand that I'd be leaving my little sister in a war zone.

Fighting a lump in my throat, I held Ari tight, not knowing it'd be for the last time. "Love you too, pretty girl."

Hana snapped a shot, squinted at the screen, and handed it back. "You see? I can take good pictures too! You should hire me instead of grumpy old Ishai!"

"His driving is bad enough." I grabbed the laptop. "What's the password?"

When she hesitated, I got annoyed. "Hana, I need to leave or else some Baathist douchebag will get away with stealing a truckload of medical supplies because your new 'friend' in the CIA only cares about finding WMDs."

"Clarke didn't ignore you," she said. "They're looking into the tip you gave."

My gut clenched. Magdala's face paled. "What?"

Ishai charged at her. "You know this how?"

Hana bolted, hopping the fence. "Because I pay attention while you sleep through lectures. Because I make the world give up its secrets while you flirt with your city girls."

Ishai's face purpled. "Me? What of you? As if all this is not to impress—"

My head felt ready to explode. "Start talking. Now."

Hana circled the pen, keeping a wary eye on her brother. "Father used to say that men who profit from destruction fail to realize certain truths. Knowledge cannot be destroyed."

It took a minute to sink in. "Are you telling me you hacked a CIA hard drive?"

She ran to me, with a pleading look. "One of Ishai's classmates was given safe passage to Ankara for identifying a security leak. They have always refused us visas because of Father, Matty, you know that better than anyone. I saw a chance for us all to leave."

Swearing my fool head off, I opened the lid. "Password. Now."

She entered it, pulling up window after window which showed how she'd hacked into Clarke's email. One had gone out last night, within five minutes of me talking to him.

From: Maj. Oswald Clarke
To: <undisclosed-recipients>
Subject: Mission Progress Report

HUMINT suggests Hussein moving cache of weaponized cholera or anthrax towards Syria. Confirmation by media source, who indicates WMD may be disguised as UN medical shipment.

The hell I had. I hadn't said a damn thing about weapons, mass or otherwise.

Either Clarke had a hearing problem or he was playing games with my intel.

Rani appeared in the pen, stroking a little black goat. *'You see, man? This is why we don't get involved.'*

I blinked him away, grateful Leah and I waited an extra day so she could get a cholera vaccine. The next dispatch wasn't any more comforting.

From: Maj. Oswald Clarke
To: <undisclosed-recipients>
Subject: ASSET PROFILE: MONGOOSE

Father was CIA asset before Gulf War. Prof of CompSci at Mosul University. Provided valuable technology intel but discovered and executed by regime. MONGOOSE wants to prove herself. Risk taker. Extremely intelligent. Morally flexible. Questionable loyalty. Offer of post-war asylum might keep her on the leash.

I stared at Hana. "Did you know about this?"

She was red-faced and shaking. "They know nothing of my loyalty."

Ishai let fly. "And you remember nothing of when father was taken. Do you understand what will happen if you are discovered? We will all of us be killed!"

Stricken, Magdala reached for Ari. "This family does not turn on each other, Ishai. God will protect us."

Hana took the keyboard, tapping keys. "I have been careful, Eema, I swear it. I—" A new message appeared on the screen. This time, it was from Gleason. Her breath hitched.

> From: Bradley Gleason
> To: Maj. Oswald Clarke
> Subject: Re: ASSET PROFILE: MONGOOSE
>
> Clarke's girl genius took two hours to hack DoD encryption. I'm not taking the fall if anyone finds out about our arrangement with Kıraç. Our mission was to find WMD. Fuck this 'hearts and minds' bullshit.
>
> Have Kıraç get rid of Gazim. Tell him to take out Clarke's girl and her family too. Make it look like a civilian airstrike casualty. Let the WH take the heat. Make sure the Pentagon plugs the exploit. Set some rules for the goddamn media while you're at it—this Cahill kid is trouble.

Five minutes later, they'd packed their belongings into Ishai's car. Hana sat in the back, staring straight ahead.

The plan was for me to hitchhike to Mosul and grab Leah while they headed for a refugee camp on the Turkish border. Things were seriously hosed—I'd missed my window on the shipment, then there was the whole cholera thing, but all I cared about was getting Ari out of harm's way. If these guys wanted to come after her, they'd have to get through me.

"How will we find you?" she said tearfully.

I looked at Magdala, then at Ari. "I was thinking you could stay with my friend band me for a little while."

Magdala grasped Ari's shoulders, drawing her back. "I would not let Eli take her—do you think I will let you?"

Let him? Right. "Leah and I can pass her off as our kid, they won't ask questions—"

"Like no one ever asked Eli about you?" she snapped.

Desperation growing, I had no clue how to respond.

"You should give her the choice, Eema," Hana said. Tears streamed down her cheeks. "I would want it."

A pair of fighters scorched across the dawn horizon. "I can keep her safe, Magdala," I said. "Just until the fighting is finished."

Magdala shoved Ari towards the car. "We will see the conditions when we arrive. Then I will decide."

They took off, heading north. I started down the highway, listening for a vehicle going my way. My nerves felt all jangly and shot. Did I have enough cash to bribe someone at the border? Would Leah go along with it? Even if we didn't get ourselves thrown into a Turkish prison in the process, what the hell was I going to do with a seven-year-old?

It was getting light. The highway was deserted. The ground sloped away on both sides. Hills of sand and scrub led to barbed wire, a desert expanse spiked with oil derricks. Out here, there were no mine warning signs, but the southern side was littered with rusty cylinders poking out of the sand. In the distance, platoons of Iraqi soldiers were laying more. They'd all be dead by the first night of the war.

I snapped a few shots, if only so someone other than their mothers or wives or kids would remember who they were. The whine of a motor came up behind me. I turned and stuck out my thumb.

An F-15 screamed overhead, fifty meters off the pavement. A white semi went barreling past, a torn UN banner flapping on the side. The truck's slipstream knocked me flat. Damn thing had to be doing a buck-twenty.

Another F-15 popped up from the mountains, coming out of a barrel roll. The pilot banked sharply to the left. A burst of fire came from its belly. Two hundred yards ahead, the truck swerved. The missile locked. I ran for the gully.

The fireball bloomed an instant later. I threw my hand in front of my face. The shockwave must've set off the mines, because the sand started exploding.

The pavement became one giant blur of grey and tan, air choked with sulfur and burning rubber. Diesel burned my eyes and throat.

What was left of the trailer was strewn all over the road, a twisted mass of burning scrap. The driver's body was on fire by the edge, the same guy taunting Tish the day before. There were enough pieces of him to be sure.

A silver Toyota screeched to a stop, gravel skidding under the tires. The driver poked his head out the window. It was Rani. He was himself again, all whole, chewing on that checkered scarf he wore, same as he'd always do when we'd go tearing off after something big, *'fuck yeah, boyo let's go!'* It occurred to me at that point that I'd lost it, but then I heard it. This evil metallic rolling sound, as a dislodged Claymore came rolling down the road. It did a long, lazy curl under the car, clattering onto the detonator. Boom. There I was, watching my best friend explode all over again.

I smelled burning sulfur, I saw the mines going up, I saw the sand fly, but it didn't make a sound, as if I was floating about ten feet above. Then I saw a woman running into the minefield.

Leah.

A flood of sick panic hit. I screamed at her to stop, but she kept getting farther away. Then a shower of sand went up and she disappeared from sight. Truth be told, I haven't got the first fucking clue what happened after that.

The muezzin was calling evening prayers by the time I stumbled into the cantina in Mosul, dehydrated to the point of hallucination. The desk clerk stopped me. "Your bill is unpaid. You cannot stay here." Then he handed me a note. "This came for you."

It was Ishai's handwriting on the envelope. "When?"

"Two days ago."

I rubbed the grit out of my eyes. "What day is today?"

"Friday."

Last I knew, it was Tuesday.

My stomach knotted when I unfolded the note.

> We are safe, no thanks to you.
> I have never seen my sister so upset.
> Do not try to contact any of us again.
> To you, we are dead.

Tish, Rosie, and Dinosaur Dave came out from the bar, gawping at me as if Moses himself had crawled out of the desert.

Tish gave me a long, hard, stare. "Don't worry, she's fine."

"She?" My head was somewhere about three months in the past. Rani was the one missing. "I'm confused."

"You're both complete nutters is what you are, the pair of you. Leah tried to go running into the minefield after you. I barely stopped her. What's the matter with you? One dead friend isn't enough?"

Bits and pieces came back. Something kept pulling her away. "You weren't there, none of you were really there."

"Bloody piss we weren't," Tish shot back. "You were supposed to be finding my supplies. Then I get a call that you were there when the fecking Air Force blew them up. What did you think we'd do, leave you there?"

If all that was real, if it wasn't in my head… "Is she all right? Did she get hurt?"

Exasperated, Rosie lit a cigarette. "Of course your little copaine was not all right."

Tish shot Rosie a look. "She was a wreck. I sent her home."

Dinosaur Dave stuck a tumbler into my hand. "Thought you'd done it this time, mate."

The water tasted oily and stale, and I choked when I remembered how all this started. "Shit—the village—the cholera outbreak…"

The oddest expression came over Tish's face. "It's not quite that bad. Some of the village children got dysentery from the contaminated tanks. Touch and go, but Leah's replacement shipment got here last night."

My heart stopped. I felt it. "Leah's what?"

Tish borrowed Rosie's Gauloise, taking a deep inhale. "Emergency airlift, courtesy of some upstart little aid group in London. My man there is calling her a miracle worker. Do us a favor—when you finish groveling, give her my thanks."

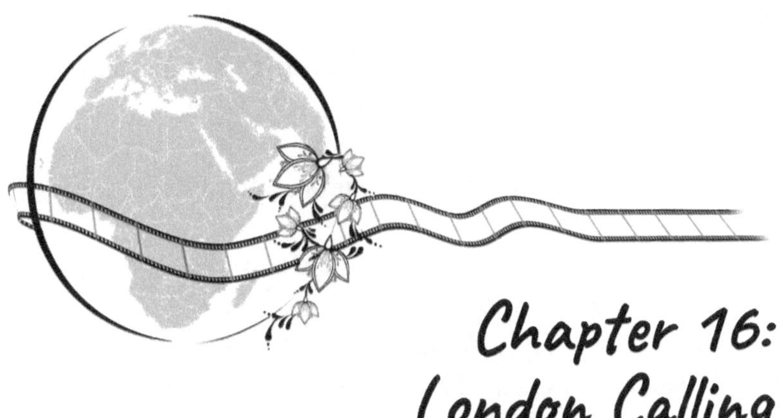

Chapter 16:
London Calling
JANUARY 2003
LONDON, U.K.

Three convoys and a cargo flight later, I stood at the door to a Canary Wharf flat, working up the apology I'd been rehearsing for the past thirty hours. I'd already delivered some form twice to Leah's mother, at least whatever I got in before she hung up on me. On the third try, Dale took pity and told me where Leah was.

After I knocked, a shadow hovered under the door long before it actually cracked open. Clouded by sleep, her face was shrouded in darkness. Hair loose and tousled, all she had on was a blue T-shirt of mine, which barely skimmed her hips. "It's four a.m., Matty."

The second I saw her, I felt drunk. Drunk on life, drunk on love, drunk on the promise of a new beginning. If I kissed her, she'd feel how sorry I was, wouldn't she? Fighting the urge to find out, I leaned on the frame. "Can I come in?"

Her expression was still—almost serene. "You should go," she said softly.

That was when I heard a voice in the background, a man's voice, telling her to come back to bed. Somehow, I found mine. "Did it help?"

An eternity passed before she said anything else. "You should go," she repeated.

I had no one to blame but myself, but it still felt like someone hacked me off at the knees. Maybe a foot or so higher. "Let me talk to the guy," I finally said.

She rested her forehead against the door. "It's none of your business who I sleep with."

"I didn't say it was." I ground the heel of my hand into my eye. "Leah, I've been living with the fact that I wasn't there when you needed me with Jason. Maybe I've been going about it all wrong, and I'm sorry, but for my own sanity I need to know that whoever you've got in there isn't going to hurt you again."

She fought it, but her chin went wibbly. "I thought you were dead, Matty, three days I thought you were dead."

The guilt and shame of it all were killing me. Before I caught the transport here, I'd spent two days running between refugee tents on the Turkish border. There was no sign of Ari. So whether or not Leah realized it, I knew exactly how she felt.

She didn't resist when I drew her into my arms, so I exhaled into the top of her hair, feeling like I couldn't hold her tight enough. "You have no idea how sorry I am."

The lights flicked on. A short guy with an over-broad mouth that made him look like the Joker stood by the bed, buttoning a starched pink shirt. "Well now, I'm guessing you're the bloke she was getting smashed over last night." He tucked the shirt into his pants. "Must be going, love—early call with the Hong Kong office. Impending crackdown in China, you know how those bastards are. It's been fun."

He brushed past me with a curt nod. "Save yourself the trouble, mate. Totally frigid, that one."

Small relief competed with the urge to deck him. "Go fuck yourself."

The flat was cramped, a modern studio with a kitchenette, a suede couch, and a glass slider to a balcony running the length of the wall. Outside, moonlight glistened on the Thames. I slung the rucksack off my shoulder. "Nice place."

"The owner is a friend of my dad's," she said, taking a glass from a maple cabinet in the kitchen. "He's in Thailand. He's a lawyer for Amnesty—that's how I met—"

"You don't need to explain," I said, feeling raw as day-old steak.

Leah was usually a neat freak, but the place was covered in large-scale maps and charts, notebooks and scraps of paper. "Tish thinks you're a miracle worker," I said. "How'd you get the shipment through?"

She filled her glass, surrounded by an air of hangover and defeat. "Same way I do everything. I asked my father for help."

It couldn't have been further from the truth. Dale gave her one name, an Iraqi ex-pat living in London who'd done some refugee work. Somehow, she got an NGO on board, leveraged that into a group of wealthy donors who financed the lift, and convinced a couple of MPs to sign off on the whole thing.

"Let me get this straight," I said. "You started this by telling me the only way you managed to circumvent a Baathist strongman and sanctions imposed by two of the most powerful countries in the world is because of your dad?"

She stared at the floor. "Tish said you were beyond help. I had to do something before I started to believe her."

I leaned on the counter. "Leah, sometimes it feels like there's so little in the world that I can change. I swear, I'm never going to let myself get like that again."

She gazed out over the Thames. "Are you sure?"

I knew how hollow it sounded. "My dead best friend is my new co-pilot. It takes some getting used to."

"You were yelling at him too." She was twisting her hands around the glass, like she wanted to throttle me. "I mean, in Portuguese, I think—I couldn't understand, but you kept saying his name. PTSD is nothing to be ashamed of, Matty. You need help."

I scratched my head. "Leah, shrinks give me hives, but if that's what it takes, I'll go find one right now."

A wan smile warmed her face. "I'm going to hold you to that."

Awesome.

I moved closer, hands coming to rest on the sides of her face. But she drifted away, into the main part of the room, and stopped short at the bed. Stuck in the middle of the rumpled comforter was a bright red condom wrapper. I couldn't tell if it had been opened or not, and I told myself it didn't matter. *You screwed up, asshole, not her.* But then she saw me looking at it and burst into tears. "Matty, what's wrong with me? What the hell was I thinking?"

I reached for her, but retreated when she pushed me away. "Nothing's wrong with you. Which is more than I can say for him."

Arms wrapped around her waist, she went to the slider. Her voice was barely a whisper. "I didn't know how to cope with the idea you were dead, and then when it turned out you were alive, I couldn't deal with that either. I knew he was manipulating me over it but I didn't care. I just wanted to stop feeling everything at hurricane force for one night. To prove I could be with someone and not get hurt."

I shook my head. "Seriously—I get it. You don't have to explain it to me."

"Yeah, I do," she said. "You've been acting like I'm damaged goods since Christmas. At least this would've made it true."

If she'd slapped me, it would've hurt less. "Tell me that's not what you think."

She stared at me dully. "Forget it."

"No." From behind, I slipped my hand under her shirt, letting it rest on her stomach, feeling her breathe. I thought I got it, that she didn't want to feel like a victim. Now I wasn't sure. "I'm a guy, Leah. I can't read your mind."

She sniffled. "The last thing you needed was me adding onto your problems."

"I'll always have problems. That doesn't mean I don't care about yours."

She sank to the edge of the bed. "You really want to know?"

"I don't want you thinking what you were thinking, put it that way."

Fingers curled around her toes, she took a deep breath. "Afterwards… it was dark, I was crying, but I don't think he knew. 'We'll get married and everything will be fine,' he said. 'He'll see you're mine now.'"

Seething, I wiped my hand over my face. "Leah, if I ever see that guy again…"

She squeezed her forearms over her ears. "I know, I know, I told myself not to listen but then you started acting like you couldn't bear to touch me, and—" Her breath hitched. "I mean, I know, I told you not to, but there was this voice telling me you were disgusted with me because I let him do it."

"Seriously?"

With a hurt look, she drew up her knees. "I figured you of all people would understand the evil head voice."

For me, it was simple—the guy needed a rusty spike driven through his balls. But for her, it was coming to terms with the fact that someone she trusted had done something unforgiveable. And that, I did understand.

I sat next to her on the bed. "Can I ask you a personal question?"

"Have we been discussing the weather?"

"Pretend we could go back in time a few months. If I asked you whether you liked sex, what would you say?"

"Like…physically?" Her face got pink. "Put it this way. When we were living together, any time you'd come out of the shower with a towel around your hips, let's just say I'm glad you couldn't tell what I was thinking."

Now she tells me? "See that's what I mean. How come? Because we might've ended up in bed together? Would it have been so bad if we did?"

She rubbed her shoulder. "It's like this. I'm the Catholic daughter of old school liberals, so hello, mixed messages. Plus, I grew up in a town and a time where sex was literally a life and death thing for like, everyone I knew. I lost my virginity when I was barely fifteen because I thought it would stop everyone else telling me how I was supposed to feel about it. Myself. Something. So far, I've decided is that sex is messy and confusing and if there's a right and a wrong way to do it, I have no idea which is which."

"The wrong one is the fun one?"

She poked me. "Helpful."

"So make love with me and we'll figure it out."

She arched her brow. "Hooking up with two guys in one night? Pretty sure that'd make me a whore in anyone's book, Matty."

I flopped onto the mattress. "Good, we can both be whores. Where are those condoms?"

With an uncertain expression, she came and straddled me, bare thighs against my hips. "If I said let's go for it, right now, you'd say—"

"Yippee?"

"You're such a guy."

Most of the blood in my body was headed out of my brain, but it eventually dawned on me what she was doing. It was a way to regain control, over her body, over her heart, her life.

"Yep." I slid my hands to her waist. "Give me a break, I'm a preacher's kid. I'm as screwed up about sex as they get."

She went quiet. "Ask me, it's the one thing you're not."

I took her hips. "So let's make a deal. Show me what it feels like to be with a woman I'm madly in love with, who loves me as much as I love her, and I'll show you what sex is supposed to be like."

Mid-giggle, she froze. "Wait a sec—did you just… you love me?"

I sat up, burying my face in her neck. I hadn't meant to put it 'out there', but I wasn't sorry either.

She rose, opened the slider, and stepped out onto the balcony. I followed, grabbing the duvet. It was barely above freezing, and daylight was a red thread on the horizon, disappearing into the far end of the Thames.

"They gave me an offer to stay in London," she said. "One of the donors works with an NGO doing aid work in north central Africa. They're revamping their approach and looking for a contract liaison—a pair of fresh eyes to go in-country and talk to locals and aid workers, then come back and tell the money people what's needed. Right now, half of the aid gets skimmed off by warlords and goes into weapon sales. I mean—you know."

It was probably closer to three quarters, but it didn't seem like a helpful thing to say. "Yeah."

She grasped the railing, shivering in the cold. "God, if we could get it to the people who need it—women could start businesses, girls could get proper schooling instead of getting married off at thirteen, babies could get the medications they need…"

I pulled her down with me into the papasan chair on the balcony and wrapped both of us in the duvet. When I'd stepped off the plane at Heathrow, anything short of her slamming the door in my face would've been a victory. "Sounds perfect for you. What's the problem?"

Downcast, she nestled into my arms. "It's really my dad they wanted—they'd envisioned this whole father-daughter return to their roots thing. I mean, I wasn't even sure how I felt about that, and maybe ten years ago, he would've been up for it, but now…" Her voice trailed off. "He convinced them to give me a chance on my own."

Now I got what was bugging her earlier. "Which is it? That your dream job came with a leg up from Dad or that you'd be working for a bunch of clueless white guys?"

"Both?" She wrinkled her nose. "Plus, I'd have to put off law school."

"You've been looking for an excuse to do that for months."

Her mouth opened, like she wanted to protest. "My dad—"

"Wants you to be happy," I finished for her. "Dreams change. Jobs change. I'm taking a break from mine, right?"

She lifted her head off my chest. "Seriously?"

Wasn't like I was going to have much choice, once word got around about the meltdown I'd had. I slipped my hand under her shirt, caressing her belly. "Haven't you been telling me I need it?"

"What about the magazine? You only got a couple days of footage."

"They got exactly what they wanted and only had to pay half my per diems. Trust me, they're thrilled."

She got quiet. "Can I see your photos?"

Most of them, she already had. What she was really asking was if I'd taken any after I'd run off. God knows I had. But only one I could show her.

I got up, went inside, dug the Nikon out of my bag, and scrolled to the photo Hana took. My heart hurt looking at it, so I crawled back into the chair with Leah. "This is Ari-eil. Ari for short."

She wet her lips and blinked twice. "She's beautiful," she whispered. "Why didn't you tell me you have a daughter?"

"Sister." I frowned. "Half-sister, technically. Why'd you think she's my kid?"

She traced the frame with her finger. "The way you're holding her… there's a picture of me and my dad this reminds me of."

My insides got all twisted up. "Yeah, well… *her* father doesn't give a damn that she exists."

Leah got quiet, as if she was putting it all together. "Ari is the reason you hate your dad so much?"

Among other things. I pinched the bridge of my nose. "Her mom is an Iraqi widow. Bastard doesn't exactly practice what he preaches, does he?"

She caressed my cheek. "But that's not your fault, is it? Why didn't you tell me?"

"Look at your father," I said. "Now look at mine."

She sat back. "My dad was a forty-five-year-old married man when he started his affair with my mother. She was barely twenty. He didn't leave his first wife until after DJ died." She shook her head. "I don't have to like everything someone does to love them. Do you?"

Heaving a deep, frustrated sigh, I knocked my head against the frame of the chair. "It's different, okay?" I didn't know how, it just was. "You saw what things are like there."

Leah's head came to rest against my chest. "Where is Ari now? Is she safe?"

"Wish to god I knew." I shook my head. "I need to go back. Keep looking."

She hugged my waist. "We both know that's a bad idea."

I knew she meant because of my mental state. But there was another reason, tucked deep into the lining of my coat: my spare memory card. There were photos of the truck after the missile hit, and of Gleason, Clarke, and the others arriving on-scene. Later, there was a long-lens video of Gleason in the mountains somewhere, machine-gunning a bloodied, kneeling Iraqi, cheered on by a light-skinned foreigner with flowing black hair, a crocodile jacket, and silver aviator sunglasses.

Somehow, I had pictures of an extrajudicial execution I couldn't remember taking.

Losing my mind honestly scared the shit out of me, worse than any gun battle or shelling I'd ever been in. Given the photos, I must've been lucid some of that time—and decided whatever I was doing was more important than Leah or Ari. Something I'd blocked out. I was only sure of one thing—what I'd uncovered was big. Dangerous. Too dangerous to tell Leah. It had too many holes that needed filling. Under ordinary circumstances, there's no way I would've let it go. But in lieu of letting it kill me, I did.

With the winter air surrounding us, the calm of pre-dawn London, her breath was a calm flutter against my cheek. "So what are you going to do?"

Photojournalism wasn't exactly a steady income. I was forever having to find ways to make ends meet. "Wait tables, bartend, medical guinea pig—"

"If you grow a tail I'm not going out with you."

"I draw the line at manning the Sears photo booth."

She got quiet after that. "Matty, I hear what you're saying, but you're saying it because you think it's what I want to hear, and it's not. Everything I know about you tells me you don't think you have a choice. You'll be back in the field before long. But I can't sit and watch you self-destruct every time. You're not good for me."

The way she said it, she threw it out as a challenge. "You don't want someone good for you." I nibbled her neck until I found her pulse. "You want someone you can fix."

She made a little noise, somewhere between pleasure and assent, craning her neck for more. "I'm not convinced you're housebroken, let alone fixable."

"Sure I am." I slipped my hand under her shirt. "And besides, I am good for you. I'm the guy who convinces you to do what you want to do instead of what you think everyone else wants you to do."

She wet her lips, pulling away slightly. "What I wanted to do put me in Iraq with a crazy reporter, remember?"

More or less. "I can make you happy, Leah." I went the last few inches, caressing the underside of her breast, the curve, spreading my fingers wide, like a shield over her heart, a promise not to break it. "Give me a chance to prove it."

She burrowed farther into my chest. "I need to think about it."

I kissed her forehead. "I'm not going anywhere."

So there we sat, curled up together, watching the London skyline over the Thames, more than friends, but not yet lovers, and right as I was about to doze off, the moment the first rays of dawn broke over the river, I heard her murmur "yes".

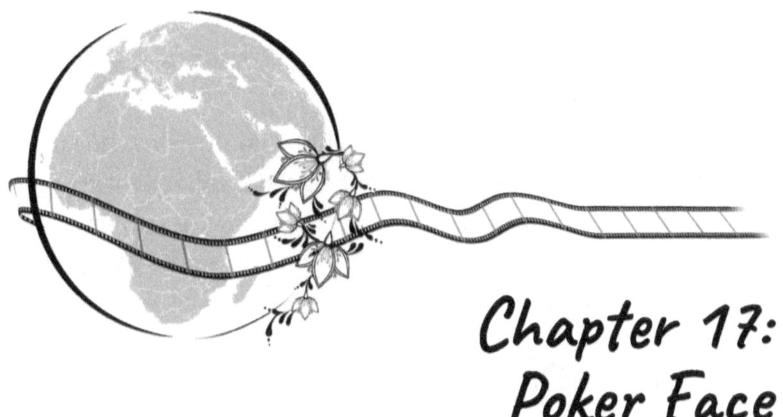

Chapter 17: Poker Face

MEDITERRANEAN SEA
PRESENT

I have to get out. Have to warn Leah.

Coming off a hunger strike… sucks. Two mouthfuls of beans last night, and I spent the rest of it puking my guts out. This morning, I managed to choke down some rice and lentil stew from a rations packet, the salmon-colored 'humanitarian packs' that litter half of Afghanistan—most of which are tainted with fun stuff like arsenic or cyanide or anthrax courtesy of the Taliban. Never thought I'd be desperate enough to eat one.

The numbness in my limbs is disappearing. My teeth hurt. My head is clearing, but that means the walls are closing in. I walk box letters around my cell, spelling out poems I memorized as a kid. *Invictus, Annabel Lee.* Kipling's *If.* Thomas, Tennyson, Whitman. It's a way to slow my mind, to render the time meaningless, to keep a tenuous grip on sanity. To stop freaking out about whatever Leah is doing.

The beanhole slides open. Orlyk is on the other side. "The fuck you doing, man?"

I finish my 'Y'. Won't hurt for him to wonder. "Working on my plan for mass terror and world domination. You'll like it. It involves sheep."

"Funny." A smoke trail curls out of his nose. "You're up to something. Don't think you have us fooled, eh? Gleason wants to talk to you."

Gleason hasn't shown his ass on board for a while. The last time wasn't one of my better days. "Lucky me."

Orlyk puts me in a hood and shackles and drags me down into the bowels of the ship. When they pull off the hood, it's not the usual interrogation room. There's a wooden plank set across two sawhorses, plus three sets of straps dangling on the ground. And a gallon jug of water resting near a towel. The hair on my neck rises. I know what it's for.

Gleason started his career as Special Ops during the Gulf War, bailed on the military, made a fortune on Wall Street, which gave him a front row seat when the South Tower came down while his younger brother was in a stairwell on the 49th floor. He's calculating, shrewd, and mean as a snake on hot coals.

He sits in near darkness, only a bare bulb for light, shuffling a set of cards, which he sets face-down on the plank. It's not just any deck, it's the Iraqi 'Most Wanted' cards made up during the war. "You like to gamble, Cahill?"

"Not when the house rigs the game." Chains clinking, I turn the top card. It's the Nine of Spades, a potato-faced Iraqi with a wooly bear mustache, beady eyes and thin-lipped sneer.

"Tell you what." I flip the card at Gleason's barrel chest. "I'll bet you a free trip out of here that you and Kıraç blew this guy's head off while I was up on the hill taking pictures."

"You've got balls, I'll give you that." Gleason lights a cigarette, blowing a smoke ring in the air. "Rashid Gazim."

All I can do is stall for time. Give Leah a chance. I've known from the beginning there's no way he'll ever let me walk out of here. "What about him?"

He pushes a copy of my photo across the plank, the one I can't remember taking. "Head of Tribal Affairs, misappropriating UN relief from his own people. Gave them some cholera-laced water in the process. But I'm not telling you anything you don't know, right Cahill?"

A month after the Iraq War started, Leah and I were in Africa. I'd gotten my hands on a copy of *The Guardian*, where they'd printed the entire Most Wanted deck in a full-page spread. Saddam as the Ace of Spades, all that. Imagine my surprise when in the third row, I saw the guy whose execution I'd witnessed.

Gazim was supposed to be their smoking gun. The proof that Iraq was a hair trigger away from having nukes or some advanced, head-of-a-pin neurotoxin capable of ending life as we know it because that's what the idiot had told them. They'd believed him because they were all caught up in their own grief, rage, and hubris, and when it didn't pan out, they made him pay.

Kıraç had been their backup plan, an arms dealer with connections to the Russians, Saudis, and Turks. Somebody who could get his hands on the kind of WMD that'd scare the fence-sitters into supporting the war, but after I'd gotten wind of things, Clarke got cold feet. That's when Gleason had gone into cleanup mode. He'd kept it quiet enough that on paper, Gazim 'survived' the war. "What's your point?"

He taps the photo, near Kıraç's head. "You know, it's funny. Half the U.S. Government is looking for this bastard. Nobody can find him anywhere. Lord knows he ain't returning my calls these days. Yet you seem to be able to find him whenever you want. Except now, when thousands of lives are at stake. What gives?"

I hold up the shackles. "Seriously?"

"See, I don't think that's the problem. I think we haven't convinced you to tell us what you're hiding yet." His eyes lift, towards the board. "Easy enough to fix that."

Sweat breaks out on my forehead. "If you idiots are so convinced I can find Kıraç whenever I want, put your money where your mouth is. He's the one guy on the planet who wants me dead more than you do. Use me as bait. Let me out."

He snorts. "Right."

I lean forward, elbows resting on my knees. "Think about it. I'm the reason he's in hiding. Best case, you flush him out. Maybe you even come out the hero. Stop the attacks. Worst case for you, he puts a bullet in my head and gets away, which saves you the trouble of doing it yourself."

He contemplates his cigarette. "This is the part where I'm supposed to get stupid. You convince me I'm in control of the situation, but somehow, you live long enough to burn me."

"I'm willing to deal," I say. "What, you think I'm a saint?"

"I think you're a devious little fuck." He pushes his tongue into his cheek. "Don't worry. Thanks to your little woman, we've got all the bait we need."

My heart starts to pound. "What?"

His grin turns mean. "Seems her finding out about you was good for us after all. We put it out through channels that she's figured out what you were up to. Cooperating with the feds. Getting ready to turn over everything you had on Kıraç. I expect he'll come after her soon enough."

My mouth goes dry. "Leave her out of this."

"Relax. We've got eyes on her. She's safe, for now." With a squeak, he sits back in the chair, blowing a ring of smoke through his nose. "Whether she stays that way is up to you."

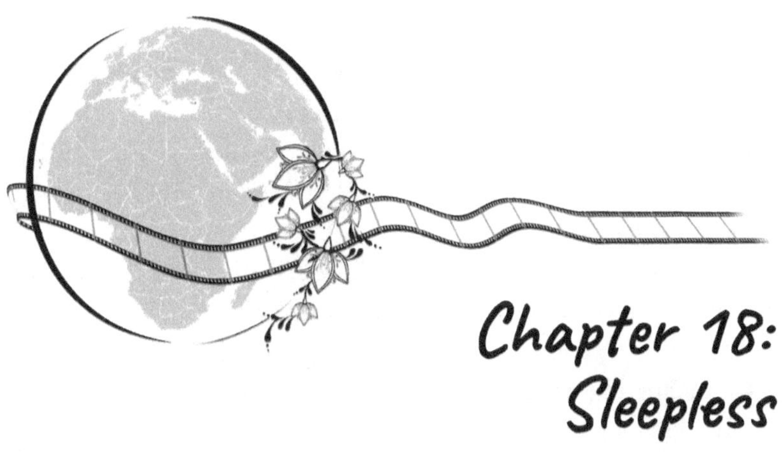

Chapter 18:
Sleepless

PROVINCETOWN, MASSACHUSETTS
PRESENT

Leah

The kettle's whistle prods me awake. I sit up in the hammock and rub my temples, regretting the two gin and tonics it had taken to steady my nerves after Jason. The ship's wheel clock on the carriage house wall says it's after three in the morning. Time to get back to work.

Slipping fragrant chamomile into the pot, I wake my laptop and sort through the stack of CDs on the shelf. Our lives together, memories in silicon. It's killing me go through them this way, looking for clues of things he never told me about. Signs he was in deeper trouble than I ever realized. The risks he faced weren't just bombs or bullets. I'd been focused on his mental health. Our government locking him up, violating his rights… it wasn't exactly on my radar.

Where do I even start? The end? The beginning? How far did it go?

I settle into the hammock with my latest clue, a nineties-era photo I found in a shoebox labeled *Family*. Matty, who can't be more than seventeen, is awkwardly holding an infant swaddled in an orange blanket. Next to him is a teenage Iraqi boy with a wild cowlick and cheeky grin, next to a tween-ish girl with long dark hair and brooding eyes, a puffed-up mongoose kit crawling up her shoulder. On the back, in spidery Arabic, it reads: *Wadi Dusyan, 11/02/1995, Ishai, Ari-eil, Matthias, and Hana.*

Ishai, our quiet, studious driver. Ari-eil, the lost baby sister. Hana, the middle sister, he'd never mentioned much about.

My mind wanders back to the mystery woman with the mongoose in Cairo. She'd be about the right age now. Is it her? Is she the hacker?

The knob on the door twists. Left, then right. I bolt off the hammock. Full-on panic mode engages. Then my dad shuffles in, clad in a frayed bathrobe and moccasins, scratching his stomach.

"What's the matter, girl? You never seen an old man in pajamas before?"

Cute. "What are you doing up, Dad?"

He rubs his whiskers, the same way he does when mom catches him sneaking a cookie. "Can't a father come check on his little girl?"

"Dad…"

Pulling a face, he waves his hand. "I can't sleep." He shuffles over to his Catalina, which is dry-docked in the middle of the room, its mast forlorn on its side in the cockpit. He climbs the step, plunks down onto the gunwale, and after shoving aside a coiled line, he fishes into the small hatch and comes up with a clam shell ashtray, a lighter, and small baggie of weed. "Tell your mother and I'll put you straight over my knee."

I raise an eyebrow. "Tell Mom what? That I'm not the only one married to an occasional pothead? Since when do you keep a stash in the boat?"

"Since when are you Miss Goody Two Shoes?" With surprising nimbleness, his gnarled fingers roll a fresh joint. "Matthias was always willing to share. It's his, not mine."

A sense of hurt descends. I thought I knew all Matty's hiding places. The day we left for Cairo, I got rid of everything. He'd promised that after we got back, he'd try a real therapist again, that he'd stop self-medicating. Had he lied? Forgotten?

"Just take it easy," I sigh. "Knowing Matty, it's not exactly 60s pot."

A night wind is coming off the water, rattling the windows and oversized door. His expression grows distant. "I spent my life trying to change the things that killed your brother, Leah. In the past twelve hours, I've come to see that I failed."

I climb into the boat, resting my head on his shoulder. "You didn't, Dad. I promise."

Never one for cuddling, he shifts forward, reaching for the clam-shell and lighter. From the angle I'm at, I can see inside the hatch. There's something shiny near the edge. A dark, heavy plastic bag. A film bag. The farther I reach, the more I find. There have to be dozens.

He peers over my shoulder. "Well now, what have we here?"

Pulse racing, I pull out the first one: *RELIEFNET TRIP WITH LEAH: MOROCCO-SUDAN*

It was the first trip we took as a couple. As partners. But the prints I find inside aren't the ones I remember. Most of the shots are blurred or out of focus—the only thing they have in common is a male figure with long dark hair, usually near the edge of the frame. None capture enough of his face for anyone to recognize him. A shadowed profile. Eyes obscured by the smoke of battle, or hidden behind the glint of silvered sunglasses. "I'm not sure yet."

Dad lays the joint aside, shores up the knot on his robe, then pats his pockets for his reading glasses. "Right then. Let's get to work."

The first thought that occurs to me is that somewhere in this stack is Matty's nude photo of me, so uh… no. The second is that Dad isn't the only one so desperate to see things improve that he fooled himself into ignoring other dangers that lurked. And the third is that it's not just the impossible task of finding something which can free Mat-ty—it's how badly my memories of our relationship get tainted in the process.

After gathering the envelopes, I head to the hammock. "Thanks, Daddy," I say softly. "But I've got it from here."

Chapter 19:
Moonstone Promises

Matty stood behind me at the rail of the Gibraltar ferry. Morning sun swathed the city in warmth. The hillside rising from the port glowed, an immense terrace of white buildings flamed orange.

I felt giddy, taking in my first sight of Africa. Amidst honks and shouts, men in white robes bustled around stacks and stacks of mysterious bushels and crates. The air smelled of fish and the sea and spice. Though I wasn't sure whether I'd come to Africa to find myself or lose myself, this was where I needed to be. I had a job. I had a mission. I had a new boyfriend who'd gone almost two whole weeks without trying to kill himself.

Maybe I shouldn't think about that.

"So what do we do first?"

With that funny left eyebrow arch he always got when he was messing with me, he surveyed the chaos below. "Street begging? I could rent myself out as a male prostitute—how does my ass look in these jeans?"

He'd been ribbing me about the 'slave wages' I'd hired him at—the NGO, ReliefNet, needed promotional material for donors, I needed a guide, so it was perfect. But the detour through Morocco was our own. "I'd do you."

He waggled his eyebrows. "Say the word, sweetheart. For the right price, I'm yours."

"Sold." My heart was, at least. My mind wasn't so sure.

To me, what happened in Iraq didn't need forgiving; it'd been far beyond his control. Yet what scared me was it'd been beyond mine as well. I'd been naïve enough to assume his troubles weren't stronger than both of us. Since then, I'd spent hours poring over the DSM—dissociative flashbacks, hallucinations, psychosis. If I could figure out what happened, I could keep it from happening again. Couldn't I?

He nuzzled that secret spot behind my ear, the one that always sent a jolt straight to my toes. He nudged me around with a whispered caress, his restless body pressing me to the railing. God, but the man could kiss, kisses that started with my mouth, my face, my neck, but took over my whole body. My toes had adopted a permanent state of curl and he'd managed to convince my brain that oxygen wasn't nearly as important as it once believed.

With a hitch in his breath, he broke the kiss and shifted backwards. "You're too much for your own good."

Stifling a giggle, I shifted my leg to hide the ridge inside his jeans. "Are you sure the doctor didn't give you Viagra by mistake?"

An odd look came over his face. "Positive."

He really had been trying. The morning he got back from Iraq, he made some calls and disappeared for the day, returning with a vial of pills, a bottle of wine, and a stash of condoms. Not that he'd made any effort to use them, that night or since. Oddly, his libido had finally woken up on the flight to Malaga.

Beneath the shrieks and squawks of seaport gulls, we debarked into the marketplace, amidst shouts and voices in Arabic or French, smells of shisha and burlap, spice and earth, striped tents crammed together in a maze. Men in western clothes butchered meat while women in robes plucked chickens with lightning speed. The pace of it all was dizzying. The second I stepped off the curb I had to dodge a motorbike driven by a skinny pre-teen who was balancing an oversized basket and two siblings. With a tinny *peep-peep*, he zipped into the maze of stalls.

Matty grinned. "A few weeks in London and you've forgotten which side the rest of the world drives on?"

"Road, sidewalk, same difference," I replied, mentally counting my toes.

A grocer, mahogany skin tanned to leather, brandished a long, curly zucchini at Matty. "Control your woman!"

I bit back a retort, expecting Matty to have a better one, before realizing he hadn't heard a word. He was staring across the market with that numb look, the one he always got when he saw Rani. Disheartened, I reached for his cheek. "Did you even take your meds today, Matty?"

That brought him back. With a long, slow exhale, he dropped his forehead to mine. "Leah, you've seen me—I can't function on those things. They're in my pocket. I swear, I'll take one if it gets bad."

I hooked my thumbs into the straps on my backpack. "Can he hear me?"

"Who?"

"Rani."

His expression turned rueful. "You mean the figment of my imagination between the two guys hacking up codfish?"

Gently, I turned his jaw. "Tell him it's okay to let me watch out for you sometimes."

"Nope." After a quick kiss, he pulled me into the sea of market stalls, weaving between teetering stacks of tagine pots with domed lids and shelves filled with cone-shaped piles of spice. "My turn to take care of you."

We were heading to a spot in the Atlas Mountains, a couple of hundred miles south. "When we get there, I could teach you some yoga. The breathing exercises might help."

"Real men don't do yoga." Wearing an impish grin, he turned down a hidden aisle. "And not the kind of heavy breathing I had in mind."

Outwardly, I was playing it cool on the whole sex thing. We'd made a pact to stop blaming ourselves for things we couldn't change, and we were finding our way back to normal, whatever that was for us. But 'normal' for Matty was a Russian model. Or someone like Rosie, not a head case who flinched when he kissed below her navel. In desperation, I'd snuck off to a naughty shop in London, where the very nice, very gay proprietor sent me away with a tube of cherry goop and some tips on the finer points of a proper blowjob. "Think how flexible I'll be when we're done."

"Yoga it is."

In the doorway of a lime-washed dwelling, a man in a white crocheted skull cap, T-shirt and grocer's apron sat on the stoop, smoking a cigarette. Recognition lit Matty's face. "There's Mehdi."

Mehdi was a BU grad like Matty and, as of a few weeks before, me. He'd returned to Morocco to run the family business. We'd be hitching a ride on his trucks, which were heading south to pick up a winter harvest, our transport to my first stop with ReliefNet.

The two exchanged greetings. His wife, Yasmin, came downstairs, a wild-haired baby on her hip and a belly full of another. She beckoned us towards a tiled courtyard inside, where an emerald green parrot was doing tricks on a perch. "Come, come. I have breakfast."

She had mint green tea with tons of sugar, flat crepes called *msemmen* with honey and figs. She smacked Matty's hand as he stole a hot one off the pan. "You have not changed."

He licked honey off his finger. "Can't help it. Your mother spoiled me."

Yasmin passed me a sugar-dusted beignet with almond spread, revealing an intricate lotus design on her palm. "My mother was a henna girl in the market. And the best baker in five stalls."

Mehdi poured tea from a pot with a long necked spout, creating a field of steaming bubbles. "Yasmin was seven, Matthias and I were eight. I was helping Father unload a shipment of grain when I saw a filthy, sopping wet boy with blond hair stealing the *amlou baghrir* her mother set out for us."

I stared at Matty, licking spread off my thumb. "Why were you wet?"

"Jumped off the ferry," he said, reaching for more. "First time I ran away from my folks. Or second. I forget."

"The ferry, as in the one we came in on?" I said. "You're lucky you didn't drown."

"Let's just say it was better than the alternative."

Mehdi raised an eyebrow—almost as if he was asking whether Matty needed a rescue from the whole conversation. Once I noticed the way Matty was absentmindedly rubbing his tattoo, it dawned on me that little boys did not jump off moving boats in busy ports without good reason. I squeezed his hand. He squeezed back, winked, then made a shameless grab for my beignet.

Yasmin gave him a sympathetic smile, bouncing the baby on her hip as she flipped another crepe. "He was so wretched my mother scooped him up and made us all a second breakfast."

I popped a date into his mouth. "Is this what you do? Travel the world looking for kindly women to make you breakfast?"

With a wink, he drained his tea. "I have no idea what you mean."

Mehdi took the baby from Yasmin. "So where will your travels take you, my friends?"

"Three stops in Mali," I said, ticking off our scheduled stops on my fingers. "Then a couple in Niger, which is cool—I've wanted to visit there since I was little."

Matty's brow furrowed. "You have?"

"Don't you remember?" I asked. "That whole story about my dad's biographer tracing a slave route back to an Igbo village? Why do you think he told you to take lots of pictures?"

He rubbed his eyebrow. "Uh…"

"Seriously?"

We'd had this long, amazing conversation the night I accepted the job, after I told my parents. I'd let my entire identity get bound up in this trip, as if working in Africa would magically fix the way I'd always felt like my father's daughter on the inside, but never looked like her on the outside. I wasn't there to be anyone's savior, white or otherwise. I could finally just be Leah, whoever she turned out to be.

It'd all spilled out, twenty years of being the girl with no box to check on the form, of feeling like I'd betrayed whichever half of me I didn't pick, of being afraid somebody would call me a liar whichever I did. Of strangers making comments that I acted like one or didn't act like the other. Matty listened patiently. Or at least I thought he had.

"Sorry," he murmured, giving me a quick kiss that made it better. "Told you, it's those stupid happy pills." As if sensing I was about to point out that he should be *on* the stupid happy pills, he steered the subject to the trip. "After that it's Chad, then we head to Sudan."

Something unsettled came over Mehdi's face. "You may wish to rethink the last part of your journey. I hear reports from our suppliers of unrest in the south."

Matty slurped his tea. "What kind of unrest?"

"Your kind," Mehdi replied. "Come. You will need supplies."

We drove for hours on a poppy-lined highway, passing smoky tagine shacks and kids selling everything from hashish to honey out of flatbeds. The Atlas Mountains were a purplish shadow on the horizon when we said goodbye to the trucks and set out on foot.

Ten miles later, we were nearly there. The air tasted sweet. A warm breeze rushed past my cheeks. I could hear the water. Finger to his lips, Matty pointed to the eastern ridge, where a Barbary macaque paced the branches of a windswept cedar. We were close enough to see the yellowy tufts tipping its ruff and spot the tiny baby clinging to its back.

Matty raised his camera, reeling off a few shots before turning it on me.

"Nobody is going to pay for shots of sweaty old me," I pointed out, transfixed by the monkey.

"You're dating a photographer," he said, smiling. "Get used to it."

He'd gone quiet after returning from his supply mission with Mehdi, but since we'd struck out on our own, it was almost serene being around him. Or it would've been, if it wasn't weirding me out. 'Serene' and 'Matty' were two words that didn't belong in the same sentence.

"So what did you find out about Sudan?"

He scratched his neck, as if deciding whether to admit checking into it. "There's some heavy fighting in the Darfur region, near the border with Chad. Doesn't sound safe for you to be there."

I had a job to do. People were expecting me. A lot was riding on this for ReliefNet. "Who is it safe for? The people who live there? You?"

He put down the lens. "Are you mad?"

"Maybe I am." It was irrational; on some level I knew that. Or it was perfectly rational, just delayed, it was the fit I should've thrown when he'd shown up on my doorstep without explaining a damn thing. "Would you go if I wasn't here?"

A massive flock of rock birds took flight from the trees, pursued by a red-tipped kestrel. The raptor dove. The flock split and curled like eddies in the ocean, moving as if it had one mind. He raised the lens again. "Doesn't matter. You are."

"What happened to us being a team? What happened to not patronizing me?"

"What happened to trusting me?"

"I trust you a hell of a lot more than people seem to think I should."

He looked down at his sneakers and kicked the red earth. "Then trust me when I say you wouldn't be helping anyone by going. There's a decent chance you'd make things worse. I'm not coddling you, I'm telling you flat out that you don't have the experience and you'd be putting us both at risk."

The kestrel alit on the ridge, lowering its head. I watched it, willing tears to stay out of my eyes. There was no arguing with anything he'd said—what was wrong with me?

Iraq had made clear there was so much I didn't understand about the world. At first, Matty had been there with answers when I had questions, he'd pushed me to do things I didn't know I was capable of doing. Then all of a sudden he was gone, and all I had left were people who were convinced I was a liability. I nearly let them convince me too.

Matty turned my chin. "I'm not leaving this time, Leah. I promise."

Truth told, I was finally, properly and utterly terrified of what I was getting into with him, and instead of confronting that, I was picking a fight to avoid the issue. I sniffled and wiped my nose. "Thought you said you can't read my mind."

"Only when it's obvious." He smiled at the macaque. "Come on. Let's go around so we don't disturb mama."

Though it seemed to roll off him, it gnawed at me as we picked our way through the scree leading up a narrow trail. Darfur, my job, the nagging feeling I was keeping him from his. Or whether that was actually a bad thing.

The view from the top was breathtaking, a narrow canyon of red earth and rock, the wider desert beyond, hues of tan with wide swaths of dusky green. Dozens of small waterfalls washed over the sunlit rock, collecting in a lazy swirling pool fifty feet below. Even in winter, the valley was lush, surrounded by cedars, roots zigzagging out of the rocks.

Matty took my waist. "This is home for the next few days. How'd I do?"

The longer we stood, the farther the rest of the world drifted away. Here it couldn't touch us. "Wow."

We climbed down into the red rock canyon, which had been worn smooth by the river and wind. The sun was disappearing, and there was a chill in the air, so while I pitched our little tent on a sandy spot by the shore, he got a fire going with wood from the banks. The flames popped and crackled outside, over the falling water and twilight song of desert insects.

"We should have marshmallows," I called, spreading our sleeping bags inside the tent. He'd opened some sweet-tasting contraband wine he got from Mehdi, and it'd gone to my head. "Or hotdogs on sticks. Do you give out merit badges?"

"Dinner's started," he called. "Moroccan lentils. Yasmin's recipe. Gonna jump in the water and wash off while they're cooking."

After the long hike, both dinner and a swim—theoretically—sounded good. Given that it wasn't much above fifty degrees, the latter probably involved hypothermia. On the plus side, it'd also involve cuddling and blankets and the fire. "Hang on, I'll grab my suit."

The tent opening rustled. His fire-warmed arm wrapped my waist, and we fell in a tangle of torsos and limbs. "No suit," he murmured. After rolling me to my back, he set to the button on my shorts. His kisses took the chill from my neck, light and warm, like spring rain laced with wine. Eyes closed, I explored the taut muscles of his back, feeling the sinews contract. He lifted my top, hands spread wide over my belly, and his breath tickled my navel. "Relax, Leah. I'm not in a hurry."

"Come on, I'm totally fine," I protested. "I didn't flinch!"

His eyes twinkled in the dusky light. "If you were wound any tighter, you'd bounce off the canyon walls. I'll race you. Last one in does the dishes."

He crawled out of the tent. By the time I caught up, he was standing in ankle deep water on a rock ledge, bare ass to the breeze.

He was lean and strong, with a fading tan that highlighted all the little scars he'd collected over the years. I slipped off my sneakers and joined him on the ledge. It dipped and disappeared into the pool, smooth rock and cool water soothing my tired feet. For the first time, I let myself look at him, *all* of him, those seen-it-all grey eyes, proud chin, the light sprinkle of hair on his chest, the path of it leading down to his groin. He wasn't the boy I'd grown away from, he wasn't some midnight mistake—he was just Matty, as naked in form as he usually was in soul.

He let me take a good long eyeful, then beckoned me closer, enveloped by the mist from the falls. Pulse racing, I plunged into the spray, pressing my body to his. The water soaked my clothes, chilling my skin. "Matty, it's freezing."

"Could've fooled me," he murmured. We kissed again, a kiss that tasted of dusk and rain. My hands slipped from his back to his ass. His cock stirred against my hip. "God, you're beautiful."

Fingers spread wide, I slid my hand down the outside of his thigh, up the inside. His breathing turned slow and shallow, so I took him in hand. I wanted to taste him, to feel him surrender. I wanted him to pull me onto the ragged side of life and see how long we could teeter before we fell over the edge. *No turning back from here.*

Every move was a little seduction. Goosebumps rose as he fingered the edge of my top, so I lifted my arms. He slipped the wet shirt over my head, exploring each curve on the way, grazing the side of my breast. Down, down he went, my ribs, my waist, slipping to my hips, tugging down my shorts with agonizing slowness. As they fell to the mist, he drifted behind me, hard against the small of my back. Swaying to some unheard melody, he kissed my neck. A warm frisson went to my core as he released the clasp on my bra. One hand caressed my breast. The other traveled south. Gentle fingers dipped into my undies. My legs went weak when he found what he was seeking. He held me tighter. "Is this okay?"

I reached backwards, cupping his head, and kissed him. "Matty, we promised," I whispered. "No bad memories, no holding back…"

"I'm not," he said, lips warming my neck. "Savoring." Then in one fluid motion, he stripped me bare. Nothing left between us, not even night air. The kestrel screeched. As it echoed off the rocks, he grinned, took a step towards the ledge, and back-flipped into the pool.

"Showoff," I said, as he surfaced, holding my underwear.

"Little bit," he chuckled. He slicked his hair, watching me in all my nakedness. "Now you're ready for a swim."

I was ready for *something,* but it sure wasn't a swim. Especially not with the huge underwater shadow weaving around. Shivering, I sat on the ledge, dipping my toes into the water, and pointed behind him. "Something's about to eat you."

"There are some big-ass carp in here. They're harmless." He drifted closer, then reached for my ankles. With a wicked, hungry expression, he spread my knees and nestled between, warming me with his body. "Unlike me…"

My nipples went taut at the first brush of his lips. With agonizing slowness, he worked his way down, from the hollow of my throat to the tops of my breasts, then my navel, making it clear exactly what he was hungry for. I leaned forward and breathed *don't* into his hair. "I like doing it. Getting it, not so much."

Brow furrowed, he climbed out, and sat next to me, steam rising off his body. "Here's the thing. I'd love a chance to change your mind, but I'm not sure if A, you're thinking about what he did and don't want to say, or B, you never had anybody who really knew how to get you off, or C, somebody convinced you that you're supposed to be shy about it."

None of which I had any intention of admitting to. "D, I'm freezing, and you need to hurry up and ravish me before we both catch our deaths?"

Chuckling, he wrapped me in his arms. "Yes ma'am." He walked us both towards the blanket by the fire, nuzzling my neck the whole way. After guiding me down to the soft flannel, he nestled on my side, cupped my cheek with one hand and slipped the other between my legs. "If you don't like it, tell me and I'll stop, okay?"

Maybe it was the wine, maybe it was him, but no surrender was ever so sweet. As an aftershock ripped through me, he wrapped my legs around his waist. His face was flushed, hips rocking, every inch of his need pressing against me. "Tell me you don't want to wait anymore. Tell me you want what I want."

What did I want? My skin, slick against his, the weight of him on top of me, every breath *please god please*, let this be the one where he thrust himself inside. "I want you."

He groaned. "Don't move. I buried the condoms in my bag so I wouldn't get ideas."

I played with the stubble on his jaw, wet bristles tickling my finger. "We've both had this particular idea since November, remember?"

Grinning, he pressed into me, just the tip. "Do I get points for trying?"

As the last rays of sunlight left the canyon wall, we made love at the water's edge, filling each other in every sense. The stars came out, the desert sang its song, and the world fell away, until all that was left was warm sand and the drowsy comfort of his arms.

He'd promised to show me what sex could be like. Sex with Matty was stolen moments at the edge of a Moroccan lake, it was the wash of relief and not being able to get his clothes off fast enough when he came home after a trip, it was waking up at three a.m. when the sheets were drenched and he was shaking and knowing only one thing could make it right.

Lying on his chest, I ran my finger over the raised white ridge on his left pec, drunk with the promise of places I hadn't yet seen, stories I hadn't yet heard. "Where'd this one come from?"

"No clue." He brushed grains of sand from my temple, and gave me a tender kiss, more at peace than I'd ever seen him. "It means everything, by the way…you being out here with me."

I nestled in the crook of his arm, in the grip of his spell. "Getting sappy on me?"

"I'm serious. This is my life, Leah, and it's a lot better now that you're part of it." He smoothed my hair, and together we watched the stars, billions and billions of them, more than I'd ever seen. Then he rolled over, rooting in his bag, setting his camera on the blanket.

"Already?" I giggled, thinking he was going for another condom. But there was a small silver ring in his palm, little scrolls carved into the band and a shimmering white moonstone in the center.

It suddenly occurred to me that I'd barely been single a day since I was fifteen. "Uh…what's that?"

A shy smile crossed his face. "Not what you're thinking. Not yet at least."

I let out a breath. "Okay, good."

He rolled the band between his forefinger and thumb, letting the firelight play off the stone. "The guy in the market told me moonstone is said to reveal truth. I'm giving it to you as a promise—no matter what you say, you don't trust me, and I don't blame you. But you know how I feel and I want to show you that whatever you need me to do, I'll do."

I slipped the ring onto my finger, contemplating it as the fire crackled. Was he right? Was it the real reason I'd flipped out on him earlier? It all came to the same thing, the fear that I'd let myself fall and then one day, I'd turn and he wouldn't be there.

My throat got tight. "I need you to promise that I'm never going to find you like I did that first night. No car running in the garage, no empty bottle of pills. No phone call telling me that you closed your eyes and walked into crossfire."

He blinked twice. I could tell it wasn't what he was expecting. "I can't always control it, Leah—you've seen that yourself."

I sat up, knees to my breasts, and traced a circle in the sand. "I get that your job has risks and I can live with that. I get that life has hurt you in ways I can't always understand and I can't always fix. I get that the reason you run off to war all the time is because it's easier than being at war with yourself. I get all that. It's part of why… why I love you. But I can't love someone who thinks he's beyond help."

He went quiet, and I wasn't sure if he was watching me or the stars. "You couldn't have possibly been this beautiful the day we met," he said, reaching for his camera. "I would've never let you out of my sight."

I raised my eyebrow. "The magic Matty truth ring says you're changing the subject. And you really are nuts if you think I'm letting you take a picture of me like this."

Smiling, he took off the lens cap. "If you want that promise, I need something to remember when you asked me to make it."

Searching for all the bravado I could muster, I stretched out on the sand. "Okay. Let's give it a shot."

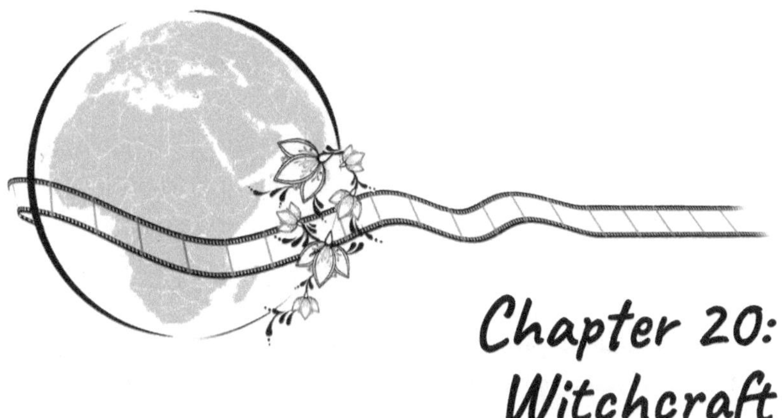

Chapter 20:
Witchcraft

FEBRUARY 2003
MOPTI REGION, MALI

The turboprop jostled and bounced as the pilot made a graceful skim over the plateau. Matty nudged my arm, pointing over the left wing. A herd of giraffes craned their long necks to nibble an acacia tree. A family of elephants splashed in a brown river. Fishermen in a cream-sailed pirogue were casting nets.

Content, I rested my head on his shoulder, captured by the lazy peace of the country. We were arriving at our fifth stop, a field hospital near the Niger border, courtesy of a Chadian bush pilot named Bobo. It'd been a month since we'd left our canyon hideaway, shag-happy and exhausted. Even Matty's PTSD seemed to have eased. He'd been teaching me Arabic, meeting the aid workers and locals, taking photos. I'd filed my first two dispatches with Relief Net on a stopover in the capital, and there was talk of extending the trip. Life, quite simply, had become perfect.

Mud brick dwellings rose on the far side of the plateau. Bobo bobbled us to a landing on a grassy strip at the edge of the village, near an enormous mudhole, where a man stood waist-deep, making bricks. Others were smoothing the same mud into the cracks of a nearby hut, climbing nimbly up the walls using wooden pegs which jutted from the surface. Though it was barely nine, a scorching wall of heat hit me as soon as Matty opened the door. Our liaison, Dr. Geffen, was waiting.

Fodi Geffen was a native Malian, who'd left to get a medical degree in Paris, then returned to found a network of rural health clinics. Stretch-legged, with wild hair and deeply intense eyes, he greeted us with a massive outstretched hand. "*Bienvenue à Sangha, Monsieur and Madame Atkins.*"

"*S'il vous plaît, appelez-moi Leah.*" I overlooked the married thing, since he'd introduced himself to me directly instead of to Matty. Which was the opposite of every other head of station we'd met so far. I kept reminding myself that overworked aid workers simply did not have time for twenty-one-year-old newbies from the home office asking dumb questions, but it was hard not to notice that no matter what I asked, they'd direct every answer to him. Matty's solution was to pretend he only spoke Portuguese and wander off with his camera. Mine was that I was just going to have to try harder. Mostly because becoming less young, less white, and less female wasn't an option.

The last month had been eye-opening. The aid sector was a business, a cut-throat one at times, drowning in its own do-gooder impulses and red tape. Not to mention there were some *seriously* weird people working in it—so far, we'd met Jesus himself seven times and Mary Magdalene twice.

Then, at our last stop in Sikasso, the head of station had put together a glossy presentation about how great the place was doing, complete with handouts. I walked out thinking I'd finally figured out how to do my job. Until Matty sat me down and showed me the real story his camera had captured, and waited for me to realize I'd gotten rolled.

'*Ask me, the home office set you up to fail*', he'd said. '*They want to be able to say Dale Atkin's daughter thinks they're already doing everything right. Convince you to get a few quotes from him and they're gold. Make up your mind if you're going to let them or not.*'

"We're looking forward to meeting you and the rest of your team," I said to Dr. Geffen. This visit was going to be different. We'd been practicing.

Dr. Geffen beckoned the nurse over. "Please, this is Dima. I regret, we are the team for now. The others left yesterday for Chad. There is a refugee crisis on the border."

In the capital, we'd come across open air weapons bazaars, Kalashnikovs and grenade launchers hanging with belts of ammunition inside brightly colored tents. Matty engaged the dealers, where had they come from, who was buying, who was their competition. Whatever story he'd been chasing in Iraq had started the same way, and truthfully, I wasn't sure how I felt about it. "In Darfur? It's gotten worse?"

"It was bad to start." Dr. Geffen extended his arm. "Come. I will show you the village."

While we unloaded the plane, Matty talked in low tones to Bobo, until Dr. Geffen was called away on an emergency. We ended up wandering into the animist section of the village, which was closest to the field hospital. Most people spoke Bambara, a local dialect, which meant getting by on gestures and the few words Matty knew. Ten minutes in, I gave up on my questions in favor of kicking around a ball of tied-up rags with the village children, which was more fun anyhow.

My favorite were the hedgehogs, which darted in and out of stacks of drying river reeds scattered between dwellings. Smoky three-stone cooking fires smoldered inside, the source of the persistent cough plaguing most of the women. Many had visible tumors in their chests or throats, something that had started soon after a chemical plant had been built upstream. I was under strict orders not to mention the plant—orders I was both dying of curiosity about and had every intention of ignoring.

The clinic's ultrasound had been broken for months, with no hope of repair. The dwellings were open to the air, with clay pots and gourds perched in pass-through cubbies in the walls, which, given the unholy spawn-of-Satan bloodsuckers buzzing around, was behind the astronomical malaria rate. Once Geffen returned, we spent a long time talking with the wives in the village. Matty, whose mind was clearly elsewhere, dutifully kept shooting.

The tour ended at the council hut, four short stone pillars topped with bundles of tied sticks. A group of men sat cross-legged below, amidst a heated argument, which, near as I could tell, involved the sand pit outside, the fox tracks running through it, and the local shaman/healer. The village chief, a gnarled man in a crimson *kufi* cap and purple *dashiki*, oversaw it from the doorway of his house, flipping away flies with a switch made of pure white horsetail.

One of the councilmen crawled out, calling something to the chief, whose wife came out with a handful of shot glasses and a wide-bellied gourd. At his nod, she sloshed yellowish liquid from the gourd into the glasses. "*Banjiki*," the chief said proudly, picking three of the glasses with his spindly fingers.

Rotgut would've been an understatement. My eyes watered at the first sniff. "Am I supposed to drink this?" I whispered to Matty. "What is it?"

"Distilled palm wine." He tossed his back. "Don't worry, it'll come up sooner or later."

I held my nose, did likewise, and *oh dear god* the burn. The council cheered and laughed. My eyes were crossed when they poured me another. Coughing, I tried to wave them off.

With a mischievous grin, the chief took the gourd, pointed to my feet, pantomimed drinking the shot, then hopped on his left side. Everyone laughed.

Matty chuckled, steadying my arm. "He says the first shot went to your right leg. He doesn't want you to fall over."

Dizziness and probable mercury poisoning aside, they made us feel at home, feeding us a breakfast of bean cake and millet mash fried with plantains. The chief, Moussa, talked of easier times when he was a boy, when the cows were full of milk and the river held so many fish he could nearly walk across without sinking in. And then came the plant upriver.

That was as far as we got when a heavily pregnant girl appeared by the hospital, groping her way along the wall.

No more than seventeen or eighteen, she clutched her belly, blood staining the saffron yellow *pagne* she wore. Her legs were skeletal and bloodied and she made a pained, plaintive cry for help. Dr. Geffen and Dima ran for her, and all hell broke loose in the council hut. The shaman leapt up and thunked his head, gesticulating between her and the fox tracks.

Geffen and Dima guided her towards a boulder, where she squatted. He shoved his hands under her *pagne.* Dima prodded her belly, asking rapid-fire questions. The girl heaved through answers between contractions.

"Her pelvis is that of a child." Geffen lifted her, carrying her towards the clinic. "We will need helpers." But as Dima beckoned the women, the chief shook his switch. They retreated. Geffen scowled, jerking his chin at me. "You—come with us."

Though suffering the effects of the *banjiki,* I ran for the clinic door. "Why won't he let them help?"

"She is a bad omen." Dima turned her back to the shaman. "From another village. He has been warning them of an outsider surrounded by death."

"So? It could be us!" I was scared for her, frustrated, and helpless. "Tell them that!"

"Her husband turned her out," Matty said quietly, his eye to the lens. "Four pregnancies, no baby. They know her here. The chief says she's cursed."

Hot tears welled up. I wanted him to be joking, or wrong, or for it to somehow be untrue. For a teenager in labor to walk from god-knows-where, only to be turned away again… "It's not right."

Geffen carried her through the main doors to an operating table. Dima started an IV. Geffen pushed a syringe of something into it. The girl's face relaxed. He glanced up from his preparations long enough to catch my eye. "Ms. Leah, you will not survive here if you approach it this way. Your cultural values do not apply. If you want to help this girl, find a way to work within hers."

God, it hurt, hearing him say that. *That* was the lesson here? That I needed a lecture on colonialism? I got it—life here was inextricably defined by who'd oppressed you in the past. The British, the Portuguese, the

Dutch or French, or more recently, America, which damn well should've known better. I'd had no illusions of shared experience, only my own, gained from a lifetime of hiding in plain sight, something I couldn't do here. I'd been raised by parents desperate to shield me from the racism they'd experienced, despite the system designed and determined to thwart them at every turn. Fine, I was new at this, but I knew enough to realize that bringing our messed-up 'cultural values' here wouldn't solve a damn thing. But why was only half the population worthy of the liberation so desperately sought? How the hell was I supposed to 'find a way' to work with that? Why did women have to wait?

I started to wonder if maybe I wasn't cut out for this after all. And I told myself it wouldn't help getting pissed at a bunch of withered old tribesmen. Maybe my American eyes couldn't make sense of what they'd seen. Either way, I couldn't turn off the way it made me feel. In short? Fuck the fucking patriarchy.

Ba-deep, went the monitor at Geffen's side. I took the girl's hand. She looked at me, barely registering a change of expression. "What's her name?" I said. "Will her baby be okay?"

"She is Cisse." With a flash of his scalpel, a crimson line appeared across her belly. "And I think she has come in time."

Next thing I knew, I was staring inside her, rippling uterus and all, the baby squirming in a caul. Geffen stuck his hand inside. I swallowed, nauseous from the *banjiki*, the blood and the smell. "How do I tell her?"

"*i denkura bè kènè.*"

Cisse squeezed my hand. Then came a tiny squawk. A moment later, Geffen placed a crying baby girl on her chest. A tear rolled down Cisse's cheek. My adrenaline faded into a sense of awe. "How do I ask if she's happy?"

"*i bè bo neema.*"

She nodded, caressing her daughter's face. Then Geffen plopped her placenta into a tray and offered it to her. Overwhelmed, and certain I was about to be sick, I went outside.

Matty was sitting in the shade beneath a spiny baobab tree, scribbling in his notebook. I made it ten feet before I threw up.

"I warned you about that stuff," he said, frowning. "You okay?"

I wasn't. I was exhausted, drunk, hot, and smelled like the wrong side of a goat. I was covered in mosquito bites and sunburn, traipsing around places I'd never understand, not to mention watching a teenager being cut open in front of me, and to top it off, my period had started and there was blood running down my leg. Shaking, I wiped my mouth. "I hope you don't want kids anytime soon."

He closed the notebook. "Plans to subject anyone to a childhood like mine? No."

At the time, I didn't think much of it. It wasn't the first hint of that nature he'd dropped, and as someone without an ounce of maternal instinct, it was a relief to have it in the open. "That was disgusting," I said, dropping down beside him.

He handed me a tin of mints. "See one birth, you've seen them all."

"I mean what happened at the council hut." I rattled the tin. "They would've let her die over some silly superstitions about foxes? Come on."

He tucked the notebook under his butt. "When you live like this, watching your children die year after year, people need explanations for why."

Feeling suddenly defensive, I popped the mint into my mouth, bit down hard, then rummaged through my backpack for my toothbrush and a tampon. "Because they don't have screens on the damn windows. Because they don't have enough to eat, because people keep starting bullshit wars, because people treat other people like property. Because instead of doing something about the freaking *chemical* company making them sick they go all Salem Witch Trials on a teenage girl."

Staring up through the thick branches, he ran his hands through his hair. "After I lost my faith, I used to sit out at night, watching the stars, begging for something to fill the void. There was this one time, I'd gotten some serious shit from this shaman in Tanzania. I had no idea what it was, and I was pretty sure it'd worn off when all of a sudden, I started feeling my soul again. Except it wasn't just mine, it was the soul in the jackal that had been sniffing around all night, the soul in the rocks, it was a soul in every grain of sand. They were all alive and conscious, and I looked up at the stars and finally felt part of the world again."

He must've noticed the way I was staring, because he scratched the fuzz on his neck. "Course, right after that, the jackal turned into the shaman and ran away cackling, so…"

Matty liked to downplay his spiritual struggles, but the way he'd grown up had left an indelible mark, an awareness of things human eyes couldn't always see. In a way, I was jealous.

I ran my finger over the spirals of his notebook and told myself to chill. "What were you writing?"

After glancing over at Bobo, who was kicking the turboprop's tires, he craned his head, resting on the baobab. "Notes for Jack. He's been talking about getting back into field work but can't seem to find the right story."

I thought he'd meant the chemical plant, until he closed his eyes.

"God, Leah—some of this stuff, you can't imagine. The Sudanese government is paying the rebels to go rampaging through villages on the south. Weapons are pouring in at rural airfields. Someone needs to get on this. Might as well be Jack."

"You want it to be you," I said softly.

"ReliefNet wants us out here for another two months, remember?" He shook his head. "Don't worry. I'm not going anywhere."

I told him to go. It was the only thing either one of us could do. I could see it on his face. The story had grabbed him and wouldn't let go. And me, I was surrounded by women making it on their own, facing longer odds than I'd ever dreamed, and it left me with a desperate desire to prove I could do this job, *any* job without relying on my boyfriend or my father or basically anyone male.

But Matty was equally desperate to prove he was serious about the promises he'd made. At first it was no. Then 'hell no'. He was convinced I was testing him.

"For crying out loud, I'm not helpless," I said. "My stops and contacts are all planned."

"This is Africa. Plans change."

"I got myself out of Iraq, didn't I?"

That almost shut him up. "No, Leah."

With a sputter, Bobo started the engines. Matty's head turned, gaze lingering. I turned his chin back until he met my eyes. "I'll meet you in Chad. Three weeks. If you give me your spare camera, I can take the photos myself. They won't be as good as yours, but they'll be good enough. You get to do your job, I get to do mine. That's how this works."

A low noise rumbled out of his throat. He picked up his bag, slung a second camera off his shoulder, and waved at Bobo. "You're as nuts as I am—you know that right?"

"That's why you love me."

Together, we ran to the runway. The drone of the engine lowered a notch. Bobo hopped out of the cockpit and opened the door. After a few minutes of haggling, the deal was done.

Matty took my waist. "What am I going to do without you for three weeks?"

Hot, dusty wind from the propellers blew my hair all over my face. I brushed a wayward strand out of my eyes. "Just come home, okay?"

"Always will, if it means coming home to you." He laced his fingers through mine, kissing the ring he'd given me. "Consider it a promise."

Second thoughts slammed home. "You've got your meds? And you remember your breathing exercises—"

"Yes dear."

We kissed, and he headed up the steps. At the airframe, he turned, with the oddest expression on his face. "Do you want to get married?"

Had to be the noise from the engine. There was no way I heard him right. But he just stood there, hands shoved deep into the pockets of his jeans.

My voice came out like a squeak. "What happened to 'not yet'?"

He came down two steps. "It's later."

I didn't move. "You're crazy."

He took the last two, cupping the sides of my face. "My job, you take the shot when you've got it. I've got everything I ever wanted."

I stood there, dumbfounded, heart pounding. "Why now?"

One hand slid to the back of my neck, bringing my forehead to his lips. "That story I told? About feeling my soul again? The only other time was those nights with you in Morocco."

"Matty—"

"Just think about it," he said, backing up the steps. "Maybe this is the life you want too."

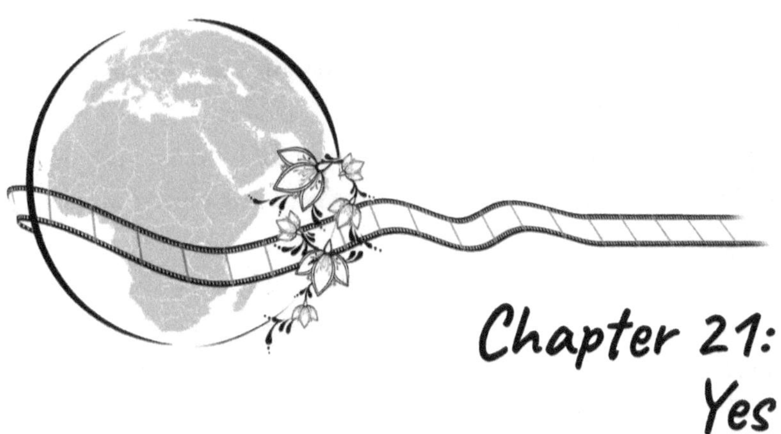

Chapter 21: Yes

MARCH 2003
ABECHE REFUGEE CAMP, CHAD/SUDAN
BORDER

This was Africa—plans change, Matty had said, and boy was he right. My feet had barely hit the ground when ReliefNet's entire operation pulled up stakes, heading for a refugee camp in Chad, on the site of a Catholic mission. Reports said five hundred people a day were streaming over the Sudanese border. So off I went with the others.

Three months before, I'd been running around Boston with protest flyers. Now I was stumbling through the remotest place I'd ever been, no roads, no buildings save for a lone church, swimming in an endless sea of displaced people, most with nothing but the clothes on their backs. Sometimes less. What little water we had came from the Chadian government, which did nothing but lie and demand bribes. Food was growing ever more scarce.

Worse, I wasn't even sure I was helping. They needed doctors, nurses, engineers. I was a go-fer, running between senior staff, making lists, begging for supplies. By day I wandered the camps holding hands with lost children, searching, often futilely, for their parents. By night I fell asleep in a dusty field crowded with other aid workers, surrounded by the sounds of sobbing, of singing. Quiet voices, harsh ones, fighting, lovemaking. Sometimes there was gunfire. The army would come into the camps, waving their weapons, shooting into the air. The third night, a group of rebels crossed the border and marched off a hundred boys before anyone knew what had happened. I watched people take in children they'd never laid eyes on before; I saw a dying mother not recognize her own son.

It was the most soul-draining, dehumanizing three weeks I'd ever had, and near the end, the mission priest found me sobbing in the nave of his church. *Yes, you are empty. God has made you such so he may fill you again.*

Empty. In some ways, I was. But I was more confused. I thought about law school and my father and the partnership he'd always planned for DJ instead of me. And then I thought about being here, about feeling needed and helpful, as if I was making a difference, and then I wanted Matty there to help me make sense of it all, but in my thirst for independence, I'd sent him away.

The next day, the twenty-third after we'd said goodbye, I awoke to the same priest shaking my arm. "You have a visitor."

When I flew out of the tent, Matty was picking his way through the blankets, limping and clutching his side. *What happened…they told me you were here…are you okay… I'm fine,* and then he closed his eyes and folded me into his arms and for a few brief seconds it was all right.

But he wasn't alone. Behind him stood a Sudanese woman in a tattered and singed purple robe, her face bearing the marks of ritual scarring, and she carried with her a girl of maybe two. Though the woman's arms were covered in weeping burns, she clung to the child as if her soul depended on the contact.

Matty's face was haunted. "Her name is Nyali. Nyali Waleed." He kicked the dust. "She needs a doctor—they hurt her, bad, but she doesn't want anyone to touch her. I told her you know what it's like."

I wanted to curl up into a ball. What happened to me wasn't the same, not even close. "You think being held down and beaten by soldiers is the same as—?"

"For fuck's sake, Leah." Clearly itching to say more, he tugged at the scraggly growth on his face. "Who's closer, you or me?"

My mind went on autopilot. Matty survived his job by reaching into the depths of his soul, holding fast to the things that made him furious about the world. I was only beginning to understand what my job would take from me. "I can get her registered while they're treating her," I said numbly, offering to take the child.

But Nyali clung to the girl more tightly, forehead to the little girl's cheek. "No."

"She had a husband and four boys too," Matty said, his jaw shaking. "Dead, the whole goddamn village. I couldn't…we were too… there were so many…"

One man with a camera couldn't stop an army. I knew it, even if he didn't. Closing my eyes, I let the rising sun warm my face, searching for some sign of hope in all this. "The medical tents are this way."

But Nyali wouldn't go. She wanted to work. '*My girl needs food*', she said. We finally got her to agree that if she let the doctors dress her burns, we'd find work for her. She wasn't fine, not by any stretch, but it kept her occupied, it kept her from feeling so goddamn helpless, and at sunset, she hugged her daughter, told us she'd come find us tomorrow, and went into the church.

Matty collapsed onto the far wall, dragging me down with him. "God, I missed you."

"You too," I said, burrowing into his chest.

The priest had been right, I was filled again. It was the feeling I wanted to come home to, it was the warmth of trust rewarded. We'd survived apart, but we were stronger together.

So as we huddled together in the gathering dawn, I told him I loved him and took a deep breath. "Were you serious about what you asked before you left?"

He held me tighter and whispered *yes*.

"Then that's my answer," I whispered back. "Yes."

Chapter 22:
An Uninvited Guest
SEPTEMBER 2003
PROVINCETOWN, MASSACHUSETTS

Matty

Leah looked like Aphrodite at the shore. She was barefoot, in a gauzy white dress that fluttered in the sea breeze. Her hair fell in stray wisps around her face. Behind her, the bonfire crackled, flames leaping against the dusky sky. The sun was just beginning to set.

I snuck up behind and kissed her neck, running my hands over her bare shoulders. "No bride should be alone on her wedding day. 'Specially one as gorgeous as you."

She stole my beer and took a sip. "Shh. I escaped. Be quiet or they'll find us."

'They' were the hundred and fifty guests milling around her parents' beachfront like Ginsberg's proverbial angel-headed hipsters. The day was a blur. Champagne and beer were flowing, and I'd had my share. Smooth rocks glowed cherry red at the edges of deep sand pits, where beneath the canvas and seaweed rested a good half-ton of lobsters and clams, corn on the cob and linguiça. Me? There was only one thing I was hungry for.

More in love with her than ever, I turned her towards the sailboat moored at the dock. We'd spend the next ten days sailing the rocky coast of Maine before heading back to Africa. "Say the word and I'll carry you on board right now."

Two very naughty fingers walked up my crotch. "My mother would have kittens."

I nipped her earlobe, exploring the fasteners on her dress, calculating how long it'd take to get her out of it. "Your mother has been riding the Xanax Express since five o'clock this morning."

"And thank god for that."

Leah and her mother had had a knock-down-drag-out row after we came home and said we were getting hitched. We knew it was fast, we knew Leah was taking a leap with me, but we both just…knew. Half the Atlantic seaboard had heard them hollering at each other. Dale went into the carriage house long enough to grab two highballs and a dusty bottle of Glendronach. *'I put this down the day she was born. You appreciate her for who she is. That's all I can ask.'*

Dale treated me more as a son than my father ever had, but at the moment, I had a sneaking suspicion he was the reason Leah was off by herself. When the caterers uncovered the clam bake, he'd made a crack about paying for the wedding by selling his law practice. When Leah realized he was serious, she wasn't happy.

"Are you upset with your dad?"

Her body went slack in my arms. "Seriously, what does he think? That I'm going to jump on the mommy track and follow you around with a pair of slippers?"

Dale was old school, no two ways about it, but that wasn't why he did it. I nibbled her earlobe. "Nobody told me I get slippers with this deal."

She gave me an indignant poke in the ribs. "I'm still going to go to law school—I can defer my admission to Columbia for a year. Haven't I been saying that since I took the job?"

I held her tighter. "Your dad sees what everyone else who loves you sees—working with ReliefNet makes you a thousand times happier than some law job ever could."

"It's working with you." She faced the ocean. "You get that, right?"

Husband and wife, Leah and I stood together, swaying to Jimmy Buffet until I caught a glimpse of a woman standing atop the far dunes. Waist-length dirty blonde hair, navy skirt down to her ankles. It was my mother.

"Hope to God I'm seeing things again," I said, blinking.

Leah traced her toe through the sand. "Don't be upset. She wanted to see her son on his wedding day."

"You talked to her?"

She hesitated. "Her face… I mean, you told me what happened to her, but… I think I might've been staring."

From a certain distance, my mother was beautiful. It wasn't until you got up close that you noticed the scars. When that nutjob cabbie shot her all those years ago, his bullet had taken her right eye and made a mess of her cheek. Scrambled her brains along the way, if anybody asked me.

"Don't worry, she's used to it," I said. "What did the little doormat have to say for herself?"

Leah tipped my face to hers. "She made me to promise I'd never lose faith in you, not even if someday, you deserved it. I told her she didn't have to worry."

Seething, I took a walk over the dunes and found my mother, who stood with her face to the ocean. "I don't recall sending you an invitation, Gabriella."

Her expression was peaceful when she turned. "God has many angels watching over you, Matty. I'm never as far as you think."

"Spare me." I scanned the cars parked along the road. "Where is he?"

She held out her wrists. "Do you see chains? I am a free woman. Despite what you have always believed."

"I believe a man should be responsible for his actions. Especially his kids."

She turned her face skyward. "If only you knew."

Whatever. "Look, if you want me in your life this bad, go convince the sonofabitch to get his daughter and her mother out of Iraq. File the paperwork with immigration and bring her here. I'll take care of her after that. Until then, I'm not your son. I'm going back to my wife."

She took my hand, running her thumb over my wedding band. "You will *always* be my son," she said. "God answered my prayers for you with Leah. May he protect you both."

As she disappeared over the dune, I stood there, hands in my pockets. Truthfully, I wasn't even certain Ari had survived the war. In fact, I was pretty sure she hadn't.

All I wanted was to start building a life with Leah, to settle into a quieter routine, to leave behind the endless airports and haggling and wars. As soon as I finished the story about that damn arms dealer.

I was almost to the road when a six-foot-five wall of muscle stepped out of a Bronco. Close-cropped dark hair, a leathery tan and a desert squint.

"Congrats, yo," he said in a Down east Mainer's drawl.

When he held out his hand, it revealed the Glock holstered under his coat. I'd been places where a piece was normal wedding attire. P-town wasn't one of them. "Are you a friend of Leah's?"

The bones in my hand crunched, and his smile faded. "You don't recognize me?"

"You and half the people here. Wedding day hazard." But once he fished out a pack of Marlboros, it dawned on me where I'd seen the guy before—the rookie spook I'd shared a smoke with at the cantina in Mosul, right before everything hit the fan. I tapped my noggin. "Sorry, man, I got some gaps from that trip. It's Quinn, right?"

With a distant nod, he lit the butt. "Call me someone who has your wife's well-being in mind."

Leah was down by the water, giggling with one of her bridesmaids about something. "If that's a threat, you'll have to tell me what I did before I tell you to go fuck yourself."

"Drop your investigation of Adnar Kıraç."

The first I'd heard of Kıraç was when somebody had told him to kill my little sister, and for all I knew then, maybe he did. So not only was that a no, it was a hell no. What I'd found since only got worse from there.

Billionaire financier, playboy… Kıraç was Turkey's shadiest arm's dealer, son of a Russian oligarch whose family traced back to Ottoman royalty. He was also a total psychopath. The day of the massacre in Nyali's village, I'd been there because I'd heard he planned to sell a fully armed Apache to the Janjaweed. Since forty-million-dollar helicopters under embargo to unfriendly nations didn't exactly fall off the back of trucks, I was pretty damn curious about where he'd gotten one to sell. His 'technology demonstration' was to lay waste to the entire place. If Nyali hadn't taken me and her daughter off to see a herd of cattle that he'd shot up for practice, we'd have been dead too.

I drained the rest of the beer, hoping to wash away the disgust in my throat. "Man, you've got *seriously* shitty taste in friends."

"You might not care if we get hit again, but after what happened to Jenna, I do."

"Who the hell is Jenna?"

"My fiancée." Quinn pushed his tongue into his cheek, as if he didn't know quite what to make of my memory problem. "Point is, I'm willing to be 'friends' with anybody who helps us keep this bullshit off our shores."

"So if he vaporizes a bunch of Sudanese villagers, that's all right with you?"

If he'd heard me, he didn't let on. "I used to hear that cockpit tape in my sleep, you know? That crazy co-pilot, calling on God…" He stared over the water. "Some guy in a bar downtown told me they sometimes get pieces of the aircraft washing up around here. You know what they found of Jenna? Her suitcase."

"Doesn't make Kıraç one of the good guys."

He knelt, picking a few slipper shells off the sand. "Kıraç is a problem, and if it were up to me, he'd be on the business end of a Predator, but he's valuable to the right people."

"Then they're stupider than I thought."

He reached into his coat and withdrew a glossy photo. "Trouble is, Kıraç's problem is with you."

The shot had been taken our last day of the trip. Leah was in her red ReliefNet windbreaker at the bottom of a jungle ravine somewhere with a couple of Sudanese kids. It was taken from the cliffs above, where a sniper had a 50-caliber rifle trained at her head. Kıraç was standing behind him, polishing his glasses on a bloody rag.

My guts flipped. "What the hell is this?"

He slid a second photo out from behind the first, of a breathtaking brunette dancing with a man in a gilded ballroom, that gaudy, over-done style favored by the Russians. The man was Kıraç, and a sense of nausea swept through me when I realized who the girl was. When I saw the fear and desperation behind her eyes. *Oh Jesus Christ, Misha.*

It was that wire service photo she'd emailed me about years ago, except I was damn sure it'd never seen daylight before today.

She was investigating the same guy. That's what'd happened to her. Why she'd died.

Staring out over the water, Quinn folded the photos in half. "Kıraç knew she contacted you, Cahill. He's kept his eye on you ever since. So he knows you got a habit of going off the deep end when you lose somebody you care about. You seem like a decent guy. I wouldn't wish what happened to me on anyone. Wasn't your fault the last time, but it will be the next. I managed to talk the crazy bastard out of blowing your wife's head off. This time. I won't be able to do it again."

The entire world started to spin. "What do you expect me to say? Thank you?"

"Don't fuck with him—he's a ghost. You won't even see it com-ing." There was an edge in Quinn's voice. "He's hoping you don't back off. He's got ideas already. Last one I heard about? Honeymoon mur-der-suicide. Daughter of prominent local attorney killed by unstable husband."

Feeling like someone had dumped dry ice in my veins, I swore at him and walked away.

I couldn't talk to Leah, not until I calmed down and figured out what the hell to do, so I found Jack on the porch. "Jesus, Cahill, you're as white as an Eskimo's balls," he said, cracking a lobster claw. "If you've got cold feet, it's too late."

Jack's time in Vietnam had ended under mysterious circumstances, and he'd been drunk enough once to tell me what they were. Everybody in this business had regrets. I sure as hell didn't need any more.

I grabbed the scotch next to him and gulped it down. "You ever sit on a story because it got too dangerous?"

He pulled a hunk of meat out of the claw. "Unless your brain is in your ass—which is something I've often wondered by the way—I can't see how that would fix anything."

"You think I want to be talking shop at my wedding? I'm serious."

For a long moment, he watched my face, then picked up the glass, rattling the cubes. "No. But there's a few I wish I had."

The newness of the gold band on my finger hadn't worn off. What it meant. Whatever I'd gotten myself into, job one was to protect Leah. I fished into my pocket for a pen. With one eye towards the street, where Quinn was watching me from his Bronco, I leaned on the doorframe and wrote a single word on a cocktail napkin. Jack raised an eyebrow. I folded the napkin over. "If anything ever happens—"

Sara Jacenko, Leah's maid-of-honor, came around the porch. "She's looking for you, Matty—her dad wants to give a toast before you two sail off."

I knew what I had to do. I'd wait until we were alone, the two of us under the stars, and then I'd tell her everything. We had a very serious problem and we needed to figure out what to do. Together.

But then Leah came up the path with some friend from high school, talking about me 'saving' Nyali Waleed and her daughter, as if I was some kind of hero, instead of a guy who went off to look at some dead cows.

The napkin went into my pocket. Jack, who was watching, shook his head. Before Leah spotted me, I snuck off to the clam pits.

Kneeling, I set the napkin atop a red coal. The edges caught first. The ink glowed orange, then flamed. The word disappeared, as if it never existed.

Janus

If I'd told her, she would've talked me into continuing the story. She would've told me I owed it to Rani to finish what he and I had started. That I owed it to Misha. She would've reminded me how her father had stood up to threats and intimidation and still managed to keep her safe. She would've made me feel like together, we could do the impossible: we could bring down Kıraç and all the people who created him.

It would've gotten us both killed.

So instead, I found my wife on that beach, held her close, and told her she was my world. Then I carried her onto the boat to make love. And let all my secrets float away on the tides.

Chapter 23:
Board Games

MEDITERRANEAN SEA
PRESENT

Gleason's been out in the hall, chewing over his next move with Orlyk and Wade, and he comes back twice as pissed as when he left.

"Let's start over." He settles in the chair. Whatever's going on, he's got more to gain by letting me wonder. "I want to know what put a bug up your ass about Kıraç in the first place. Why you started investigating. I want your source."

He already knows what and why—those are easy.

Kıraç, as I knew him to start, was simply 'SG', for 'sunglasses'. In Sudan, that was what made the connection—Bobo the pilot had said the weapons flooding the local airfields had come in on a fancy Gulfstream. He was jealous of the pilot, a Turk with flowing black hair, who always wore a blue crocodile skin jacket and silver sunglasses, even at night. Just like the guy who shot up Nyali's village.

Even his name remained elusive for months. He operates behind a byzantine labyrinth of fake identities and shell corporations, which had a disturbing habit of linking to *both* CIA and Russian intelligence, who hired him any time they felt like arming some tin-pot warlord to the tits and didn't want to get caught doing it. He has a gift for bribes, for disguising payoffs and kickbacks as legitimate charges, for brokering deals that swept away embargoes and restrictions. They were the two faces he showed the world. So in my notes, he became Janus.

After Quinn had told me about Misha, I'd tried to drop it, I really did, but we fed ourselves off the same chain of people, which meant our paths kept crossing and my subconscious fought back. Leah had tried to pretend she understood why her new husband woke up mumbling his ex-girlfriend's name, but it affected us both. Kıraç getting away with Misha's murder was everything that was wrong with the world. Eventually, I realized that in giving up my investigation, I hadn't kept Leah safe, I'd just shut my eyes to the danger. Even then, it was a decade before I captured his photo again. And years more before I had anything that might stick.

Now, who's the source that made it happen? That's the part that's about to suck. Because it's not a question I have any intention of answering.

"Ever hear of the First Amendment? Reporter's privilege?"

"You're not in the US, genius."

He goes for a pack of cigarettes next to the water jug, chain-lighting a fresh one. "So tell me, Cahill. From what I hear, you're the guy who always gets the story. No matter the risk or cost. God chose *you* to shine light on all the shit that happens in the world."

"Not how I'd put it."

He pushes a photo across the board, the one of Leah in Kıraç's crosshairs. "I thought you smartened up after Quinn warned you at your wedding."

My nuts clench. "Screw you."

He snaps the lid off the water jug. Cigarette clenched between his teeth, he pours some over the cloth, enough to drench the fabric. "What was it—about four years? You were content to follow the little woman around, snapping pictures of huts and little round bellies, hoping she wouldn't notice every time you snuck off to stick your nose in something."

That, I don't answer. She'd noticed.

With a *squelch*, he wrings the cloth, letting the water drain onto the board. "For a guy with ties to Iraq, you didn't spend much of the war there."

If he wants me to sweat, it's working. "Had better places to be."

Up to that point, I'd managed to avoid the whole post-war clusterfuck. I was convinced Ari was dead. Tish and Dinosaur Dave were gone too, thanks to a Green Zone bombing back in 2003. The whole place was one bad memory. The Iraq I knew no longer existed, replaced by madness built on sand.

"Then the insurgency started, and all of a sudden you showed up on my radar again. Waziristan, Diyala—what gives?"

I shift in the chair. "Guess I got restless."

What I'd really gotten was a tip that Kıraç was up to his old tricks. That he'd hooked up with a civilian contractor named Bradley Gleason, and the two of them were making a killing—literally—by fueling the insurgency. It was the perfect arrangement: Kıraç got to spread more explosives and guns and chaos around the world, while Gleason, jaded and embittered by the war, got to practice his two favorite pastimes: making money and taking out his frustration on war-trapped civilians.

"Pretty sweet assignment that rag of a magazine gave you," he says. "Considering your little meltdown during the last one. What I can't figure out is why they kept hiring you afterwards when you went diva and walked off the job a second time. How about that?

Diva? I walked off, yeah, but I had a damn good reason. If that's where he's going with this, things just got worse. Much worse.

"I get my assignments the same way I got you." I shrug, feigning that I'm more concerned with saving my ego than saving my ass. "I'm good at my job."

He slides a black tag across the board and flips it over, my press credentials from that trip. "Not good enough."

Chapter 24:
Sierra Tango

OCTOBER 2007
PROVINCETOWN, MASSACHUSETTS

There are days on the Cape where the clouds seem to weigh down the ocean, when the sun's up there somewhere but it seems like it'll never break through again.

I'd been back from Iraq for a few days, though I wasn't sure where they'd gone. There was a plateful of Leah's molasses cookies on the porch swing, but I couldn't remember her bringing them out.

The screen door banged. Dale shuffled over, carrying two tin cups and a battered pot, from which he poured boiling coffee sludge that'd probably been through the war with him. "Drink up," he said, with a nod to the cup. "You're bleeding, by the way."

When I looked at my thumb, I'd pressed the edge of my carving knife into it. The unfinished plover, a sea-pitted, bird-shaped knob of driftwood, was covered in blood. Dale lifted the knife and replaced it with a dishtowel.

It was the sand swirling over the path that was getting to me. A gust of wind off the water, and I'd start tasting the way that damn Iraqi sand stuck in my throat. The sky would turn yellow, the scrub pines became date palms.

A gull screeched. I choked down the coffee, which took the edge off the numbness.

Dale settled on the rocker, watching plovers scurry from the waves at the shoreline. "First time I got busted by the Army, it was two months after I'd arrived in France. I was in the Wire Corps, 45th Infantry."

"I didn't get 'busted', I got a censor's boot up my ass."

Dale took a noisy sip of coffee. "You got your idealism stuck up there too, son."

Getting my credentials yanked was a blessing, even if I was pretending it wasn't. The embedded system wasn't meant to allow journalists to cover the fighting; it was set up to humanize the people fighting it. Great, right? In one fell swoop, the military kept the press from screwing up their war and transformed us all into propaganda-spouting robots. You could talk about nineteen-year-old Corporal Gilly Tavarez proposing to his sweetheart in a rowboat somewhere in the Ozarks and the little baby girl he'd never met, but you couldn't show the medic digging her photo out of his pocket so he could see it one last time before he died. To me, that was as human as it got.

With the IED situation as bad as it was, going out 'cowboy' was suicide, so I'd taken an embed for *Rolling Stone* with the 13th Marine Expeditionary Unit, a counter-insurgency team in Diyala Province. Fifteen guys as batshit as I was and a Master Sergeant named TwoFer. I was their 'GDR', their Goddamned Reporter, which became Gutter once I proved I wouldn't slow them down like the last guy. Or maybe it was the dirty jokes. But then two months in, the unit lost four guys in a triple ambush.

Afterwards, TwoFer ordered me to wipe my card. Not because I shot stuff that put us at risk, or wasn't following the rules, but God forbid the folks back home get an idea of what war actually looks like. War was the toddler caught in the crossfire, bleeding and shaking her dead mother. War was the lifeless eyes of the Marine slumped next to me. War was the line of Iraqi policemen who appeared every morning, heads chopped off or holes drilled through their skulls. War was two splayed legs with a head sitting on top that told you which body was the fuckwit who blew himself up. I was sick and goddamn tired of risking my life to have some desk jockey in the Green Zone go and make it all pretty. It wasn't.

I walked off the assignment, spent the day dodging insurgents, and saw a few things I wasn't supposed to in the process. When the Army found me, they put me on a transport to BaseOps in Doha, took my passport and press credentials and locked me in a room for two days. The military didn't tell anyone, so the magazine called Leah and told her I'd been captured by Al Qaeda. When the Army finally let me go, I was barred from the country. I was sure Leah was going to tear me a new one, but when I Skyped her, she broke down and sobbed.

Dale was just watching me, patiently waiting for me to come back from wherever I was. "More coffee?"

Leah would talk about watching her dad in court. He'd be the most congenial guy in the room, even with bitter opponents, always an anecdote or some story from his life to share. It usually turned out to be a trap. I knew better than to think I'd be getting out of this one. "45th Infantry, you said?"

He shuffled his feet, scuffing his moccasins on the floorboards. "They'd farm out us black guys whenever a unit got thin. Lieutenant Murphy, my CO, ordered me to take my Garand and shoot out some Klieg lights at the German fortification. 'Sir, I can't, sir', I said. 'Why the hell not, Private Atkins', he said. So I showed him my clip. 'Sir, they never gave me any bullets.'"

"Good to know the Army hasn't changed in sixty years."

He looked deep into his coffee. "He hollered for a while, then hauled me off to the back of camp. 'What kind of fool goes to war without bullets', he wanted to know. Told him I wasn't ever going to shoot nobody anyways."

Dale and me, we could always talk, but he never mentioned the war. It was as if someone opened a valve and it all came pouring out, his two crazy years stringing Allied wire across occupied France and Germany. I closed my eyes, listening to him ramble. Maybe in sixty years, I'd be ready to talk about the stuff I'd seen too.

The ambush had happened in a Shiite village in northeast Iraq. We'd been patrolling some orange groves when a motherfucker of a sandstorm had come up. Thirty seconds later, the Husky mine-clearer at the front of the convoy disappeared in a two-hundred-foot fireball, until the storm swallowed that too.

There were insurgents in the hills with Stingers, more in the village with rifles and grenades, sand blasting hard enough to flay your skin. A six-foot tire had come hurtling out of the storm and smashed the HumVee, so we fell back. TwoFer was screaming into a radio over the wind, *get us some air support*, like Apaches could fly in that shit. When it was over, two guys were dead in the HumVee, another was slumped by the wall. Gilly had a round sneak under his vest, into his pulmonary artery. Two inches left, it would've gone in my ear instead.

The Cape was getting dark. A shaft of light fell outside the porch in the shape of the window above, Leah's bedroom when she was a child, her refuge when she'd run out of ways to deal with me. We hadn't seen each other in months, and she'd flown all the way home from Kampala because she needed to see for herself that I was okay, or maybe because she knew I wasn't.

Dale tested the edge of my carving knife on his thumbnail. "Scary thing, being in a war without a way to defend yourself."

"I guess."

Fear I could control. Moments like that were purely reactive anyway. The shot I snapped of the medic working on Gilly had been pure instinct, but TwoFer needed someone to unload on after all that. I wasn't thinking straight when I walked off, but damned if I was going to give up the card and turn back. If it hadn't been for the storm, the insurgents would've gotten me for sure. By the time it'd lifted, I was two villages away, where a whole new horror was waiting.

Dale kept up a slow, steady rock on the swing. "We had a reporter or two at Dachau," he said. "A lady even—married to Hemingway, people said, though she didn't much like it when they put it like that."

The trap clicked shut. He knew that would get my attention. "Martha Gelhorn? You met her?"

Squeak, rock. Squeak, rock. "Didn't seem right to me, the Army letting a woman see what the Germans did there. 'Course, Leah calls me old-fashioned when I say things like that."

They'd liberated Dachau, he'd told me, the first ones there. The last mile, they'd walked in silence, past thirty-nine boxcars of emaciated bodies. A lifelong Baptist, by the time they'd reached the gate, he'd concluded God must surely be dead too. When the Germans came to surrender the camp, he watched his CO raise his rifle and fire.

"Some of those fellers never seen a black man before." Dale's voice was flat, emotionless. "I helped round them up. I'd do it again. Whatever you saw that's eating you, don't let it."

Whenever I closed my eyes, I saw bodies. A desecrated mosque. I should've known—there'd been complete silence when I'd walked up. The whole village was gone. Women, kids, some naked, most shot through the head, lying amongst smashed beer bottles and half-smoked Winstons. There was drug paraphernalia, along with a scrawl of graffiti on the wall. *Eye for an eye, motherfuckers.* My hands had never shaken so bad taking a photo.

But when I'd gone to leave, I'd heard a metallic crunch, a shell casing stuck in the tread of my boot. When I pried it out, it wasn't the stuff the Marines were using. This was high-end alloy-jacketed ammo, stuff only contractors could afford. I pocketed a few and made for the hills.

Not two minutes later, an Apache had popped up and fired a couple of Hellfires into the mosque. Somebody wanted a cover-up. They'd get it over my dead body. Trouble was, I wasn't out chasing leads, I was bleeding on the porch, listening to an old man tell war stories.

The blood-stained plover in my hands was ruined, so I chucked it into the hydrangeas. "Gonna go scrounge a fresh piece. Thanks for the coffee."

The house phone was ringing as I headed down the stairs. Dale cleared his throat. "Don't shut her out, Matthias," he said, with an eye to Leah's silhouette in the window. "She needs you too."

From the second she'd gotten off the ferry, she hadn't been herself. There was something weighing her down, something that had nothing to do with me. Even Dale could see it.

The message was clear: stop being a dick and go talk to her. "Yes, sir."

Hoping to redeem myself, I jogged across the road and hunted the water line until I found what I was looking for, a weathered piece of beech with four stalks. Then I walked back, whittling a little giraffe. She loved giraffes.

But when I came up on the house, I heard the porch chains squeaking, along with Leah's mom. She sounded upset. "If they didn't tell Jason to fire on the mosque, then why did he? Don't they have computers?"

Asking Dale about computers was like asking me to do brain surgery. "Court martial might be a formality," he said. "What did Connie say? Have charges been referred?"

"I don't know, she doesn't know." Her voice rose. "They're claiming he was on drugs—what is she going to do?"

My first thought was that whatever was going on, it couldn't happen to a more deserving guy. The second was that once Leah found out, it was going to be a rough night. The third was that there probably hadn't been that many mosques 'accidentally' fired on in Iraq last week.

I hopped up the porch. "What's going on?"

Marybeth yanked her cardigan around her shoulders. "Where did you come from? The last thing they need is you making it worse."

Dale put his withered hand on hers. "We'll work it out, my darling—I'll drive you over."

It wasn't about making it worse. Leah and everyone else deserved the truth. So I headed across the road, to the high point of the dunes, which was the only place to get a signal out there. Then I dialed a guy I knew in BaseOps, an Arabic translator forced into his third tour by a stop loss order. It tended to make him more talkative than he should've been.

When he answered, he sounded groggy. "Yo, man, it's the middle of the night. What gives?"

"I need the scoop on an Army captain up on charges. Name's Jason Barnes. Drives an Apache."

"That guy? Eh, the usual—dude can't operate his flight computer, hit a wedding party or something. High as a freaking kite to boot. Can I go to sleep now?"

As much as it would've made my day, something about this didn't smell right. "After you give me the coordinates he was supposed to hit."

He snorted. "Right. This place is a shithole, but it's better than Leavenworth."

I called up the mosque photo on my phone and hit send, which was a stupid thing to do, but I'd gotten careless. "Check your email and tell me again. And remember, as embedded press, I'm required to carry equipment which geotags all my photos."

Another long silence. "Jesus, Cahill, warn me or something next time."

"I am. By the time the rest of BaseOps wakes up, that photo will be on every wire service. Get me the info and I'll hold it until you've had a chance to get coffee."

"Stay out of it, man," he finally said. "These guys have bigger friends than you do."

Which was what made them worth going after. "With that gut you've been working on? Nobody has bigger friends than me."

"You funny, white boy." He cursed me out in Arabic, then added, "Hey, that reminds me—how come I never knew you had a sister here? She ever find you?"

Everything went grey. "What?"

"Your sister. Iraqi chick."

Somewhere in the pit of my stomach, I found my voice. "She's— not… when was this?"

He went quiet. "Never figured you for the type to cheat on your wife with the local tail."

My heart was pounding. Could Ari be alive after all? "How old? What did she look like?"

"Twenties? Real hottie. Big rack. Caught me in the Green Zone couple of months back after she saw me with a couple of reporters. Wanted to know if I knew how to reach you."

Ari would've been almost twelve, so twenties meant Hana. "Do you still see her?"

"Nah, just that once. Think she came in with some spooks."

Dammit Hana. I pinched the bridge of my nose. "Look—get me in touch with her and I'll sit on the mosque photo. Permanently. Deal?"

"See what I can do." *Click.*

Make a deal with the devil and it'll come due in the end. My hands were shaking as I plunked down on the dune. It could all turn out to be nothing. I needed to think, so I picked up Leah's giraffe. And for the first time in a long time, I prayed.

I'd been working on it for a while when a message came in on my phone, a blank sender line with a wire service address.

THREE MEMBERS OF SIERRA TANGO PRIVATE SECU-RITY DETAIL KILLED IN DIYALA PROVINCE YESTERDAY. OWNER, BRADLEY GLEASON, VOWS TO CONTINUE OP-ERATIONS.

The article had a photo of Gleason, flanked by Quinn, Orlyk, and Wade, and—from the back—a man in a blue crocodile skin jacket. I cursed. If they didn't already know I was onto them, I had a bad feeling they would soon.

What I had was evidence the military was covering for a security contractor who'd murdered two dozen women and children, and that they'd used my wife's rapist douchebag ex to do it. And to get the story out, all I had to do was risk her life and say goodbye to the chance of ever finding Ari again.

Jack was right. Life had a funny way of making this job personal.

'*Won't bring those people back*, gatao,' Rani's voice said. '*Dig into it a little more. Let Barnes sweat for a while. Guy deserves whatever he gets. You kidding me, for a chance to find your little sis?*'

The voice flew away in the wind when I heard Leah calling for me, her footsteps rustling through the dunes. The moon was a silver shimmer through the clouds. She had on my favorite T-shirt and a pair of yoga pants, hair blowing loose in the breeze, but the rest of her was all knotted up, I could tell.

"Hey gorgeous, what's wrong?"

She flopped next to me on the sand. "What do you say we both quit our jobs, steal my dad's sailboat, and go find some uninhabited Caribbean island to shipwreck ourselves on?"

Running off to Shangri-La wasn't the first hint that she wasn't as enamored with ReliefNet as she used to be. She'd always relished being one of the few girls in a boys-only club, but lately, the boys' club was using her lack of a law degree as an excuse to hold back her career.

I held up her giraffe, twiddling it by the leg. "Only if Walter can come."

"Hi Walter." She took the carving and sat up. "Just think, no endless strategy meetings, no more acronyms I can't remember because they all have fours in them…"

"Fours?"

She waved me off. "You know, like NUW4Peace, IDP4Darfur, all those. It's like… a thing."

"You live for acronyms."

"Ssh." She ticked off another finger. "No more phone calls that my husband is dead, no more fellating the Ministry of Travel guy so I can get a flight home…"

I raised an eyebrow.

She poked the ticklish spot on my side. "Hey, you were dead."

As moonlight broke over the dune, so did a sense of relief, of broken isolation, of safety, of home. Maybe the world was going to hell, maybe it'd been there a long time already, but Leah and me—together, it couldn't touch us. "Not quite."

When I kissed her, her smile faded. "I heard you outside with my parents. What's going on with Jason?"

I rolled onto my back in the sand, but kept her close. What was I supposed to tell her? He was the reason she hated coming home. The reason she froze sometimes if I touched her wrong. She didn't hate him, she hated the memories, but I hated him enough for both of us.

"Put it this way. Hurting you is no longer the worst thing he ever did."

She got quiet and burrowed against my chest. "Come back to Africa with me," she whispered. "Like it used to be."

I should've listened. Leah was four years and three wars gone from the sheltered idealist I'd told to stay away from Darfur. She'd proved me wrong then and I had no doubt that she'd prove me wrong now if I gave her the chance, but they'd already threatened her once before.

Instead, I exhaled into the warmth of her hair. "Got a few loose ends to tie up, babe. A month, tops, then I'm yours."

I should've realized it went way beyond the justice I'd never been able to give her. I should've know Barnes was just the guy who'd taken the fall, and for god's sake, I should've remembered that photo of Kıraç's rifle trained on her head. Because the choice I made brought justice to no one, not those villagers, not even Leah.

Instead, it damn near got her killed.

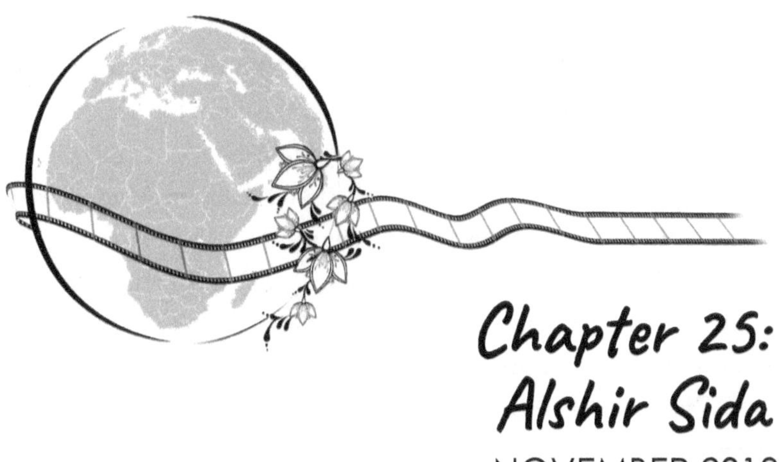

Chapter 25:
Alshir Sida

NOVEMBER 2013
KITGUM REFUGEE DISTRICT, UGANDA

Leah

Stay in aid work long enough and Something Bad is bound to happen. You wake up in the middle of some tribal war and find out the entire government was executed by rebels. Or a massive earthquake swallowed everything but a naked *boda boda* guy who insists his zebu calf can ride in your lap. You consider yourself an expat, because you're mad at your own country for doing fuck-all to help, because it helps you feel one with the stateless people around you, even if you have a choice and they don't, and you're cool with the idea that your friends are mostly alcoholics and adrenaline junkies with raging untreated PTSD. You're supposed to joke about it, slough it off like it's no big deal. But privately, you wonder when your luck will run out.

The 'road' between IDP camps was a tar pit of muddy ruts and overgrown trees, along with a river or two that'd gotten lost for good measure. I was out with a team doing wellness checks, the beginning of a three-month field rotation. In theory, the war in Darfur was long over, but a fresh offensive was brewing over the northwestern border.

We were responsible for monitoring the situation, making sure a bare minimum of people starved to death or got killed in the process.

Dieter Janzen, the Belgian leader of ReliefNet's outgoing team, was navigating the ruts in a beat-up Land Cruiser. Muddy water sluiced onto the floorboards from a run of fifty-caliber bullet holes in the side panel. Since they'd been there longer than I had, I was more worried about his driving, which had me clutching the chicken handle for dear life. "Yo, Janzen—it's a long walk to Kampala. Just sayin'."

"Where's your sense of adventure?" Dieter's claim to fame was he'd once *personally* guided George Clooney around the camps. Every wide-eyed recruit heard the story, over a long night drinking *waragi,* the local moonshine. With predictable results. "Did that husband of yours take it with him to Syria?"

"Turkey." Even that, I wasn't sure about. Matty had been secretive the past few months, always vague about where he was going or what he was doing.

"Ah yes, civilization." Dieter gunned the engine. With a squeal, the mother of all warthogs shot out of the mudhole, tusks-first. Muck went flying, the cruiser lurched and we pitched forward into the crater.

Rubbing a bump on my head, I opened the holey door and stepped into the muck. "Remind me—what I was saying?"

Dieter cut the engine. "Don't look so glum, fellow do-gooder. I shall capture the beast and for its impertinence, it shall be tonight's feast."

It wasn't the mud or the damn pig, it was burnout, pure and simple. I'd spent the last three months arguing with corrupt government officials determined to block everything we did, and I'd spend the next three dealing with the fallout. Life here was half police state, half pirate ship, and the captains were all war-crazed and drunk.

November was the rainy season, so a sun-shower and drenched Ugandan soldiers greeted us at the gate. Music blared from an olive-green Jeep. Inside the barbed wire, little boys were chasing each other, wearing brand-new T-shirts proclaiming '*SUPERBOWL XLVI*

CHAMP NEW ENGLAND PATRIOTS', which undoubtedly would've been news to the Giants.

Amidst a sea of circular canvas tents, entrepreneurs hawked their wares: portable clay stoves, yams and cassavas, freshly killed chickens, children's shell trinkets and everything imaginable made out of a gourd. The field station was off to the side. With a shifty look towards the medical tent, Dieter rolled up our reporting forms and stuck them inside his vest. "Let's split up. You hit the school, I'll take the clinic."

Nyali, the Sudanese woman who'd escaped with Matty from the Janjaweed, worked as a nurse here. "Nyali and I need to go over vaccine inventories."

"Forget it," Dieter said, wiping mud from his forehead. "That looney old nun whips out a rosary and runs off to the chapel the second she sees me."

Under the patter of rain, Nyali flipped back the tent opening, wearing a bold printed skirt with a sash tied over her chest. Her face bore the ritual dot marks of the Nuer, and her arms would always bear scars from the attack, but she'd made a new life here.

"She prays for you because you are an unfaithful snake." Nyali waved a syringe full of yellowish liquid at Dieter. "Come, inside with you now. Perhaps your wife will remain stupid for another few months, *insha'Allah.*"

I had no idea Dieter was married, and it must've shown. "Oh stop being so bloody American." He loosened his belt and dropped his trousers. "I've got news if you think yours is faithful once he's out of your sight."

"Matthias is a good boy." Nyali swiped Dieter's backside with an alcohol pad, then jammed in the syringe. "He never come to me for one of these. Don't be rotten or next time I'll let your *kanjut* rot right off."

Like the places we worked, emotional lives in our world ranged from dysfunctional and messy to outright warzones, and most of us barely noticed when people drifted in and out of the comfort of each other's beds. Given that sex was like oxygen for Matty on his bad days, and god knows we'd both had opportunities, maybe I would've worried, but he had a real thing about cheating because of his sister. Me? I was madly, truly in love and that didn't change with whatever continent he happened to be on. Still, I'd be lying if I said there weren't nights when sleeping alone really sucked.

"I'm going to the school," I said, rolling my eyes. "Try not to fall into anyone's vagina while I'm gone."

Dieter wasn't a bad guy—his father and grandfather had been big-time Belgian colonialists, and I think in his own way, he was trying to atone. We bickered, but I liked him.

Nyali sniffed the air. "You see Nya Jean, you tell her come home. There's an evil smell on the wind."

Nya Jean—Jeannie—was her surviving daughter, and while I didn't put much stock in evil wind smells, given the rumors of fighting, it made me nervous. I guess maybe it was the same thing.

Face to the rain, I trudged off to the school, a round hut with a reed roof, one of the few permanent dwellings in the camp. Jeannie, twelve now, was alone in the schoolyard, where she liked to hang out and challenge the boys to races. If her mother told her about an evil wind, she would've thrown her head back and shot off to outrun it.

She ran up to show me the still-healing *gaar* marks on her face, six rows of pencil-sized dots across her forehead which dipped lower at her nose. "I am beautiful now," she said, gingerly touching her skin. "Like Mama."

"You're always beautiful." I knelt for a hug. *Gaar* marked her as someone brave, loyal, and worthy of respect. She'd been begging her mother to do it for months.

Little girls grew up too fast the world over, but nowhere faster than here. Dr. Geffen's admonishment to work within the local culture always stuck with me, but it'd never been easy. I'd learned to accept that however I saw myself, people here saw me as white. In the years since,

I'd worked side by side with the nuns I'd written about, the ones who'd chafed under Vatican authority, who served the poor and the sick in defiance of what they'd been told to do. I'd held the hand of a dying Carmelite sister who'd asked me to pray for her soul because she'd long since been excommunicated. I saw too many child brides yanked out of school by their fathers, held down and mutilated by their mothers and aunts. Traditions like those didn't need to be respected. They needed to be killed. Preferably with fire.

Sister Mary Nwosu, the elderly African nun who ran the school, shuffled out of the hut, bare feet red and swollen from the mud. Her gnarled hands trembled over a set of beads. "The devil is testing us, Leah. He keeps coming for my girls."

Apparently, the trouble had started that morning, when a father had come to collect his thirteen-year-old daughter, intending to marry her off. "You know how Shayla loves school, Leah," she said. "She cried, begged, pleaded, but her father threatened to curse her if she wouldn't go."

If the chickens didn't lay, it was a curse. If a cow keeled over, it was a curse. Fuck curses. "Didn't you tell her there's no such thing?"

Mary Nwosu's thumb rolled over her beads, red seeds worn shiny with use. Jeannie skipped over. "Sister tried—he cursed her too. Then the rain started and her feet swelled up."

Word got around. Other parents arrived, some frantic, for the man's curses were said to be powerful indeed. Now, only Jeannie was left.

"Matty taught me a counter-curse," Jeannie said matter-of-factly, twirling as the rain fell on her face. "They couldn't do nothing to me."

I frowned. "Counter curse?"

Face as stern as a twelve-year-old can muster, she steepled her fingers. "*Seus jogadores sao mais lentos do que os burros uma perna só.*"

Loosely translated, 'your footballers are slower than one-legged donkeys'. In Portuguese. "Show me where they live," I sighed. "Nobody's cursed me in a month or so. I'm due."

Since Sister could barely walk, Jeannie led me to the far reaches of the camp, the marginal area used as a quarantine during cholera outbreaks, and even farther out, the graveyard, where crooked stick-branch crosses rose from fertile soil. She stopped cold beneath a thick-trunked mangosteen tree, where the ground was covered with sweetly fermenting fruit.

Beneath the *drip-drip-drip* from the leaves, adult voices were cajoling another little girl. '*Minoo, Minoo, where have you gone? Come in from the rain!*'

Minoo was Shayla's five-year-old sister. If she'd run off, it wasn't going to improve their father's mood. I looked at Jeannie. "My little instigator. Have you and your friends been playing hide-and-seek in the cemetery again?"

She pulled me behind the mangosteen. "You can't let them find her. Alshir Sida is here. You know what *she'll* do."

For the children here, there was no shortage of bogeymen lurking outside the fence. For the younger girls, Alshir Sida—the 'knife lady'—was one of them.

"Run back," I said, watching the trees. "As fast as you can. Bring your mother and Dieter. Tell them what's happening. Have them bring soldiers."

Jeannie sprinted off. "Fucking hell," I muttered under my breath. Long since banished for her practices, Alshir Sida never returned alone, but I didn't dare wait, not if she had Minoo. Alshir Sida, Shayla's father—the only thing they'd be getting was a piece of my mind and a muddy boot to the ass.

The voices led into the forest, past a break in the barbed wire. An eerie sense of stillness cut through the mist, broken by the drone of insects and the croaking of bullfrogs around the Nile-fed lake. Though crocodiles lurked beneath the thick mat of papyrus and water hyacinths, a battered aluminum skiff bobbed at water's edge.

The smell of a smoky campfire led west. I found Alshir Sida squatting in a clearing, running a crude scalpel through a sputtering flame, which hissed and popped under the rain. Near skeletal beneath her indigo *thawb*, she rose, cold hatred on her face. "Yes, yes, they said yous would come. It is past time yous get what's coming to you."

Matty had taken the ghoulish photo of her which hung in every aid station and camp in a fifty-mile radius. Nyali had made the case to the local councils and I'd sweetened the deal with extra development aid. If Alshir Sida blamed us for getting kicked out, I was A-OK with that. "Leave. Now. Or I'll have you arrested."

Really, I wanted her thrown in with the crocodiles.

She slid her knife through the flames. "Think yous helping them, don't you? Nobody gonna want a dirty girl like you."

"That'd be news to my husband."

"Him? He no good," she said, a singsong in her voice. "That boy a ghost, baby doll. He'll make you a widow, he'll make you a corpse, but he ain't never gonna make you no mother."

The fire spit an angry spark at my feet. Suddenly, there were tears in my eyes and I didn't know why. A few weeks ago, he'd told me he had a lead on Ari, but then it hadn't panned out. Since then, it seemed like there was so much left unsaid. Something was going on with him—his heart or his mind, I didn't know. Whatever it was, he'd shut me out.

I was standing there, frozen, when Dieter came crashing through the brush by the eastern shore of the lake, following closely by Nyali and Jeannie. "Run, Leah!" Crazy-eyed, chest heaving, he stumbled over and yanked me away by the arm. "It's a trap. The soldiers at the gate, they're gone. I heard them say—"

I never did find out what. Suddenly there were armed men everywhere, guns pointed at us, others firing in the air. Rebels spilt out of the hills and out of the trees, too many to count. Nyali told Jeannie to run.

She was the only one who got away.

Chapter 26:
What a Fool Believes

PROVINCETOWN, MASSACHUSETTS
PRESENT

Dust motes slow dance in the air as morning sun streams into the carriage house. The film bag's contents splay haphazardly over the teak. My hands won't stop shaking. Thousands of photos, miles of negatives, I'd almost convinced myself there's nothing here, until one single photo tore that theory to shreds.

It's a long-lens shot. Black and white. Grainy. Nyali, Dieter, and I are in the skiff on the lake, blindfolded, surrounded by rebels. My head fills with the smell of gun oil, of hyacinth and sweat. I feel insects crawling my skin, hear the growl of a croc, the rebels laughing, taunting us in Acholian. I hear Nyali singing softly to the souls of her sons and Dieter begging for his life. They shot him the third night. We didn't know why.

Matty couldn't have taken the photo—he was half a world away when it happened. It was clipped to a perfunctory *Guardian* article. *Three foreign aid workers kidnapped in Uganda's Kitgum District. Two freed, Belgian man killed by rebels.*

I never expected to walk away. NGOs didn't pay ransoms—even if they had the money, it would've given kidnappers carte blanche on everyone else. At sunrise on the fourth morning, the rebels threw Nyali and me back into the skiff and pushed it out into the center of the lake. I thought for sure they meant for the crocs to get us, but Matty was there when it reached the far side. He was the one who'd stripped the blindfold from my eyes, the bonds from my wrists. *I'm sorry, Baby, I'm so sorry.* It's one of the few times I've ever seen him fall apart. It was the last day I ever spent in the field.

There's a label on the outside of the bag, scribbled in an angry scrawl:

Janus: Damn it, remember next time!

Swallowing hard, I force myself to look through the spilled collection of photos. Some are personal: our trip to Morocco, our wedding, my graduation from Columbia. The photo of him and Ari is here, along with his nude of me. But the rest are war photos, things the papers here would never print, the things that keep him from sleeping at night. Sudan, Iraq, Syria—they span the length of our marriage and then some. Yet there are gaps, like whatever links them, there've been times when he put it aside. The last was after my kidnapping.

It's not that I'd been careless. It wasn't bad luck or chance.

The man in sunglasses came after me. In order to force Matty to drop the story.

And he did. For years. Until Syria. Until Ari got hurt. Until the story forced him to choose between protecting her and protecting me.

Reeling, I put my head down on the gunwale. I don't have time to be angry. I can be angry later. He needs me, Ari needs me. If they get away with silencing him, they'll keep going. Other journalists. Other activists. They'll know there's nothing standing in their way.

Part of me wanted to believe his detention is simply 'national security' gone mad. That in keeping it secret, someone was trying to prevent exactly what happened two days ago, when the attacks in Montreal hit the world's panic button. But if it were true, I wouldn't have the marks on my neck that say otherwise. Nobody would be threatening to send his sister back to the war that almost killed her. There's more, but I'm not seeing it yet.

These photos are Matty's entire career, all the things he cared about, the things that make him insane, his half-assed claims of objectivity notwithstanding. But they're a jumbled mess, neither his usual methodic journalism nor enough for a legal indictment. He wasn't there yet. But somebody was convinced he was close.

I re-arrange the photos. Janus, the two-faced god of Roman mythology. Someone playing both sides. Whatever Matty uncovered in Syria, someone doesn't want the world to know. Some else has a personal stake in this. Someone with enough power to silence a journalist.

Dad is right. The law won't save him. The law is what they're using against him. I need a new plan.

Dad taught me that building a case is a meticulous exercise in building a fortress, digging a moat and filling it with dragons, buttressing the walls against every possible angle of attack, built with language that's just as arcane. I only have one shot at this. If that.

Ten minutes before I have to leave to catch the ferry, as I'm making a third attempt to log onto the court's website to file the petition, the carriage house door cracks open. My mother pokes her head in. "Like your father, at it all night."

Right now, she's the last person I can deal with. I tug the halyard, raising the sail enough to block her view, and start uploading files. "Busy, Mom."

She sets a steaming china pot of chamomile on the gunwale. "Too busy for tea?"

"Mm hmm." I keep my eyes on the progress indicator. "Along with whatever mother-daughter bonding you were hoping for when you came out."

She climbs into the hull anyway, shoving my notes onto dad's ham radio setup. "This is why God owes me grandchildren. You'll end up with a daughter as stubborn as you, if there's any justice in the world."

I sweep the photos into my bag. "In my experience, there's very little."

She reaches out. "Let me give your hair a trim before you go," she says quietly. "You won't have to stop working."

I grab my laptop, with its spinning cursor, and hop out. "Lay off my hair, will you?"

She twists the ring on her finger. "Leah, all I ever wanted was to spare you from the things your father and I went through."

"It's not 1968 anymore, Mom."

"I'm not talking about the color of your skin."

The filing still hasn't gone through. Frustrated, I slip on my shoes. "Neither am I. Some of us don't have the luxury of giving up the fight."

"I didn't, Leah." A bitter note creeps into her voice. "Life burnt it out of me."

I slam the lid and stuff the computer into my bag. The Wi-Fi has always sucked out here. I'll have to try again on the ferry.

She picks up a photo I've missed—one I'd taken of Matty with his feet dangling over the canyon wall in Morocco. He's staring into the sunrise, at peace with the world. It's always been my favorite picture of him. My hope for the future.

She reaches out, rubbing my shoulder. "Don't you realize, when you started talking about this troubled, passionate idealist you'd met, I saw myself and Daddy?"

"Must've missed it while you were yelling that I was ruining my life." I take back the photo. "Gotta run. The benefit is tonight. I need to catch the ferry."

"Jason said he'd drive you. He was hoping you two could talk."

Ugh. Some days, I wish she'd get a clue. *Hey guess what, Mom, Me-Fucking-Too.* "I'm good."

She picks up the teapot. "I get it, Leah. You need an outlet for your frustrations and I'm it. But you need someone on your side."

"I needed *you* on my side." I nearly choke on the words. Fine, it was *my* choice not to tell anyone, but I made my peace with it a long time ago. Somewhere in the *months* of silent treatment, the *years* of treating Matty like Paris of goddamn Troy. "Guess that was too much to ask."

She catches my hand. "I am on your side. I'm telling you that if you don't start letting people help you, you will fail."

Maybe she's trying to help, but I've had it. "Nothing would make you happier, I'm sure."

I go into the house to say goodbye to Dad, who's in his study. For some reason, he has my diploma off the wall. "I told your mother I was right about Matty the day your acceptance came." He runs his knobby finger over the gilding. "Columbia was the place for you. That boy knew what lit your fire."

After the rebels had let me go, Matty had waited until the plane home to tell me my dad was in the hospital—the stress, his heart. Between that, survivor's guilt over Dieter, and getting panic attacks whenever I thought about returning to the field, I'd spent the next three weeks at his bedside, filling out applications. To local schools. Schools we could at least sort of afford. Matty had other ideas. *Columbia or nothing*, he said. *You're not making that mistake with me.*

At first I'd gotten mad—what the hell did he have to feel guilty about? Couldn't he see I was done with aid work forever? *Maybe you are, maybe you aren't,* he'd said quietly. *But you were never meant for small things. You won't be satisfied unless you're in the thick of a fight that matters. I've spent years watching you struggle to prove yourself to egotistical assholes who only care about names. Fuck if I know any other way to fix it. We'll manage. We always do.*

Dads sets my diploma on the desk, next to a photo of DJ. "I used to think you were unfocused. Flighty. But I'd forgotten what it is to be young. To have too much passion. It's what your Matty has always seen in you." He takes my hand. "Learn to channel it and you'll be unstoppable. Don't give up."

I kiss the top of his head, which smells of bay rum, and try not to cry. "I won't."

With a harrumph, he peers through his reading glasses, flips through his rolodex, and hands me a card. "Lucky said he'd drive with you to DC. Call him when you get to Boston."

Lucky was my occasional bodyguard when I was little. I don't need a sixty-year-old Marine following me around, especially not one who still calls me 'Pigtails', but my dad has that thing going on where he's seeing me in braces and a schoolgirl outfit. "No time, Dad. Gotta fly."

"We'll buy his ticket."

I take the card to humor him. "I have miles."

Mom comes in, all red-eyed and sniffling, and gives me a stiff hug. "Can we drive you to the ferry terminal?"

Feeling guilty, I kiss her cheek. "I walked halfway across Gaza once," I say, shoring up my bag. "Where were you then?"

"Worrying. Promise you'll be careful, sweetheart."

"Always."

There's a storm brewing offshore, which makes for a rough ride on the ferry, and somehow, I'm not surprised to find myself completely locked out of the court e-file system. Fighting the urge to throw my laptop into the Atlantic, I turn on Izar's encryption program, then make a call.

It connects on the second ring. "Jack Solomon."

Jack hasn't been Matty's editor for ages, but they're still close. He and his clove cigarettes and flak jacket now haunt the Back Bay, snogging heiresses and collecting royalties off a polemic Woodward biography he wrote. "It's Leah."

He sighs. "Leah, I've had a lovely morning. Please don't say you're calling to tell me he's dead."

Is it so much to ask that *one* other person on the planet believes he'll come home? For a second, I hesitate. Jack was the one who called Matty about the job in Cairo. If it was *anyone* else, I'd wonder, but Jack's been the closest thing to a father Matty's ever had. Somebody was using him. "Actually I might've had a break."

"With reality?"

"Cute. I need a favor. For Matty."

"Anything."

"Fire David Gernham and hire me."

Jack is a lead plaintiff in the ancient suit against the DOJ on the indefinite detention provision. They're screwed and they know it—none of them are currently being detained, so they have no standing. Matty is, but he's not part of the case, and they'll never give me a joinder claim. On his own, he doesn't have time to make it through the courts, and anything I file will get quashed regardless. What I need is a way to jump into a case that already exists. As Matty's editor and confidante, Jack could have a reasonable fear the government might come after him next. It's thin, but win or lose, it puts my evidence into the record.

Jack clears his throat. "Leah, you'll be a fine lawyer someday, but Dave —"

"Has thirty years' experience as one of the top Constitutional scholars in the country. I know. Please Jack, I'm begging."

Another long silence. "He's my friend too. But we're playing a long game and we're losing. This affects all journalists."

"I have good reason to believe it's being applied to one in particular."

More silence. "How good of a reason?"

"Video. Pictures. Documents." A lump wells in my throat. "I can't say more over the phone, but put it this way: I can solve all your problems with standing."

The honks and engines of the city grow muffled, as if he's gone indoors. "Dave will be glad to hear it. I'll put you in touch—you two can put your heads together."

"No." I swallow the lump. *Play hardball.* "We do this my way or you lose the case."

"Remind me when you passed the bar again? Do you have any idea who you'd be up against?"

"He's dying, Jack," I blurt out. "You know what he's like. Today, tonight, I don't know. They're watching me, blocking everything I try to do. The only way to save him in time is if you do something that'll force a hearing. Fire Dave."

A long, slow exhale sounds out of the phone. "I hope you're as good as Matty says you are."

"Yeah, me too." I drop my head to the gunwale. "Jack, he was working on something—something big. Something to do with refugees. With these attacks, maybe. Does the name Janus mean anything to you?"

Silence. "No. But if it did, I'd tell him he was a damn fool for it to mean anything to you."

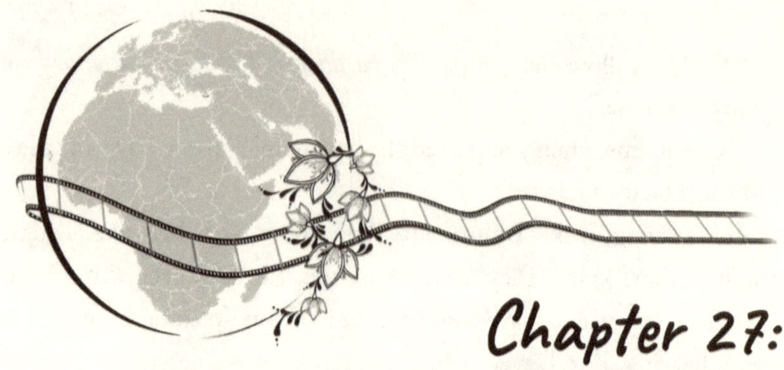

Chapter 27:
Water Water Everywhere
MEDITERRANEAN SEA
PRESENT

Matty

Smoke streams from Gleason's nostrils like contrails. He's flipping pages of a glossy travel magazine, which show panoramic photos of an Istanbul palace set high above an azure Silk Road coastline. Palm trees, formal garden, and an Olympic-sized pool, filled fresh that day. A shadowed figure overlooks the scene from the highest minaret, light reflected from the silver sunglasses in his hand.

"Look at this asshole," Gleason grunts. "Some life, eh?"

The pictures rekindle something ugly inside me too, but he keeps playing with the straps on the board, like he's itching to take it all out on me, so I just shrug.

He flips to the first page, which has my byline. *The Two Faces of Anatoly: Turkish Philanthropist Seeks to Conquer the World.* "So how did your wife feel when she found out that while she was kidnapped in the jungle, you were living it up like some old-style Caliph?"

After a decade chasing a phantom gun runner, I thought I'd finally cracked it. Secret meetings in the foggy dockyards, blindfolded car rides into Roman ruins—they led to an invitation from Kıraç himself. *'Come to my place'*, he'd said. *'I will show you I am not a monster. I simply stand in a doorway of the world created by those in power. Ask anything you like. Bring your camera.'*

What I found was that he truly lived like a sultan. Thousands lived in the compound, less employees than serfs, and they all revered him. There were women too—take your pick, he told me, they will refuse you nothing. When I'd said I wasn't interested, they showed me the picture of Leah.

The article was the trade I made for her life. From then on, I was on record saying Kıraç was a good guy, an honest-to-fucking-god humanitarian. His efforts to 'eradicate' child soldiers, to bring 'peace' to Sudan. Every word, every click—they cut a piece of my soul.

"Leah doesn't dwell on stuff she can't change," I finally say. "She leaves that to me."

Gleason leans back, hands clasped behind his head like a boss. "Only a pussy would let Kıraç get away with what he did to your wife." Then he leans down, reaching for something under the table. "He thought he put you in checkmate, but it ate you, it gnawed like scorpion venom through your skin."

Prickles crawl up my back. "So?"

"You're not a pussy, are you, Cahill? Jason Barnes found that out."

The simmer in my gut goes to a boil. "That piece of shit deserved what he got."

He chuckles. "Funny how those 'principles' of yours go out the window when somebody pisses you off." He sets a folder next to the water jug on the board, then lays out a series of documents. "Your investigation into Kıraç was based on classified information from a Syrian hacker who used the handle M0ng005e."

My neck breaks into sweat. Mongoose is Hana, and all this started because she had a thing with Kıraç, who she'd met after joining a women's unit of Kurdish rebels. She was desperate to escape the war, desperate for someone who'd love her the way she was, damage and all. It had taken months to convince her who he really was, and by the time he'd caught up with both of us in Cairo, it was too late.

I pick up the closest printout, a CNN-Asia tweet stream:

> **@Presidency_Sy** Aug 12
> Government communications satellite down
> after collision with camel.

"Who says nerds aren't funny," I say. "Never heard of him."

Gleason raises an eyebrow. Then he gets up and raps on the door. It squeaks open, admitting Orlyk and Wade. "Funny thing, that. We thought *she* was dead. Except now she's sending messages to your wife."

My head goes all light. "What?"

He gets in my face. "You've got five seconds to tell me how that little pain in my ass is threatening to fuck everything up from beyond the grave."

"Come on, man."

"Four."

I rub the shackles on my wrists, praying for an escape that won't happen. "I had bunches of guys who tell me stuff."

"Three."

Fuck it. *YOLO.* "It ain't my fault you're not as covert as you think you are."

He takes a half step back. Then he charges me like a rutting bull. Lightning-fast, his hand strikes my throat. The air stops. Pain seizes me from eyes to toes. My feet lift off the deck, my back hits the board. I try to roll off, but Wade holds me down.

"Stop," I wheeze, as somebody tightens the strap on my feet.

"That was for one lie." Gleason tilts the board down. "You won't like two."

Leah and Ari, Leah and Ari. It can't last forever.

My lungs won't inflate. The straps are too tight. Rage, fear, desperation—it all floods out in a last gasp of madness. "You committed treason, asshole. Me or someone else, it's a matter of time. Remember when they put the needle in your arm."

The black hood comes at my face. I fight but they hold me down. Everything goes black, and they throw something soft on top. I suck in a breath and hold it, knowing it'll be my last for a while.

Adrenaline gives me the shakes. My pulse is pounding in my ears. The mask gets wet, then drenched. I count to ten, then twenty. Thirty. Thirty-five. My lungs are going to explode.

My body rebels, I give in, but the air doesn't come, all I suck in is wet mask. Water flies up my nose, down my throat, can't tell if I'm breathing in or out. The pain is unbearable—fucking hell, isn't drowning supposed to be peaceful?

The black goes supernova, to brilliant white. My thoughts go all fuzzy, then stop. They rip off the mask. Spasms wrack my body. The board wrenches sideways. I get sick.

"Where's Hana Maloof?" Wade blows cigarette smoke into my face.

"Hell if I know," I cough.

"Hit him again."

I brace myself. This time I only make it to ten. "She must be getting close," I sputter. "You and Kıraç are going to pay for what you did."

Gleason lights a photo of Leah with his cigarette. The edges curl, her image blackens. "Whether we get Kıraç or whether things start going boom, I win. Either way, I don't care. Funny though, I could've sworn you did. You're the one who made it personal. You're making me do this to you, because you couldn't let it go. Now why's that?"

Throat burning, gasping for air, I can't stop choking. He reaches for the mask and I panic. "You killed my friend."

Chapter 28:
Lost & Found

ONE YEAR AGO
TURKEY-SYRIA BORDER

Right up until the day I found Ari, I thought she was dead. The Green Zone lead went nowhere. Dagen, the Kurdish bookseller, who I'd run into in Turkey, told me they'd gotten caught up in the invasion. Guess I lost hope after that.

ISIS had been vanquished, its fighters flung to the winds. In liberated villages, markets once commandeered into bomb factories now bustled with perfume shops and women in colorful dresses. The human tide of refugees surged anew, as those who'd been desperate to escape before took their chance. Since few reached their promised destinations, the US, Russia, and Syria were too busy sucking off each other's dictators to care.

Nobody benefitted more than the human traffickers. I'd been chasing one particular group that had a bad habit of selling their charges to militias and criminal gangs or pushing them into the Mediterranean and letting them drown.

Between runs, they were lounging under a stand of pistachio trees, waiting for the all-clear signal from the Syrian side of the border, which was heavily guarded by the Turkish Army, not to mention a series of trenches and fences, watchtowers and minefields, all surrounded by an endless sea of packed tents. Since they weren't going anywhere, I was snapping shots of a kid in a blue hoodie, who'd made a jungle gym out of an old truck parked beside the sprawling pink brick orphanage on the wrong side of the border.

Traipsing footsteps came up between the rows of tents, but I was focused and paid them no heed until someone clapped me on the back. Someone who smelled of Russian cigarettes and pickled herring. "*Moy drug,* if this is big story you came for, you are looking in wrong place, eh?"

I hadn't seen Aleksei for a few years, but he never changed. Lopsided grin. Spare butt behind his left ear. Last I'd heard, he'd gone over to the dark side and was working for RT, Putin's propaganda channel. "Hey man, how's tricks? And by 'tricks', I mean whichever ones you paid for lately."

Stroking his chin, he made a great show of peering around me. "Something is wrong. Did you slip your collar? Where is little woman?"

"Home—she's a lawyer now." Squinting, I kept my Nikon trained on the kid in the hoodie, who'd noticed me and was showing off. "Well, she will be. She's taking the bar exam tomorrow."

Aleksei almost looked impressed. "And you are here?"

"Eh, you know. Wife trying to study, says I'm driving her nuts and would I please take my ass somewhere else." Something caught the kid's attention, and he scrambled down, out of view. "Except she's *my* wife, so instead of suggesting a bar or a football game, she says Turkey."

If it'd really been that simple, I would've found an easier way to get out of her hair, but Leah's real problem was that watching the world ignore yet another refugee crisis was messing with her head. She hated law school, never made peace with herself for leaving the field, and the shitty corporate law job she'd started a few weeks back wasn't helping. Three years ago, she'd left a place she loved and come home to a country she barely recognized, which for some inexplicable reason was re-fighting battles her parents thought they'd won. The short version?

She barely knew which way was up. My coming here, shining some light on the situation… this was what she needed.

One of the traffickers signaled Aleksei. He jerked his chin. "They will take us across for fifty Euros. What do you say—like old times, eh?"

For the people desperately trying to cross the other way, it'd be ten times that much. A seat on a raft would be another thousand. Fifteen hundred if you wanted a life jacket. I lowered the lens, trying to see where the kid went. "Can't man, sorry."

Scanning left, I found him, clinging to the waist of a thirtyish man in a green T-shirt, sobbing. His father was just as anguished. There were other men standing behind them, with other children. The whole thing was odd, because there were never any grown men here, only orphans and the few women that cared for them. Their fathers had all been killed, and too many of these kids lived with the memory of watching it happen.

Some gruff words passed between the men. The father disentangled himself, with a wary eye towards an olive grove on the far side of the orphanage.

Aleksei grunted. "You can't? Why not?"

Because I promised Leah I'd stay on the safer side of the border? I was about to make up a manlier excuse when the camera caught another face in the group. Dark hair, hawk nose, proud Russian face. Silver sunglasses and that damn crocodile jacket. Plain as day, it was Adnar Kıraç.

Mouth dry, my hands got sweaty. I dropped the camera. "Shit."

Kıraç started towards the olive grove, where a rust bucket Toyota truck was idling by the edge. I crouched low, ducking out of sight behind a string of laundry hanging between tents. The sickness started to twist into something darker, something fueled by long-steeped anger, and before it got away from me, I stuck the lens cap on. *No way. Not again.*

Aleksei furrowed his brow. "You look bad."

I fumbled in my pocket for my phone, then punched up a Skype connection. The camp on this side of the border was run by the UN, so there was service, even if it was spotty.

Leah picked up on the second ring. "What's wrong, Matty?"

My heart rate started to slow as soon as I heard her voice. I craned my neck, peering around a damp blanket hung on a clothesline. After licking his thumb, Kıraç peeled a wad of Euros off a large roll and gave them to the head trafficker. Everything about it struck me as wrong. If he was paying the man's passage, it wasn't out of the kindness of his heart. Bastard didn't have one.

Closing my eyes, I rested my head on the canvas. *Let him be someone else's problem.* "Nothing's wrong," I lied, fixed on the truck. Though the driver's face was turned, she wore PKK fatigues, with an olive scarf covering dark, shiny hair. "Just miss you."

"Okay, *now* I'm worried," she said.

"Funny." Truth was, her worrying was the last thing I wanted. The past decade had been a lousy time to be a journalist. Or a journalist's wife. Leah had always taken the risks of the job in stride, but even she had her limit, and somewhere towards the end of her third year, she'd hit it. I'd been hanging around with some White Helmets near Ghouta, a freelance assignment that'd ended the day before a couple of them had been kidnapped and beheaded by al Nusra. I hadn't even realized it'd hit the news back home until I'd gotten a call that Leah'd had a breakdown in class and was in the hospital with chest pain.

Eventually, they diagnosed her with anxiety, but long story short, it'd screwed with her job prospects and the medical bills put us even deeper in the hole, which was the only reason I was taking the chance of working in Syria in the first place. Now she'd taken a job she hated because it paid well enough to keep me in places where my head was more likely to stay attached to my shoulders. Basically, we went to sleep one night and woke up in an O'Henry story.

Memories, arguments, tears—we shared a lot of all three, but in the end, we'd made a pact: she'd start looking for a job that was more 'her' and I'd stay out of Syria. So far, I'd held up my end, but her job was running her so ragged she'd be lucky if she didn't end up with a relapse. "Did Voldemort give you enough time to study the last couple of days?"

She tittered. "That's the Dark Lord to you. And surely you jest."

"Leah…"

"It's fine. I'm ready." Her voice was tight, but then it softened again. "This morning's photo was my favorite, by the way."

Make a pact with an attorney and it's bound to have a few codicils. One of which was that the first picture I took on any given day was for her. I was doing my best to keep it interesting—night sky long exposures, macro shots, old darkroom tricks I dug out of the recesses of my skull. This morning, I'd made friends with a rock hyrax. The truth? I hadn't had this much fun being a photographer in years. "You say that every day."

"Because it's true. You're flying back today, right?"

"Depends." I switched ears, since Aleksei was parading in front of me, pretending to lead himself around on a leash. "Do I get to see this lacy red underwear you've been teasing me with?"

Okay. So the pact had its perks. With a hopeless roll of his eyes, Aleksei gave up and wandered off towards the orange grove.

Whatever Leah said after that went in one ear and out the other when the kid broke free and ran after his father.

One of the two goons with Kıraç reached into the Toyota's bed and came up with a semiautomatic, which he aimed at the kid. Wide-eyed, the father lunged between them. Kıraç barked at his man, then ordered him to stand down. Permitted one last goodbye with his son, the man disappeared into the grove.

Without meaning to, I exhaled into the receiver, and told myself I needed to put the whole thing out of my head. "Sorry, babe, what was that?"

Her voice got a suspicious note. "Matty, what's going on?"

Kıraç opened the driver's side door, greeting the woman with a kiss. Elation broke on her face. Time stopped.

Hana.

"Leah... I gotta go."

Hana was long gone by the time I'd made my way through the gullies, minefields, and trenches. The smugglers claimed they knew where she lived, which amounted to a high stakes game of truth or dare, with a decent chance they were planning to sell me to al Nusra. For the chance of finding Ari... I was desperate enough to take the risk.

Castello Road, the only route into Aleppo, was a dusty two-lane highway lined with burned vehicles and bombed-out shells of buildings. It was packed with refugees heading north, pickups and people on foot, carrying everything from mattresses to pots and pans. Reconnaissance drones and Russian Sukhoi-34 fighters buzzed the road almost constantly, scattering the column of refugees. Thunderous artillery barrages echoed off the hills. We counted fifteen, twenty, a minute.

We were riding in a truck with tinted windows, where I was doing my best to be invisible at each checkpoint we passed. Every now and then, my finger slid towards the call button on my phone, but I couldn't do it. In a couple of hours, I'd either be able to call Leah and tell her I'd found Ari, or someone else would call and tell her I was dead. There was no sense destroying what little peace she had in the meantime. Second thoughts? Oh yeah.

As the smoking ruins of the city came into view, so did the last rebel-held checkpoint. Near a wall of rubble, the driver, a scrappy desert jackal named Amar, stubbed his Winston in the ashtray and took his foot off the accelerator. "I cannot stop. Roll out here or there will be trouble. Head south, until you see a wall of three red Israeli tour busses standing on end. They shield those who live there. You will find the woman you seek at the Mar Assia church."

The last checkpoint commander was suspicious, so I did as he said, not a moment too soon. Even as I scrambled over the first pile of twisted iron and stone, I heard the truck stopping again. Angry voices, laughter, someone being pulled out of a car. "You have the foreign journalist, no? We want him. You take us to him, we pay. If not, we kill you."

War doesn't just trap the poor and the powerless, it attracts the disaffected dreamers, the sadistic and disturbed. Showoff Iraqi insurgents, Yemenis hiding from drones, entrepreneurial Algerian kidnappers, the odd Brit or American. Pimple-faced Saudi kids looking for a rocket shot to Paradise, who wouldn't have the foggiest clue what to do with one virgin, let alone seventy-two. It beat washing dishes in some Riyadh mall, watching your fellow Muslims get blown up on the news. Here you could be Iron Man, you could get off the freighter you'd hopped in Cairo and be a hero. You could sit on the side of the road with a carbine between your legs, harassing whatever poor slobs happened by, and if you felt like it, you could shoot them. Destiny was yours, right up to the instant it fought back and killed you.

The Christian quarter was a maze of tight-knit apartments, narrow alleys reeking of open sewers and trash, cratered ruins from time and war. Concrete dust and ash choked the air. I'd known my way around, once, but one pile of rubble was the same as the next.

Finally, I saw the buses, standing like sentinels in the street, taking the occasional *plink* off an exhaust pipe or headlight reflector. The snipers ruled Aleppo. Only the foolish and desperate strayed into the open.

An ancient church in an ancient city, Mar Assia stood at the end of the street, like an elder surveying the ruin of its children. Dim light filtered through the bombed-out sanctuary. A chlorine smell lingered in the air, masked by wisps of incense which trailed skyward. I ducked under the rubble of a collapsed arch and made my way down the transept. The sanctuary walls were pocked with bullet holes and stained with soot. Twisted shrapnel from cluster bombs had embedded itself in the columns. I dug out a piece, then moved closer to the window to examine the markings. Russian.

It was reporter's instinct that made me pull out my Nikon. Dropping gas on a church was one more atrocity in a war full of them, but it was either kept documenting them past the point of being numb or let those committing them win.

I'd gotten off maybe a dozen shots when voices came around the far side of the wall. American voices. Familiar ones at that. "We've been watching this goddamned church for hours," Orlyk grumbled. "Gleason's right. I vote we call in an air strike and get this over with."

"We're not bombing a goddamn church," Quinn muttered. "We're not even sure Kıraç's here."

Last I knew, these guys were BFFs with Kıraç. Now they wanted him dead?

"It already got bombed," Wade said. "You got a better way to cover our tracks on this whole thing? We're made, genius, and you're in on it too."

Creeping closer, I switched my old Canon to video mode, hit record, and set it up on a hidden ledge. It wasn't more than an afterthought, but one that'd come back to haunt me later.

The last voice, Colonel Clarke's, came slow, and sounded almost robotic. "Maloof's little sister sneaks off to the hospital every few hours. We grab her, use her phone to send a message that their mother is dying, then we give her an address that'll minimize civilian casualties. If Hana is with Kıraç, she'll come. Gleason will handle the rest."

Sick and lightheaded, I made my way to the sacristy, where a crack of light was visible under the door. All I knew was that Ari was alive. That it wouldn't be for long, unless I did something. Beyond that, I had no idea what they were up to. And what the hell was I going to do if Kıraç was inside?

When I listened, I heard Ishai, who was reading aloud from a Bible.

Quietly, I knocked. "Open up—it's Matty." The conversation stopped. I tried the handle, but it was locked. "You're in danger."

A chair scraped the floor. After what felt like eternity, the door swung open. A sense of the surreal took over. He was my oldest friend, but I barely recognized him. A silver pectoral cross, a black shirt, and a cold, thousand-yard stare. Somewhere along the way, he'd lost his left eye. "And you are many years too late, Matthias. I do not need you to protect my family."

My world stopped when Ari stepped out behind him. Or maybe it'd stopped back then, because in my head she was seven, not the grown woman in front of me. One look at her made me wonder if she'd slept since then. She still wore our old man's wooden cross, which pained me, but not as much as her troubled green eyes, which had surely seen more than anyone ever should. An hour ago she'd been a ghost in my head, but the impossible had happened: she'd come back to life.

A lump swelled in my throat. "Hey, pretty girl."

Gaunt and sleepless, she stepped forward and kissed my cheeks. "It is good to see you, brother."

Flooded with relief, I held her tight. "You have no idea."

Magdala limped out of the back room, pale and feverish. I helped her sit on a threadbare stool by some heavily singed choir robes. Her foot was wrapped in filthy bandages, misshapen and swollen. "What happened?"

Emotionless, Ari knelt in front of her mother, re-wrapping her shattered foot. "Assad, the Russians, who can say? Our priests here were martyred in the same attack. Ishai has taken over as laity."

Magdala's foot was bad, verging on gangrenous. "Has she seen a doctor?"

The noise Ari let out was half laugh, half sob. "Dr. Alatassi runs an underground hospital near al Jalbri. I begged him to tell me what to do. I stole instruments, removed fragments as he instructed. Yet her fever only gets worse."

The idea of her out there ducking the snipers made me ill. It started to hit me how dire this was. From here, it was roughly thirty miles to the Turkish border, which meant half a dozen checkpoints, all of which would have heard by now that there was an American journalist free for the taking. "We all have to get out of here."

"Here is where I am needed." Ishai circled me, while Ari drifted closer, holding his gaze. "Why have you come, Matthias?"

I smoothened Ari's hair. Whatever it took, I wasn't leaving her this time. "It's Hana—do you know where she is?"

Ishai stayed tight-lipped. "With Ioannis, I imagine. Or her PKK friends. We see very little of her these days."

"Ioannis?"

"The man she is dating."

I knew most of Kıraç's aliases, but that one felt too personal to be a coincidence. "Tall? Long hair? Always wears sunglasses?"

Ari got all dreamy-eyed. "He is… handsome, yes? Very kind. He has helped many of our friends escape from the conscriptors and obtain passage to safety. She helps him by providing documents for the UN, and in the meantime, he keeps their families safe. Once Eema is better, he says we can go too."

"It's a lie, Ari. That's not even his real name. He's a bad guy. A really bad guy. A killer. Here, I can prove it." I turned on the Nikon's display and called up the shot I'd taken of the father and his son at the border, the one with the goon pointing a rifle at him. "Is this 'kind' to you?"

Her face grew troubled. "We know them. Ishai, isn't this your friend Tal Morsia? Did you know he had plans to flee?"

Ishai, who stood by the rubble of the sacristy wall, glanced briefly, as if it pained him. "The death squads have been hunting him. I am not surprised."

"There are American soldiers outside searching for Hana," I said. "If they see her or Kıraç anywhere near this place, they'll call in an airstrike."

Ishai turned away. "Then she is as great a fool as ever. There are others I must warn. The rear entrance is shielded by rubble. Use it. You will be gone when I return."

Artillery pounded in the distance, explosions no more than a few seconds apart. "Come on, man—we grew up together. First time I kissed a girl, you were the one I told. It's been fourteen years. Stop being pissed at me so we can figure this out."

Magdala turned her face to the sky. "My children had such dreams of rebuilding Iraq. Ishai, your curse is you give up your dreams too easily for others. Hana's is that she fights too hard for hers."

Ari worked on her mother's foot, saying nothing. I sat beside her. "How about you, kiddo? What's your dream?"

Her cheeks flushed. "Here we do not dream. Here is where we die."

I'm not sure who took it harder, me or Ishai, who finally met my eyes. ""Her best friend Maira was killed in an airstrike yesterday," he said. "Her dream is to heal. To no longer feel helpless. I have a friend who can get you to the border. Promise me Ari will learn to dream again on the other side. Do that, and you shall have my forgiveness."

I embraced him, the brother I thought I'd lost. "If it takes my last breath."

If I'd known they were the last words we'd ever speak in this world, maybe I would've said something different. Maybe there was too much to say.

As he walked out the door, I stared at Ari. "A priest? Really? What happened to architecture?"

"You would have liked his wife," she said, head lowered. "He says she is waiting for him in heaven."

"I'm sorry about your friend," I said, aching for her. For everything she'd suffered over the years.

"Sister." Her voice was strained. "Maira was grateful for the place Hana did not want in our lives."

Saddened, frustrated, pissed—the walls were closing in. Ishai was out there risking his neck and I was inside feeling useless. That's when I remembered that I needed to grab the Canon. If I was lucky, Gleason's grubby minions had been stupid enough to say something incriminating.

Ari was picking bloodied fragments of bandage from her mother's foot. I got up, listening over the pile of rubble. It was the usual street sounds, foot traffic and quiet conversation. "You okay if I run to the sanctuary for a minute?"

A hint of her old mischievous self poked through. "I am no longer a child, Matty. If you like, take two."

The voices had gone when I got there, so I scooped the camera and bailed, rewinding the feed as I walked. From the timestamp, I'd been inside less than five minutes, but they'd bugged out in a hurry ninety seconds ago. *Fuck.*

I ran up the altar steps and threw open the sacristy door. "Yo, get your stuff, we gotta—"

Everything in me went cold. Kıraç leaned against the credenza. Though he wasn't doing anything more than fiddling with a few cones of incense, I knew that look of his, like a cobra about to turn.

Shoulders tense, Ari finished rewrapping her mother's foot. She greeted my return with a forced smile, as if she was desperately trying to figure out what to believe. "Ioannis has come to ask Ishai for permission to marry Hana, Matty. Isn't that wonderful?"

He'd overdosed on cologne for the occasion. I recognized it, a musky scent called Sultan, a favorite of the human traffickers and kidnap gangs up north. "Where is she?"

"She is… close." He fixed on my camera. "It is an unexpected pleasure to see you again, Matthias."

A split second. That's all I had to decide. A drone could be there in under a minute. An airstrike in two. "Whatever you cooked up with Clarke and Gleason is off. They want you dead."

"I see." It was like a stone landing in still water. "When you next inform them of my whereabouts, perhaps you will be good enough to send my regrets. Your wife, is she well?"

Ari stopped breathing. I knew she'd seen it, seen the venom behind the mask. She rose, helping her mother stand. "Ishai will return soon, Eema. We must go."

Without taking my eyes off Kıraç, I lifted Magdala into my arms. Partly because she was in too much pain to walk, partly so Ari could run if she needed to. "I didn't come here looking for you, Kıraç. You gotta know that."

He lowered his glasses before climbing over the rubble. "For your sake, I hope that is true."

Kıraç went off the way he came, and the rest of us climbed through the hole in the sanctuary wall. Protected by the three standing tour buses, the neighborhood's trapped residents were venturing out in search of provisions. Ari knew where Ishai's smuggler friend lived, so after Magdala stubbornly found herself a makeshift crutch, we set off for the end of the street.

Taking my hand as we walked, the way she did when she was little, Ari ran her thumb over my wedding ring. "You are a husband now?"

For now I am. Until she finds out I'm in Syria and decides to divorce me.

The bar exam would be starting in five hours. The last thing she needed right now was a call from me. By the time we got across the border, it'd be over and done. "For a long time now. Her name is Leah."

Ari fiddled with her cross. "What does she know of me?"

When I hesitated, her face fell. What could I say? That she was a picture I couldn't bear to look at, an empty place in my heart, one even Leah didn't dare go? "She'll know a lot more soon. Promise."

At the corner, a white truck was parked near a bombed-out kebab shop. Ishai sat in the driver's seat, grasping the wheel. Ari must have seen the blood first, because a strangled noise came out of her throat. His head lolled unnaturally to the side. A pair of silver sunglasses fell off, revealing a massive void where his good eye should have been.

She let out a cry and ran to the truck. Magdala wailed and fell to her knees. I saw the Sukhoi jet before I heard it, and I was at a dead run after Ari when I heard the click. For the briefest second, all sound stopped, as if it'd been sucked into a vacuum.

The ground buckled. A wall of scorching air slammed me like a Mack truck. By the time the fireball erupted, I couldn't breathe, couldn't hear, could barely see. Ari was on the ground, bloody and still. People's mouths were open, like they were screaming, but I couldn't hear a thing. They kept pointing at the roof. Something whizzed past my ear. Debris rained down. Burning fuel choked the air. There were body parts next to me, brains in my hair. I wondered idly if they were mine.

When Ari's foot moved, it snapped me out of my stupor. I stumbled to the burning car and tried to lift her. Couldn't do it. Massive pain wracked my chest. Her face was bloodied, her left side torn open from hip to breastbone. There were sirens, but they sounded under water.

My head broke the surface when a rough pair of hands grabbed me by the armpits, hauling me out of the line of fire, and when a camera lens banged my face, I realized it was Aleksei. "My sister," I gasped, pointing at Ari, who was lying in front of a wall of rubble where Ishai's truck had been. From beneath the rubble, the horn still blared. With a grunt, Aleksei ducked low and dragged her back.

There was blood everywhere, gleaming bone, a purplish twist of intestine. I wadded her skirt and pressed it as hard as I could over her side. "We have to get her to a hospital."

Magdala didn't answer. She sank to her knees, near catatonic, fixed on the rubble covering her only son. Grief would come later.

When I tried to suck in a breath, pain stabbed like a hot knife. Broken ribs. Couldn't hear a damn thing out of my left ear. Something was trickling out of it. Nausea and vertigo threatened to suck me under. The FSA rebels Aleksei was traveling with were launching mortars at the sniper positions. A group of White Helmets arrived, a few guys I knew, who hurriedly loaded the wounded into jeeps and trucks. Aleksei took a few shots, then stopped long enough to load Ari into the back. "*Spasiba*, my friend."

With a shrug, he exchanged words with the driver, tapped the fender, then went back to shooting. "You would do it for me."

As the truck jostled off, Ari's side gaped open. I scrambled over, struggling to put pressure on the wound before she bled out. *God please, no, don't do this.*

At the bridge, a band of al Nusra fighters were stopping every driver. One was pulled out and shot. *Crusader, crusader,* the fighters shouted.

I reached for the cross around Ari's neck and snapped the worn leather. Magdala glanced up with red-rimmed eyes. "You would have us deny Him now?"

It was getting harder and harder to breathe, like a boulder rolled onto my chest. As the fighters threw the body over the bridge, I pocketed the cross. "No. They would."

The rebels took us to the underground hospital, where the driver dumped Ari onto a bare spot of floor near the wall. There was no electricity and the floor was covered in blood from whoever had been brought in before. Trash bags and bloody clothing were piled up the walls. Dr. Alatassi came running over. There was a flit of recognition when he saw Ari's face, but only as a man who knew death. Clutching my ribs, I staggered to her side. "Please, will she—?"

"Out of the way," he said, kneeling at her side. "You too, need attention."

"I'm fine." I wasn't, but it didn't matter.

Alatassi cut through the dressings, setting aside her identification paper, and poked inside her. After a minute, he pulled down his mask. "I am sorry, old friend. Her injuries are not survivable."

Vertigo made the walls swim. The shakes set in. "Don't say that. Please, I'm begging."

He took me aside. "She will lose one kidney, along with her spleen. The liver is damaged and her intestines perforated. It will turn septic. We have no antibiotics, no anesthetics. I could stabilize her, but she would have a painful death awaiting. I can ease her way out of this world, —that is all. Perhaps in your country, she would live."

I seized on the only part I could deal with. "If I get her to the US, she'll have a chance?"

"I meant no guarantee."

"Please, do what you can." My vision started going black. I braced myself on the wall, struggling for air as I dialed Leah's mobile.

"What do you think you can do?" Magdala's pain broke through her stupor. She seized Ari's cross, which I'd unknowingly wrapped around my hand. "I saw how your Immigration treated my Ishai. How your CIA lied to my husband, to me, how they abused my daughter's trust. America turned her back on us many years ago. Ari will not be permitted."

I hit redial. The hard truth was that getting the whole family to the States was no longer a problem. It was just Ari. "Leah will know. Ari is my sister. That has to count for something. If it takes a blood test—"

"A test will show nothing," she snapped. "You share no blood with Ari-eil."

I stared dumbly. "You're saying Eli isn't really her father?"

"I am saying he is not yours."

Words wouldn't form. "You're lying."

Face purple, her hands clenched into manacles, as if she was grasping for anything that would keep her grief at bay. "You were an orphan they took from São Paulo. You have always tried to blame your failings on him. They are entirely your own."

Her words changed everything and nothing. "Ari is my sister. I don't care about blood."

Groping the walls in blinded grief, I made my way outside and prayed for enough reception to reach Leah. Then I heard Gleason talking with Orlyk. "Clarke says we got Maloof at the church, boss. Still checking on Kıraç."

My knees buckled. Grief, relief… they both hit at once. Hana was dead too? Had she even been there?

Gleason didn't sound convinced either. "That brother of hers—the priest—he knew what we hired her to do. Hell, he recruited half the guys for Kıraç. I wasted him, but the mother and sister knew too. I'm not leaving a set of loose ends to hang around our necks. Find them and take them out."

The knot in my lungs yanked tighter. I made a beeline for Ari. "Where are her papers?" I wheezed.

Alatassi kept stitching. "Check the cabinet by the bags. A Kurdish family was brought in this morning. There was a girl of seventeen who no longer has need of hers. We have not yet had time to clip the corners."

My vision started tunneling out. I stumbled over the bags. There was a stack of bloodstained three by four cards in Arabic, each with an eagle wet seal. In the state Ari was in, the picture was close enough. Magdala was the problem.

With a dull scalpel, I sliced the upper right corner of Ari's card, then switched it with the dead girl's. We piled the bags of bloody clothes over Magdala. Right after that, I must've passed out, because I woke to Alatassi digging a scalpel into the side of my chest.

He wiggled his finger in, then two. If I'd had any air, I would've screamed, but with an audible whoosh, my lung inflated again. With a haggard expression that made me suck it up, he stuck a short length of tubing into the incision, popped in a few stitches to keep it in place, and closed it off with a clothes pin.

"Your lung collapsed," he said. "This is all I can do. Release the pressure when you need it."

Gasping and woozy, I sat up. Ari was on the floor next to me, still as the grave. "Is she…?"

He checked the wound on her side, which was packed with dressings. "Alive, for now. I cannot say what will happen in transit."

"Transit?"

From a dark corner of the room, a fighter in olive fatigues emerged, a woman, but not Hana. She helped me up, while two of her colleagues lifted Ari onto a makeshift litter. A fourth carried Magdala, as easily as if she'd been a child. "It has been arranged."

They had a truck waiting, which sped off down the wasteland of Castello Road. When we rolled up to the first checkpoint, it was manned by four guys in black pajamas. The driver, a broad-shouldered Kurdish woman named Leyla, got out. They exchanged words, too low for me to hear, but when she started towards the truck, the head pajama guy jumped her. More or less, I thought that was it.

Like a wolf shaking rain from its coat, she threw him off her back, twisted around, and hooked her dagger under his throat. She nicked his jugular with a deft flick. A rivulet of blood trickled onto her hand. She chortled. "Now, do you let us pass as you have been instructed, or do you meet Allah having been killed by a woman?"

She slid behind the wheel and sped off, clearly relishing her triumph. I cradled Ari's head and prayed. "Who told them to let us through?"

"A friend. That is all you need know."

I had a hunch, a sick one, which grew as she sped through the rest of the checkpoints with no more than a wave. A mile from the border, she turned off the road, heading west. Under the cover of an olive grove, a small band of female guerillas was waiting.

Hana, clearly not dead, met us at the side of the road. Though stoic, she was covered in grey dust from the explosion, and tear tracks betrayed her.

Magdala sat up and wept, beating her fists on Hana's shoulder, repeating Ishai's name over and over. Grief and rage barely contained, Hana climbed into the back with us, embraced her mother, then bent to kiss Ari's forehead. "They will pay for what they have done."

"She won't last much longer," I wheezed, as the mongoose bopped into the truck bed, unaware and unconcerned. "She needs a hospital."

"There is a facility near the border." She regarded me slowly, as one would do with a ghost risen from the grave. "For many years, my brother told us you were dead. I would trade his life for yours in a heartbeat."

Kıraç came out of a canvas bivouac, heading for my side of the truck. Disgusted, I closed my eyes. "So would I."

He came to the liftgate. "I control these mountains. Your path across the border is secure. I owe debts to no one. Now we are even."

I would've torn his head off, but I could barely see for the spots. "Man, we ain't even close."

As the truck sped off, Hana opened a laptop and set some government documents next to her on the truck bed. "That was ungrateful, even for you."

This was his fault, all of it. "Your boyfriend is a bad guy, Hana."

Her eyes stayed on the screen. ""Ioannis never abandoned Ari-eil. Can you say the same?"

"His name isn't Ioannis." Releasing the clothespin, I tried to inhale, but every breath stabbed. "It's Adnar Kıraç. Arms dealer. Human trafficker and slave trader on the side. Go on, look him up."

"Yes, he sells weapons. He sells them to us," she said irritably. "Your government says they will help, but they are always lies. If it is not Assad slaughtering us, it is the Russians or Turks. If it was not for Ioannis, we could not fight back."

"He sells to you so he can sell more to them." I grabbed the corner of her computer screen, which showed a database of birth, death, and marriage records. "What the hell did he get you involved in anyway?"

She grabbed it back. "I am saving our sister. If Gleason learns any of us are alive, we will be killed. Beyond that, it is not your concern."

The truck jostled over the ruts, leaving me clutching my ribs. "These guys you helped Kıraç get over the border. They had you making false documents for them. Did you ever ask yourself why?"

"The west has abandoned us. What else are we to do?"

"Come on, Hana, you're smarter than this. If that's all it was, why would the Americans want you dead?" I went for my camera, to show her the video. It was then I realized I'd dropped both cameras at the scene. *Shit shit shit.* "Somebody got wind and shut it down."

She slammed the laptop shut. "The world is fickle and cruel. Those I have created documents for are all friends of Ishai's. I know what you fear. They are good men. All of them." She picked up the papers. "I cannot go with you. You must give the people at the hospital these papers. We knew the family they belonged to for many years. Maira was a good friend of Ari's. If she resists, tell her she must live the life that was stolen from her friend."

The border was in sight, with the field hospital complex on the other side. As I reluctantly took the papers, my phone signaled an incoming Skype connection from Leah.

Her voice was frantic. "Matty, where are you? Are you hurt? Who's this girl?"

Before I could reply, Hana grabbed the phone and hung up. "Don't be a fool."

I wrestled it away and redialed. "You're not the only one with connections, Hana. Mine are actually legal."

"Say nothing," she repeated. "Or you will get us all killed."

"I can't lie. Not about this. She's my wife. She'll know."

Hana glanced sideways. "Say nothing. They know you are here. They are listening."

Chapter 29:
Sex & Candy

FOUR DAYS LATER
HANSCOM AIR FORCE BASE, MASSACHUSETTS

Leah, who hadn't lost her touch, pulled off one of her miracles. When the C-130's rear hatch opened, she was in the hangar, along with two surgeons, an ambulance, and a shipment of relief supplies. The painkillers they'd given me in Jordan had long since worn off, so it hurt like a sonofabitch when she hugged me, but I was too fucked up to care.

She reached for my face, hands trembling. "You said you weren't hurt."

"Nothing that won't heal." The left side of my chest was one massive bruise, not to mention the giant tube hanging out of it. If I'd known she'd be there, I would've found a way to put on a shirt. "I thought you'd be in New York."

Lips pressed together, she watched the surgeons wheel a gurney up the ramp. "We have a lot to talk about, Matty."

She was dressed in yoga pants and a hoodie instead of one of her buttoned-up lawyer suits, so maybe I should've figured it out, but I didn't. All I saw was that she was mad and had every right to be. As soon as we were alone, I could come clean. "Yeah, we do."

Her friend Sara Jacenko, the relief doc who'd flown home with us, came to check the valve on my chest tube. Sara's field rotation had just ended, the supply plane was her ride home, and without hesitation, she'd agreed to shepherd a critically injured refugee to a new life. She was facing the reaming of a lifetime when the home office found out, but the way she put it, after six months in a refugee hospital, regulations weren't the only thing she felt like smashing.

Sara, who'd been maid-of-honor at our wedding, stretched her back. "Well, you're right. He's an idiot. But he's more afraid of what you're going to say than of flying with a collapsed lung. Go easy, okay?"

Leah's sideways glance put that idea to rest. "Sara, if you get in any trouble…"

Sara poked her shoulder. "Then I know a good lawyer."

Leah shuffled her feet. "I can get you a name if you need it."

They rolled Ari down on a gurney, small, pale and heavily sedated. Magdala, now Amira by her false papers, hobbled to the end of the hatch, then stopped, as if taking it all in.

Sara's face clouded. "You save the ones you can save and that's supposed to be enough. Fuck that. This was a chance to show those pricks in Washington exactly what they've been ignoring. I wasn't about to pass that up."

The taller doc jogged over. He held out a plastic cup with two Percocet in it. "Guessing you'd probably appreciate a few of these." He stuck out his hand. "Ethan Rhodes. I've been following your blog. Guess us doctors aren't the only ones who sometimes get too involved, eh? Maira's in good hands. Dr. Parisi and I will take it from here."

I swallowed the pills, unsure of what to say. "Thanks."

A smile ghosted through Sara's exhaustion. "I've been trying to talk Hawkeye and Trapper John here into a rotation for months. If it wasn't for you, I might've had to sleep with one of them."

Parisi shone a pen light into Ari's eyes. "How easy does she think we are?"

Rhodes pressed some buttons on the ventilator Ari was hooked to. "Well, before, I might've said yes for some M&M's and a hand job, but now…" A few more beeps and button presses, and Ari's face relaxed. Her breathing became easier. "I'm in."

Women, men, sex, candy… doctors who had what they needed to do their jobs. It was all so damn normal and suddenly I couldn't keep it together anymore, just leaned on Leah's shoulder and bawled like a baby. I could barely remember my own name, never mind the last time I'd slept, but for that brief moment, I thought the worst was over.

Her embrace was stiff. Sara came up behind us. "He's an idiot, but he's *your* idiot, Leah."

Leah closed her eyes. "Yeah, I guess he is." Wiping my cheek with her thumb, she exhaled a deep, warm breath on my forehead. "ICS has some paperwork for Maira's mother, and there's an affidavit you need to sign. I was going to do this on a humanitarian medical visa, but those documents you sent said her brother worked for the coalition in Iraq, so I switched to an asylum petition. I filled out as much as I could."

The instructions were full of dire warnings about penalties for falsification. Disbarment. Perjury. "Maybe we should go over these at home."

A shadow fell behind one of the crates, and Anthony J. Nance oiled out. "I'm afraid that's not possible, Mr. Cahill."

A cold sweat broke out, seeing him there. The way he was looking at me. "Senator."

"I'm due in Washington for an intelligence briefing on these air-strikes," he said. "The administration's showing its usual truth allergy on the matter, so it's a fool's errand, but I promised your wife I'd see the paperwork to a friend in Immigration who owes me a favor."

Leah stuck her hands into the pocket of her hoodie. "I was getting nowhere until I ran into my friend Cole at a coffee shop. I guess I must've mentioned what happened to your sister during the war. I don't really remember. I was pretty upset. Next thing, Cole called me and told me to get the papers ready and told me Senator Nance would push it through."

"My staff know I like to help where I can," Nance said.

"He convinced some of his donors to sponsor Maira's medical bills." Leah added, a note of apology creeping into her voice. "It's the only way we could make this work."

Nance held out a pen. "I've got copies in my office. There wouldn't be anything wrong with the forms now, would there?"

Swallowing hard, I added my signature above Leah's. "No sir."

He swept up the papers, then handed them to her. "If you'll be kind enough to go get the mother's signature, I'm going to borrow your husband and see if we can't get at the truth about the Mar Assia strike."

Worn out, but firm, Leah steadied me. "No. Matty's in no condition to answer questions. We have a long drive ahead of us. We'll call your office tomorrow. It can wait until then."

"I'm afraid I insist. The Russians claim we're responsible for the strike. Right now, we have nothing to contradict their false narrative. Our allies want answers."

"It's okay," I mumbled. "You can go."

She crossed her arms. "Actually, I want to hear this."

The conversation she and I needed to have was different than the one I needed to have with Nance, so I pointed out that the sooner she got 'Amira's' signature, the sooner we could get on the road, and she reluctantly went off to do her thing.

Nance walked behind the crates, as if he expected me to follow, and since I was too messed up to think straight, I did. "Look, the guy you want is—"

"Adnar Kıraç." He set my battered-to-hell Canon on the crate. The lens was shattered and the case was smashed. The memory card slot was open and empty.

The air went leaden. I sucked in a breath, which was easily the worst idea I'd had in weeks. "Where the hell did you get that?"

Gone was his congenial manner. "Forget that. Worry what'll happen to that sister of yours if you ever breathe a word of what you caught with this damn thing."

The hangar went grey. He knew. He knew everything. "She's not—"

"Ari-eil Maloof. Cahill, if you prefer. Born October 21, 1995, Mosul, Iraq." He grabbed the end of my chest tube and yanked. "I was CIA then. Magdala's husband was one of our assets. So was that useless father of yours."

Pain made my knees buckle. "He's not my goddamn father."

He gave an exasperated grunt. "He's also not your problem right now. *Your* problem is what will happen to Ari-eil should Gleason find out she's alive. You breathe a word of whatever you *think* you know and I'll get out of his way."

There's an instant of clarity that comes when you're standing next to a bomb that's about to detonate. It's transient and fleeting, and you know what comes next is going to suck. Whatever the reason Gleason turned on Kıraç, Nance was at the center of it. He was the reason Ishai had died under a pile of rubble, why Ari was hovering between life and death, and he'd dragged his ass up here to make sure I knew he had the power to decide which brother she stayed with. The only reason he'd agreed to help her was so he could use her as leverage. To shut me up.

Trouble was, whatever he thought I'd seen or overheard on the video…I hadn't.

He'd tipped his own hand without knowing. Which meant he was approaching this as mutually assured destruction. If he figured out I had nothing, it was over.

I took a stab in the dark and prayed. "What I caught? You mean you blackmailing Gleason?"

He was too slippery to admit it outright. "Personal tragedies led Gleason and his compatriots to make a series of poor decisions, which fortunately, were discovered before anyone got hurt. The taxpayers shouldn't have to foot the bill for cleaning up their mistakes."

"Guess I can have my memory card back then."

He glowered. "I know you have copies. Since you were kind enough to send them to me."

I did?

Hana. It had to be Hana. "Fine. So I keep my mouth shut. Then what? Kıraç isn't planning to let this go."

"That's what drones are for."

"You'll have to find him first," I said. "Ain't easy. Trust me. He finds you."

"We're the U.S. government. Perhaps difficult for you to believe, but we have better ways of finding people than some pissant reporter."

Leah was coming back. "Fine. You take care of it your way, I'll take care of it mine."

He yanked on the tube one last time, digging his thumb into my rib. "Don't even think about bringing her in on this. I'll have Justice slap charges on her so fast your head would spin. I'd be willing to bet the current administration would relish the idea of sending Dale Atkins's daughter to prison."

He let go just before Leah jogged around the corner.

She stopped short. "Matty, what's wrong?" She handed the papers to Nance without so much as a thought. "I'll get Sara. You're white as a sheet."

All gentlemanly and pleasant again, Nance tucked the papers into his coat. "Those ribs must be murder. You should get him home."

They were loading Ari's gurney into the ambulance. I knew then I wouldn't be there when she woke up. *If* she woke up. Leah stroked my hair. "It's going to be okay, baby."

No. It won't. Not until this is over.

She helped me into the car, and I only meant to close my eyes for a second. Except when I opened them, I saw skyscrapers. Trouble was, they weren't the ones I was expecting.

Moonlight reflected off the Prudential Tower. "Wait, Boston? Don't you have to be at work tomorrow?"

"No. I don't." The light in front of us turned red. "Matty, do you have any idea how I spent the past four days? It wasn't at the office, and it wasn't taking an exam. What I really need to know? How *you* spent them. Why the hell were you in Syria? Have you been there all along?"

"No." Trapped and sinking, I rubbed my ribs. "Just happened."

"I deserve an answer, Matthias. Right now."

I was shell-shocked, in pain, and grieving. Every time I closed my eyes, I saw Ishai's face. Every time I opened them, I saw Ari. Rani. Leah was the only one left unscathed, and I was desperate to keep it that way. "Since when do you give ultimatums?"

"You know what? Never mind." Voice breaking, she put her head and arms down on the wheel and sobbed. "How can I ever trust anything you say again?"

The cabbie behind us laid on the horn, but in my head, what I heard was the one on Ishai's truck, the way it kept blaring after the strike. I fumbled with the door handle, and more or less fell out of the car, because it was either that or suffocate. "Guess you can't."

I ducked into the T station and hopped the turnstile. Maybe she came after me, maybe she didn't, but I walked half the streets in the city that night, knowing I'd broken everything. Every overpass, every set of train tracks, they all had one voice, a voice I'd learned to shut out over the years. Over and over, it said the same thing. *Do it. Do it this time. Make sure you never hurt her again.*

Somewhere on the BU overpass, I called Jack. He picked up on the first ring. "Where the hell are you, Cahill?"

Everything inside me felt dead. I stood, staring over the edge. "I promised her, Jack, I promised her I wouldn't do it."

He let out a long exhale. "Stay where you are. As soon as I can scrape her off my floor, we'll be there."

Chapter 30: Manny

SIX MONTHS LATER
PROVINCETOWN, MASSACHUSETTS

Ari recovered slowly and fitfully, beneath a veil of secrecy I didn't dare lift. As far as Leah or anyone else knew, she was just another face in the world's latest diaspora. Kıraç was still at large, and if the way Nance was harassing me was any indication, the search was going about as well as I said it would. Leah's second try at the bar was in ten days, but we were still in a bad place. Syria had broken a lot more than my ribs.

My world had shifted. Grief…isolation… life felt like I was stumbling around in a dark room, bumping into the furniture because nothing was where I expected. Even the weather was off-kilter. The day I got the Cairo job, it was a balmy fifty-four degrees, so I'd gone out on the porch for some winter sun. Leah was fretting around the kitchen, sounding as if her nerves were about to shoot through the kitchen window. "Does this suit look okay, Mom? Should I button the jacket?"

Senses dulled from lack of sleep, I rested my head on the slats of the porch swing, listening. She had an interview that morning, one in a long string that'd gone nowhere because it was obvious to everyone it wasn't what she wanted to be doing.

We'd always been able to lean on each other, to share a smile or a joke, but lately, we were like two strangers who shared a bed. Not being able to tell her the truth was killing me. About Ari, about what'd happened to Ishai, what Leah had really sacrificed. Any of it. About how all of sudden, my folks weren't my folks or the distant, awful memories of São Paulo that'd started coming in streaks. If I couldn't blame their bad DNA for messing me up, was it life with them or something before? Did I have other parents, maybe brothers and sisters out there somewhere? Without Leah, I couldn't made heads or tails of what any of it meant.

"Leah, stop," her mother said. "Julie adores your father. You would've had this job months ago if you swallowed your pride and let him call her then."

"Not helpful." Her heels clacked on the kitchen floor. "Will you keep an eye on Matty? I made him a sandwich—see if you can get him to eat it?"

Silence. Her mother sniffed the air. "Put on your other suit before you go. And tell him I don't want him smoking that stuff in the carriage house."

A mug clanked on the counter. "It lets him sleep." Leah's voice was brittle. "Not much does at this point, in case you hadn't noticed."

Like a fast-burning fuse, the attack in Syria had reignited my psychosis. I'd wake up dreaming I was that mutilated kid Rani and I found, or I'd see Ishai in the window of a shop, and boom, the glass would explode and there'd be bodies everywhere. A little weed took the edge off the flashbacks, off the constant pain in my ribs. It let me work. If she thought I slept, fine. Unfortunately, I was out.

The screen door banged, and Leah emerged. I sat up. "Knock 'em dead, counselor."

She fiddled with her mom's Audi key, then went down the stairs. "Seventeenth time's the charm, right?"

I met her at the car. "Listen," I said. "You graduated in the top ten percent from Columbia Law. You have a decade of field experience as one of the most passionate, committed human rights geeks I've ever met. They're interested in hiring you, not your dad. Quit telling yourself you haven't earned it."

Her eyes were watery when she tiptoed up to kiss my forehead. "Bye."

Things would be better once she got through the bar. At least that's what I kept telling myself. Deep down, I knew the only way they would was to tell her the truth. To end the devil's pact I'd made with Nance. To do whatever the hell it took to cut through Hana's grief and rage to convince her to see the light, because she was my only hope of bringing Kıraç and Gleason to justice.

Trouble was, six months of hell later, six months of tapped phones and emails hacks and the paranoia of unseen eyes watching everywhere I went, I was no closer than when I'd started. I had photos, but no context, no second source. The only one I'd said anything to was Jack, who laid it out in stark terms: unless I was willing to accept the risks to Leah and Ari, I was well and truly fucked.

Glancing over my shoulder, I took a detour into the Post Office, jangling my key ring. I rented two boxes here. The one in my name had the usual junk mail and flyers, along with a second notice that we were late on Leah's student loans. The second box, which I'd rented with a fake ID, had a thick envelope with postmark from São Paolo. A Brazilian passport for Leah. In case nothing else worked and we had to run.

Eyes closed, I leaned on the wall of P-town's burlesque theatre, rubbing my wedding ring. Maybe I was assuming too much, that she'd even be willing to come with me.

After dialing up the VPN on my phone, I fired up WhatsApp. At the top of my contacts, it read: ***M0ng005e** is **offline***. Our last conversation, from three days ago, was still in the window.

> **Was hoping you thought more about those pictures I sent. Can we meet?**

> **They prove nothing. Leave me alone.**

The frustrating—and dangerous—part of dealing with Hana was that the depth of her denial varied minute-to-minute. I could never be sure whether I'd caught her on a bad day or if I'd caught her in bed with Kıraç. On the plus side, once she figured out he'd been gaslighting her, I was pretty sure she'd castrate the sonofabitch.

My eyes were on the phone, so as I rounded the corner of the mailboxes, I didn't see Nance standing by the windows. "You're rather focused this morning, Matthias," he said. "Anything we might find interesting?"

With a swipe of my thumb, I sent the conversation to the trash. "Hang on, I'll forward it. It's a copy of the Constitution. Try reading it sometime."

"Your ability to find humor in our situation is impressive."

The last time he'd come sniffing around up there, he'd demanded my notes. Recordings. Photos. That was *after* the third interview with men in suits who wouldn't tell me who they were (and hadn't seemed to know about each other, either). It'd taken Nance a week to realize everything I'd given him, I'd already published on my blog. The problem wasn't that I wasn't cooperating; it was that they were clueless.

This time, apparently, he'd prepared a speech. "Mr. Cahill, you of all people should understand the unique dangers this country faces with this utterly unqualified buffoon in the Presidency. A civil war between the FBI, DOJ, and CIA has been brewing since his election, reducing our ability to respond to threats like Kıraç. The administration is failing. I and a handful of like-minded colleagues have been doing our best to prevent something terrible from happening. It's time for you to get on board."

I rubbed my nose. "That part where you just confirmed the whole 'deep state' shadow government conspiracy bullshit… can I get that on the record?"

His expression didn't change. "It would be unfortunate if certain elements of the first government learned what you know. Given their hostility towards your profession. Perhaps you'd be interested in seeing the dossier they're keeping on you."

I know a threat when I hear one. "What do you want, Tony?"

He reached into his pocket and withdrew a tablet, calling up a document on the screen. "This is the copy of the President's daily briefing. This is the most classified document in the entire government, so of course, so you're going to forget you've ever seen it once this conversation is finished."

Curiosity got the better of me. It was a report that the Paris police had raided an apartment. The man they were looking for had escaped, but had left a fake EU passport at the scene. "Okay, so?"

He scrolled to a picture of the suspect. My picture, specifically, of the man kneeling in prayer before he climbing into a leaking raft. "Six months ago, you interviewed this man on your way through Turkey. We know you've been in contact since. We want to find him."

He was right, I knew the guy in question, a husband and father whose wife and two daughters had barely survived an ISIS massacre last year. The rest of his family hadn't been so lucky. "Man, if you think this guy is an Islamic State supporter, you're so far up the wrong tree the other dogs can't even hear you barking."

"All the same, you know this man and you're going to help us find him."

"Congress shall make no law respecting an establishment of religion, or prohibiting the free exercise thereof; or abridging the freedom of speech, or of the press; or the—"

"I'm aware of the First Amendment. This is a matter of national security."

I wiped my hand over my face. "Do you even hear yourself?"

"We're going to require a list of your sources," he said. "Names, known aliases and addresses, how to contact them."

At that point, I swore at him and walked away. I didn't want the world to start going boom any more than he did, but it would've meant them going after people like Nyali Waleed the way they were going after me. After Magdala and Ari. People who couldn't help him. People who'd been through enough and deserved to have peace.

Needing a little peace myself, I hit the Army-Navy store. Dinah, the owner's daughter was helping two little kids pick through a seashell bin. "Your wife around?"

"Feds came sniffing around last week. We're out." Straightening her leg prosthesis, the result of the IED she'd stepped on in Iraq, she jerked her head towards the pier. "Try the pier. The *Antonio Jorge*. Tell Manny I sent you. If he offers you anything stronger, tell him I'll kick his ass. And I'll kick yours twice as hard if you take it."

The fentanyl epidemic was hitting the vets around here pretty hard. "So would Leah."

In the winter, the pier was deserted. The artist shacks were boarded up, the yachts were dry-docked, so it was just a few hardcore fishermen. Manny, who turned out to be a six-two lobsterman, was out piling up his traps. Inside the cabin, he opened a wooden panel in the bulkhead, revealing one hell of a stash. "You know what you want or I gotta figure out what's wrong with you?"

"Who says anything's wrong with me?"

"All Dinah's friends got something wrong." He laid three bags on the bulkhead, and I could tell from the smell they were out of my price range. "Depression, PTSD… this one helps you sleep, that one's great for bone pain."

Rubbing my ribs, I dug out my wallet. "Yeah, all those. Whatever's cheapest."

He was anxious to get out on the water, so we made the exchange. As I was leaving, he stuck a sample joint into my shirt pocket. "This one's on me. You're a mess, bro. You give that a try, see how it fixes you right up. You won't go back to this cheap shit."

"Thanks, I think." I gave it a polite sniff. "Happy fishing."

I was halfway down the pier when Jack called. "You're off to Cairo, Matt—the bloody-minded Egyptians are at it again."

It was a bailout job. The networks had gotten wind that the government was preparing a new crackdown ahead of their rigged election, but to save money, they'd been using stringers, Egyptian kids with cell phones and big dreams, and before any more of them ended up dead or jailed on trumped-up life sentences, they wanted me to go babysit.

"Leah's got the bar next week," I said, wondering when—not to mention how—the hell I'd gotten to be one of the old guys. "I promised I'd be here this time."

"It's ten grand for five," he said. "Can you afford to pass that up?"

What I couldn't afford was another transgression. I took a seat, legs dangling over the pier, staring into the ocean. I was barely functioning in a sleepy tourist town. How the hell would I get through a crackdown in Cairo?

The right answer was obvious, even if I had to think about it for a while. "Can't do it."

"Probably a good call, from what I'm hearing. Fucking Egyptians. I'll let the guy at the network know. Things all right?"

I snorted. "If you don't mind living in a country without free press, they're great."

He didn't say anything for a long time. "She'd want to know, Matt. Tell her what's going on." *Click.*

I was about to hang up when I heard someone else on the line. Specifically, someone breathing. *Oh what the hell.*

But then I realized, whoever it was, they were breathing fast. Breathing heavy. The connection wasn't great, but the sound was higher pitched, like a woman. A scared woman.

It could've been Leah, or Ari, or even Magdala. But I only knew one who could hack though the VPN on my phone. "Hana?"

"I believe you, Matty," she whispered.

"Where are you?" I said, through a sudden case of cottonmouth. I hopped down, under the pilings, gripping the wet wood so hard the barnacles came off. "You safe?"

"Not for long. I can give you what you need. We will make him pay. Yes?"

"Yes." Renewed unease washed over me. I didn't have a clue what changed her mind and trusted it even less. But I had to find out. "I'll meet you. Anywhere."

The connection broke, but one last message came in. *Tomorrow. 9 PM. Cairo.*

Banging my head on the pilings, I hit redial. "Hey Jack? Changed my mind."

An hour later, with my flights arranged, I sat down at my favorite spot on the shore with my laptop and notes to plan the article. To dig out whatever shred of objectivity I could find. To figure out how the hell I was going to verify Hana's info. To shut out all the ghosts in my head and get it written.

This place was magic, a wind-swept well in the dunes. The half-buried remnants of a campfire marked a reminder of the nights Leah and I'd spent out there. It was low enough to be hidden, high enough to hear the ocean through the scrub pines. That sound, man, it was peace.

I fished Manny's joint out of my pocket. The walk into town had pissed off my ribs, and going through the photos I needed to go through was going to throw my subconscious on red alert. There was no more getting around the risks. ICE would be all over Ari, probably within hours. Kıraç and Gleason would come after us, which meant that between Nance and the rest of the Pentagon, CIA, and NSA officials I was about to implicate, we were in deep shit. It meant they'd crank the propaganda machine up to eleven, crow like drunken cocks about fake news, and send the darkest corners of the internet digging into every photo I ever took, every word I ever wrote. Professionally, I wasn't worried, but there were things Leah needed to hear from me, not some bot on Twitter. As my head started to clear, I realized Jack was right. When she got home, I had to tell her everything.

I took a few hits, then ran back to the carriage house for some shots I'd archived, and stopped to take a leak while I was there. That's when I saw two pregnancy tests in the trash. And almost threw up. If they hadn't been negative, I would have.

Reeling, I hauled my stuff back to the beach. What if it had been positive? Why two? Did she want it to be? Nobody in their right mind would think of me as father material. Would this be the last straw, would she leave me?

Half-stoned and lightheaded, I found Rani's old St. Frances medal in the box of photos. I remembered the last time he'd worn it, the day we'd gone into the *favelas*. He couldn't shake off the thing with the kid, so we'd hiked up to the cliffs overlooking the city and passed a joint.

You want kids someday, man? Nah, he replied. *World's too fucked up. Just like us.*

Leah had always felt the same way. Hadn't she?

Lost twenty years in the past, I took another hit. That was my mistake.

Suddenly, I couldn't focus. Colors grew bright, my vision distorted. All the sound stopped, like it had right before that missile hit. The whole world started throbbing, then wrenched away. Everything I touched turned to fire and a laughing demon sprung up in its place, a demon with a thousand faces. The harder I tried to fight, the more he burned. The more I fought, the stronger he became, the more he tore through everyone and everything I loved.

I don't know how long it lasted, but by the time I got straight, the air smelled like ash and burnt film stock. A blast of February wind hit my bare ass. In the fire pit, I could make out the blackened and curled edges of some old photos.

Christ, what had I done?

That's when I noticed Leah sitting cross-legged in front of me, eyes red as the desert sun. I blinked twice. "Are you real?"

When she started sobbing, I reached for her, but she pushed me away. "I can't do this anymore, Matty."

By her side, there was a grey shoebox, which she pushed across the sand. When I opened the lid, I found a Bible, some happy pills… and her wedding ring. All the air sucked right out of my lungs, seeing that ring off her finger. It was the moonstone I'd given her in the desert— the only one she'd ever wanted. "Don't, Leah please—"

"These are the three things I've ever seen help you." Her voice broke. "Pick one, pick all three, but for god's sake, pick something, because you're killing me."

That moment was everything Jack had warned me about from the beginning, it was why he was on his fourth wife, along with every other guy I knew in this job. So I put the ring on her finger where it belonged, told her I was sorry, then we buried the pills and the Bible with the ashes under the sand.

We were both wrung out and raw, so somehow the conversation we desperately needed to have turned into a messed-up fuck on the beach. As she lay in my arms, everything felt wrong, and I started to doubt whether I could ever make it right. It wasn't just the secrets. It wasn't her dashed hopes of a baby, if that's what they were. Or my fear of it. It was this crazy life we were leading, it was the families I'd seen in town and on the beach, the things they took for granted that we couldn't. Lately I'd been feeling the weight of the life we were missing. Maybe the world wouldn't give up on war. But we could.

"I got the job," she said softly. "So long as I pass the bar."

As the shadows grew long, I told her I loved her and made up my mind. Cairo was my last job. Retirement. If she wanted kids, we'd figure it out. Maybe in a year or two… when things calmed down…

"Shit, what time is it?"

Her arms tightened around my waist. "Jack called. I know about Cairo. I'm going with you. End of discussion."

Chapter 31:
The Mongoose
CAIRO, EGYPT

The kid in the Adidas T-shirt danced atop the police tank, a triumphant silhouette in the noxious air. Grinning, he waved his arms at me. "You make me famous, eh?"

Death to Sisi! Death to the dictator!

Like ants swarming a grasshopper, they knocked him down. The hive picked up his chant. It washed over the fallen, the bleeding, even as the police beat anyone they could get their clubs on. The way things were going, the kid didn't have worry about getting famous. He needed to worry about getting dead.

Crackdown or not, my mind was elsewhere, and the photos I'd been taking were crap. The eighteen-hour trip had been murder on my ribs and even raising the camera hurt. Eyes burning, I fixed on the window of the museum, chewing a vinegar-soaked rag to blunt the gas.

Lit softly by the gallery lights, Leah was inside with her review books. Her hand was on her stomach, which had been bothering her all day, and it was messing with my head. As in, my head kept forgetting that people were shooting at me in favor of wondering about things like diapers and whether pregnancy tests were ever wrong. The longer I watched, the less I wanted to be out here playing Baghdad Bob for the network.

A teenage girl in a checkered hijab was working the crowd near the museum, waving a handmade sign. *Sisi, get out! This is our Egypt!* The police charged, she ran, and crashed right into the window near Leah, who reacted by tossing her books away and going for her sneakers. She was pissed off and sick of studying, and wanted to be where the action was, but bodies were piling up. Hopping on the wall of the lotus pond, I sent her a text:

(Stay put Leah)

(And get away from the goddamn window)

My mobile rang, then next thing I knew, bullets were spitting into the pond. Three more dug into the pavement before I realized they weren't rubber. Searing hot pain flashed across my left biceps.

I beat it into alley behind the museum, swearing at myself. It was a rookie mistake, forgetting to turn off the damn ringer. Oppression 101—shoot at the journalists.

Since I knew she'd be freaked, I called back. "Hey, babe." I examined the gash, which felt like it went three rounds with a blowtorch. "How's the studying?"

"Are you okay?"

So far tonight, I'd been shot at, gassed, and nearly took a hunk of highway overpass to the head. I had my name and her mobile number scribbled in permanent marker on my forearm, for reasons neither of us wanted to think about. "Far as you know."

"Butthead. I'm coming out."

Reaching into my vest, I took out the picture I'd taken of her in Morocco. To me, it was never about what she was or wasn't wearing; it was a reminder that we'd always come out the other side of whatever shit we'd been dealing with. A reminder of how she'd given me a second chance I didn't deserve. Tonight, I was praying she'd give me another one.

"Leah, it's bad. Stay where you are. There's nothing you can do."

The curator's son, Saleh, came up behind me, a gas mask popped up on his head. "*Sahabi*, is that your wife? Man, I had no idea she had tits like that."

Fuck me sideways. Okay, so it was partly about what she wasn't wearing. "You mind, Sal? I'm talking to her."

"Come on." He jumped on me like an overexcited puppy. "CNN wants us on the roof of the City View Hotel in five."

"Busy." Covering the receiver, I scanned the crowd for Hana, who was already an hour later than she'd said. "Find somebody else."

Journalist or soldier, the two guys you don't want sitting next to you are a private fresh off the transport and the old vet looking to ride it home. Whether by skill, luck, or my mother's damn angels, I'd made it this far. If Hana delivered, after tonight, I'd have something to show for the hell I'd put Leah through. I'd be able to make good on my last promise to Ishai, to give Ari the chance to dream again. With any luck, it'd get Nance off my case. It meant the end of old nightmares, it meant new beginnings.

I walked off down the alley. "Sorry," I said to Leah.

She didn't sound happy. "Since when are you showing that to people?"

"I wasn't, I just… needed to see it, okay?"

"Matty, just come home," she said softly. "You can have the real thing."

"God, you have no idea." The smoke, the gas—I'd had enough. "How's your stomach? Did that tea I brought you help?"

"Yeah, better," she finally said.

"Liar." I could practically hear her rubbing her midsection. "How about I scrounge up some of that honey candy you like?"

"I'm okay."

She wasn't. We weren't. I wanted all this behind us. "Hey, listen—can you see my blog?"

"It's been running like a ninety-year-old turtle with a piano on its back."

"Check your flights while you're at it."

"They're looking for observers down in Suez," she said. "The military says eleven dead, but Amnesty thinks it's higher. Maybe we should—"

"No." The only reason she was here at all was I was fairly certain she would've divorced me otherwise.

Leah was in the middle of a full-tilt—and futile—pitch to convince me that I needed babysitting more than she needed to pass the bar when Hana appeared on the far side of the alley. It would've been a relief, except for the nervous, folded-in set to her shoulders. When she skulked up, face obscured by the lace veil over her hair, her blouse was torn, dirt on her knees, and she had a nasty-looking shiner on her left eye.

Kıraç? I mouthed, covering the receiver.

"I would have killed him, not ratted him out to you," she replied. "The police raided our camp this morning."

Leah finally gave up. "You realize I'm going to make a shitty lawyer if I can't even negotiate with you."

"You only suck at negotiating when you're wrong."

Leah was quiet for a minute. "No internet. They must've pulled the plug."

Which meant the network guys were freaking out. "Let me go deal with that, then I'll come find you."

"Will you be long?"

Glancing at her photo, memories stirred. Desert moonlight on her curves, the slickness of water on her skin, watching her casting her doubts to the sand, giving herself up to me and my lens. "I'm staring at a naked picture of my gorgeous wife. Part of me is."

"I happen to like that part. Try not to get it shot off."

The connection went dead, so I inspected Hana's bruise. "So if Kıraç didn't do this, and nothing I sent made a dent in that thick skull of yours, what exactly led to this change of heart?"

Through the tear gas and smoke, a line of police in riot gear marched across the end of the street, shields and masks lowered, batons at the ready. Hana held her breath until they passed. "Come. There is someone waiting for us."

"You sure you're all right?"

Her voice was bitter and dark. "When my brother's killers taste the fear I have tasted, then I will be 'all right'."

She took me to the Kasr El-Dobara, a stone-spired church two blocks east, set up as a makeshift hospital. Casualties groaned in the courtyard. Bodies of those less fortunate, tied in white sheets, lined the edges. Beside the sanctuary wall, a young father was reading a book to the boy in his lap. Hana's mongoose, now grey in the muzzle, was curled up next to them. I recognized him as Ishai's friend Tal Morsia, who I'd last seen being torn away from his son at the Syrian border. The rest of the night's crap melted away. They'd found their way together.

When I raised my Nikon, Hana stepped in the way. "You mustn't. If Kıraç learns we are here, he will kill us."

Tal met us at the fence. Wary and mistrustful, he kept his son behind him. "You are her friend, the journalist? She says you are angry with her. That you think her a great fool."

"Only if she thinks that." I slipped the boy one of Leah's honey candies. "She's pretty cool, right? For a girl."

Between that and the mongoose crawling up my jeans and sticking its nose into my pocket, it convinced Tal we were all on the same side. His wife had been killed early in the war, but he'd stuck around, equal parts death wish and stubborn attachment to home, which lasted until some piece-of-shit death squad commander decided to target his six-year-old son. "But so many have drowned on the rafts. I thought I had purchased a path to safety. All Kıraç delivered were lies."

"Lies I believed." Hana's voice was bitter.

What I'd seen at the border was even worse than it looked. They were about to enter a smuggling tunnel when Tal was told they'd been compromised. Men loyal to the death squad commander were waiting at the far end, and others were fast coming up behind. Another tunnel was in progress, but it was small, barely large enough for a child Ninan's size.

Believing they'd both be killed otherwise, Tal agreed to separate, and soon after, was captured. Held for weeks. Tortured. One day, he was dragged from his cell, certain he was being taken to be executed. Instead, Kıraç was waiting, claiming he'd paid the ransom for Tal's release.

"He was… enraged." Tal's hand shook as he smoothened his son's hair. "Kıraç said American commandos had attacked and killed his men at the tunnel exit. He said Ninan was alive, but the Americans had sold him to slave traders. He said together, we would make them pay, that my son—" His voice broke. "He would contact me once he knew more."

For months, Kıraç had dangled false hopes and near misses, manipulating him into fits of rage and despair. The meetings began to come with strings attached. Odd requests, like obtaining a job handling baggage at the airport. A sick sense hit my gut. "Please tell me you knew something was up."

Through the tear gas and smoke, the blare of a horn grew louder. Another ambulance inched its way through the throngs. The paramedics gave up and leapt out, carrying two bloodied and limp forms. The crowd erupted beside the iron church gate. Four guys dragged in the Adidas Kid, now lifeless, one holding each limb. Some started sobbing, others prayed. The police came and tried to break it up, but the students formed a wall around the vigil. Candles were lit.

Tal tilted his candle towards Hana's. "That I was being manipulated? Yes. I told myself I had no choice." He held the flame to his thumb, perhaps needing something to cut through the numbness. "Three weeks ago, I was given a package by another man and told where to put it on the plane. When I refused, he said he wife and daughter would be killed. We were living the same hell. In that moment, I believed I would never see my son again."

Someone lit the candle in Hana's hand, but if she noticed, it barely registered. I tipped mine to hers, wondering where her mind was. "So is this where you came in?"

She'd been focused on something across the square, but she faced me, jaw shaking. "Where I came in? To do what? To discover the man I loved was a monster? That he had sold my friends and their children to Daesh? That I helped him do it?"

Tal reached for her, but she spun off by herself to the far side of the prayer circle. Troubled, he stroked Ninan's hair. "He had been taken to a Daesh camp near Raqqa. There were many others, mostly Yazidis and Christians, but Ninan was the only one she could get out. Even I do not know fully what they went through to get here. Only that my nightmare ended where hers began."

Nance had been right about everything. It was a cruel, ugly, cynical plan that had Gleason's fingerprints all over it—they'd targeted mostly Christian and Yazidi refugees who wouldn't get the same scrutiny as Muslims. Kıraç had long made a game of weaponizing fear. Gleason meant to weaponize love. He was out to prove no refugee could ever be trusted. If there were others, it meant the plan was still in motion. That they meant to carry it through one way or the other.

Reeling, I ducked around the vigil and went to Hana. It was starting to sink in, how explosive this was. Five minutes ago, this was a story linking dirty US money to arms deals and human trafficking in Syria. I'd never known the endgame, and made the mistake of assuming it was financial.

It wasn't.

They wanted successful attacks. They wanted atrocities.

They wanted a narrative they could point at for generations.

"I need all the names of Kıraç's other victims," I said. "Descriptions. Documents. Everything you have. Help me find them. Help me stop it."

She didn't answer at first. "These men are our friends. With America, it is shoot first, and ask no questions. They will die with the world believing them to be terrorists. I will not betray them again."

"People will die, Hana."

She let out a bitter laugh. "After the way the west has treated us? You expect that I care?"

Jesus, what happens if I fuck this up? "You wouldn't be here otherwise."

Her eyes narrowed. "Perhaps I want Ioannis to suffer."

"Great. Me too." I opened the Nikon's memory slot and popped out the SD card. "Copy whatever you've got onto that. I'll make sure the world sees it. But everything hinges on whether you're both willing to go on the record."

She reached for the card. "Will it convince them to rescue the women and children Kıraç has sold?"

I knew she already knew the answer. "What about your YPG friends?"

She looked away. "We are too few and our enemies are too strong. Do you not think I tried them before you?"

Tal spoke up. "I have a sister who remains in Syria. Last night, she went to the terrorists' camp to see what she could learn. So far, we are three. Four, if you are with us too."

"And we will be two again after your sister gets herself killed." In shame, Hana lowered her head. "Matthias, these are women I helped dress for their weddings. Children I helped come into this world. What have I done?"

It was obvious that it was killing her, so I kissed her forehead. "Where is Kıraç now?"

She went stiff in my arms. Her eyes locked on something near the museum wall. "There. Behind your wife."

My whole body went cold. Kıraç flashed a cruel smile, sniffing Leah's hair, then sauntered over after Hana, who scurried into the middle of the prayer circle. He went after her and something snapped. At the last second, I saw the knife in his hand, and barely dodged the swing. The mongoose jumped off Hana's shoulder and sunk its teeth into Kıraç's neck. He cursed and dropped the knife. The mongoose chittered away in triumph.

Sniper fire spit from the rooftops. Hana seemed frozen. "Go!" I shouted. She grabbed Ninan and ran off, the mongoose close at her heel. Right then, Kıraç's fist caught me square in the gut. A white-hot light exploded behind my eyes. I heard a metallic scrape, and realized he'd picked up the knife. I couldn't get a breath, but as my vision cleared, Leah was watching, hands over her mouth.

Kıraç spoke right in my ear, a mocking tone in his voice. "I had forgotten how beautiful she is. I will return for her later."

With that, he skipped off after Hana.

Leah ran over and helped me out of the line of fire. The betrayal and confusion on her face almost killed me. It dawned on me that she might've seen me comforting Hana. How it must've looked. "She's just someone I know," I stammered, fighting to breathe through a haze of pain. "That guy…"

Her hands were shaking as she took my camera. "It's fine, you can tell me later."

The square was chaos—tanks and APVs rumbling around, Sisi's murderous thugs, bullets, rubber or not. Kıraç wasn't the only psychopath out there. All she had was a pair of swim goggles and a scarf over her face. I could've throttled her for coming out by herself.

She fumbled with Yusef's keys, unlocking the service door. "What were you thinking, going after that guy?"

I mumbled something about a flashback. Even behind the goggles, from the way her eyes filled, I knew she didn't believe me. Didn't know why I'd lie. Didn't like the suggestions her mind was throwing at her.

"Stop looking at me like that." It was past time to come clean, but I didn't have the words. "You know I'm no cheat. She's a source. A friend."

The dusty basement was a maze of metal crates in fading green paint, mysteries which hadn't seen daylight in five thousand years. I paced between the crates, mind racing. Hana hadn't given me anything concrete. I barely knew more than I did an hour ago. Only that something terrible was coming. And that I didn't know enough to stop it.

"Matty, where are you, what's wrong?" Leah took the camera from my hand, caressing my temple. "Are you in trouble?"

How do you tell the woman you love you're the reason she almost died five years ago? That she witnessed a colleague's murder and gave up a career she loved? I couldn't forget seeing that ring off her finger. She didn't need one more reason to leave, she needed a reason to stay, and I had nothing to offer. So I lifted her onto a crate, captured her mouth and told her I needed her, because everything in me was screaming I'd already lost her.

But then I heard the breaking glass upstairs, the looting, and I heard Yusef screaming for help. Groaning in frustration, every inch of me protesting, I let my weight drop onto Leah. "He's going to get himself killed over a clay jug or something, isn't he?"

Leah sat up, reaching for my T-shirt. "I'm coming too."

I kissed her, snagging my shirt. "Stay. I'll only be a few minutes."

Frowning, she covered her breasts. "Seriously, what has you so spooked?"

I rested my forehead on hers. "I don't know where to start."

She bit her lip. "You could… you could tell me how you feel about this."

At first I thought she meant Hana. Ari. The fact that the world was about to start exploding. Then I saw where her hand was. On her stomach.

The room started to swim. "God, Leah, I—"

Glass shattered upstairs. Yusef screamed. So I closed my eyes and kissed her. "I love you. So much, but right now, I am scared to death. Lock the door behind me. I'll be right back. Then we'll talk. I swear."

At the first-floor landing, I stopped, resting my hand on the wall. There's this photo of a lonely, confused man on a beach in Phuket, wondering where all the water's gone, because he doesn't have a clue that a tsunami is about to race back in and drown him. That was me.

Leah's pregnant? Christ, what the hell have I done?

Looters were streaming in via a rope ladder dangling from the museum's dome. Shattered glass covered the limestone floor, raining down on the Amenhotep statue. They ran to the museum door, throwing it open. Yusef was on the second-floor landing, all wide-eyes and crazy hair, having a tug-of-war over a mummy's head, hysterical as bandages unraveled. I bounded up the closest staircase and dragged him away. He fell to his knees, sobbing as the head crumbled to dust in his hands. "Ain't worth it, man."

I got him to his office and locked him in. When I made for the stairs, mixed in with the looters, I spotted a guy in tactical gear. Then two more. "He's there," one shouted.

On instinct, I spun around, expecting to see Kıraç. A fleeting sense of relief hit me, thinking they'd finally caught him, but there was just a terra cotta vase. Then it shattered.

The shards fell slowly, as if time had stopped. At the sound of the shot, I realized it. They weren't here for Kıraç. They were here for me.

Two more guys ran up the stairs, three from the mummy room. All my exits were blocked. Desperate, I hopped up onto the railing and made a leap for the rope ladder. Pain exploded in my ribs. On pure adrenaline, I pulled myself up, hand over hand, until I reached the jagged hole in the domes. The looters had gotten up here somehow—I could get down, melt into the crowds.

I collapsed on the roof, groaning. My vision swam. The roof was covered with a grid of lighting and ventilation structures, domed sky-lights and steaming vents. Feeling like a rat in a maze, I dialed Leah. She picked up the instant the call connected. "Hey, where are you?"

"Out." I ducked around the roof structure, searching for a hiding spot. "Needed a smoke."

A gasp came from the phone. It was a code phrase. She knew. "Can you get some aspirin while you're out?" *Can you get away?*

"Stores are closed, babe." *I'm probably screwed.* "Check my bag. Side pocket. Should be some there."

Leah's voice trembled. "Matty, what's going on?"

"I got your back, baby." After waiting for the footsteps to fade, I rolled around the side of the structure, heading for the edge of the roof. *Where's the goddamn fire escape?*

"Is this about—?"

"Stop." Somewhere on the other side, I heard the crunch of gravel. "You don't know anything. I haven't told you a thing, right?"

"Matty please…"

For God's sake don't give them a reason to come after you. "Say it, Leah."

"Would I be asking if you did?"

A single, glowing red dot appeared on a nearby rooftop—camera, sniper rifle, who knew. One of the commandos had reached the top.

"Matthias Cahill, you are charged with providing material support to terrorists under the Patriot Act. Surrender yourself immediately. This will be your only warning."

The fuck?

The other footsteps drew closer. Hoping for a dumpster, anything, I glanced over the edge, but it was fifty feet straight down, to where a police gang was brutalizing a protestor. Nauseated, I rested my skull on the bricks and prayed.

"Listen to me," I said to Leah. "Put on my sweats. Tie the biggest goddamn knot in the waist you can because there are gangs out here who will make you regret it if you don't. Then get your ass to the embass—"

My first thought was that a cobra had fallen out of the sky and sunk its teeth into my neck. The pain was blinding. My legs, arms, nothing worked right. Gravel crunched next to me. I groped for the phone. "I love you. You know that, right?"

She was sobbing, but it sounded far away. "You promised me, Matty, you swore you'd always come home."

"No choice," I said, but it all came out wrong. "You were the only home I ever knew."

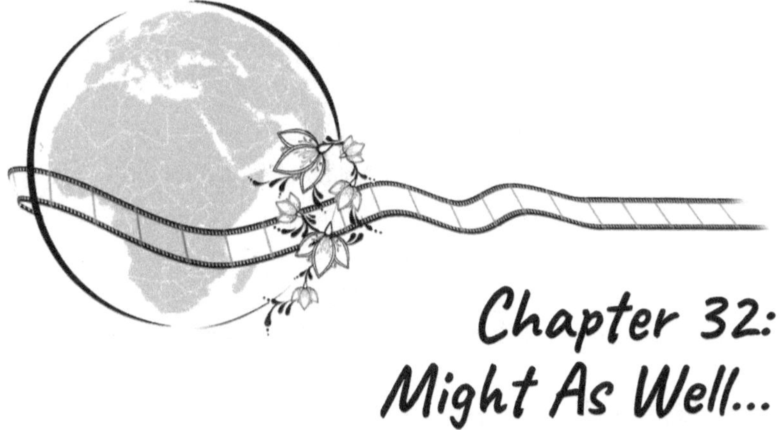

Chapter 32:
Might As Well...

MEDITERRANEAN SEA
PRESENT

The world spins at a distance. Lost spirits take roost in the darkness. Under an ink-black sky, Rani and Ishai are kicking around a striped melon. Gilly Tavarez sits on the dock, fishing. By the water's edge, Tish and Misha are passing a joint on the hood of a HumVee, pointing at me and laughing about something. With a welcoming wave, Ishai boots the melon in my direction. I'm about to kick it when I realize that everyone here is dead.

Rani runs over, troubled. "Shit's real this time, boyo. You don't belong here yet."

He thrusts his hands at my chest with the force of a mule kick. I can't draw a breath, until a rush of water spews out of my throat. A blinding light flashes by. Retching, I sputter out a lungful and collapse to the floor.

Wade is swearing his fool head off. "You didn't notice he stopped breathing?"

Gleason gets in his face. "You questioning me?"

"Yeah. I am. You kill him, Nance gets another thing to hold over our heads."

Gleason slops the wet mask on my chest. "We're done. Sonofabitch told us everything."

"Told you what?" I splutter.

The swinging bulb casts ghoulish shadows on his face. "Where to find that baby sister of yours."

I didn't, I know I didn't. I made stuff up. "You're lying."

"232 Seaver Street. Dorchester. Apartment 3B." He backs off, settling into the chair. "'Course she's not there now, is she? You told her where to run if things ever got too hot. You told us that too."

Everything goes numb. Quinn raises a bottle of brown liquor and takes a deep swig. "He's full of shit. Nance let it slip about your sister."

I cough another mouthful on the deck. "When you two get your stories straight, let me know."

Gleason yanks my hair. "ICE is on their way to pick her up. By this time tomorrow, she'll be back where she belongs."

Empty and defeated, I put my head down and pray. "Leah will stop you."

He heads for the door, chuckling. "I'm counting on her trying." He waves his cigarette at Quinn. "Lock him in his cell while I figure out what to do with him."

Quinn doesn't bother with the chains or the hood. I'd make a break for it, but my arms and legs are all pins and needles and between my ears, there's only buzzing. "What's he want with Leah?"

He shoves me forward. "Walk."

Find your head, idiot. Stop thinking like a prisoner. Or a guy who's about to lose his wife. Start thinking like a reporter. You know his weak spots.

"So three women pay the price for what you did?" My tongue feels thick and slow, swollen from salt water. "Bet your fiancée would be real proud."

"Say another word about Jenna and I'll break your neck." He turns left instead of right at the sally port, then pushes me towards a steel-runged ladder leading into blackness. "Climb."

My claustrophobia picks a bad time to act up. Can't breathe, can't think. Fifteen rungs up, I whack my head on a metal hatch. Quinn climbs up beside me and grabs the handle. The sea wind rushes in as he opens the hatch, a roar drowned by the engines. I scramble out and collapse on the deck, gulping air. The wind on my face is like life itself.

He climbs out, dragging me behind the bulkhead, out of sight. "That mosque up in Diyala… the one your wife's ex took the rap for blowing up? You never found out what that was about, right?"

"Your boss covering up for the fact you all got whacked out on PCP, then raped and murdered a bunch of civilians? Sure I did."

With a soulless expression, he sinks down next to me. "Sarin. The stuff Kıraç is using. That's where it came from. We found these 152mm shells—old, rusty, leaking. Clarke made the mistake of picking one up. Gleason blamed the village kids who brought us there. Ain't none of us been right since."

Understatement. "I didn't smell any chemicals when I was in there."

"We got orders to cover the whole thing up because the precursors came from a US company with the right connections. Let's just say we didn't like it much. Gleason kept a few 'souvenirs'. Said you never knew when they'd come in handy." He stares off into the distance. "Overheard him and Wade earlier. He's got cover from Washington now. They sent him to figure out where Kıraç's planning the next attack. Orders are, 'make it bigger'."

Nausea rolls me over. "You grow a conscience all of a sudden?"

"You gonna help me or not?" His eyes shift sideways. "Tell the truth. You know how to find Hana."

Months without a whiff of freedom, now this? *Nope.* "Sorry."

He digs out a cigarette and lights it. "Too bad, because he's close. Somebody spotted her crossing out of Kurdish territory an hour ago. If he kills you and gets her, the only thing standing in his way is your wife." He bangs his head on the steel. "The plan is for Hendricks to arrest her for harboring a fugitive, then stage a jailhouse suicide."

I press my thumbs into my eyes. It's a moonless night, as black outside as it was in the tunnel. "Why are you telling me this?"

"Because I didn't sign up for this shit." He gets up, peering around the bulkhead. "They're transferring another detainee tonight. The rendezvous point is a couple miles off the Syrian coast. How far you think you can you swim?"

Towards the east, there's a faint glow on the horizon. Land. Civilization. "*That* far? No way. Grow a pair. Stop him yourself."

"I got family too." Knuckles white, he grips the railing. "Lucky me. I get to see this through the bitter end."

I pull myself up the rail, fighting vertigo. "So what do I get to do? Drown?"

"Same thing that got you here. 'Cept this time, put out the goddamn story. Warn people what's coming. Give them a chance."

He's setting me up, I know he's setting me up. Buried deep inside is kid who's looked over a rail before, and found the sea more forgiving than the monster on board. But this isn't the Gibraltar ferry. These monsters aren't my old man. Shore is a lot farther away. I'm too wasted for this.

I swing a leg over and swallow hard. The swell is up. One good gust and the wind will rip me right off. Swirling black water rushes by.

Just come home.

I always will.

*Promise me you'll never do anything
like you did that night.*

You want that promise,
I need something to remember it by.

If I jump, am I keeping my word or breaking it?

The wind carries shouts. Searchlights fire up on the deck, sweeping the water. Footsteps pound. First thing I see is the barrel of an M4. Then Gleason behind it.

He makes a 'hands-up' motion with the gun. "The hell is this?"

Quinn tries to cover. "Chill, a'right? The moron made run for it when I tried to give him some fresh air. Where's he going to go?"

"You tell me." The barrel swings his way. "You think I don't know what this is? You think you can burn me?"

Quinn raises his hands, as if he knows what's coming. "You think you can control Kıraç. You can't. You're both crazy."

Gleason's finger twitches on the trigger. Quinn makes a lunge for the gun barrel. A blinding flash comes out of the muzzle. Pain sears my eardrums. Quinn crumples to the deck like a bloody rag doll. I know he's dead. I know I'm next.

I let go.

The fall in blackness lasts longer than I thought. The sound of the sea rushes up, so I suck in a breath, but the cold and the force of entry knocks it right out. The water churns from the wake, so I kick for the surface before the screws suck me under.

My head breaks the surface. *Goddamnit, it's cold.* A searchlight sweeps over me, but only once. The sound of the engines grows fainter.

Disorientation sets in. Panic. I can't find the lights. I'm miles off shore, bobbing in the middle of the Mediterranean. There's a very good chance I'm going to die.

A swell comes up beneath, pushing me to the stars, and when it crests, I spot the glow of civilization on the horizon. A crazy, unstoppable rush of euphoria floods through me. I roll onto my back, watching the stars, whooping and laughing like a fool. "I'm free, baby, I'm free!" I shout to Leah, as if she can hear me.

In response, a wave washes over, pushing me under. Sputtering and sobered, I find my bearings and swim.

Exhaustion has long since set in. My arms and legs are too heavy to move, and I'm starting to think Quinn had the right idea when I spot something bobbing on the waves, which turns out to be one of those deathtrap inflatable rafts the smugglers use. What's left of one, anyhow. Then closer to shore, a light appears. Not a searchlight, just a point of brilliance in the dark. A flashlight. Maybe a cell phone. Voices, speaking Syrian Arabic. I call out, but the sound is a croak. A small fishing trawler breaks through the night mist. The light points my way again. Exhausted, I wave my hand, afraid to hope they're friendly, too desperate to care if they're not.

A line slops next to me in the water, but I don't have the strength to grab it. Someone hauls me out. Spluttering, I collapse on the deck. A young girl comes over and sits cross-legged in front of me. "You are safe," she says in Arabic. There are other shadows on the boat, people, most wet, shivering, and traumatized. The world spins, like it's growing and shrinking, going backwards and forwards all in the same moment.

The captain drapes a grey blanket around my shoulders. There's a phone on his pocket. Coughing out a mouthful of salt water, I crawl to my hands and knees. "Please… I need to call my wife."

Chapter 33:
Hope & Dreamers
BOSTON, MASSACHUSETTS
PRESENT

Leah

Lucky pulls up to the Orthodox church near the Arboretum, driving the same rumbly green Ford he's had since I was little. As rain plinks the hood and the skies open, he scans the parking lot. "You sure about this, Pigtails? Could be a trap."

Ari—or at least someone pretending to be her—texted me that she's here. Since it's the *only* thing that's gotten through my phone in hours… yeah, my working theory is that it's a trap. Between that and spotting Ryan Hendricks lurking around the ferry terminal, I decided my mother was right. Lucky may be in his sixties, he's also six-four, two hundred and thirty pounds, and much better at losing creepy pseudo-CIA agents than me.

My phone rings once, with an unknown number, then immediately disconnects. Which it's done three times in the last five minutes. "I'm not letting them send her back, put it that way. You sure you're up for this?"

Looking mildly insulted, he shifts out of park, turns up the volume on his police scanner, and checks the hand-held video camera we brought to document any potential shenanigans. "Meet you around back."

The rain intensifies as I run across the lot. All I've ever known is that Lucky had been there when DJ died. It's the reason I knew he wouldn't go anywhere. But I had to ask.

Though it's barely nine a.m., the small sanctuary is unlocked, with candles burning on the altar. In the rain-darkened vestry, Maira—Ari—sits on a bed roll near the corner, reading a textbook. The weight of broken trust and secrets washes over me, and for a moment, all I can do is watch, struggling to overcome the hurt and betrayal. Truth is, I don't know what to feel. Mostly that I want a do-over for the whole damn last year.

In that quiet, frozen moment, clarity begins to dawn. She's not the toothless little girl in the photo anymore. She's the same age as I was when I met Matty. Have I been sleepwalking all that time? Which generation was on watch when this became a country where a powerful few could silence a journalist? Was it my father's? Mine? Was it inevitable when the planes hit the towers, or did we miss our chance to stop it? Did the country succumb to its fear, or was it slumbering right along with me? The girl who'd grown up believing in the law is suddenly wide awake.

The last stair creaks under my feet. She startles, dropping a textbook and grabbing an aluminum crutch like makeshift clubs. "Who's there?"

"It's okay, Ari-eil," I say. "It's Leah."

Her mouth opens to a little 'o'. Drawing a pained breath, she struggles up, clutching her side. "Please, if you know—what does that mean? Is Matty free?"

"No, he's not. Not yet at least." Tears well up. She's always been as guarded with me as I've been with her. "I want that as badly as you do, but from now on, I need the truth. Why didn't he tell me? Why did he keep you a secret?"

"You would have to ask him." She rubs the scars on her arms. "A year ago, I woke up in the strangest place I have ever seen, in pain

I could have never imagined, to people calling me by a name that wasn't mine. I had lost my sisters, my brother and the one who survived treated me like a stranger." Head bowed, she grasps the cross around her neck. "Perhaps I am a reminder of things he would rather forget."

"Losing you haunted him, Ari. He wasn't ashamed. At least not of you."

She kneels to collect her bed roll, redness rimming her hazel eyes. "Eema told him my injuries were his fault."

Her mother limps out of a small library off the vestry. "Tch. I told him a truth he should have been told as a child. Be thankful I was kinder to you."

Ari reaches for a thick school text. "A truth which wouldn't have brought Ishai back. Instead you made Matty feel as I have my whole life. As a shameful secret best hidden."

The comment registers deeply on her mother's face. "I die when she says these things. I don't know which of them is worse. A girl ashamed of her birth, a boy ashamed of the man who gave her life. When you have lost so much, such things should seem small."

Mothers, daughters, fathers, sons… people the world over lead messy emotional lives. That I understand. This, I don't, and we don't have time for it. I yank the zipper on my bag. "Trust me, I'm aware of Matty's issues with his father."

"The man who raised him, yes. But Eli is not his father."

"Huh?"

Magdala slips her book onto the shelf. "Matthias was a toddler they found wandering in São Paulo. Alone. Abandoned. For how long, I don't know. Some time, I believe."

Something wrenches in my gut, spreading into a sense of sickness. "So they just…took him?"

Her mouth opens, then closes. She raises a finger, then lowers it. She's not sure whether she wants to defend them. "They convinced themselves it was God's plan. The child they had prayed for. But the tighter they clung, the more he pulled away. By the time Eli confessed it to me, he'd known for many years what they did was wrong. He'd come to see Matthias as a test… one he had failed."

I'm too shocked to say much of anything. "Of what? His humanity?"

She purses her lips. "I have asked myself many times if it is really so different from when I took in my daughter's friend to raise as my own. When no one would help and no one else cared, what were they to do?"

Being an aid worker means figuring out how to cope when your own powerlessness punches you in the face. You get drunk. You cry. You pray, if that's your thing, or go off and scream at the sky. You don't kidnap a child. "Matty never knew any of this before?"

"No. And it was never my place to tell him." Head low, she rests on the shelves. "In three days, I had lost three children, and I believed I would lose the fourth. Each of them viewed Matthias as a brother. Sometimes I forgot he was not my own. In my grief, I lashed out at him for being the one who survived."

Learning something like that would throw anyone for a loop, never mind Matty. The idea he might've had another family out there… the question of what happened to them or whether they'd abandoned him and why. Or whether he'd been stolen. How different his life might have been. The nightmares he'd been having, mumbling in his sleep in Portuguese—suddenly, it made sense. Everything did. Except whatever made him so scared of telling me that he decided to go through it alone.

Struggling to pull it together, I riffle through my bag for their asylum forms. "Immigration found out about your false papers and denied your petition. I wrote an appeal, but they're going to deny that too. Whoever has Matty is using you against him. Our only hope is to prove that. I need to know what he was hiding and why."

"Hana and Matty swore to bring Ishai's killers to their knees," Ari says. "He said none of us would be safe until that happened."

A bitter taste comes into my mouth. "Well *that* plan worked out great."

She stands, a protective expression on her face. "He was afraid you didn't love him anymore. Do you?"

Guess I can see why she'd wonder. "Yes, I still love him. Very much." My vision blurs. "But he's put you in danger. Pack a bag with some warm clothes. I have a friend outside who can protect you. Otherwise, by this time tomorrow, the government will have you on a plane to Syria."

Her face pales. "We'll be killed."

My phone buzzes, then disconnects again. I fight the urge to smash it on the floor. "I'm not going to let that happen."

Ari goes to pick up her overstuffed school bag, but drops it, clutching her side. As I reach for it, her breathing is labored. Gritting her teeth, she fights through the pain. "There is a man in your government who knows who I am. A very powerful man. A senator. He told Matty that if he ever told anyone, we would be sent back and you would end up in prison."

Her mother sucks in a breath. "For God's sake, Ari-eil."

Ari whirls, as if she's no longer able to contain the fire inside. "Because of that man, you are a widow. Because of him, I have never known my father. Because of him, Hana lives as a ghost. Because of him, Matty may never come home. Why are you protecting him?"

"I am protecting you." Magdala crumples her bedroll into a ball, as if she means to strangle it. "Hana is the worst of both her parents. Her father a fool who believed he was smart enough to fix anything. Her mother, a fool who believed she could fix any man." She curses at her bag, which stubbornly refuses to close. "We should have listened to Ishai about her Ioannis."

"Wait, what? Who's Ioannis?"

"My Hana's betrothed."

"Matty said it was not his true name." Ari hesitates. "A few days before he was taken, Matty came to me in the hospital. He thought I was asleep, and I pretended because otherwise I knew he would leave. He had no one else he could talk to. He was... very upset. Much of what he said I could not understand. But I do remember a name: Adnar Kıraç."

Ioannis. Janus? *As in Matty's code name for his story?*

Lucky pokes his head into the vestry. "I was coming to tell you there's a squad car on its way," he says, in that deep Southie accent of his. "They were supposed to detain you and your friends until Immigration could get here. 'Cept somebody got on the line and ordered them to stand down."

The hairs on my arms stand up. "Why would they do that?"

"I wouldn't stick around to find out." He tips his cap at Magdala. "Pleased to meet you, ma'am. Leah tells me you're family. My word as a Marine, you're safe with me."

We all make a mad dash for the truck. Lucky shoves the cab door open with his foot. "Get in and get down."

The three of us huddle together, knees to our chins. I rest my cheek on the glove compartment, feeling powerless. Magdala grips my hand, with surprising strength. "I have never known a man of courage who was not prone to mislaying it at the wrong time. Matthias wanted to tell you." She wipes a tear from my cheek. "But he is a man, and therefore a fool."

Lucky glances in the rearview mirror. "No greater fool than a man in love."

The truck lurches forward, then turns a corner and picks up speed. The sound of wet roads comes through the floorboards, struck by the metronome of windshield wipers. I watch raindrops trace squiggles on the windows. "Where are you going?"

"Best if you don't know," he answers.

"They can't leave the country."

"Your father knows how to find me." He turns a corner. "Though I expect he'd be a lot happier if you came along."

Craning my neck, I peer out of the rained-streaked window. The autumn blaze of the Arborway rushes past, chased by the flashing blue of a silent cruiser going the other way. I slide my hand to the door handle. "I expect you both understand why I can't."

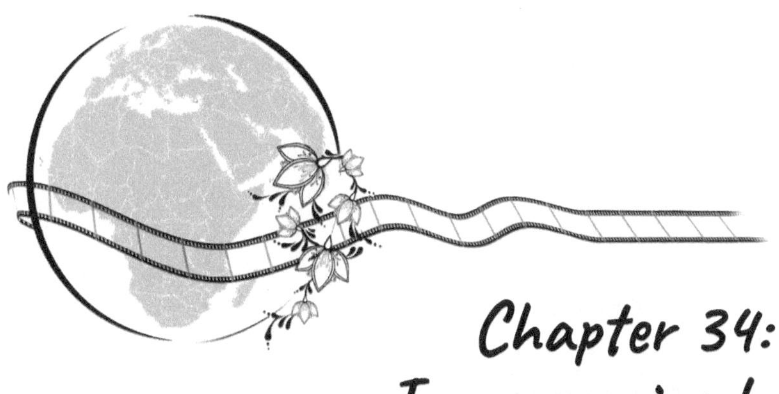

Chapter 34:
Incommunicado

WEST KURDISTAN, PRESENT

Matty

Leah, for crissakes, answer the phone.

Sand crunches under the boat. Someone starts weeping. A squall came up, forcing us to land here. A craggy landscape rises ahead, shrouded in dawn mist. No one seems to know where we are. Turkey, Syria… hell.

Other survivors straggle ashore. Everything from the minute I hit the water is a blur. My throat burns with massive thirst. When I'm not heaving, I'm hallucinating. It's like every hangover I've ever had rolled into one, but the only thing I've drunk is salt water. A lot of it. Three rounds on the waterboard, a leap in the drink…

Eyeing his phone, he captain helps me out of the surf. "You are not well."

The battery is down to the red. Leah, Ari, even Jack…they're not picking up.

Not even voicemail?

Confused and fearing the worst, I dial the last number my fogged-up head can remember. *Hana. Hana will know.*

Right about then, I realize the buzzing sound isn't in my head. Wade's drone makes a low skim over the beach. Stumbling, I make a run for some scrub by the rocks. The call connects.

"Who is this?"

The connection is shit, all dropped packets and road noise, but I'd know the impatience in Hana's voice anywhere. "It's Matty," I croak.

She exhales. "It worked? Leah was able to obtain your release with what I sent?"

My gut knots up. "Wait, what? You got her into this?"

"As did you." Her voice goes brittle. "Perhaps you expect me to save the world by myself."

"Bullshit. I spent six months begging you to help. And six months after that in hell."

"Yes, and until last week, I believed hell was exactly where you were. Much has changed." Her voice grows muffled, as if she's talking to someone. "Where are you now?"

"Dunno. They turned on each other and I jumped ship." A dehydration cramp slices through me, dropping me to my knees.

While I'm retching, the drone makes another pass over the beach, hovers, then turns in a wide circle, heading out to sea to return to its master.

It begins to dawn on me. Whether it spotted me or not, Gleason's not convinced I drowned.

Someone comes up behind, slipping my arm around his shoulder. Dizzy, I turn my head and see Rani. He helps me towards a crevice in the rocks. "Come on, man. You can't stay here."

Hallucinations are the least of my worries. I can barely work up enough saliva to talk. The ringing in my ears, waves lapping at a body on the sand… now there's a motor. Struggling to focus, I peer around the crevice. A grey fog hangs over the Mediterranean. A few hundred yards offshore, the hulking shadow of a ship appears through the mist.

Swallowed by hopelessness, I rest my head on the rock. "They're coming after you. After all of us. Leah, Ari, your mother… I don't know if they're alive or dead, I can't get through—"

"Nor I. Your government is up to some tricks."

The tingling in my fingers and toes is moving up my limbs. "Can't you fix it?"

"They will know. Get rid of this phone and run as if the devil himself were after you." She curses. "When we left, I thought Ari was safe."

"Left where? Who's 'we'?"

Her answer comes slowly. "My sisters and I are retrieving the last of what was stolen from us."

My head feels like pea soup. "You mean like a rescue? From Kıraç? You know where he is?"

She sucks in a breath. "Only a fool or a drunkard would use that name when certain to be overheard. Which are you?"

A guy trying to stop a lot of people from getting killed. I close my eyes. "There's another attack coming, Hana. A big one."

She goes quiet. "We had a source close to Kıraç's Daesh allies. What happened in Montreal… she would have warned us had she been able. If she has been discovered, Kıraç will know Tal and I sent her. I fear the worst."

Her words spin through the fog in my head. "I spent fourteen years walking in the guy's shadow, Hana. This is what he does. He makes it personal. He wants to hurt me and he wants to hurt you—"

"But Ari and your wife are the ones he can get to," she finishes.

I close my eyes. "Yeah. Wherever they are, that's where the attack will happen. We have to warn them."

"I will do what I can. May our brother watch over them."

The battery indicator blinks. The drone's low, buzzing whirr returns, hovering outside the crevice. "If I don't make it home, tell Leah I died trying."

Chapter 35:
One Nation...
WASHINGTON, D.C.
PRESENT

Leah

Henry, the Smithsonian's mounted elephant, glows a festive purple. Sapphire light bathes the rotunda, along with a hypnotic school of laser-projected fish and starburst in harvest yellow. Beneath, dozens of attorneys and society clients mill between mountains of food, along with copious check-loosening alcohol. A string quartet is plucking Vivaldi for all they're worth, a mostly a futile attempt to drown out what's happening outside on the National Mall.

It started as a Resistance march that'd been planned for months. First, the permits got yanked without warning. Then warrants came down for the leaders, which broadened into a shield to arrest anyone they wanted. The jails overflowed, which should've been the end, but the people in charge were determined to prove it, so they 'kettled' the rest into commandeered school auditoriums and hotel ballrooms, crowing as if they'd won some sort of victory. At that point, every bridge-dwelling, chest-thumping, alt-right troglodyte in creation hit the D.C. streets.

It's like getting that phone call about a loved one who's been an addict for years. You watch the doctors work with your hand over your mouth, and it suddenly hits you that they're not coming back this time. Your stomach craters, and you decide that maybe God exists after all, and you'll do anything, anything at all if he'll just let you fly to a time when it wasn't too late to fix it. Our drug is rage, our drug is fear. Listening to the chants and shouts, my head is stuck fifteen years in the past, in another city, at another protest. Any time I blink, I see Matty kneeling on snow-covered bricks, desperate to warn anyone who'd listen of what would come next. Yet here we are, America 2018, one more failing state with badly drawn borders. This has been coming, and it's been coming for years. Why couldn't we stop it, why couldn't we fix it?

My current hideout is by the caterer's station, which is stacked with foil-covered trays and overflowing with the canapé of the moment, spicy scallops in lettuce cups. One of the waiters is trying to pick up a tray without touching the leaves, looking as queasy as I feel. He's handsome and slender, with greying dark hair and luminous blue eyes, a striking hue I've only ever seen in Kurdish people. On a nostalgic hunch, and needing something to occupy myself, I rearrange one of the trays so the leaves don't touch the sides. "Here, take this one."

A fine sheen of sweat glistens his brow. "Why did you do that?"

"You're Yazidi, right?" I rub the scar on my wrist. "The lettuce thing… you remind me of someone."

His head tilts. Something flickers in his expression, and his breathing becomes measured. "I see."

As a rowdy crowd of demonstrators marches by, a memory starts to bubble up. Another protest. Not Boston this time. Cairo. "Have we met? I swear I've seen you before."

"You are mistaken." He turns abruptly on his heel, as if he can't get away from me fast enough.

Frustrated, I bite into a scallop. "Right. Good chat. Thanks."

Julie, who's not about to let ten thousand cawing nativists spoil her party, gives my cocktail dress the once-over. Discreetly, she slips behind me, fastens the clasp, yanks the zipper the last inch, then hands me a champagne flute. "Much better. Jade is your color."

Tipping the flute, I drain half. "Matty's favorite."

"Next time, dear, he'll be here." She gives my waist a squeeze. "How are you holding up?"

"Depends," I say. "Are we counting helping my sister-in-law escape from the feds? Or that the only reason they haven't arrested me yet is they're hoping I'll lead them to the other sister-in-law? Or that PACER refuses to let me file the petition that might save my unlawfully detained husband?"

The official explanation is that the system is clogged because of an overnight series of deportation raids. On the surface, it's exactly the same heartless, wearying, bullshit that's been going on for months. Years. Trouble is, I've also been asking, and every other immigration attorney I know has been able to get their cases filed. Earlier, Julie sat me down and told me she'd turned over the rest of my clients 'just in case'. So instead of doing the *one* thing I suffered through law school to do, I'm at a party, feeling paranoid, targeted, and useless.

A proud gleam comes into Julie's eyes. "Then you'll have to explain why I got a call from Olivia Forrester a bit ago, demanding to know why the upstart first-year associate I hired thinks she's taking over Jack Solomon's case."

My breath catches. "Are you serious? It went through?"

"My dear, you've outdone yourself. The kind of billable hours we're talking?" She raises her flute, expectant of a toast. "Of course, she wasn't inclined to allow it, even after I said I'd mentor, but once she found out you're Dale's daughter, she insisted on meeting you."

I'm not sure whether to dance or get sick in my purse. "Meet me? Like…here?"

"She'll be here soon." With an airy *ching* of our flutes, Julie gives my flip-flops the side eye. "Now that that's settled, let's hope our clients find your fashion sense endearing."

Settled? Right. My head is suddenly jumble of legal arguments—that somehow, between now and whenever 'soon' is—need to turn themselves in a coherent defense of Matty's life.

"Breathe, dear," Julie chides. "I read your filing. The law is on your side."

"Like that matters these days." Inhaling deeply, I close my eyes until my heart slows. Which works, until I open them and see Jason walking into the center of the rotunda.

Julie eyes my frozen reaction. "Someone you know?"

Someone I wish I didn't. I down the rest of the flute. "Will you excuse me?"

I cut Jason off at the bar. "This is a private function."

He fiddles with a pair of onyx cufflinks, then snaps his sleeve. "I have a ticket."

At least he seems sober. "Yesterday you looked like Pigpen. You expect me to believe you had two grand to throw at the Smithsonian?"

He laughs bitterly. "Right."

I scan the room, every busboy, every waiter, until I spot Ryan Hendricks watching from the opposite balcony. "Guess I know who paid."

The quartet switches from Vivaldi to Haydn, a heavier strain. Jason shuffles his feet. "I thought about what you said. We need to talk. Somewhere private."

"There is no 'we' anymore, Jason." My dress suddenly feels too short. I tug it down. "This is as private as it gets."

He gives his bowtie a frustrated yank. "Lee, four days ago, my only plan for the day was to stay drunk enough to get to the next one. Then a friend I haven't seen in five years shows up and asks if I want one last shot at serving my country. I ain't here for you, and I certainly ain't here for that piece of shit husband of yours."

"Then leave."

"Not until we talk." He steals a glance at Ryan. "Henny got me thinking I'm getting my bird back. Turns out, all they want is a glorified taxi driver."

"A what?"

"Rendition pilot." He grimaces. "I'm not supposed to ask questions, but something is going down. You don't even want to know how many attacks they've thwarted over the past few days, Lee. They've got a bunch of refugees rounded up, but none of the bastards will talk, so I get to fly them someplace where they will."

The air this close to him is suffocating. "Here's a crazy thought: maybe they're not talking because they're innocent. Does due process mean anything to you?"

He sets his jaw. "Since when do terrorists have rights?"

Oh for fuck's sake. "Remember the first time we broke up? You and Ryan, freshly sworn lieutenants, mouthing off about the Iraqis you were going to kill? I got upset, Ryan called me a commie bitch, you called me a traitor…"

"Upset? You flipped. You threw my ring at me in front of the entire detachment."

We saw the world differently, I'd always known that, but it'd been a raging red flag that maybe we saw it *too* differently. "Didn't you swear an oath to defend the Constitution? All enemies, foreign *and* domestic? Pretty ironic that the commie bitch traitor is the one who's actually doing it."

"Christ, I forgot how self-righteous you are." His voice drops. "Look, whatever the hell you got yourself into, I got dragged into it. I'm done. I'm sick and tired of being the fall guy."

"You fell a long time ago, Jason." Fighting emotion, I bite my cheek until I taste blood. "Go home."

I make a beeline for Julie. She eyes Jason, who's gone straight for the bar. "I'll presume I don't want to know."

Deep breath. "It's nothing."

"Marvelous. I've hired the one attorney in DC who can't lie." She waves her flute towards the rotunda. "If you can stop watching the Mall for two minutes, there's Izar."

Instead of his usual tunic, he's wearing a sapphire ceremonial coat, loose trousers, topped off with a matching cap embroidered in gold around the brim. It's dress for a chieftain, not a poet. "Let me guess—you bought him that outfit."

Julie pinches my elbow, turning me towards the White Boys' Club gathered by the rhino. "Behave or I'll stick you with Joe Winthrop and his new client instead." She gives a curt nod to Mr. Godderall, the other founder, a creaking mountain of a man leaning on a silver-knobbed cane. "Even God himself is wondering how Joe managed to land an international financier at this point in the tax cycle."

Joe, whose ego has an annoying habit of alerting him whenever people are talking about him, is with an olive-skinned playboy in a gauzy linen shirt and couture jeans, the type convinced the world and everyone in it exists for his pleasure. Fortyish, with sharp cheekbones and close-cropped wavy hair, he looks my way, then slides a toothpick with four stuffed olives into his mouth.

"Charming." There's something familiar about him, but I can't place it. "Who's that?"

"I'll never remember his name," she says. "Come to think, maybe I *should* introduce you—supposedly he's done some work in Africa with child soldiers."

Law school refugee or not, I've stayed involved with ReliefNet over the years. "If this guy is a player on the NGO scene, I've never run into him."

As the orchestra launches in a furious rendition of Holst, he saunters over and kisses my hand. "A most pleasant evening to you, Mrs. Cahill."

Boarding school manners. A continental accent, like something out of an old movie, which means it's fake. "Have we met?"

His grip tightens. Lingers. "Regretfully, no. I've had dealings in the past with your husband. His death was…a great shame."

I pull free. "Matty is alive. Whoever told you otherwise was mis-informed."

He makes a dramatic bow. "My apologies. He spoke of you with great passion. Now I see why."

Joe sidles over, with a smug tug at his cummerbund. "Leah At-kins-Cahill, Kristos Aydemir. Associate pain-in-the-ass, meet my new favorite client."

"Go spin." I face 'Kristos'. "What kind of dealings?"

An enigmatic expression shadows his face. "The feature he wrote on me raised my profile in the philanthropy community considerably. You have not read it?"

My palms feel all clammy. Something is going on here. Matty doesn't do fluff biographies. He takes photos. He investigates things. Things that put his sister in hiding, nearly got us both killed, and stole his freedom. "Apparently not."

"You might find it interesting." He tips his martini glass, swallowing the last dregs of gin. "Your husband's work is very powerful. I purchased a set of his Yazidi tribal photos for my private collection."

Seriously, Leah. Paranoid much? Matty had taken the photos in question a few years ago, in the Sinjar Mountains. Barren landscapes with dawn silhouettes. Three wives having ceremonial tea in a lavish-ly decorated red tent, which earned him a prestigious award, opened doors with collectors and gave us a bit of financial breathing room. "The *National Geographic* series?"

He makes a noise with his tongue, and gives a connoisseur's squint. "My tastes lie elsewhere. There is beauty in the destruction of war, no?"

Nope. I take it back. This isn't normal. And it doesn't feel random. "Most people don't think of that aspect of Matty's work as display art."

His smile turns wolfish, just a hint of bared teeth. "As I said, a shame. Perhaps he would have found it a safer career. Good evening, Ms. Cahill."

Julie stares at me as 'Kristos' and Joe walk away. "What was that?"

Get a grip, Leah. Adnar Kıraç did not fly to Washington, D.C. to attend your company party for the sheer pleasure of taunting you. He is hiding in a cave somewhere halfway across the world. How many rich creeps like this have you met over the years?

"Nothing," I reply, drawing a shaky breath. "Skeevy Joe has skeevy clients. I'll stick to Azerbaijani hackers and my secret in-laws."

Julie swirls her flute. "Careful or you'll start reminding me of your father."

"He'd have a clue what he was doing." I shift my weight. "I need to ask you something. That chemical company you pointed me towards… When I was home, Dad hinted that you had history with them. He told me not to waste my time. He seemed to think that you might've accidentally put me on a false trail."

In that bare moment, she suddenly looks her age. "Perhaps I did."

"You didn't," I say quickly. "They're in it up to their necks. It's like… I have this weird feeling he was trying to throw me off."

She sets aside the flute, then sinks into a chair, staring distantly at the elephant. "My son would be the same age as you—the fifth in our neighborhood to come down with leukemia in a year. It was the same blighted Baltimore neighborhood where I grew up, because of course it was designed to keep us in our place. The Elcola plant went up on the river the year I got married. The first pipes they put in lasted less than a month. Which was more than the first three attorneys I convinced to take the case." Her voice trails off. "Dale was the eighth. I knew about DJ, of course, so when the threats to you and your mother came rolling in…"

Sadness overtakes me. "I always thought my dad was fearless."

"Oh, no, dear. They realized it was easier to buy off the judge and jury and that was that." Recovering herself, she squeezes my hand. "You're in a long-haul fight, Leah. The system protects itself. It's set up that way. This won't end once you get your husband back. I hope you realize that."

Remind me not to come to you for a pep talk. "I need a minute with Izar."

He stretches out his arms as I approach, the sheen of his tunic brilliant under the rotunda lights. "Has ever a strutting peacock looked finer?"

"Julie outdid herself." I kiss his cheeks. Glancing towards the unwanted complications at the bar, I slip my phone into his pocket. This is the safest place for me to try to contact Hana again, because if anyone comes after me, they'll have to do it in view of a federal judge and a roomful of attorneys who'd crawl over rusty thumb tacks to impress someone. "They're still hacking me. Can you fix it?"

With a Quixotic grin, he doffs his cap. "And yet I thought this event would be a chore." Bare moments later, he hands it back, rather pleased with himself. "And there. The mouse lives to fight another day."

Delayed messages are starting to pop on the screen, missed calls and voicemails. "That's it?"

"It helps when the cat has grown old, fat, and lazy."

I fire up his anonymizing browser, and send up what I hope is a signal flare to Hana. Then I notice Jason watching from the bar, spinning a coin, an empty tumbler near his wrist. "Let's move someplace else."

We end up in the Hall of Mammals, where Julie is with an elderly Korean woman, who she introduces as Min-ne Alexander. "You three have much to talk about," Julie says. "I must say, we've never assembled a finer collection of dissidents, defectors, and spies."

Dissidents? Is that what Matty and I are now?

Izar certainly qualifies, but I wouldn't have thought Min-ne, with her elegant grey-streaked hair and delicate hands, had ever strayed outside Embassy Row in her life. She takes my hands. "I met my Robert in 1951, after he was captured near Kaesong. Let us say, our courtship did not go as my PRK handlers had planned."

Julie has a satisfied set to her mouth. "At Robert's funeral last month, Min-ne told me she'd lost the only person who understood what they'd been through. I told her I knew two."

Over champagne and artful crudités, Min-ne spins a love story for the ages. Recruited at nineteen, she was sent to help turn American POWs, but the atrocities she witnessed led to her to defect. In the process, she orchestrated the escape of a dozen men, her future husband among them. Normally, I'd be rapt. Between watching the door for Judge Forrester, the fact that there are at least three men in the room who are watching *me*, none of whose intentions I trust, I'm only half paying attention until Min-ne takes my hands again. "You must prepare yourself, if your husband returns," she says. "A man imprisoned this way will never truly be free."

My stomach flips. I'm expecting Izar to disagree, but head bowed low, he's scribbling verse on a cocktail napkin.

"I… I haven't thought that far ahead."

In my sleep-deprived, scared-shitless brain, it almost seems like a joke. *A lawyer, a poet, and a spy walk into a museum…* But what's the punchline? I'm no trained spy. I'm not the Azerbaijani reincarnation of Leonardo da Vinci. I'm just a girl who followed a boy with ten times her passion into the desert and came out his wife. The longer I watch Izar and Min-ne struggle to cope with the endings of their relationships, the more I realize how terrified I am of mine.

Shaken, and needing to pull it together, I excuse myself and find refuge in the Ocean Hall, which is dark and shadowed beneath the massive blue whale. I sink to the floor behind the wall of an exhibit. Bringing Matty home has always been the endpoint, my all-consuming goal, but what then? We were at rock bottom before, and nothing I did could fix it. What if we had even further to fall?

Something moves behind a column to the rear, by the predator wing. The red emergency lights reflect off a pair of sunglasses. Though the light is dim, it looks like Joe's client. My first thought is that, so help me, if *one* more person can't leave me alone for two minutes, I'm going smash open the nearest exhibit, be it a meteorite or a mammoth tusk or a sabretooth squirrel and beat them to a bloody pulp with it.

The second is that maybe I'd better quit reacting emotionally and figure out who he is.

In the browser search, I enter the name he gave me. *Kristos Aydemir*. Halfway down the search results, I find an article in a luxury travel magazine with Matty's byline. *The Two Faces of Anatoly*. I click the link, but before it comes up, Julie appears in the passageway in her best power pose. "Leah?"

I scramble up. "Sorry, I'm here."

"So we see," she says curtly. "I told you she was here somewhere, Olivia. Rumors are making the rounds that they've called in the National Guard outside. I'll have to leave you to it."

Forrester is behind her, fiftyish, dark-skinned and impressively broad in the shoulders. Broad everywhere really, and a good six feet if she's an inch. As Julie bolts, Forrester extends her hand. "Your father is the reason I went to law school, Ms. Cahill. It's a pleasure."

In theory, drawing a black federal judge who idolizes my father should be a good thing. In reality, it means as of thirty seconds ago, she's scrutinizing everything I do. It's the way I talk, my body language, whether my arguments are as sound and soaring as his. From the first day of law school, it's been the game I've had to play.

"He'd be honored," I say. "You can imagine how he feels about this. Neither of us ever thought I'd be here appealing for the safety and freedom of American journalists at home."

I'm so caught up in a thirty-four-year-old case of how to be Dale Atkins's daughter that I don't see Senator Nance until he flicks on the lights. "Yes, well, Ms. Atkins, your husband's situation isn't nearly the travesty you'd like everyone to believe."

Chapter 36:
Revenge of the Deep State

WASHINGTON, D.C.
PRESENT

Seeing Nance, a jolt shoots from my heart to my feet. "What are you doing here?"

"Perhaps you don't remember cajoling me into buying a ticket," he says, though his tie hangs loose, and he's unshaven, as if he found out at the last minute. "This unfortunate—and might I add desperate—petition of yours is a mistake. You're jeopardizing the rest of your clients. Not to mention thousands of other refugees."

It occurs to me that Julie still thinks he's one of the good guys. I sidestep Nance. "Your honor, my client doesn't have time for political posturing. I'd appreciate it if the senator removed himself, on the grounds that his concerns over his 'signature issue' don't constitute standing."

Forrester dons a set of reading glasses. "Denied. You mention him in your filing."

Fine, that was a long shot. "If this is an official response, shouldn't we be under under oath? Have it recorded?"

Nance, who clearly realizes what I'm up to, produces a rolled-up sheaf of papers from his suit coat pocket. "Leah, had I done half the things you've accused me of, the perjury trap you're trying to set would be the least of my worries. I presume you would prefer candid answers to official ones."

I raise my right hand. "I have nothing to hide. You?"

Forrester pushes my hand down. She sweeps a printout onto a display case, beneath the skeleton of an ichthyosaur. "Tell me, Ms. Cahill, has it always been your belief that the U.S. Government kidnapped your husband?"

I lean on my stitches, needing the pain to bite through my frustration. "The State Department led me to believe he had been captured by a faction of the Egyptian military."

She pushes the glasses down her nose. "You believe you were intentionally misled?"

"I can only say someone went exceptional lengths to hide the truth." I flip through the filing until I find the photo I snapped at the hearing. "Three days ago, I received an anonymous tip directing me to a classified Senate Armed Services briefing. When I got there, the committee was discussing an unnamed Section 1021 detainee code-named Lotus 12."

Expression sour, she turns the page. "Is that where this nonsense about Jack Solomon hiring you as his attorney came from?"

"The statute authorizes indefinite detention of anyone associated with a known terrorist element, and since it makes no effort to define that relationship, the government may do so freely. Based on the dates of detention, Lotus 12 is Mr. Solomon's long-time associate Matthias Cahill, a freelance journalist and United States citizen. Therefore, Mr. Solomon has renewed concern about the government's intentions towards him."

"Quite a leap, counselor," she says dryly.

Nance clears his throat. "Your honor, Ms. Cahill has a history of emotional breakdowns where her husband's professional activities are concerned." He slips another page into the stack. "If you'll enter these medical records into the case."

Asshole. "I've got someplace you can stick them."

Forrester doesn't touch them. "Make your case, Ms. Cahill."

"My client's detention is based not in any wrongdoing, but is wholly related to his work as a journalist. This is nothing short of a direct attack on the First Amendment, and with it, democracy itself. Based on work product he left behind—"

"Bullshit," Nance interrupts. "Cahill had direct knowledge of imminent attacks against US interests. Names, places, perpetrators. He was given ample opportunity to cooperate before action was taken."

"Was Mr. Cahill ever afforded the presence of counsel during these 'opportunities'?" I say. "Or were they more you like you blackmailing him with threats to deport his sister to Syria and have me disbarred?"

Nance gives the stubble on his chin an annoyed tug. "Your honor, I've known Ms. Cahill for some time. While her reaction to the situation is tolerable, her misguided assumptions are not. Her husband's links to the current global security crisis extend far beyond what she knows."

Without another word, I set my phone on the glass, activating a video. Ari, Magdala, and Lucky appear on screen, along with a copy of today's *Boston Globe*. In halting English, hands clasped so tightly their knuckles are white, the two women lay their nightmares bare.

"Ari-eil and Magdala Maloof are also my clients, your honor," I say. "I recorded this shortly before they were forced to flee a deportation order meant to silence them forever. I intend to amend my filing to request immunity for them from the Attorney General, as they have direct knowledge of a criminal conspiracy to cover up the involvement of a top defense contractor and several high-ranking officials at the Pentagon in provoking the current security crisis, including violations of the Hatch Act, Arms Control Export Act, and the Espionage Act."

Nance rubs his nose shamelessly. "This would be the same Attorney General who signed off on torturing this information out of your husband?"

Don't react. For god's sake, don't react. "As a result of these illegal activities, Matthias Cahill has now been detained for more than 183 days without charge or trial, and further, has been denied access to counsel. As his legal representative, I petition for his immediate release on the grounds that as a US citizen, his detention is flagrantly unconstitutional and criminally motivated."

Quietly, Nance lays another set of papers in front of Forrester, who skims them. "According to this, Matthias Cahill is not a US citizen."

"Huh?" I snatch the paper.

It's a grainy and blobby photocopy, which turns out to be a kidnapping complaint dating to the late 1980s. There are photos of a tow-headed boy who's about nine or ten, along with a birth certificate in Portuguese from the year Matty was born. *Elijah and Gabriella Cahill, wanted for unlawful flight with an unrelated minor child.*

My heart starts to pound. "No way. This is a mistake."

Nance shrugs. "Guess you're not the expert on blackmail you think you are."

A metallic taste floods my mouth. Mistake or not, he just gutted my case. "I—I don't understand."

"Think about the places he grew up. Iraq, North Africa, Soviet Yugoslavia. Now ask yourself what the CIA might do to learn what his parents had seen."

Forrester folds her glasses. "I'm going to ask you a question, Ms. Cahill. And you're going to think very carefully about your answer before you give it. Were you aware of your husband's immigration status when you filed this brief?"

Matty's last chance at freedom is collapsing in front of me. "In *Rasul v. Bush,* the Supreme Court upheld that detainees had a right to challenge their detention regardless of citizenship."

"In all dominions under the sovereign's control," Nance finished. "As a foreign-flag vessel in international waters is not."

Forrester taps her foot. "Ms. Cahill?"

I fight to keep my voice from breaking. "He's always held a US passport and traveled with it freely. If the government didn't question his citizenship, why would I?"

She sweeps up the response claim. "If I were to issue a release order, presuming you could even provide us with someone it could be issued to, which seems unlikely, as you've failed to specify one in your complaint—"

"Your honor—"

"I am sympathetic to Mr. Cahill's plight. It seems clear something terribly wrong has occurred, but the fact is you have provided me with neither jurisdiction nor a respondent to do anything about it. The three of us are on shaky legal *and* ethical grounds meeting this way to begin with and you know it. I will not issue a ruling which would be overturned in an hour and I don't believe it's in your husband's interest either. If there is a better case to be made, I strongly suggest you present it. Now." She throws her glasses onto the display case and turns to Nance. "As for you—"

Throughout her diatribe, he's been staring at his phone with a troubled expression. "Unfortunately, all this just became moot. Earlier tonight, Matthias made an attempt to escape. He murdered a guard, then jumped overboard. He's presumed to have drowned."

All the colors go grey. My mouth tastes like I bit down on a spark. "No."

Mouth set in a line, he flashes the phone, which is paused on a night vision video. A dead body is slumped against the ship's rail, splashed black with blood. "I'm truly sorry, Leah."

The room starts to swim. Matty's no killer. I know that.

But he'd jump given the chance.

He'd jump if they were trying to get rid of him.

It could be true. You know it could be true.

Half-blind and shattered, I bolt, heading for the darkened rear staircase. The sound of angry chants rises from outside, and I can't take any more, so I collapse right there in a puddle on the marble.

You couldn't save him. The same way Dad couldn't save DJ. All you can do is make it mean something. Find a way.

I scroll through the documents on my phone, and call up one I wrote on the plane. The one I prayed I'd never have to send. The one I prayed Matty would be able to write himself.

Jack picks up on the first ring. "Leah?"

My hands won't stop shaking. "I'm going to send you something. Something I need you to publish. You'll have to act fast. It needs to get out before they have a chance to discredit it. If you're not in a public place, I need you to get to one first."

He's quiet for a long time. "If they're covering their tracks, you know where they'll start."

I push my hair out of my face. "It's too late. Call me back."

Numb, and needing a quiet place to grieve, I head up the stairs, past the atrium, into the Egyptian exhibit. A few sarcophagi, a few mummies… where it began is where it ends.

The phone rings again. I sink to the floor between two glasses cases and hit answer. "That was fast."

Pops and gaps fill the line. A woman's voice breathes an *Amen.* "Matthias was able to reach you?"

When I realize who it is, I bolt up. "Hana? He's alive?"

"Last we spoke, yes. He said he had escaped. They will kill him if they find him. I cannot be certain."

A pang slices through my stomach, leaving me doubled up and shaking. "Where is he? Is he okay?"

"That is unclear." She hesitates. "I do not know him as well as I once did. Would you expect that upon gaining his freedom, the first thing he did was drink himself blind?"

Nauseated by whatever prompted her to ask, I draw up my knees. "Not if he knows the people he loves are in trouble."

"Then the alternative is worse. When we spoke, his words came with great difficulty. Our medic thinks he may have been poisoned."

Poisoned means he's still going to die, which I can't deal with. Breathing deeply, I search for an alternative. "They said he jumped off the ship. I've seen similar stuff with refugee kids who almost drowned. Either way, we don't have much time. How do we find him?"

"Leave that to us."

"No." I push myself up. "I'm coming to you."

"To do what? Lead them to us and get us both killed?"

"We have to trust each other, Hana. They'll kill you both the second they find you. You need someone who can get the story out. You need me. Give me a way to find you."

She's quiet for a minute. "Matthias once told me you never forget a detail. That your Immigration would seize on any discrepancy to deny Eema and Ari. Maira and Ari were like sisters for many years. Our families traveled together. They had little to share, except secrets. I believe what tipped your government off was the name of the village Eema gave you where we fled just before the war. This was where Maira and Ari's lives diverged. Do you remember it?"

I'd spent hours helping them prep for those hellacious 'reasonable fear' interviews. "Pretend I do. If you're afraid someone's listening, all you just did was tell them I can find you if they make me."

"Then I suggest you not give them the opportunity. If you meet me at the real location in twelve hours, I will know Ari is safe."

Matty's out there, hurt and being hunted, and she's talking in circles. "They're safe. In hiding. I have no way of asking her where the hell you mean." Frustration makes me kick a mummy case. "Besides, I'd need a miracle to get there under a day. None of which helps us find Matty."

An exasperated sigh comes out of the phone. "You have bigger problems than your husband. He believes Kıraç is looking for revenge, and may have planned the next attack at your location. Likely soon."

Time slows. My world shrinks to a pinpoint. "Does burying the lede mean anything to you?"

"We have done what we can to stop it. If what Matthias says is true, it may not be enough. He gave no details. I said I would warn you and I have. Ask if someone has ever warned me before they dropped a bomb or missile on someone I love. I will wait for you until sundown tomorrow. God be with you."

The line goes dead. I try to breathe, but I can't.

An attack. Here.

It means what happened downstairs wasn't a coincidence. It means my reaction to the creep downstairs wasn't paranoia. It means he's—"

A shadow falls across the galley entrance. The red light of an exit sign reflects off a pair of sunglasses. I try to run, but he's on me in a flash, knocking me into a case. My head hits the stone wall. Everything flashes white, then grey. Consciousness starts to slip away, until I feel his hands on me, so I scratch and claw at whatever skin I can find. He flips me onto my stomach and kneels on my back, hands around my throat. I can't breathe. Can't move. Can't feel my fingers. The last bit of fight slips out of me.

He bends low, to whisper in my ear. "Allow me to introduce myself, Mrs. Cahill. Perhaps you know me as Janus."

Chapter 37:
Eight Legs Bad

WASHINGTON, D.C.
PRESENT

The room swims into view. There's something over my mouth. Duct tape, I think. There's a dull ache in my shoulders, which I go to rub, and realize I can't move my hands. Or my legs. The only light comes from a floor-to-ceiling window to my left. The remaining walls are lined with cases full of creeping, nightmarish insects, and when I see Kıraç peering at a terrarium full of tarantulas, that's when panic sets in.

Any hope of escape drains the minute he turns. He strides over, reaching into his pocket. He waggles a glass vial near my nose, snaps off the top, and bites the cap off a hypodermic syringe. I twist and try to roll away, but the needle bites into my neck. My body temperature shoots up a hundred degrees. Everything starts to go blurry, twice as bad as before. My mouth and throat feel like I swallowed every last grain of the Sahara. *What did he do to me?*

He loosens the tape, which stings like hell. Looking quite pleased with himself, he hops onto a glass case. "Not to worry, Ms. Cahill. Simply an injection of atropine to counteract the sarin. Belladonna. Nightshade. Call it what you like. It will allow you to live."

"Fuck you."

He wanders towards the window, where the obelisk of the Washington Monument overlooks the Mall. "Your husband and I once had a most interesting conversation. About you. What he fears most is losing those he loves, but for you, it is different. You understand the power of that fear. How it can be manipulated. Wielded as weapon. Watching them die, knowing how their deaths will be used to finish tearing down everything you hold dear… this will be the worst for you, no?"

The crowds swim and swirl. They've only grown since earlier. There are police and barricades and a line of National Guardsman stretching down the Mall, every one of them somebody's mother or father, daughter or son. "Why are you doing this?"

"Ah, but what am I doing? We are alone, here, having a conversation. What is to come, others will do." His reflection in the glass is impassive, almost thoughtful. "It is said the greatest trick the devil ever pulled was to convince the world he doesn't exist. No. It is knowing how easy it is to turn a man into that which he despises."

The tape chafes my wrists. "I despise psychopaths, but you don't see me turning into one."

He chuckles. "You are just as Matthias described you." He gestures at the window. "Gleason's man out there—the one with the ginger hair. I am told he is a friend of yours?"

My vision is getting worse and my head is about to split open. What I *can* see is the Kurdish waiter's reflection in the window, creeping closer from the direction of the Egypt exhibit, brandishing a brass gallery pole. "If you mean Ryan Hendricks, we hated each other from day one."

Kıraç faces the Mall. "Mr. Hendricks is waiting for a signal. When the attack begins downstairs, he will trigger a series of explosions. The story that will be sold to the public is a cell of refugees carried out the attack, and all but one escaped to fight another day." He jerks his chin towards the protesters. "They shall have what they wish. An enemy to fear."

If Ryan is involved, does that mean Jason is too? He's a lot of things, but this? No way.

I work my fingernail under the edge of the tape. "Your mothers must be so proud."

"You too will have your role to play, Ms. Cahill. You are the witness." He watches me struggle, with maddening bemusement. "At first they will see you as Cassandra. Then as a traitor. Yet you will persist, because your husband's memory will dictate you must. When the chaos clears and the investigations begin, do you think America itself will survive?"

The waiter peers around the tarantula case, nearly close enough to strike. But then, from down the hall, towards Egypt, comes the sound of my phone vibrating. Kıraç turns. Desperate, I kick both feet at his legs. "Yeah. I do."

The waiter winds up and swings the pole, but it glances off Kıraç and into the display, sounding a *clang* that reverberates off the stone and down the halls. Kıraç momentarily goes down in a rain of shattered glass and spiders, but scrambles up and launches himself at the waiter. They scuffle. Downstairs, the quartet of strings hits a sour note, then stops cold. People start shouting. Someone screams.

Spiders scuttle every which way. A cockroach hisses. The waiter swings again. Blood gushes from Kıraç's temple, staining his white shirt. He no longer looks amused. "This is the choice you make? There are thousands of them and one of her."

The muscles in the waiter's arm vibrate with tension and rage. "We are many. But even one is enough."

I turn to run for the phone, to call for help, but it's as if someone hammered a hot nail into my foot. Fiery pain shoots up my ankle. A scorpion darts away. "Bastard!"

Seizing the distraction Kıraç snatches a shard of glass and jams it into the waiter's chest. I scream. The waiter's mouth gapes. After a satisfied, triumphant smirk, Kıraç careens off towards the rear exit.

I hobble towards the injured man and drop to my knees, pressing my hand to the wound. "Oh god—it's going to be okay, I'll get help."

"It is not so bad as it looks," he says, though his breathing is labored. He peers at my ankle. "You are stung."

My mouth tastes funny, but my foot isn't swelling. Much. "I've had worse." Down the hall, the phone buzzes again, and whether it's Jack or Hana or even Matty, we have bigger problems. "There's an attack coming downstairs, we have to find out who, we have to stop it."

He grips the shard, then grimaces. "There will be no attack."

"How do you know that?"

"Because two hours ago, I sank the bomb and the body of the man who would have delivered it into the Potomac." His face contorts in pain and he pulls out the shard. "Downstairs, you remembered me. From Cairo. You were right. But it was not the first time we met."

"Huh?" Cursing everything that creeps or crawls, I hop on one foot towards my phone. "I don't understand."

"My name is Tal Morsia." He follows. "The scar on your wrist… I gave it to you."

Between the atropine and the damn scorpion, my head is a mess, but the memory flashes through, from just before the war. "You were the man in the truck. Near Mosul. The rotted lettuce…"

He slumps against the wall. "Three days later, my sister lay dying. Then a medical shipment arrived that saved her life. The rumor was that the young American woman had arranged it. Barely out of her teens, yet more powerful than the great Saddam. We never forgot."

My phone shows three missed calls and a series of texts from Jack, each more concerned than the last. Trembling, I call up Matty's story and hit send. "The guy you killed—there are more of them. Kıraç said they're outside waiting for a signal."

"I will tell you what I know. Where to find the body. Then I must disappear. We both know that if I try to do more, I will never see daylight again. I have a son, to whom I promised to return after I had avenged him to Kıraç."

He needs a lawyer. A good one. Which right now, is not me. "Tal—"

Grimacing, he clutches his ribs. "There is a pistachio tree which stands near my home. My sister and I would sit in its shade for hours with our books." He turns his face towards the sky. "We swore an oath that one day, we will read with our children beneath that same tree. That we will rebuild our broken country. By this time tomorrow, that is where I must be."

Those who see past the impossible are too often derided as dreamers. They may be the only ones who can save us. "Where is she now?"

A combination of pride and grief twists his face. "Likely, she is dead, or will be once Kıraç contacts his men. She has been helping those he sold to escape. If by God's miracle she evades capture, she will reunite with the YPG in Rojava."

The only reason I'd heard of Rojava was because of emails from my friend Sara during her field rotations. It was a city in Kurdish Syria, site of a small refugee camp, mostly populated with women and children from Mosul. Many of them had been there since the start of the war. "YPG—the Kurdish Women's Protection Brigade? Do you know a woman named Hana?"

His eyes crinkle. "Who do you think talked me into this madness?"

The cavalry pounds up the steps—Nance and Jason, followed closely by Ryan. Everyone starts shouting at once. Squinting, Ryan swings a gun at Tal. On instinct, I jump in front. Ryan's finger moves to the trigger.

Jason makes a desperate hack at his arm. There's a sharp crack. The bullet skips off the marble and *thunks* into a door casing. "Whoa whoa *whoa!*"

Ryan shoves him off. "You crazy, Dino? That's the terrorist. Can't you see she's in on it?"

My legs wobble. "No. But you are." Desperate, I stumble towards Jason. "He's got a detonator… a cell phone… I don't know."

"Nice try, law school. The FBI is on their way."

My stomach lurches. Hana gave me twelve hours, which doesn't exactly include time for interrogations. "Jason, you have doubts about him, I know you have doubts—"

Ryan gets in my face. "Jesus, look at her. Look at her eyes. She's on drugs. Her pupils are huge."

Jason looks between us. "Dude, so are yours."

Nance smoothly disarms Ryan, then lifts a cell phone from his rear pocket. "I'll take that."

Relief mixes with confusion. "What are you, the Lebanese James Bond?"

"Twenty years ago, perhaps." He chops Ryan's skull with the butt of the gun, watching dispassionately as he crumples. "Had Mr. Hendricks not been so hasty with his own dose of atropine, this might have gone differently. Where is Kıraç?"

Everything hurts and I can't think. *Do I trust him? Do I have a damn choice?* I point towards the tarantulas, slowly backing away. "That way. Down the stairs. Dark hair. Bloody white linen shirt, blue jeans."

With a curt nod, Nance punches a number into his phone and makes a call. But when I go to help Tal up, he follows. "Where do you think you're going?"

"He needs a hospital. Beyond that it's none of your damn business."

"Have you made contact with your husband?"

Okay, no more trust for you. "Ten minutes ago, you told me my husband is dead."

"Yes, and I would still believe it if you were not standing in front of me as if you have someplace you desperately wish to be. You're on the no-fly list by now. Best of luck."

Maybe Nance is bluffing, maybe he's not, but there's only one way I'm getting to Turkey in time. Swallowing hard, I look at Jason.

"Downstairs you told me Ryan jacked you into doing rendition flights. He had it all set up."

"Yeah, and?"

It means I'm out of chances. It means climbing into a flying tin can with someone I can't stand to be near. "If you want your wings back, I have evidence that could exonerate you. The mosque in Khanaqin—"

"Where is Matthias?" Nance cocks the hammer on Ryan's gun. "I'm afraid I insist."

Exhausted and dizzy, I limp for the stairs. "No. You don't get to insist on anything, because five minutes ago, I sent a story to Matty's editor. *Matty's* story. The one where he knew you were involved in covering up a planned false-flag chemical attack on Americans, except he couldn't prove it. Well guess what, I did. So not only am I walking out of here, but I'm going to be doing it with an immunity agreement for myself, Matty, his sister, her mother, this guy here, who stopped what you couldn't. Somebody get me a goddamn pen."

Nance gives me a withering look. "I do wish you'd leave the blackmail to the experts. You've nothing on me that can't be explained."

In the movie version of my life, this is where the music swells and I let him have it. Where I list every bribe he took, every name, every dollar amount down to the cent, but my foot is screaming and the lights are blinding and my mouth tastes like straw and I can barely come up with my own name, let alone anyone else's. Lightheaded, I force my eyes to focus. "It's coming out. All of it. You can't stop it." All the blood rushes to my head. The floor swims too close. "All they'll say is you… you knew."

Chapter 38: Old Mistakes

NORTHERN VIRGINIA
PRESENT

The Potomac rushes by in a painful blur of light. I force my eyes open but can't get my bearings. Moving. Car. The driver's face swims into view. Jason.

"Welcome back," he says.

A fake pine air freshener swings from the mirror, and it's making me dizzy. I close my eyes and swallow my revulsion. "Did they find the sarin? Where's Kıraç?"

With a dark look, he flips my phone across the seat. "Nothing's gone off, put it that way."

The atropine is wearing off, but my foot won't quit throbbing. "Where are you taking me? Where's Tal? The waiter?"

"How the hell would I know?" He glances at a GPS on the dash, then veers to the right, exiting the highway onto a rural road. "You gotta give me something, Lee. From my end, the night my father died, the girl I loved since I was six was too busy cheating on me to pick up her phone and for some reason, she thinks I'm the one who's a dick."

He comes up to a stop sign. I jam my shoulder into the door. "I don't have to defend myself to you."

"God no, not you." He hits the child lock. "You'll defend anybody to the death, except yourself. Now sit your ass down. You need help.

Mine's all you've got." His face clouds. "You look like hell. There are some tissues in the door pocket."

Tears blur my vision. Up ahead, the tail fins and blinking lights of a small airfield come into view, a short strip lined with dozens of Pipers and fancy Gulfstreams, most with corporate logos. "Just drive, okay?"

Glancing in the rear view, he gets that uncomfortable expression he always got whenever he made me cry. The leather-wrapped wheel makes a *squinch*. "You're literally killing yourself to save your husband. My ex-wife's idea of 'helping' was to serve me with divorce papers the same day I lost my bird."

I crack the window, needing fresh air. I'd done everything to put Jason in the past and forget him. Matty still went quiet any time we drove past the Barnes' house on the way to my parents. He'd find some excuse to take me into town if he found out Connie was coming over. Deep down, he'd always hate Jason for what he did. He'd hate what I was doing now too, but he'd understand. The same way I understood what it must have cost him to write that article on Kıraç. And if he didn't, it was too damn bad for both of us.

A few hundred yards from the airfield gate, Jason pulls off the side of the road and parks behind some trees. A second pair of headlights comes on across the way. They blink once, then twice more.

"That's the all-clear," Jason says. "You want a pilot, you tell me everything about Khanaqin. Right now."

Nance gets out of the car, dragging behind a semi-conscious hooded man in an orange jumpsuit, and from here, I can't tell who it is. "Not until we land."

"Why the hell not?"

Because I don't trust you. "We're doing this my way. Either you want your wings or you don't." Since I know what the answer is, I go for the door handle, but the damn child lock is on. "Let me out."

After some shady side-eye, he gets out, slams the door behind him, and leans against it. "You can sit there."

Cursing him, I crawl across the seat, but Nance is close enough that I can see his prisoner is Tal, which is simultaneously a relief and… not. He and Jason exchange a few words, then a folded sheet of official government-type paper. They open my door, but block the way.

"What's on those papers?" When in doubt, litigate. "Is Tal under detention? Why did you drug him? Has he been offered a lawyer?"

Nance suddenly seems far older and tired. "The papers are your flight plan. In exchange for his help preventing the attack, Mr. Morsia has requested to return home for which, last I knew, legal representation was not required. He's groggy from the morphine I gave him after tending his wound."

"You're a doctor now?"

"A field medic, back in the day."

None of this computes. "Where's Kıraç?"

He doesn't answer right away. "He escaped. Which means he had help."

It takes a heartbeat to sink in. "Oh god I'm going to be sick."

"I've contacted an old friend in the Mossad. One with a personal stake in Mr. Kıraç's capture. I don't think we'll hear from him again."

"That's not justice."

"I didn't claim it was." He fishes an IV needle and a plastic pouch of clear fluid out of his pocket, then grabs my arm. "You were stung. This will help."

"Get away from me."

He shows me the label. "Benadryl. Leah, your stunt accomplished its purpose. If I wanted you dead, I'd have permitted Gleason's man in the ambulance to take you from the museum."

"Huh?"

Brow quirked, he holds up the needle. "Preferable to the bullet in the head you'd have received otherwise, I'd say. Yes or no?"

It's a trick, I know it's a trick. "Listen, Agent Double-oh-Nothing. You've known what happened to Matty from the beginning. Every meeting you and I had since then. Every time I begged you for help. You stood there and lied to my face."

"Yes, I did. And now I am doing as you've asked. It would help if you stop fighting me."

"Yeah, I bet it would."

He sighs. "Did it occur to you to ask how I knew where to look for that kidnap complaint? Because I'm the one who filed it. The day I met a frantic American preacher in Iraq whose boy had run off in Mosul. His mother was convinced the Republican Guard had gotten their hands on him."

Part of me wants to argue. *Needs* to argue. Except it's so Matty it hurts. I look away and close my eyes. "Yeah. He did that to me once too."

"They found him playing in the river with the Maloof kids. His father beat the tar out of him for it. Let's just say I didn't approve."

He stands, pointing at a white and blue Gulfstream at the edge of the field, which bore a logo reading *Bayard Foreign Marketing*. "That one is yours. Fueled and ready. Mr. Hendricks was kind enough to make arrangements in the course of his treason." He fishes into a black bag and comes up with a set of handcuffs and chains, which he drops onto the ground. He holds the end of the bag open towards my face. "Unfortunately, his handlers remain in position. We'll have to keep up appearances for now."

I've been tied up against my will once in my life. Twice, including tonight. Which is more than enough. "If you think I'm going to let you tie me up and throw me on one of your torture planes, you have another think coming."

Jason throws up his hands. "Oh for fuck's sake." He shoves Nance out of the way, then pins me down on the seat, throwing the fuse on everything I've buried for years. I kick, I scream, I fight, but I can feel his hands everywhere, my breasts, my waist, between my legs. Cold metal bites down on my wrists.

Nance clears his throat. "Mr. Barnes, I said treat her like a prisoner, not your prom date."

Jason jams the hood over my head. "She didn't make me work this hard at prom."

I kick at what I hope is his groin. "Fuck you."

Nance grabs my feet, lifting me off the ground, and shoves me into the cab. "Best to save this performance for the security gates."

The flashback subsides. Tears stream. The second they take the cuffs off, I'm going to scratch both their eyes out.

In the end, the guard at the gate lets us through without incident, and somewhere in the stifling, inky blackness under the hood, I force myself to remember why I'm doing all this. Because way back when, I fell for a guy who makes me believe that no matter how bad things get, there are more people on earth who want to build it up instead of tear it down, and that for whatever cosmic purpose the universe brought us together, we haven't finished it yet. Even still, when Jason comes out to take off the cuffs and hood, I'm too shattered to do more than roll over and stare out at the madly spinning, fucked up world.

He taps my hip. "Quit sulking. Nance said he didn't know who was watching. Told me to make it good. Get your ass in the cockpit and tell me where the hell we're going."

We're not even off the ground yet. And besides, the one who knows is Tal, who's surfing a serious morphine haze and talking to his dead wife in the next seat. "East."

Jason swears at me under his breath. "You haven't changed a bit, you know that?"

I draw up my knees, covering my bare legs under my dress. "Neither have you."

After flipping me the bird, he retreats to the cockpit. Five minutes later, we're in the air. As we level off, he's talking to himself, fiddling with the controls. "All these fancy avionics and no IFF," he grumbles, tapping the 3D GPS. "Redundant control devices, night vision terrain maps..."

Resigned, I get up and sit in the co-pilot's seat. "Were you this freaky the last time I flew with you?"

He runs his finger down the manual. "The last time I wasn't worried about flying head-on into a transoceanic heavy that doesn't know I'm there. Or an F16 launching a missile up my ass. You get the idea."

When I notice his hands are shaking, a hazy memory of an email from my mother comes up. "Didn't that almost happen to you once?"

"Couple weeks before the mosque thing, yeah." He punches something into the nav computer. "A patrol incursion. I was returning to base. All of a sudden, my instruments lit up like a Christmas tree, and next thing I knew, an S-75 tore by my left window."

"Did it affect you? The way the military said?"

He flicks a switch overhead, shutting down a flashing orange light outside. "What, you mean my own mortality confronting me at Mach 3 or the fact they found Ativan in my system?"

"So it was true?"

His eyes stay trained on the sky. "I hit what I was told to hit."

No emotion at all, just flatness in his voice. On an intellectual level, I know his side. Nobody ever said war is pretty. A pilot with doubts is a dead pilot. You follow orders and trust your command. Trouble is, I spent a decade living and working with people who'd borne the brunt of that thinking. "How many people were killed? Thirty-something?"

"Twenty-four." His glance slides sideways. "Which you knew. Don't start with your bullshit, Leah. Let's have it. What exactly do you think you know?"

"It was a cover-up," I say softly. "A massacre committed the night before by some rogue security contractors. The same guys who are doing all this to Matty. They used you to destroy the evidence, make it look like an accident. Somehow, he found out. He was investigating."

His hands freeze on the yoke. "Are you telling me your bastard husband knew I wasn't responsible?"

My hackles fly up. "Responsible for what? How many other missiles did you fire?"

"Spare me." His knuckles go white. "What did I ever do to him? For crissakes, he's the one who ended up with you."

Ended up with the mess you left. "Think *real* hard, Jason. Think about the last time I saw you."

"You think I haven't? You think I don't wonder about you every time I get a call from my wife's lawyer? You think I don't ask myself why it didn't work out with you and me?"

"I don't have a clue what you think."

It's a lie, a lie that feeds into the fiction he spun for himself about that night. The one where it was just makeup sex after a bad fight, where his cheating slut of a girlfriend was only crying because he was willing to take her back. It's a lie that's stood for all these years, partly because I made a choice to let it. In his own way, Matty never stopped trying to get me justice. He never understood that justice for me was that the one person who matters knew.

Jason tilts the yoke. The wings dip left. "Tell me. Right now, or I'm turning around."

"You won't." My eyes sting. A lump pains my throat. "You're here for the same reason I am. Because there's nothing at home to go back to."

I run out of the cockpit. I want to collapse in a seat and cry myself to sleep, but I can't, not today. Past is past. I'm not a victim. I'm not a fool. I'm a woman with one last chance to undo her husband's mistakes. I don't have the luxury of wasting it.

A red thread of daylight is unraveling on the horizon when Jason comes out. With a deep exhale, he takes the seat across.

"Who's flying?"

"Autopilot." He wipes a hand over his face. "You flinched when I hugged you at Dad's funeral."

Gnawing discomfort takes root. "Jason —"

"You barely said a word after I left your place the night before."

I draw up my knees. "We don't have to do this."

He drops his head to his hands. "For god's sake, why didn't you say something, Lee?"

"No." The lump returns. "You don't get to put this on me."

When he finally looks up, his eyes are rimmed red. "I'm sorry. That's all I wanted to say… I'm sorry."

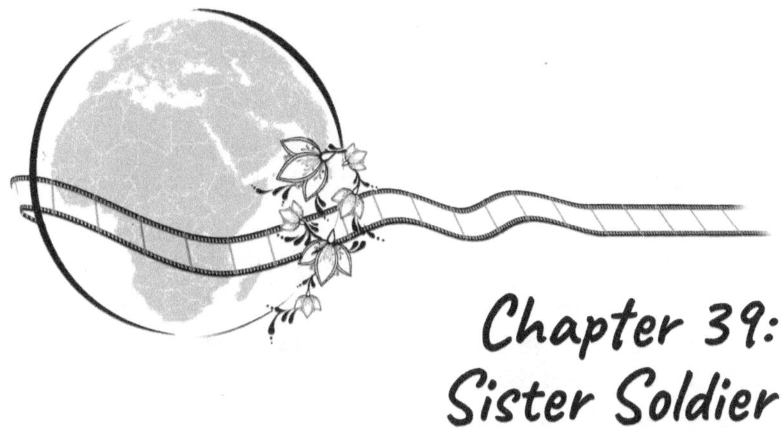

Chapter 39:
Sister Soldier

WEST KURDISTAN
PRESENT

Jason taxies the Gulfstream to a stop at the end of a bomb-pocked airstrip, where after some coaxing from Tal, the rebels were kind enough to let us land. Shimmering waves radiate from corrugated metal lean-tos, which ramble between busted shipping crates and burned-out vehicles.

Near the control tower, a young boy peers around the corner. Tal, who's been anxiously scanning since we touched down, fumbles with his seatbelt and bolts for the fuselage door, chest heaving with emotion and pain. The boy sprints towards the plane, followed by a pair of women in olive drab fatigues and rose print headscarves. The taller one, I recognize from the night Matty was taken in Cairo.

Jason, who's barely said a word since his apology, shields his eyes. "Do all YPG chicks look like these two? I'm suddenly feeling very into Kurdish separatism."

Unwanted, unhelpful feelings of jealousy bubble up. She's prettier than I remembered. "Go ahead. Tell them that. It'll be fun watching you get your ass kicked."

We follow Tal out of the plane. His sister, Shaza, looks worse for wear, haunted and bruised, and she shrinks from her brother's embrace. They exchange some inaudible words. Tal's face darkens. Shoulders slumped, he kisses her forehead. Hana comes to the base of the steps.

Her wary, mistrustful expression probably mirrors mine. "I received word from Ari. Eema says without you, they would have been taken."

I trust Lucky, but the confirmation is welcome. As she makes fast tracks for a white Nissan truck near the tower, I limp after her. "Where's Matty?"

"When I know, so will you." Her gaze lingers on my ruined cocktail dress, then shifts to Jason, who's caught up. "Who is this?"

"Uber for commies and refugees." He yawns, stretches, then goes for the driver's side of the Nissan. "Where are we?"

As Tal and the others climb into the truck's bed, she hip-checks Jason out of the way. "A place strange men are not welcome."

"Women can drive in Syria?" Jason appears genuinely surprised. "Turkey. Wherever the hell we are."

"Rojava." Turning the ignition, she revs the engine impatiently. "Drive, think for ourselves, yes. We are fortunate no one has yet tried to bring democracy here."

Ninan pipes up, bowing towards a mural painted on the side of the control tower, of a mustachioed man who reminds me of a Kurdish Tom Hanks. "Apo says a society can never be free without women's liberation."

Tal tousles Ninan's hair. "I see Shaza's friends have been taking good care of you in my absence."

Jason comes around to me. "Are we good?"

"I'll be fine. You have to find someplace to refuel anyway."

He tugs the bristles on his chin. "Not what I meant, Lee."

I knew it wasn't. "Look, I appreciate what you said... what you did... but..."

He kicks the tire. "Okay. Yeah. I get it. Have a nice life and all that."

"I'll hold up my end," I add quickly. "I mean—it's all in the stuff I sent to Matty's editor anyhow, but I'll give you everything he had on your case. What the Army did wasn't right."

He glances at the sky. "I'll keep my phone on. Call me when you find him, okay?"

When… if… seeing Jason will be the last thing Matty needs. I climb in beside Hana. "We'll manage. Probably not smart to stick around."

He gives the plane a dark chuckle. "Know anyone interested in a $250 million CIA jet?"

Hah. Har har. "Where will you go?"

"I've got a Navy buddy at Souda Bay. Crete. Figure I can hang out while this blows over. Clear my head. Get my life together, maybe." He turns, hands in the pockets of his tux. "See you around, I guess."

The moment hangs in the air, bound by old scars and fresh hurt. I could make this easy. Grant him the absolution he seeks. Except it's the same mistake I've made with him all along. If he wants his life back, great. But it can't hinge on me. "See you."

Hana winds the truck through mountain checkpoints. Twilight is gathering when we come to a grove of trees, shielding a larger group of women in fatigues, laughing and grunting their way through a series of obstacles built on the rugged terrain, which leads to a rushing river. Beyond it, a stand of brown canvas tents sprawl around a crackling fire. Hana waves at the leader and rolls the truck to a stop. The two confer through the window in Kurdish. Neither sounds happy. When Hana turns back, her face is grim. "I am told that an unconscious foreigner was found on the road to Idlib."

I'm going to be sick. "Alive?"

"Then? Yes. Now, it is impossible to say."

The shakes set in. "Who found him? Bad guys, good guys?"

"We think they can be reasoned with. If not, we will fight. In the meantime, you are welcome in our paradise. Have Shaza introduce you to those who stay behind. Pray for us."

"I'm going with you." My eyes prick. "Being this close… not knowing… it's killing me."

"Then go with Shaza." She gestures towards Tal's sister, who's in the back of the truck, staring listlessly into space. "It does no good for either of you to sit and be attacked by your own minds."

"I can't even imagine what she's been through."

Hana, who was halfway to the glade, spins around. "What she has been through?" She gestures at two twentyish women with long braids who are fighting their way across the river. "Paisa was studying to be a doctor in Ankara, until she angered her father for refusing to marry and he sold her to Daesh. She has saved the lives of countless brothers and sisters in our struggle. Katya will not even tell us what she endured at their hands, but we see it in every battle she fights. Shaza returns to us a hero in our eyes and nothing less. You are only welcome here if you see that."

With that, she stalks off. Tal walks towards the fire, shaking his head. "Hana is angry at the world. She was too harsh with you."

"She wasn't," I say. "Your sister has amazing courage. I wish I knew her secret."

Face lit warm by the fire's glow, Shaza sits next to me. "The secret is having a stronger vision of the world than the one for which your enemy is fighting. That is a faith which will never fail."

Chapter 40: Indivisible...
WEST KURDISTAN
PRESENT

Matty

Wherever I am, it's dark. My limbs feel like lead. I hear water falling into a basin, then someone wringing out a rag. Like Pavlov's dog, my throat closes up. "God, please, not again."

"Ssh, baby, you're safe," Leah whispers, bringing a cool washcloth to my chest.

I make it as far as my elbows. Woozy. "They've got Ari—"

"No they don't." She guides my splitting head to her thigh, then caresses the bristles on my jaw. "She's safe. I swear."

Eventually, it sinks in. The woman I love is cradling my head in her lap, washing months of hell from my skin. Reaching for her face, I pull her lips to mine and kiss her, kiss her like I never stopped. The sweet taste of her mouth, the curve of her cheek, they're as real as they've ever been. "You're the most beautiful thing I've ever seen."

With a hitch, she breaks the kiss. A stifled sob, another, and she loses it, weeping, like she can finally let herself fall apart. We both do.

We stay like that, clinging to each other, until someone walks by outside. Leah moves away, kneeling by a bed roll. "I scrounged up what

I could." She dumps out the contents of a paper sack. "Some clean clothes, a few snacks…"

Dizzy and disoriented, I sit up. Wherever we are, the ground is pitching, as if we're still at sea. "Leah, I swear to God, I was going to tell you everything that night."

She's wearing a ruined jade dress with some camouflage pants underneath. She strips them off. "I borrowed these—they're too big—you've lost more weight than I thought."

I reach for her waist. "I know I should've done it before…"

"Please don't." Jaw wobbling, she sorts through toothpaste and a toothbrush, a razor, socks, sports drinks and snacks, a first aid kit, plus a package of molasses cookies, which she shoves aside.

I raise an eyebrow. "I can't have my cookies?"

She wrings out her cloth and moves behind me. "Have whatever you want."

What I want is for her to stop treating me like one of her damn refugees. I get that she's in self-preservation mode, but… fuck. I squint at the lantern, which feels like someone is trying to squeeze my brains out my nose. We're in a canvas tent, the walls lined with prayer rugs and cooking utensils. The flap is open, leading to darkness. It should feel like freedom, but it's like any minute, Orlyk is going to pop up with the pepper spray. Groping for balance, I find the safest looking corner. "Where are we?"

She reaches for the lantern key, and the tent dims. "Rojava. With the Kurdish Women's Protection Brigade. You were in bad shape when they got to you. There's a woman outside named Paisa you need to thank. She saved your life."

A shaft of light falls across the tent flap. A decrepit mongoose sticks its nose in, followed by Hana. She waves a flashlight in my direction. "I heard voices. It is good to see you awake, Matthias." As the mongoose climbs her shoulder, a smile flits across her face. She shows me a tablet, the browser opened to the Globe homepage, which has a big red banner. "I thought you would both like to see this."

MISSING PHOTOJOURNALIST MATTHIAS CAHILL FOUND ALIVE IN NORTHERN SYRIA.

Multiple confirmed sources indicate Cahill was detained without charge or trial for the past six months at a US "black site" after uncovering evidence that the recent sarin gas attacks were orchestrated by a splinter cell of the American intelligence and military community, intended to stoke support for stalled anti-refugee legislation.

DEVELOPING STORY.

It hits me like a deep-sea wave. *It's not over. Not even close.* "Oh god."

"We had to get out in front," Leah says. "Jack's on it. Your whole report will be up as soon as they can finish vetting it. I didn't have a choice."

"What about Gleason and the others?"

"They have paid for their crimes," Hana says, without elaborating. She rubs the cross around her neck. "May our brother rest. I will leave you in peace."

As Hana retreats from the tent, Leah presses the cloth to the knot on my temple. Her hands are shaking. A thousand inane questions fill my head, buzzing like drunken bees. "So… uh—how did the bar go?"

She lets out a short, unhappy laugh. "Super. Everyone kept telling me it was what you'd want, so I spent eighteen hours locked in a room taking a test I didn't give a damn about taking. Oh, and let's not forget that halfway through the second day, the friend I'd bribed to babysit my cell phone came running to the proctor and said CSF found your body floating in the Nile. Or what was left after the crocodiles got you."

I wince. "So, third time's the charm?"

"I squeaked by the second." She takes my arm, rubbing the washcloth over my biceps. "Honestly, it helped," she says. "They'd sent a photo. No tattoo. If they were going to all that trouble to screw with me, I figured you were probably alive."

I reach for her hand, but she pulls away. "Come on, Leah."

She sinks to her knees, skirt falling over my lap. Her face is streaked with tears. "I missed you."

I finger the hem of her dress, but can't make myself touch her. Alone in my cell, I used to close my eyes and imagine the velvet warmth from her skin, the heartbeat fluttering beneath her breast. But as the months wore on, the honeyed taste on her lips became poison, the hands groping my body turned to shackles. What if this was another nightmare, another trick?

She takes matters into her own hands, unzipping the dress, easing it over her shoulders, then peels down her bra. Her torso is bare, nipples drawn taut, and all of a sudden, I'm not focused on the water.

"Relax," she whispers, one hand on my sternum, the other reaching over my head for the basin. "Let me finish."

At first, it works. She brings the washcloth to my chest, never taking her eyes off mine. She works her way to my arms, my neck, my face, but I can't take it. Every touch is agony. "This is as clean as I'm going get, okay?"

Tearful, she slaps the rag into the basin. "Fine."

Way to go, asshole—you haven't seen your wife in months, she gets naked, and you make her cry. Fighting every impulse, I take her hips and pull her on top of me. Our kisses become frantic, heated, but when she slips her hand to my crotch my whole body seizes up and before I even realize what I'm doing, I shove her off.

A shocked look crosses her face. She wipes her nose and curses, with an expression as if she wants to hurt someone. "I never knew how it felt from your side."

When I realize what she thinks, a wave of nausea comes and goes. "They didn't… not that at least." It's the isolation. The conditioning that every touch means pain. "I'm not letting them have that power over me. Us. Whatever. Don't stop."

She sniffles. "Matty, I don't know how to do this."

Desperate for something, anything, that'll keep her from crying again, I lie back and try to force my brain to work. "Teach me your yoga breathing thing again? You know, curl my tongue, breathe through my left nostril, that whole deal. Promise I won't try to get in your pants this time."

Her nose wrinkles. "Did I rescue the right husband?"

"You're stuck with me babe, sorry."

Naked skin to naked skin, the ache and loss fades, turning to need, a stirring I haven't felt in months and before I know it we're making love. I have my wife back. My life. Here we're not prisoners or fugitives. We're falling hard in the Moroccan sand, clinging to each other for warmth in the nighttime desert, lost in a comfort embrace in the Provincetown dunes. Lost deep in ecstasy, I hear her call my name, a feverish lover's whisper. "Matty, we can't. Stop."

Too far gone, I try—and fail—to stave off the inevitable. "Too late."

She blinks. Freezes. Looks down between us. All of a sudden, she's in tears again. "I'm not on anything. I hadn't—I couldn't…"

"Hey, ssh, ssh—it'll be okay."

She hangs her head. "Matty, you know I was…" Her voice trails off, like she can't say it. "The night you were taken…you know I was pregnant."

A million things run through my head, and I'm pretty sure all of them are the wrong thing to say. "I thought you were happy about it."

"I didn't know what I was." A tear trickles down her cheek. "Terrified. Confused. Alone. I lost the baby at four months."

A cavern of loss looms over us, as if we've been stumbling around all this time, trying to find each other. "Leah, I spent the past six months thinking I was going to be the father of a kid I'd never meet. Then, last night, I found out I was wrong. If the worst that happens is we just tried again without meaning to, then as far as I'm concerned, it's the best thing to come out of this whole situation."

She shifts on my thighs, tucking her messy hair behind her ear, and tries to climb off, but I'm not letting her go. Glancing between us, she grinds the heel of her hand into her eyes. "Matty, I love you. I've never stopped, I never will. But you're not thinking straight."

Closing my eyes, I rest my aching skull on the canvas. "What else is new?"

With a soft exhale, her lips, warm and reassuring, touch mine. "We're going to get you better. I promise."

"I'm fine."

She caresses my cheek. "Look at where we are. You went right to the corner of the tent like you're still in a cell. You can't stand light. I touch you, you flinch."

I bury my face between her breasts, feeling the warmth of her flush against my skin. "I'll get over it."

She strokes my hair. "I can't fuck you better."

Shag-drunk or not, there isn't a part of me that doesn't hurt. "Worth a try."

"Seriously?" She pushes me away. "I've been sitting here for the past hour finding marks on you that prove my worst fears, and the *one* thing I'm grateful for is that when you finally woke up, you hadn't completely lost your mind. We both know tonight won't be the worst. It scares me to death, thinking of what lies ahead." She catches herself, her breathing measured. "We're in deep—legally, personally. I don't know how we get out of it, and the worst is that *none of it had to happen!* You lied to me, Matty, you *lied* to me."

And there it is. She finally said what she needed to say.

"I made a choice," I say. "The only one I could make without sacrificing you and Ari."

"It wasn't yours to make." She draws her knees to her chest. "You didn't let me because you weren't ready to crawl off your cross over it. I guess I have more faith in us than you."

Outside, someone is singing, something that sounds like a hymn. I sit up, cross-legged, transported back to a time where I saw the world far differently. "The last time I ever heard my father give a sermon, it was to a parish outside Johannesburg. He was talking about marriage. Towards the end, I remember him focusing on my mother. He said he'd failed as a husband so often that the words 'I'm sorry' no longer had meaning. Instead, whenever he screwed up, he promised to be a better man tomorrow."

She lowers her head. "I never needed you to be anything other than the man you are, Matty. Why was that so hard for you to understand?"

The soft glow of dawn lights the outside. Fighting the stinging in my eyes, I force myself to get up and peek out. Two of the women are lighting a fire, laughing while they prepare a meal. Others are praying, planning, or cleaning their guns. There's not another man in sight, and not one of them cares. Whatever they're fighting for, whatever conflicts and battles—I don't feel the need to be out there anymore. It's a life, an honest life, but one I'm ready to leave behind. "Because I wanted you to have better."

Leah bites her lip. "We're not out of the woods. I made a deal with Nance, but—"

My heart drops. "Please tell me you didn't. He's—"

"Involved. I know. He's… contained."

"How? I mean—are you sure?"

She wrinkles her nose. "If you don't believe me, I can show you the text from Jack asking what it's like to have a senator's balls in my purse.'

All I can do is gawp at her. "You really are a miracle worker."

"No. I'm not." She strokes my hair. "There are outstanding charges against you for aiding and abetting foreign terrorists, espionage. Maybe even murder. All hell is breaking loose at home. They're going to throw anything and everything at us. You could face trial. They'll try to keep you under detention in the meantime."

A bitter taste floods my mouth. "Hell to the fuck no." Vertigo overwhelms me. "São Paulo is nice this time of year."

She squeezes my hand. "We can't run. Not from this. You have to trust that I won't let you down."

Even the idea of ever seeing the inside of a cell again makes me physically weak. Ill. I rest my forehead on hers. "How much further can you go to save me, Leah?"

"As far as it takes," she whispers.

"I can't. You know I can't."

"I know what I'm asking," she says. "And I know you're in no condition to make that kind of choice, so I'm telling you what it should be. As your lawyer. As your wife. I'm telling you we can beat them."

My head fills with the taste of pepper spray. Desperate to make the burn go away, I breathe into her hair. "Run with me."

"You just told me you want kids. I…I can't deal with that right now." She sniffles, then raises her eyes to meet mine. "But I know you, and if you said it, you meant it. I also know you'd never give them a life like your father gave you."

I flinch. I'd die first and she knows it. "That's low."

She's shaking as she clasps my hand. "Matty, I thought I knew you, I thought I knew *us*, but maybe I don't. Stop fighting me. Help me understand, tell me what's changed."

Brushing back the tent flap, I force myself closer to the darkened world. It's not as if it's gotten any less fucked up in the past six months. Or that I understand what's changed either. Only that it has. "All those nights in my cell, I spent them picturing it—you, me, and this little person sitting on the porch swing, watching the plovers. The way you talked about doing when you were little. It got me through. Maybe… maybe I just need to know that you can see it too."

She goes quiet for what feels like eternity. "I've been thinking about my dad. And my brother. I mean, Dad was a much better lawyer than me to start, but he never truly found his calling until DJ died." Her forehead drops to my chest. "They're going to keep doing this. Going after reporters. Anyone who tells a truth they don't like. This is a fight that needs fighting, Matty. Our fight. But we have to fight it together from now on."

Together. The magic word. I bury my face in her hair. "Okay. You win. I'm in."

Chapter 41:
Liberty and Justice for All
PROVINCETOWN, MASSACHUSETTS
2 YEARS LATER

Leah

Weathered pickets undulate like harvest wheat down the beach path. Clumps of fat beach plums droop over scraggly shrub roses. It's the remotest stretch of the Cape, a path I've walked nearly every day since we came home.

Cries of sunset gulls and terns float on the breeze, carrying the distant lap of waves on the shore. Beneath it comes a soft *step-step-step-step* thrush. A spotted blur comes bounding out of the pitch pine forest.

"Hey, Treo." I stoop to scritch his ear. He's a springer, retired from a Marine unit in Afghanistan, an old war dog like Matty. Basically, they're inseparable. "Where are they?"

With a *ruff*, he bounds off towards the water. I catch up with him by the flats, at the edge of a shimmering tidal pool stretching clear down to Race Point, beside the ruins of a chest-high sandcastle that must've taken all day to build.

"He heard you a half-mile off," Matty says. As Treo dances, tail whipping, he gets up, brushing off his hands. "Hey pal, guess who's here?"

Plum-sticky, outstretched hands blast through a turret. "Mummy!"

Matty swoops DJ up before he can finish Godzilla-ing the castle, stealing the first kiss. "Nice try, Squirt."

DJ came along fifteen months ago, courtesy of that terrifying night when Matty was freed, proving that once again, the best changes in our lives have no intention of sticking to a schedule that makes sense. He hasn't magically transformed me into a perfect mother, but even the worst days melt away once I come out here to find the two of them on the beach.

I shift him to my hip, taking a deep inhale of salty baby hair, and brush my lips over his forehead. "Daddy's jealous, little man."

Matty turns my chin. "Daddy's a better kisser."

He doesn't eat the same, hasn't regained as much weight as he should, and on cold rainy mornings, I can tell he feels it. For once, he stopped self-medicating and found the right kind of help, from an Army medic-turned-researcher who truly gets it. He still doesn't like the dark, doesn't like being alone, hates small spaces, but we toughed it out, we fought back, we healed, and somewhere along the way, I finally got to know the man I've loved for almost half my life.

Matty didn't take one shot that changed the world; he took thousands. Whether we were famous or infamous depends on who you ask. The 'case' against us collapsed the minute his story went to print. Even still, the Justice Department kept filing appeals and new charges, everything from illegal recordings to unlawful associations with terrorists, until the public outcry over the cover up and conspiracy was the straw that finally brought down the government. In many ways the damage was done, but bottom line, I kept my promise. Matty never spent so much as another minute inside a cell.

We countersued, alleging false imprisonment, torture, fighting decades of laws passed to shield the powerful and corrupt. Nance, in his usual frustrating way, somehow came out unscathed.

Standing in the student union all those years ago, if anyone told me that my new crush, the adrenaline junkie shutter fiend who'd show me how to change the world, would be happy to spend his days chasing our toddler, I would've thought they were crazy. He'll never cover another war, which is fine with both of us. He's become a sought-after lecturer on safety of journalists and press freedoms, and together with Ari and Magdala, we run an advocacy organization for refugee concerns. We fight, we resist, but for the most part, he's Daddy now. We were wounded yet victorious, tested and scarred, lost innocence we never knew we had, but we came through the other side, our hearts and souls intact.

I've come to see it as the heart of a marriage, the evolution and acceptance of each other's changes. Light is shining brightly on the dark places he suffered so long to expose, and as he always says, it falls to those who see it to decide how to act. People like Nyali Waleed, Izar Namazi and Hana Maloof. Even if the world hasn't made peace with itself, he's finally made peace with the world.

Me, I'm working on it. My dad passed last year, leaving me his share of the practice, the one he'd always said he sold, including an office overlooking the Atlantic. It's a five-minute walk from home, which of course means my mother pops in with tea whenever she feels like it. Lately, I don't mind so much. I kept most of my clients, and ReliefNet keeps sending me new ones, in no small part due to Hana, who's found her calling in helping to dismantle Kıraç's human trafficking network. Publicly, he remains at large. Privately, she's told us not to worry. Which means all that's been hanging over us are the trials.

"Julie called," I say, watching Matty's body go tense. "The ruling came down about ten minutes ago."

As Treo snurfles through a tide pool, Matty wets his lips. "And?"

We'd filed suit over the countless violations to Matty's civil rights, a long shot from the start. Ruling after ruling on detainee issues and press freedom had gone in the government's favor. The courts were stacked against us and getting worse by the day. Six months ago, we'd stood in Federal Court and argued that Gleason and his enablers had misdirected the full power and weight of the US government against Matty for their own ends. That their prosecution of him was malicious and had to end. And then, beyond the last shadow of doubt, we used the evidence Matty, Hana, and I had gathered to prove it.

I squeeze his hand. "The Supreme Court declined certiorari. They didn't want to make precedent over this mess. The Appellate Court upheld Forrester, so her DC Circuit ruling stands."

"English, Leah."

"It's finally over." I pick a windblown strand of hair from my mouth. "We're in the clear."

Elation and relief breaks over his face. He picks us up and spins me around, toppling us all into the castle. DJ squeals. "Sorry pal." Matty winks at me. "Guess we know why Mommy was late."

"I have a better reason." I smile. "Two actually."

Matty gives me a quizzical look. "What's up?"

"For starters, they gave us a favorable disposition on your civil rights suit, *and* ordered Gleason's estate to pay up."

The words erase ten years from his face. "So there's money for school? DJ and Ari?"

Ari, who still thinks America is the craziest place she's ever lived, is in her sophomore year at BU as a pre-med major. It's a happy change for Matty, getting to see her whenever he wants.

I sit in the ruins of the castle, pulling DJ onto my lap. "DJ, Ari, and anyone else who happens to come along."

Matty flops down beside me, toppling the throne. "I wish your dad could see you." He brushes sand from my temple. "He'd be proud, Leah."

I pull DJ close for a snuggle. "Finally."

"He always was." A grin breaks through. "Come on, admit it, you're bummed. You wanted the shot at the Supreme Court."

"I did not."

"Did too."

"Are you kidding? *I'd* be the one having nightmares."

With a wicked grin, he covers DJ's ears. "We've got better things to do in bed than sleep."

See no evil. Hear no evil. Speak no evil, the indelible mark on Matty's arm that guided our lives for so long. We see the world from the other side these days, but from here, we could still see it change.

"Your 'better things' have been making me queasy all morning."

Matty, finally getting a clue, cocks his head. "Seriously?"

I smile, rocking DJ in my arms. "Seriously."

Folding me into a lingering kiss, he whispers *I love you* and holds me close, then he drops his face to DJ's drowsy head, and we watch the plovers until the sun goes down.

Author's Note

A free press is the cornerstone of a free society. However, nearly half the world is denied this vital mission, and the active suppression of journalism is rising among authoritarian governments around the world. In 2017, 262 journalists lost their freedom and 65 more lost their lives in the course of trying to bring more truth into the world. For more information about the fight to protect journalism and journalists, please visit the Reporters Without Borders website at http://rsf.org/en

To every survivor of assault, especially those for whom the cost of speaking out is still too great to bear: you are not forgotten. You deserve to be believed, you deserve to heal, and you deserve to be safe. Please don't let anyone ever tell you otherwise.

Acknowledgments

Bits and pieces of this story have existed in my heart, head, and hard drive for such an embarrassingly long time, it's hard to say for certain what actually inspired it. (Though it likely had something to do with my tendency to fangirl journalists instead of movie stars and a lifelong obsession with current events.) While I've always loved this story, it was never really the right time for it. Then the election happened, and suddenly the America around me no longer made sense. Both my husband and our children were born elsewhere and came to this country as immigrants. Especially to my older son, it all felt very personal and scary. For me, writing has always been my way of figuring out things that on the surface, I can't. When I started reading back through what I'd written, it became clear that now, this was the story I needed to tell, for them.

This book would've never seen the light of day if it hadn't been for a number of people. First, to Jessica Brockmole, (who's read every dratted word of this thing approximately 9 million times)—thank you for your insights, your patience, and for always being there with a bear emoji or drimk textie when I needed it. There is no one I'd rather wear museum shoes with. Next, to Courtney Miller-Callihan—thank you for believing in this story, and for being a shining reminder of how to always be who you are. (Not to mention the pirates and always knowing how to tell a bridge where to go). To my early readers for this book, including Clovia Shaw, Cindy Aleo, Jan O'Hara, Liz Michalski, Amy Bai, and especially to my editor, Sue Laybourn, who each provided invaluable advice in shaping this story. A special thank you to my mom, Pat Kupcinskas, for being my cheerleader through the ups and downs. (You always were.)

Lastly, to my husband, Kevin (who promised to read this when it was finally a 'real book'): You blessed me with countless hours of writing time over the years, made me coffee when I was too focused to remember I wanted one, and convinced me to come up for air every now and then. There's so much I couldn't do without your support—this book is just one. I love you.

About the Author

In her own fictional world, Rebecca Burrell is a secret Vatican spy, a flight nurse swooping over the frozen battlefields of Korea, or a journalist en route to cover the latest world crisis. In real life, she's a scientist in the medical field. She lives in Massachusetts with her family, two seriously weird cats, and a dog who's convinced they're taunting him.

To connect with Rebecca,
find her on Facebook:
http://www.facebook.com/rebeccaburrellauthor

or on Twitter:
http://www.twitter.com/raburrell

Goodreads:
http://www.goodreads.com/author/show/17887040.Rebecca_Burrell

For news, author events, and more,
visit Rebecca's website:
www.rebeccaburrell.com

1. As we meet her in Cairo, Leah is considerably more jaded than the idealistic young woman who embarked on a career in humanitarian aid fifteen years before. In what ways do you see the world differently than you did a decade or so ago? Do you agree with the statement that both dreamers and cynics have a role to play in trying to make it a better place?

2. Prior to Matty's disappearance, Leah finds herself seriously contemplating the end of her marriage for the first time, and wondering whether she can ever be enough for Matty. Have you ever experienced this kind of head-vs-heart struggle, perhaps in a romantic or family relationship, or in a job or career?

3. As a biracial woman, Leah sometimes feels caught between two worlds, and only partially welcome in either. Has there ever been a time when you've felt you don't fit or feared being seen as an imposter or somehow fake? Did you eventually find your place or are you still looking?

4. Though her world is steeped in the pervasive nature of violence against women, Leah avoids dealing with her own rape. While there is no right or wrong way to deal with assault, this leads to some questionable choices, both for herself and Matty. Does Leah's decision to hook up with a near stranger seem out of character or can it be seen as an ill-fated coping strategy? Do you think Matty's desire to gain justice for Leah is colored by the violence his mother experienced, with the corresponding effect it had on his childhood? As the #MeToo movement has gained strength, why do you think Leah seems to have preferred to say silent?